The Black Sparrow

The Little Folk Saga, Book 1

by

R. K. J. Sprock

DORRANCE
PUBLISHING CO
EST. 1920
PITTSBURGH, PENNSYLVANIA 15238

Dorrance Publishing Co
585 Alpha Drive
Suite 103
Pittsburgh, PA 15238
Visit our website at *www.dorrancebookstore.com*

ISBN: 978-1-6442-6143-9
eISBN: 978-1-6442-6130-9

Preface

In a time long before we became what we are now, when animals still remembered the Druid speech and all manner of beings had a strong grasp of the natural magic that still flowed through the land, a nameless being arose. They were a plain people when compared to the power, beauty and long history of the other people who dwelled among the branches, in the streams and forests and among the animals that roamed freely. They were a people who only had a tiny fist holding to the threads of magic around them, they were a being who could change into a creature of flight at a moment's notice, but that was all. No premonitions of what could happen the next day, no ability to see the flow of magic around them and no way of sensing danger lurking from afar. These people were different from the Druids and Sprites and Fairies of the woods; they never seemed to be satisfied. They had been instilled with a want for more of all things and felt the need to achieve it at any cost and over the generations they flourished faster than any other being that walked on two legs. The other people and creatures of the lands bestowed upon them the simple name of Little Folk.

Chapter One

Falling, spinning, falling...the air whooshed in his ears, there was a hard hit on his shoulder and then he was falling again. The darkness was so enveloping that he could not tell which way was up anymore, tears escaped his eyes as he searched the blank empty space he was falling through. With arms and legs splayed out and reaching for anything to grab on to he let one cry escape his mouth, and then he finally hit the bottom.

The voice was soft and slightly raspy, the words slow, or perhaps it was his mind that was slow as the words gently caressed his fuzzy train of thought. Lance found he could not understand them. Slowly he opened his eyes and found only the blackness that was there before. He moved his right arm and found it stiff, his shoulder painful, so he moved his left instead. His fingertips slowly searched out his face and he gently touched his eyelids, he wasn't sure if they were actually open. The voice came again, slowly winding through the darkness as though a phantom spirit was seated next to him; the words were different this time but he still could not understand their meaning.

"Where are you?" Lance asked softly. For a long moment there was no answer, then he heard a soft rustle of movement and the voice came back.

"Ah, you are from the far east."

"I am from Galedin, I work in the king's court. I am a Bard." Lance caught his breath, speaking was beginning to blossom a pain in his right side.

"It is best that you do not move, you seem to have something broken in your leg and your shoulder. Your leg is quite swollen and a fire burns inside of it. I am sorry, I have no light to examine you better."

The voice had a heavy accent that Lance could not identify, some of the words seemed hard for the man to pronounce.... From the far northern kingdom, perhaps.... Lance gently rubbed his palm over his face, he still could not see.

"How do you know my words?" he asked softly. "You do not sound like you are from around here. What kingdom do you claim?"

"Why does that matter?"

"I suppose it doesn't." Lance let his hand rest on his chest and continued to shift his eyes around, searching the black void around him. A fear slowly began to form inside of him.

"Am I... am I blind?" he asked.

"I do not believe so. You are in a cave and have fallen down a very deep crevice. I have no way of making light but I can remember the way out."

"I was trying to hide from road bandits, they had weapons and were going to kill me...they took my guitar...." Lance's voice caught at the remembrance of one man ripping the guitar from his back, the strap catching around his neck and choking him briefly before it finally snapped from the strain.

"That is a shame," the man answered, and then he coughed softly.

"You haven't spoken to anyone in a long time, have you?"

"I have not."

"Why are you here?" Lance's breath was shallow as he forced the words out.

"Because I wish for peace and silence," the man said softly. "Now rest, you are in pain and need to be silent."

Lance obeyed, the pain in his side slowly ebbed away as he let his mind wander aimlessly through the dark.

Lance opened his eyes only to see nothing once again. What had brought him back to his body...the pain; someone was moving him. Lance could not speak at first, he felt hands grasping his shoulders as they held him in a sitting position. The fingers were long and thin, the nails were making little pin pricks of pain across Lance's skin. It felt like a skeleton had taken hold of him and for a moment the image of a death spirit came to his mind. Lance cried out and tried to pull away but the hands held him as pain pulsed through his body. Lance submitted and went limp with a groan.

"I am sorry but I must take you out of here before you sicken and die," the man said, his face so close as he spoke that Lance felt the warmth of his breath on his cheek. "I had hoped you would stay asleep, for this will be very painful for you but if you stay here you will die."

"I can handle it," Lance breathed the words out, he tried to put strength into them but they sounded so weak to his ears.

"I know you are a grown man but I must carry you. The way is dark and there are too many places where you can fall and injure yourself more."

"Let it be so," Lance said, his words sounding just a little stronger.

Lance felt arms tuck themselves beneath his body, one below his shoulders supporting his back and the other beneath his legs. The arms were so thin that Lance was sure his body weight would snap them, but the man held Lance against his chest and picked him up without hesitation. Lance was able to put his good arm around the man's shoulders and clasp his thin shirt, it felt very old and frail in his hand. He caught his breath at all the movement and the man paused, then he began walking. Though the man was so thin and bony, he walked with a steady unwavering strength. Lance could feel the hard sinewy muscles beneath the man's shirt, they rolled and bunched with each step like knotty bands of iron. Lance was thankful for the man's steadiness, for each step caused an ache somewhere in his body and a misstep caused grinding pain as the man would have to change his balance lest they fall, but that only happened twice in the darkness. Lance kept his eyes closed as he concentrated on his breathing...breathe in...breathe out...breathe in...breathe out....

Lance opened his eyes, at first everything was still dark but then something above him moved and the darkness turned into millions of tiny lights dancing far above him. The stars seemed to be wheeling in circles as he lay on what felt like damp earth, but at least it was soft and not a cave floor anymore.

"There are dangerous creatures about, I will make a fire."

Lance saw movement to his right as the man moved away from him. He closed his eyes for what seemed a moment only to open them again and see that the man had moved him onto what seemed to be a nest of soft branches. Light flickered off the foliage around them as the man banked the fire and tossed on a few more sticks. Lance studied the man that sat just a few paces away with his knees drawn up to his chest and his arms clasped around them. His appearance was haggard, but from exposure or old age he could not tell. His clothes were thin and looked like mere rags hanging from his skeleton body. The man's hair and beard were long and thickly matted, covering most of his face, but his nose and cheekbones were still visible as they stuck out sharply. His eyes were deep dark circles in the flickering fire light with barely a glint shining back. His skin was stained and dry like a dead leaf, his bare feet so dirty they appeared black while the rest of his skin that was not dirty shone back pale, almost sickly white. His thin arms and legs were long and almost made him look like a giant insect meditating before a warm fire. Lance could see so many bones beneath his papery skin and he could count the ribs on the man's side where his shirt had a large tear in it. The man was staring hard into the fire, a pained expression on his face. Lance cleared his throat a little but the man took no notice, he didn't even blink, Lance eventually looked away and fell asleep. Sometime later he was awaked by the sound of the man moving, he had unfolded his arms and legs but he continued to stare into the fire…was that a tear rolling down the man's face…? The man slowly brought his hands up to his ears and covered them, then he laid down on his side, his back to Lance. For a moment Lance saw his thin frame shiver and then all was still and quiet again.

The fever came by morning. Lance suddenly found words hard to pronounce while his teeth chattered and sweat rolled down his face and neck. To one side of Lance's body the thin man kept the coals in the fire banked high and the other side of his body he piled up dead leaves in an attempt to keep him warm since they had no blankets. They were still near the mouth of the cave, its darkness was frightening and yet it seemed to call to Lance as he laid there, little spasms of pain running through his arm and leg. Just inside the cave the wall sweated out tiny rivets of water, the thin man was constantly going to this to collect the water on a piece of cloth he had torn from Lance's shirt, this he would either squeeze into Lance's mouth or over his forehead.

"Thank you," Lance would whisper over and over again, the thin man would only smile a little. By that night Lance began to whisper other things but several words kept coming over and over again. "I don't want to die. I don't want to die. I don't want to die."

Falling, falling, falling. Darkness. A leather strap tight around his neck as a guitar played a sad tune in his right ear and the sound of air whooshed in his left. He tried to scream but try as he would nothing would come from his open mouth. He tried to reach and grasp something in the darkness but his arms were heavy and he could not move them. Suddenly he felt he was not falling anymore though he did not feel like he had hit the bottom. Looking up he saw a faraway light, like he had fallen into a tunnel and was now looking up at the sky. Something hit him in the face, it was earth. He looked up again to have more earth rain down on him. He was in a grave and he could not move, could not even shout to let them know he was still alive. More earth fell until he could not see the sky anymore.

Lance slowly blinked his eyes, this time there was light. The sky had wisps of feathery clouds and they reflected back the reds and pinks of the sunrise. Lance opened his mouth to speak but instead he began to cough. His throat was dry and his tongue felt numb.

"Here, drink." A hand tucked itself beneath his neck and gently lifted his head enough for him to swallow some water and not choke on it. The water tasted like sappy wood, slightly bitter but still cool to his tortured mouth and throat. After three swallows there was none left and as the thin man moved away Lance saw why the water tasted like wood sap. The man had stripped the bark from a sapling and weaved it tightly into a small drinking glass.

"I am sorry, that is all for now, it takes time for the dripping in the cave to fill the cup," the thin man said when he saw Lance looking forlornly at the small woven cup that was about the size of his fist.

"Thank you," Lance managed to say without coughing again. He rolled his tongue around his mouth a little, his teeth were not chattering anymore. "How…," Lance began, but the man put his hand up for silence.

"Four days," the thin man said. "Mostly just fever and sleeping, nothing too bad. You were very restless through the night but that was right before the fever broke. I am glad you are awake, I did not feel comfortable leaving you as you were. But we need food and I have not slept all these four days."

"I am sorry," Lance said, but the man put his hand up again.

"Do not be sorry, I don't mind helping someone in need. I hope someday a stranger may help me when I am hurt. My name is Tulley, just Tulley."

"I am Lance, actually Lancer, but I prefer Lance. Lance Graven Baxton. I work in the courts of King Aidan Kalmin of Galedin, I am his Bard. I tell him bedtime stories."

"I do not recognize the name of this king, why are you not with him now? I know Galedin is far from here."

"How can you not know his name? He is the child king of war. He is the reason for so many bandits preying upon people like me...."

Tulley shook his head slightly, the expression that could be seen beneath his hair and beard was of a pacifist. "You can tell me of this child king later. I am going to find food and then sleep for a little while." Tulley stood and his lengthy body just seemed all the taller from Lance's prone position. "I should not be gone for long and I won't be far so shout if you have need of me." Lance shook his head slightly and watched as Tulley soundlessly disappeared in the foliage around them in search of food.

Lance's eyes roamed around the little campsite. The small fire was still burning with bright red coals heaped around the edge. Leaves and earth were still heaped to one side of him, it made the skin of his arm prickle but he could not itch it for his other arm was injured and still hurt to move so he ignored the itchiness. Several feet away was another nest-like bed, where Tulley must have sat while he was sick. There were a few green sticks lying on the ground, Lance could see that Tulley was in the process of stripping them to make more woven things. The sticks were so freshly harvested that sap still leaked from their peeled sides. Lance noticed a half-made woven cup on the ground near the sticks and what appeared to be a woven satchel for it had a flap for a lid and a braided strap. Lance turned his attention toward other things, he found it fascinating how things looked so different when viewed from the ground. The tall grasses were slightly bent over their little campsite and there was one flower, amongst the grass, it was larger than Lance's head, it had yellow petals with a black face. The tree branches far above him seemed to blend its green into the blue and white of the morning sky. Lance closed his eyes. Though his stomach made protesting noises that assured him of his recovery he was still tired and wanted to go back to sleep. A moment later Lance was startled by a tremble in the ground beneath him as some creature suddenly dropped from the tree right next to him. Lance opened his eyes and saw a large male squirrel right next to him, Lance's mind raced as fear gripped his body, paralyzing him. Though Little Folk had been known to ride squirrels like steeds this was no tamed squirrel and it was looking hard at Lance with its black eyes. The squirrel raised one front leg, its paw spread out with claws as long as Lance's fingers. The squirrel swung its claws at Lance and caught his shirt front, tearing the fabric and leaving a few red marks across his chest. Lance was finally able to find his voice and cried out shrilly. The squirrel pulled its arm back for another swing and as his body screamed out in pain Lance was able to roll away from the second attack. Lance kicked at the squirrel with his good leg causing it to take a quick jump back. The squirrel cocked its head and chirped at Lance, then it bunched its body and leapt toward him. Lance pulled his arms up, even his injured one, to cover his face. He looked through the space between his arms and he could see the squirrel above him. The squirrel seemed to hover over him for a moment and just as its body began to descend another body was suddenly flying through the air. Lance watched in awe struck horror as Tulley midair tackled the squirrel and knocked it to the ground. The squirrel landed awkwardly on all four feet with Tulley clinging to its back. At first Tulley only had handfuls of fur but then in one quick fluid movement he wrapped one arm around the squirrel's neck. The squirrel began to buck around, its tail making fast twitching movements from behind. Tulley held on and kept his arm around the squirrel's neck, the animals mouth was open as it gasped and droplets of spit flew in different directions. Tulley got both feet planted on the ground and leapt up dragging the squirrel with him. The animal pawed at his arm and face but could not seem to touch him. Tulley got his feet planted firmly on the ground again and tried to unbalance the squirrel to take him down. Lance could see veins on his pale arm as he squeezed pitting his raw strength against the squirrel's animal strength. The squirrel gave one desperate twist of its body and Lance saw pain flash across Tulley's face as the squirrel got one good swipe in with its back leg, the claws scraping across Tulley's side. A few drops of blood hit the ground around them and for a moment Tulley's grip loosened. The squirrel took in a breath and suddenly its strength seemed to come back double. Lance watched as the look on Tulley's face changed, there was no longer a look of pain and concentration, his squinty eyes glinted beneath the dirty hair and a smile crossed his face. The squirrel bent down and leapt straight up taking Tulley with it. With a fierce cry Tulley tightened his arm around the squirrel's neck and swinging his other hand around he palmed the animal so hard in the side of its head that he broke its neck. Tulley and the squirrel plummeted back to the ground, the squirrel's twitching body landed nearly on top of Tulley and knocked him down. Tulley put his hands out as he fell into the small fire but he leapt up again so fast that his hair was hardly sighed. Tulley let out a small cry of anguish as he immediately rubbed his palms against the dirt then he ran to the cave to put his hands against the damp walls but the red coals had done their damage. He may have defeated the squirrel but the fire left his palms red and blistered. Tulley came back from the cave looking at his burned hands then he looked toward Lance; the smile was still on his face.

"Are you all right?" Tulley asked when he saw that Lance had moved from his previous spot. Lance looked from Tulley to the squirrel and then the pain suddenly hit him, his injured leg screaming out the loudest.

"I think I'm going to be sick again," he moaned as he let his head drop in a dead faint.

Chapter Two

"Well, I was banished by my king. My father was his Bard before me and he was a great man. His words could seduce a charging animal, his poems were actually made into book and placed in the library of the castle. Many people mourned when he passed away. So I became King Aidan's new Bard. I had memorized all of my father's work since I was a child but I could not quite speak in such a way as he could. I can play my guitar sweeter than he, but that is only a small part of the story telling and the music of a guitar can actually be done away with. King Aidan grew tired of me reciting my father's work and requested I write some of my own, but I could not come up with anything new. I could only rewrite stories that have been told already and that angered the king. So he banished me, for at least two years, I am to wander and then return to him with a new story or I can remain a wanderer for the rest of my life, but I have to return, you see. My mother still resides at the castle and there is another very dear to me. I promised her I would return."

Tulley sat several feet away from Lance stripping more sticks. He had taken off his shirt and used it to bandage his hands, the cut on his side was barely a scrape and had only leaked a few drops of blood; once

Tulley used the damp rag to wipe away the dirt it looked like nothing was even there. At first Lance was stunned when Tulley had taken off his shirt, it was not because he was so painfully thin but because his torso was actually etched in tattoos. Intricate zig-zag lighting-like tattoos ran across his chest and over his shoulders where they continued to shot across his back and down his sides. The black lines were simple, majestic and intimidating. But on his back was also two handprints, the size of a grown mans, but with long slender fingers like a woman, one on each shoulder blade, as if someone had pressed their hands on to his back, the fingers spread wide like wings.

"What are those?" Lance asked in amazement, for tattoos are painful and dangerous to get, only the very brave or the very stupid would go to the lengths of getting even a small one, and yet here was a man that had them across the front and back of his body.

Tulley did not say anything at first, he was using his teeth to bite off the thin strips since his hands were bandaged now and more like the mittens of an animal, his fingertips were still visible but his hands did not function as well as they had before. A large chunk of meat from the squirrel was still hanging over the fire, they had feasted well the evening before, at least Lance had. Tulley ate and then left the campsite for several minutes, Lance could hear him vomiting.

"When you go for such a long time with hardly any food your body cannot handle it very well," Tulley had said when he returned. Lance continued to eat that evening but Tulley busied himself with the hide and bones of the animal. Lance watched in amazement as Tulley held a rock between his bandaged hands and scraped the inside of the hide until it was white. The skull he left attached to the face of the squirrel with the rest of the hide. Sometimes Tulley would stop for a moment and in a tired gesture he would bring his bandaged hands to his face and cover his eyes, then he would sigh and continue. He carefully detached the claws from the paws and set those aside. He took the two bones from the hind legs and slowly, carefully, split one end open, he sucked the marrow from these bones and then began to run their edge back and forth against a rough stone he had found. Lance fell asleep as he watched Tulley do these tasks, neither of them speaking, the soft glow of their small fire lighting up their little campsite like how the moon made its little circle of light above them.

Tulley worked through the night on the squirrel carcass, almost every part of the animal had a use for him. Sometimes he looked over at Lance as the young man slept, his injured right arm tucked into his side and his right leg resting on the pile of soft foliage Tulley had gathered for him. Tulley suspected he knew how bad Lance's leg was, but at this point it had been five days and there may be no fixing it now....

Lance dreamed of the squirrel, how it had looked at him and screeched, so when he awoke the next morning to find the squirrel was right next to him and it was looking at him again he had to stifle a scream. His heart leapt to the base of his throat and for a moment he choked on his own breath. He calmed himself when he saw what it really was. It was the skull with the hide still attached, Tulley had made a teepee with a few sticks and had laid the hide out to dry near the fire. Lance saw that he had done much more once he fell asleep the night before. The bottom of the skull had been broke open and emptied, the hide swept away from it like a cape. On the ground near it Lance saw the two leg bones Tulley had carefully split open, now they were two bone sabers, their edges sharp enough to cut flesh.

"Tulley?" Lance softly called when he realized Tulley was not sleeping in his own bed of soft things.

"I am here, just gathering spider silk."

Lance's skin suddenly crawled at the mention of a spider. "There is a spider near?"

"There was," came Tulley's lazy distant reply. "I noticed it the other day and killed it, the spider was originally going to be part of our meal but then I killed the squirrel."

"Thank Thorndin for that," Lance said with pure relief in his voice. "I cannot abide spiders and would certainly not eat one."

"Do not thank Thorndin," Tulley said as he came back, thin strands of spider silk carefully wrapped about a stick.

"Why not?" Lance asked. Tulley did not answer but merely began to gently unravel the silk. He held an end out to Lance and he grasped it with his good hand. Lance was beginning to get used to Tulley not speaking so he decided to speak instead in an attempt to fill the void.

"You seem to have many talents. You can butcher, start a fire, find water, weave things out of bark you striped yourself. Where are you from, Tulley? What do you really do and how did you come this far to hide in some cave?"

"You talk a lot," was Tulley's answer, his voice totally void of emotion.

"Sorry, it is kind of my job."

"I do not feel like telling you what I do," Tulley said as he began to twine the spider silk into a very thin string. Lance watched with some wonder as Tulley continuously dipped his fingers into the dry dirt to keep the web from sticking to them. He made two lengths of the silk, each just as long as his arm, then he looped an end of each one around each of his wrists. Lance's curiosity finally overtook him.

"What are you doing?" he asked. Tulley did not answer, did not even glance at Lance, he merely picked up one of his bone sabers. The twisted spider silk was still very thin but not quite invisible anymore, it was a milky white and could be mistaken for a thread off a ragged piece of clothing. Tulley stood up and looked down at Lance, his lean muscles flexing, he suddenly looked very intimidating. With a slight flick of his wrist the saber was instantly embedded into the dirt by his foot, the thread of silk ran from his wrist to the knobby handle. Lance looked at the sharpened bone and then back up at Tulley, for a moment he thought he saw the hint of a smile as, with a jerk of his wrist, the saber was pulled free of the ground and suddenly back in his hand.

"Never lose your sword during a battle."

Tulley took a nap late in the afternoon, Lance watched as Tulley constantly twitched in his sleep. Sometimes a word would escape his parted lips but they were always in a speech that Lance did not understand. Lance chewed on the stalk of a grass sprout, it was the first time he had actually seen Tulley sleep. *Who are you, Old Man Tulley, and why were you hiding in that cave for so long?* Tulley's shoulders gave a violent twitch and in one fluent motion it seemed Tulley was suddenly on his feet, eyes wide and bandaged fists clenched as though he was about to be in a fist fight. Lance froze, the stem of grass still sticking out of his mouth, for a fleeting moment Tulley had a strange look on his face and it frightened Lance. Tulley looked down at Lance and lowered his arms, he suddenly looked very old again. Slowly Tulley let himself sit back down on his bed of grasses, he rubbed his hands across his face a few times and then he began to pat his ears as if they were ringing.

"Are you all right?" Lance asked, guanine concern in his voice.

"No good," Tulley said as he stood again. "I have a headache."

"I don't think boxing your own ears will help with that."

"No good," Tulley said again as he picked up his woven satchel and began to walk toward the cave.

"Where are you going?" Lance called out, suddenly afraid that Tulley was returning to the darkness and leaving him behind to somehow survive on his own. Tulley did not answer and was quickly being swallowed by the darkness.

"Wait! Are you going to come back?" Tulley disappeared and Lance let out a moan.

"Yes," came the reply a moment later.

"When?" called Lance, but this time there was no reply.

Tulley did return after the sun had set. The tiny fire had almost burned out because Lance could not rise to get more wood, he had tried and only managed to create a hot pain just below his knee that was very persistent and stayed with him for the rest of the evening.

Tulley did not say a word when he returned, he merely dropped his satchel and began to tend to the fire. He brought Lance a drink from the sappy cup and then he sat back down in his spot. Lance decided not to say anything, he was not sure what kind of man Tulley was and so he did not understand why Tulley suddenly left him. Tulley picked up his satchel and opened it, from it he took out a pipe he had carved from one of the squirrel's bones. This was the first time Lance had seen the pipe and he found himself wandering what else Tulley had created from the squirrel he had killed. Tulley then pulled a small wad of some kind of pale moss from the satchel and he rolled it between his fingers. Lance continued to watch in silence as Tulley stuffed his pipe, bent as close to the fire as he could, his face grimacing from the heat, lite the pipe and then began to smoke. Tulley looked at Lance then as if he just now realized Lance was watching him, he regarded Lance with a faraway expression for a long moment.

"Hey," Tulley finally spoke. "Don't ever eat or smoke what I have in that satchel." Tulley took several deep breaths, holding each one in for several long moments before he let the smoke curl from his mouth and nose.

"May I ask why?" Lance asked softly.

"It will most likely kill you."

Lance's mouth fell open. "But you are smoking it."

"Yes, I know. I am immune to it; it will merely help me to sleep."

And Tulley did sleep, this time there was no twitching or words from far away that Lance could not understand. There was barely even a sign of breath. Lance watched as Tulley lay several feet away, totally motionless as if he were dead. Sometimes he thought Tulley was dead but then there would be the smallest flutter of his chest as he breathed and then he would be motionless again. Lance fell asleep that night hungry and thirsty and wandering if Tulley would be alive the next morning.

The next morning Tulley was gone. Lance found he had slept a little past sunrise and when he awoke he propped himself up enough to see Tulley's sleeping place only to find it void of a body completely.

"Tulley?" Lance called softly, then he dared to call a little louder and with more urgency. Several different emotions seemed to grab him at once. Confusion, worry, loneliness, anger, fear. Did Tulley become drugged and wander off to die someplace else…did he return to the cave for good this time…if not then why didn't he wake Lance? Lance tried to prop himself up the other way and was rewarded with pain in his shoulder that reminded him of his situation and the anger he felt grew stronger. He shouted Tulley's name one more time and then stopped to take a few deep breaths. Lance laid back down and closed his eyes for a few minutes as he gathered his thoughts and beat the unhealthy emotions back, once he accomplished that he propped himself back up and looked around. There was the two woven cups Tulley had made, each full of water, there was a small pile of sticks, enough to keep the coals on the fire going for the day, there was dried meat and there was the small pile of stones Lance had been playing with the day before to pass the time, everything within arm's reach for Lance. Lance blinked a few times as he looked over everything again, then he saw the letters scratched onto a leaf with a stick of charcoal from the fire.

"Be back before dark."

"Well, that's great," Lance said softly to himself as some of the tension he felt ebbed away. Lance rolled his eyes around as he took in more of the clearing. The squirrel-hide coat with the attached head Tulley had made was gone, along with the bone sabers and his satchel of cave foliage. Lance began to feel something deep in his stomach and he let out a small moan as he came to a realization.

I have to relieve myself.

With sweat rolling down the sides of his face and neck Lance found he was not totally helpless. It was hard and slow going but he managed to crawl around the area a little. He didn't make it as far away from the camp as he wanted, when Tulley helped him up to relieve his bladder they were able to go much farther, but at least he had done it on his own and made it back without much mishap; it did take him most of the morning to do so though. Lance tried to settle back on his nest of foliage but he ached all over and now that he didn't have anything to concentrate on, the pain had become sharp and annoying. Lance began to play with the pile of stones, stacking them, knocking them against each other and eventually throwing them at nearby blades of grass. His final stone he threw aimlessly and as hard as he could, it whizzed through the air and disappeared, then just as suddenly it came back and nearly hit Lance in the side of the head.

Lance looked up and saw Tulley coming through the grass, the squirrel hide draped over his shoulders, the head of the animal perched upon his head like a helmet with a face. The two sabers were tucked into his belt and there was flecks of red on his face and body.

"You almost hit me in the head," Lance said.

"You did hit me in the head," Tulley answered.

"Oh, sor…," Lance began to apologize but the word froze on his lips when Tulley fully entered the clearing. Riding on Tulley's back, thin arms and legs wrapped around his body, was a girl, an almost naked girl.

Lance could not speak and only gaped at her as Tulley gently began to pry her hands off of him, she did not wish to let go as she held her face buried in the back of his neck against the fur of the squirrel. Tulley spoke softly to her as he gently grasped her wrists, Lance could not understand what was said but the girl answered back in a very quiet voice.

"Look away, Lance," Tulley said to him. "That dumb look on your face is embarrassing her."

Lance still could not find words but he covered his face with both hands and shut his eyes. Tulley spoke more soft words to the girl that Lance could not understand and he could hear the rustle of movement, then he heard a familiar thump of a hollow wooden object.

"All right," Tulley said. Lance peeked out from between his hands first just in case the girl wasn't ready, but he did not see the girl, instead he saw the guitar, his guitar.

"My guitar!" Lance blurted out, totally forgetting the new comer for a moment. Lance grasped his old friend lovingly and ran his fingers up and down its neck and across its body. One of the strings was gone, the strap was still broken and someone had begun to carve a name into the wood.

"Where did you get it?" Lance asked, his amazement and respect for Tulley suddenly growing.

"In a bandit's camp. I also stole a horse, and her," Tulley motioned toward the girl, Lance hadn't even noticed where she had gone. She had buried herself in Tulley's nest and Lance probably would not have known she was there if Tulley had not pointed her out. Every part of her was covered and she peeked out at him like a mouse, because she was totally motionless Lance's gaze actually passed over her face before he realized it was her. Lance was slightly startled by just how light her eyes were, they were blue like fresh water that had iced over, so pale in fact that he could not tell where the blue of her iris ended and the white began.

"Tulley...," Lance said, not able to take his eyes from hers. "What is she?"

"You can see it too, huh," Tulley said softly as he took off the squirrel hide and laid it out on the ground. "I think she has Sprite blood in her, they all had almost white eyes. She also speaks some of their words, though it is very broken and another language is mixed in. Don't stare at her eyes for too long, that's how Sprites seduce you, they had her blindfolded at their camp, and heavily guarded. We should go, quickly, I'm positive they will come looking for her."

The girl blinked and Lance was suddenly able to tear his eyes away, when he did however he had spots in his vision as if he had been starring at the sun. Tulley kicked dirt into their fire and scattered the ashes with a stick until he was satisfied the red coals were harmless. Lance could only sit there blinking his eyes rapidly as he tried to regain his vision.

"I don't know if she understands what she is doing when she makes eye contact like that, she is very young. Sprites are actually a very dangerous breed and should be left alone, but they have been beating her and I fear using her to their pleasure."

Lance sucked in his breath at that.

"Rape?" he asked, suddenly feeling anger blossom up inside of him. Tulley did not answer but instead left for a moment and came back leading a chestnut mare that had deep soulful eyes. There was no saddle, not even reins, merely a thin cord around her neck but she followed so obediently that Tulley merely had to hold the end of the cord in his hand.

"She is older but her walk is silent and graceful so it should not trouble your wounds. She has seen battle and should not spook at anything." Tulley rubbed a hand on the side of her face.

"How do you know that?"

"She has scars, like me." Tulley looked at the bandages that still bound his palms.

"I think that is the most I have ever heard you say," Lance said, a smile curling up one side of his mouth.

"I like horses," was Tulley's only reply.

It only took a few minutes for them to be out of the small campsite. Tulley wrapped the squirrel hide around the girl like a robe, tying a strip of twisted grass around her waist like a belt. The girl pulled the hood up over her face and tucked her arms in; she could have passed for an old wrinkly squirrel at a glance. Tulley helped Lance to stand and managed to get him on the mare's back without hurting his pride too much, the mare stood patiently as Lance struggled up her flank. Lance nearly passed out once he finally managed to get his leg over her back, he leaned over the mare's neck and groaned, he was sure he must look pale and sickly. Tulley lifted the girl up to place her on the mare's back as well but she squirmed in his grasp and squeaked out some words, her voice fearful. Tulley set her back on her feet and leaned down to speak softly to her without looking her in the face, the girl answered back and then Tulley stood up straight and sighed.

"What's wrong?" Lance asked weakly.

"She says she won't ride. I had the same issue when we came away earlier, that's why she was on my back."

Tulley leaned down and softly spoke to her again, she held her hands up at her sides in a quizzical gesture; he spoke once more and then turned away from her. Tulley took the mare's thin rope in his hand, tossed the strap of his satchel across his bare chest and began walking away. The girl stood there for a long time and watched them go, Lance kept looking over his shoulder at her, and she continued to stand there until he lost sight of her.

Lance looked at Tulley's bare back as he walked ahead of him, the lighting stripes and two black handprints stood out boldly on his white skin. "You just leaving her behind?" Lance asked.

"I told her she would have to walk, I cannot carry her all day, I need my strength if I have to face issues ahead of us."

Lance had his guitar tucked under his good arm and he held it tighter against his side as he thought of the bandits that may come looking for them because Tulley took something important.

"But why leave her behind if you went to the trouble of saving her?"

"Don't worry, she is following," Tulley said. Lance looked behind them again but saw nothing.

"How do you know?" he asked through clenched teeth. Lance looked back again and then he noticed her fleeting form going from shadow to shadow, not making a sound and freezing perfectly still when she thought something had seen her.

"Sprites are fast and nimble, and can easily outrun a horse. She will have no problem keeping up."

By the time it grew dark the girl had caught up with them and was walking beside Tulley, her thin arm outstretched and her hand grasping the strap of his satchel so she wouldn't get lost. Lance thought they looked like a father and daughter walking side by side. The horse, which they dubbed Hannie, had begun to tire but faithfully plodded on beside Tulley without use of a lead rope or halter. Though Hannie's steps were gentle Lance was soon laying over her neck, his whole right side a constant ache. He could feel the heat rising in his injured leg and sometimes a bile taste came up from the pit of his stomach and caused him to gag. Eventually everything began to blur together in Lance's mind, the two figures before him became one large misshapen figure, a caterpillar perhaps, its head held high as it crawled along. Or maybe a rodent sitting up...or a squirrel...its tail curled beside it as it looked at him....

Lance was lying on his back, how did he get onto his back...? Once again the stars wheeled above him and a portion of it blacked out as Tulley leaned over him. A rough hand gently slapped his face.

"Are you all right? Lance, are you all right?"

"Wh...what?"

"You fell off of Hannie, are you all right?"

"Damn squirrel, go away!" Lance flung his hand up and hit Tulley in the face. Tulley did not move, he merely grunted and tucked an arm under Lance's shoulders. Lance felt like a rag doll as Tulley lifted him, his head sagged and he could not seem to get his limbs to work, they felt heavy.

"Come on, boy, not much farther. I can smell a fire with food. There's a home nearby. Gensieco went to find it."

Lance was not sure but he thought he heard Tulley say Gensieco, who the hell was that....? He wanted to ask Tulley who Gensieco was but he suddenly could not find him, Tulley was gone and there was only an apparition next to him in the darkness, one that had an arm around him and was trying to help him to walk.... Why didn't his legs work... ? Why couldn't he lift his arms...? Where was Tulley...? Did the squirrels get him...? And the other one, the smaller one that was naked, did the squirrels get her too...?

"Damn squirrels."

Chapter Three

Gensieco looked through the darkness and picked out the tiny pinpoint of light, it was not from a lightning bug or a glow worm, nor was it star light reflecting off of dew; it was light from a fire. Gensieco stared at it for a moment longer, memorizing exactly where it was, then she pulled the squirrel face back over her own and fled back to the man called Tulley, the man who had saved her, the man she loved.

"I found it," Gensieco cooed softly when she came back to Tulley.

"Good," was Tulley's reply. Gensieco squatted down for a moment, her arms wrapped about her body as a happy feeling entered her heart and spread a smile across her face. Tulley was pleased with her. Tulley was half carrying, half dragging the young man with the dark hair. The man's head hung low on his chest and he was mumbling something in his language.

"What's wrong with him?" Gensieco ventured to ask.

"He needs a bed," Tulley said. "Which way, Gensieco?"

Gensieco started back in the direction of the homestead she had found, Tulley following behind with his burden and Hannie behind them, her feet heavy and stumbling a little. Gensieco pointed at the light once she saw it, Tulley grunted in approval and she almost giggled with happiness. He was pleased with her, no one had ever been pleased with her before.

"Get yerselfs to beds, nows. Scrams, runs, hops, I don' not cares hows, but gets to beds." Jessica playfully swung a ladle at the group of children legging behind and poking fun at each other. They all immediately scattered with shoves and giggles, they knew Jessica would not hurt them with the large serving spoon but she would be disappointed in them and nobody ever wanted to disappoint Jessica. She was the one who took them in, fed them and clothed them, nursed them back to health and loved them; she was the mother they never had. They did not call her mother, though, nor did they call her Jessica, instead they called her Mims, a name the youngest child bestowed upon her because he was not old enough to pronounce Ma'am, and so Mims she became.

"Mims, Mims! I think there's someone's knocking."

Jessica stopped the ladle in mid-swing and turned toward the front room of their burrow. Their door would have been hard to find, hidden amongst the roots of the great tree, if it wasn't for the heavily used path going in and out and a few children's toys that were always left out. Jessica straightened her hair and skirt, the children crowded behind her but with some room between their group and her. Jessica tucked one more strand of hair behind her ear then she spun around on the children and with a loud "Shoo nows!" sent them all scattering and scurrying to their sleeping quarters. Jessica then untucked the dagger from her waist and opened the door a small crack. The light from her fireplace fell onto a small squirrel with a wrinkled looking face, it was hard for Jessica to see very well but to her horror a human arm reached up to the squirrel's face and flipped its head backwards as if its neck were broken. Jessica gasped and nearly slammed the door shut thinking that some demon had come to plague her when she saw what the squirrel hide really was.

"Whys, what's you doings all alones, young misses?" Jessica asked as she opened the door just a bit more. The girl looked at her with huge pale eyes but did not speak.

"We don't mean to frighten you, ma'am," came a rough voice from the darkness. "But I have a young man who needs a bed and a doctor, he's not fairing so well as of late."

Jessica squinted her eyes in the darkness and picked out the movement. A lengthy bare-chested man with rough features came into view and a good looking young man was beside him, practically draped over his arm. The young man did not look well, his eyes closed and face pale. Jessica's lips became a thin line as she studied them. The two eldest children were still up and Jessica could sense their presence behind her.

"Bobo, Hardin, please goes and sees to the spares rooms, puts some mores blankets and suches in theres."

"Yessum," the taller of the two boys said and then quickly left. The shorter, stouter boy remained, staring hard at the girl in the squirrel hide. The man behind her reached forward and pushed the hood back over her face, completely covering it.

"Hardin, gives thems some helps," Jessica said softly. Hardin nodded slightly and then stepping out the door he went to the other side of the sickly man.

"I am Hardin," the boy said.

"Tulley," the rough man said. "This is Lance and that is Gensieco. The horse is Hannie."

"Ohs, yous has a horse," Jessica said and she smiled. Tulley caught the glimmer in her eyes and gave a slight smile back; here was a woman who liked animals.

Tulley and Hardin supported Lance between them as they followed Jessica into the homely burrow. Tulley noted the fireplace, the fuel they used had been properly dried and barely smoked. He saw children peeking at them from behind curtains that covered doorways, their eyes wide as they studied the tattoos and Lance's limp form between Tulley and Hardin. The children had clean faces and most of them had a healthy glow, they looked happy and they immediately vanished as Jessica gave them all stern looks. It was hard to say how large the home was or how many hallways it had, or children in the hallways. There was hushed voices and giggles coming from the curtained off rooms, some still had candles burning and to these Jessica bid them goodnight, the candles would then promptly go out.

"I has beens heres me whole lifes," Jessica said. "Me father, he dugs outs all these heres rooms, there was fourteens of us childrens, me beings the eldests. Everyone elses, they all decides to leaves and makes they owns lives, but I stays, takes cares of Father and Mother. Once everyones leaves, the quiets, is too muchs. Makes Father and Mother sads, so's I begins to fills the rooms again. I has no childrens of me owns, never married. Would rather beats the mens overs the heads arounds heres, theys so rottens, the wholes lots of 'em. I finds strays and abandoneds littles ones. Some I helps to births and the mother, she alls alones 'cause of thems wars. Sometimes theys so worns thins and heartbroken from beings withouts their mans that theys just up and dies rights after birthin'. When I can'ts find them babies families I keeps thems heres. Theys thirty-twos of us nows, all boys, I always sends the girls to peoples more apt to takes cares of thems. It's a littles roughs heres, in the woods. The village beings halfs a day's walks away. We works hards and makes our ways though. Everyones is healthys and happy. Heres is the rooms for yous, this was father and mothers rooms, its is large and has a fireplace."

Tulley studied the room, it was indeed large, almost as large as the very first room they came to upon entering the house. There was a large bed with a real mattress bag of weed down. There was a small table with four chairs and two rocking chairs facing a window that was shuttered close for the night. There was already a fire in the small stone hearth and Bobo was just finishing with the blankets on the bed when they entered.

"Thank yous, Bobo," Jessica said as she gave him a quick hug before sending them both back out the door. Gensieco fairly floated to one of the rocking chairs and curled up on the seat, pulling her arms and legs in and laying her head down so she resembled a sleeping squirrel. Tulley looked at Lance briefly, touching his forehead and face and then feeling the heat resonating from his swollen leg.

"He needs somes docterin'," Jessica commented as she peeked around Tulley's shoulder. "Theres is a doctor buts he's not in the near-ests village. Bobo is quites a fasts runners and cans has hims backs by nights tomorrows, wills he lasts that longs?"

Tulley leaned his head to the side and then looked toward the fire.

"There is infection in his leg, I can smell it starting to turn bad. I will go and gather some herbs that will help but…yes, he does need a doctor. So please send Bobo as soon as you can, if it helps then take Hannie, she will be well rested if they leave in the morning."

"I don'ts thinks Bobo can rides, but loves to runs and wills makes it in plenties of times. I goes and fetches somes waters, for his hots head."

"Thank you," Tulley said softly as he gently felt Lance's leg again.

It's not good, Tulley thought to himself as he felt how swollen it was. A discoloration was beginning to surface and Lance groaned as Tulley gently probed around his kneecap. Tulley looked over his shoulder at Gensieco and called her over, like a snake she lithely came out of the rocking chair and was beside him without a sound. Tulley knew she was smitten with him, he had seen that same look on the faces of many women over his lifetime.

"I want you to stay here," he spoke sternly in her native tongue. "Do not speak to the other children, stay in this room with Lance unless you have to relieve yourself and above all keep your hood and your eyes downcast. I will know if you disobeyed when I return."

Gensieco quickly nodded her head. "I promise," she said softly.

"Help Jessica if you can, I know you won't understand her words but you are a smart girl, you will know what she needs I'm sure." Gensieco looked at Tulley and fairly beamed, Tulley cast his eyes down but that only caused him to notice the bruises on her legs from when she was tied up. The sound of Jessica softly scolding some children came to them and a moment later she entered the room with a wide mouth earthen jar in one hand and the other draped with several damp towels.

"Jessica," Tulley said softly. "This is Gensieco, she's not from around here so she does not speak the same language; however, she is willing to help with whatever you need."

Jessica smiled down at Gensieco.

"Aw, she's shys."

"Yes, she won't make eye contact and she wishes to stay close to Lance."

"You speaks likes you is goings somewheres."

"I am going to fetch the doctor."

"Right nows? Dos you knows the ways?"

Tulley walked out of the room with Jessica right behind him, softly speaking so not to disturb the children that were supposed to be sleeping. By the time Tulley reached the front room and was almost out the door Jessica could see it was no use.

"Wait," she said with such a pleading in her voice that Tulley did stop and look back at her. "At leasts puts on a shirts, it's a gettings colders at night."

"All right," Tulley said, it would also cover his tattoos, he thought to himself. "I'm sorry but do you have one I can borrow?"

"Of course," she said. Tulley watched Jessica ascend back to where they had just been, she returned with a brown tunic that had gold trim. It was fine material and felt silky as Tulley took a moment to rub it between his fingers.

"Thank you," he said as he slid it over his head.

"Bes carefuls," Jessica said.

Tulley did not answer, he merely gave a slight nod of his head as he exited. The door closed and for a moment Jessica continued to just stand there looking at it, then she flung it open in one last attempt at persuading Tulley to stay but he was already gone, as quickly as a moon-beam dissolving into shadow.

Lance had painful dreams, some of them quite vivid. He dreamed he was lying on the cave floor again, everything was black and his leg hurt like he had shattered everything in it. He tried to call for help, he called for Tulley over and over again until his mouth felt like cotton and he was having a hard time breathing. He called for his mother and at times she came to him, gently speaking to him and holding his head against her breasts. He would cry when she held him and he was not ashamed of it. He told her how he had been stumbling from village to town to village to homestead asking everyone for stories he could relay to the king, but he was failing. If he failed the king would send him and her away and he was so worried that she would die without a decent place to live and he did not know how to work to feed themselves. Lance cried with pity for himself because he did not know how to do anything except be a Bard, and Bards were useless outside a courtroom.

At one point Lance felt as though there were hands all over him, cold fingers digging into his naked flesh. He could not lift his arms and the darkness around him was growing heavy with a rancid smell that made his chest burn. For a time he felt he was not part of his body any-more. He dreamed that he had left his body and was looking down at it as it lay back in the campsite near the cave entrance.... Didn't they leave that behind? For some reason he was not sad that he had left his old body behind, his new one felt light and he did a somersault in midair. He looked upwards and saw a bright sphere that was illuminat-ing the campsite, he began to move toward it, how he did that he wasn't sure because at the current moment he just seemed to be a bodiless phantom. The sphere was growing in size as he moved closer to it, it felt warm and comforting, Lance smiled as he basked in the glow, and then something grabbed his leg. Lance jerked to a stop with a cry of pain, he looked back down at his body and screamed again. Squirrels. There was six of them, all standing around his inert form below, poking at him, pulling on his limbs, their tails twitching madly as they squeaked and chirped at each other. The darkness around the campsite where his body lay was slowly advancing on him, from above, Lance's spirit form could see other squirrels on the edges of the darkness, as though they were waiting for their turn to poke at him. The squirrel that was holding his right leg in its paws lifted the limb up, sniffed it and then bit into the flesh. Lance cried out again as he not only saw this happen but somehow felt it too. The squirrel ripped out a piece of flesh from just above Lance's knee. All the other squirrels suddenly froze as they looked at their companion chew the piece of bloody meat, then suddenly they all converged upon Lance's right leg. Lance screamed as he felt himself dragged down toward the ravenous animals, he felt their claws grabbing hold of his body and hold him in place as they continued to bite into his leg. The darkness pressed closer and the rancid smell returned, this time the taste of it was in his mouth as well. The darkness finally completely submerged him and Lance felt his body shiver with the sudden chill of it. The squirrels were gone and when he looked down his leg was still intact, he wiggled his toes just to be sure. He sighed several times as he tried to take control of his senses again. What was that feeling…? Was that hunger…? His mouth felt dry, when was the last time he ate or drank? Perhaps he would find food later, he was so tired but at least his leg did not hurt any longer, nor did his shoulder for that matter. Sleep, just a while longer.

Lance opened his eyes slowly and saw only blurry shapes before him. He closed them again and scrunched up his face as he yawned. He opened his eyes again and slowly rolled his head around as he looked at his surroundings. Strange, so very strange. He was in a furnished room, there was even a small fireplace. He could see a table that still had a plate and glass sitting upon it. Though it was sparse furnishings it was still much more than he had seen in the past year. He saw movement at the foot of his bed and perceived a bird perched upon the foot rail. Lance blinked and continued to look at the creature, no, not a bird, but what…? It was in fact a slim girl perched on the rail, squatting down so her knees were drawn up almost to her ears. She had her arms wrapped around her bent knees and balanced on her toes expertly as she stared at him, then she smiled and gracefully leapt from the rail to a shuttered window. The slim girl was clad in a brown and green tunic so long that she merely had to tie a belt around her waist and it became a dress. She flung open the shutters and in a young high-pitched voice she called out Tulley's name.

"Tulley," Lance croaked, his throat still felt dry. Lance slowly pushed himself into a sitting position, his head felt funny and he had to stop for a moment to let it clear. The girl looked back at him, her eyes were light blue like the sky on a bright spring day. Something tickled Lance's memory and he suddenly smelled fresh bread, and heard his mother singing as she worked in the kitchen. Lance suddenly felt like he had more energy so he swung his legs over the edge of the bed and stood up. He hit his head and shoulder on the ceiling and the room suddenly went dim. No, that wasn't the ceiling; he had fallen, it was the floor. Lance got his hands under him again and pushed himself up, he just had to get his feet under him and he would be fine. He fell again, this time his forehead made a hollow thump against the floor slats. What was wrong with his legs, he wandered as he rolled onto his side to catch his breath. The girl had her small hand on his shoulder and was speaking rapidly, but he could not understand what she was saying other than he heard Tulley's name several times. Lance gently pushed her away and tried to sit up. He looked at what was giving him so much trouble, his legs didn't want to work right.

Lance suddenly began screaming as the memory of the squirrels tearing into his flesh came to him, the pain was suddenly there was well. The girl jumped back and covered her ears as Lance used his arms to push himself backwards across the floor. His right leg was gone.

Chapter Four

"Stay away, oh children of mine, Do not wander out
alone.
For he will take you away with him, To a place of black
and moans.

He wears a raven's coat, And whispers death in your ear.
Though men be brave and strong, just his name doth
strike fear.

He flies upon wings of death, and walks the battlefields
at night.
He slays the wicked and righteous alike, whether in
darkness or light."

Tulley audibly cleared his throat and a few of the children flinched at
the sudden noise.

"A bit dark for the young ones, don't you think," Tulley said as he
came to their little gathering around Lance and sat down beside the

rocking chair. Lance did not answer but merely sat back in the chair and began rocking. The children looked toward Tulley and he nodded at them to disperse, slowly they left, the smaller ones tripping over themselves and a few holding their arms up to be picked up by the older ones. Gensieco ran around behind Tulley and leapt onto his back, throwing her arms around his neck like a child would do to their father or favorite uncle. Tulley gently unclasped her hands and shrugged her off his back.

"Go and play with the others," he said softly in her tongue so she had no excuse to not understand him. Gensieco made a pouty face at him but Tulley did not look at her, instead he picked up the woven hat she had knocked off her head and placed it back where it belonged. "And keep your eyes down," he warned as he pulled the brim low over her eyes. Gensieco folded her arms and turned away but did not leave until Tulley said her name in a warning voice, then she quickly skipped away like an innocent child playing, her bare feet kicking up the hem of her dress-like tunic. Tulley and Lance were silent for a time, watching the children play within the safe zone of the homestead, the rocking chair Lance sat in gently groaned as it moved forward and back.

"How are you feeling today?" Tulley asked, his voice as monotone as ever. Lance had been waiting for it, it was what Tulley asked every day.

"I'm fine," Lance said, it was the answer he gave every day.

"Your tales to the children are getting sadder, scarier, darker."

"I am running out of happy ones."

"Jessica, she says you're not eating much."

"I'm fine." Lance had stopped rocking, he was looking at the empty space where his leg should've been, now just a bandaged stump; he didn't even have a knee left. What good was a piece of leg if he had no knee to bend?

Tulley glanced at Lance then he leaned back, his hands behind him as he sat on the ground next to the rocking chair and looked upwards.

"You should get inside," he said almost absentmindedly. Lance looked down at him with a slightly quizzical look, Tulley got back to his feet and brushed the dust from his pants. They were part of the clothes that Jessica had given him. Dark green pants with one pocket on his right hip, with a tan tunic and a dark green vest. The clothes still hung loose on him like his old rags had, a belt was the only thing holding his pants up, but he was filling out very slightly. Jessica continually fussed over how thin he was and was constantly heaping more food in front of him. She had begun to fuss at Lance as well for he was also becoming thin, though he was still a far cry from how thin Tulley still was. Jessica had also fussed so much about the state of Tulley's hair that he had finally let her cut it and wash it while Lance was sick. The cut was a bit uneven and much shorter than Tulley had wanted, he constantly squinted now and complained of headaches when anyone asked him what was wrong, he had let his hair cover his face so before to shield his eyes from the sun. Now he wore a woven hat much like Gensieco's, he also kept the brim pulled down low. Tulley's difference in look had frightened Lance the first time he saw him. Tulley had rushed into the room while Lance was screaming and scuttling across the floor when he finally came back to consciousness. Tulley had grabbed him by the shoulders trying to calm him but when Lance saw this clean-shaven man he only screamed the louder, calling out Tulley's name.

"Lance! It's me! I am Tulley!" the man was fairly shouting in Lance's face as he tried to hold him still. Lance stopped long enough to look at this man claiming to be Tulley. He looked so much younger than Tulley, his face still gaunt but now it was clean and the dirty hair that had covered it was gone.

"Tulley?" Lance finally whispered, then the darkness that was gathering at the edges of his vision raced forward and he passed out.

Lance shook his head at the memory of seeing the "younger" Tulley for the first time. Tulley picked up the crutches that Lance had tossed away and leaned them against the arm of the rocking chair.

"It's going to rain later," he said and then walked away.

Tulley left Lance in the chair and went to Jessica as she was pulling seeds from a stem of grass nearby. Tulley reached up and plucked some of the seeds she could not reach.

"Are yous goings to brings him ins?" she asked softly.

"No," Tulley said just as softly. "If he doesn't learn to do things on his own he will only feel more depressed and pitiful."

Jessica sighed as she picked up the basket of seeds. She looked over at Lance and they both watched him for a moment as he tucked the crutches under each arm and attempted to stand. He managed one good hop and then fell forward, flinging the crutches outward as he flung up his hands to catch himself. Jessica started forward but Tulley caught her arm. Lance lay still for a moment breathing heavily, then he pushed himself up and grasped the crutches. Tulley released Jessica's arm, nodded approval and then walked toward a gaggle of children that were venturing too far away.

It did rain that day but the clouds rolled in slowly and they could feel the static on the air. The children were all rounded up and everyone stayed in the great room where the dinner table was. The tallow candles were lit and they cast dancing shadows on the walls as the children played Tiddle Toddle, a rhyming game that Tulley had taught them, designed to teach them letters. The children had all been excited when Tulley introduced them to Hannie. They were amazed at the fact that Tulley could read and write in several different languages. They thought Gensieco was unique and though she kept her eyes down and couldn't speak the same words as them they loved to hear her talk and they were teaching each other new words every day. Then they discovered Lance could play the guitar and recite historical Bard's tales and they were begging for them to stay.

The floor in the great room was earth since it was the lowest part of their home in the tree. Most of the children were gathered around Tulley as he used a stick to gently mark letters into the dirt floor. The children would come up with a word, like tiddle, and Tulley would write it down. Then they would change one letter at a time, or add or subtract a letter to make a new word. Changing the I to an O now made the word toddle, and then adding an R on the end now made it toddler, and so on and so forth.

Lance sat in a chair in the corner watching the children huddled around Tulley. Gensieco was continually trying to climb onto his back and every time Tulley would gently take one of her hands and pull her down. Jessica was kneeling in front of Lance as she readjusted the bandages around his stump.

"Are yous hungrys?" she asked softly. Lance did not answer, did not even look at Jessica. "I wills brings you somes dinners."

Lance continued to watch as Tulley once again set Gensieco back on her feet. One of the younger boys got excited that he had come up with a word and triumphantly jumped up with his fist raised, his little hand caught Tulley right in the nose and though Tulley rolled backwards with tears in his eyes, he laughed through his hand covering his face and told the boy it was all right.

He has so much patience, Lance thought. Jessica brought a plate of food over and held it out to Lance, he took it without a word but didn't eat it. After some time he set it on the floor, took up his crutches and awkwardly made his way toward the room Jessica had given them to stay in. Using the crutches hurt his armpits and made his arms sore from his shoulders down, it would certainly be easier to have Tulley carry him to where ever he needed to go but as he was regaining some strength Tulley did these things less and less; Lance knew Tulley was trying to get him to do things on his own. Lance came to the stairs and stopped. He was breathing heavy from the effort thus far and he had actually never gone up or down the stairs on his own yet. Lance looked over his shoulder, it seemed that nobody had even noticed he wasn't sitting in the chair anymore. Lance looked at the first step and thought on what he needed to do. The steps were old, well worn and slightly uneven, but they were still strong and didn't so much as groan even when the whole horde of children ran up or down them. So many children, all different ages, Lance had no idea how Jessica did it. She was truly a matriarch. Lance struggled up three stairs and stopped to lean against the wall and catch his breath, this suddenly seemed an impossible task. Lance pushed himself forward and made it up two more stairs before he felt himself begin to lose his balance. Lance tried to lean toward the wall but his body had other plans. One crutch slipped off the edge of the stair and as he felt himself leaning toward the point of no return, he opened his mouth to shout, but there was no time to. A pair of strong hands caught him by the shoulders and pushed him back upright, the thin fingers held onto him firmly and steadied him back to a standing position.

"Would you like some help?" Tulley asked in his unhurried monotone way.

"No," Lance replied almost harshly and he immediately felt bad for it. However, Lance only made it up one more step before he lost his balance again and fell backwards into Tulley's waiting hands. Sweat had appeared on his brow and he was breathing so hard that for a moment he couldn't speak.

"You have made it halfway…," Tulley commented. "Perhaps just sit on the steps to catch your breath and try again in a little while." Lance nodded at this and Tulley helped him to sit, then went back to the children who were all looking at him with wide eyes.

"How did you move so fast?"

"Wow!"

"Did you see what he did?"

"How did he know Lance was falling when he wasn't even looking at him?"

Tulley's celebrity status had just gone up again.

"Jessica, do you know what a Sprite is?" Tulley asked the next day as he watched the children play in the safe area, now muddy from the rain.

"Only evers heards of 'em," Jessica answered as she scraped some mud from her bare feet.

"Most women have never seen a Sprite. Sprites can't seduce women, only men. Gensieco is actually partly Sprite, she told me once that her father was not from their little clan and they had sold her off not long ago because her blood wasn't pure."

Jessica looked at Tulley with a pained and then angered expression. Tulley motioned for her to look at the children playing, a handful of them were on their own, each doing their own mischief, but another handful was following Gensieco around in a tight knot.

"Why do you dress the girls like boys?"

Jessica's body stiffened at Tulley's blunt question.

"I knew from the beginning that some of the children were girls. Even with their rough clothes, short hair and dirty faces, they still look far to pretty to be boys. And Bobo, she is getting a woman's figure, no matter how many baggy clothes you pile on her."

Jessica looked at Tulley with a stony glare.

"I do not ask you of those handprints," she said, her voice showing her anger and her speech suddenly sounding just like Tulley's, the accent gone and nothing sounding plural anymore. Tulley was slightly amazed at how fast her anger came. "I know of stories about men like you. Assassins for the Rising Sun. Mercenaries, murderers, rapists. If I had seen your back that first night before you brought Lance inside I would've killed you, I would've killed you both. But Lance has no such tattoos and it was such a long time ago when those men existed...." Jessica's voice grew quieter and calmed a little. "I decided to give you a chance." Jessica momentarily looked down. "I'm glad I did." She looked back up at Tulley.

"Besides," she continued, her accent returning as the anger suddenly disappeared as quickly as it had come. "That's was a longs times agos. I'm sures yous was nevers parts of those mens." Jessica turned to look at the children.

"I keeps the girls hiddens 'cause of 'em peoples who mays wants to hurts thems. I hads a youngers sister, theres was two boys betweens hers and I, buts for our wholes childhoods we was bests friends. And thens shes was takens. Father and anothers man, theys wents to finds her. Only brings backs hers body, alreadys wrapped and readys to be burys. Father was nevers the sames afters thats, and many years laters the others mans, he tells of whats they founds whens theys wents to finds her.... I nevers wants thats to happens to anyones else."

Tulley nodded. "I understand," he said softly. "I will keep the secret safe, and I will tell Gensieco to keep her eyes down."

"Will theys be alrights? The boys followings hers?"

"She is not pure blood and doesn't understand what she is doing just yet. Yes, they will be fine. A Sprite wakes happy memories in a person, so if that person is lost in the woods those happy memories are like salvation and they become attached to the Sprite. However, they will forget to eat and drink and usually starve to death. Sprites love to see people happy, that's why they continue to do what they do. If someone they seduce dies happy then they were saved, that's how sprites look at things."

"How awfuls," Jessica murmured.

"Tulley!"

The shout was hushed and directed right at him, Tulley spun around and looked up to see Lance at the small window of his room. Lance pointed straight out across the brush and toward the main path.

"Something is coming," Lance called out. "Something big."

Jessica rushed forward calling to the children to grab a hand and get inside. Each child had another that they were to go to if trouble came, the younger ones paired up with an older one. Gensieco was left standing in the middle of the safe area looking around like a confused bird, her head constantly turning from one side to the other. Tulley called to her in her language and she instantly ran for the tree just as the others were. Tulley raced up the stairs taking two and three at a time, he had to see what Lance was seeing, and he had to get his sabers from the room just in case.

Lance was standing at the window, his hands bracing him up as he leaned forward to see better, he leaned aside so Tulley could look out the small window as well.

"There, do you see it?" Lance asked indicating an area to the south. There was something coming toward them, moving slowly and deliberately. Tulley could see black and gray fur through the branches, the grasses and short brush was easily pushed aside or beneath the feet of the creature.

"What is it?" Lance asked. Tulley did not answer right away but grabbed up his sabers that were leaning against the doorpost.

"It looks like a badger," he said over his shoulder. "Close the shutters so the window is hidden, I'm going to try and deter them."

"What do you mean them?" Lance asked as he pulled the shutters closed and then made the two hops back to the chair.

"Those bandits I stole Gensieco and Hannie from, they had a pet badger." Tulley raced back down the stairs, this time taking three and four at a time, he landed heavily at the bottom and only stopped long enough to pull a long cloak from a peg and fling it around his shoulders. Tulley fastened it across his chest and pulled it closed to hide his arms as he held his sabers.

"Are all the children accounted for?" he asked Jessica as he speed walked toward the door. The children were still pouring in and Jessica was trying to count them as they all took seats on the floor.

"Don't knows yets," Jessica said as she shushed them while she counted.

"Stay inside and stay quiet," Tulley commanded as he pushed his way out the door. Tulley made straight for the oncoming badger, pushing through the tall grasses and ducking under the brush. Tulley leapt up to a branch that was overhanging the path the badger was taking and settled down with one leg folded and the other dangling, his arms and sabers still hidden. The badger lumbered into sight, its long nose sniffing at plants and earth as it went. Its wide paws with the long claws sometimes digging into the soil, at first Tulley only saw the badger but then the two riders came into view as well. They were both wearing the short black cloaks Tulley had seen when he had sneaked into their camp, these cloaks had hoods that were pulled low over their faces. Tulley reached up and pulled the hood of his cloak lower then, after tucking his arm away again, he called out to the men.

"You a longs ways from yours homes," he stated, adapting Jessica's accent quite easily since he had been listening to it for several weeks now.

The badger suddenly stopped and looked up with black squinty eyes, it had not smelled Tulley because he had come upon them from downwind. The two men tensed, the man in the front took a tighter hold of the reins that went to the ring in the badger's nose, the man in the rear reached for a weapon at his side, Tulley saw a crude crossbow raised and called out again.

"Woah, friends, I means no harms. It's justs we don'ts gets many peoples arounds heres, I know everyones by theys face and I don'ts knows yous."

The men were silent for several long moments then the one in front spoke.

"We are searching for something that was taken from us. Someone kidnapped our youngest sister."

"Ohs?" Tulley called down, forging interest and concern. "Whats she looks likes, perhaps I cans keeps my eyes outs for hers."

"She is very slender and young of face. Hazel hair and blue eyes, very light blue eyes, with pale skin."

"Ohs? And she's yours sister, yous says?" Tulley made it obvious he was looking over their black hair, dark eyes and well-tanned skin.

"Yes, she was adopted not long ago but she is still our sister."

"I sees, I sees," Tulley said thoughtfully. "I has nots seen anys young ladies likes that's arounds here."

"Very well but we wish to look ourselves." The badger was prodded to move on and it began to walk forward after an aggravated shake of its head.

"Alrights, but yous shoulds be carefuls. A neighbors downs the ways says there is bandits in the areas."

They had just passed beneath Tulley and though the rear man was watching Tulley closely the driver pulled the badger to a stop and the badger shook its head again, nearly unseating the man. Tulley let himself fall backwards out of the tree, flinging the cape wide as he lashed out with his sabers. The rear man didn't even have the time to look back at Tulley before one saber imbedded itself in his forehead. The man in front gave the badger a vicious jab that sent the poor creature into hysterics, Tulley knew the animal was becoming perturbed with the riders and he counted on the animal fighting back. The badger turned in a tight circle and bucked twice, Tulley bounced off the badger's spinning body and after a slightly painful landing he rolled away so as not to get stepped on by the pounding feet and huge claws. The driver somehow managed to hang onto the angered animal but the body of his companion fell and was crushed, his split-open skull gushing out blood as his body was pummeled beneath the stomping feet. The remaining rider continued to yank on the reins one way and then the other, the ring in the badger's nose was beginning to spurt blood and the poor creature wheezed and growled in pain.

Tulley slipped his hands free of his sabers and dropped them to ground beside him as he crouched down, one hand snaked up and un-clasped the long cloak, that too fell to the ground around him. Tulley watched for an opening as the badger continued to spin around, the moment he saw it Tulley leapt forward, his hands aiming for the bloody ring in the end of the badger's pointy nose. Tulley's hands hit their mark and he clasped it as he brought his feet down on the badger's sagging lips trying to stay clear of the sharp teeth. The badger froze for a moment, stunned and surprised at somebody clinging to his face, the rider seemed even more stunned.

Tulley looked the badger in the eye, whispered, "I'm sorry," and then pulling with his arms and pushing with his legs he ripped the nose ring free and fell backwards, the ring still in his hands. The badger screamed in pain and gave one huge jump, Tulley once again landed painfully but as he saw the creature rise up he gave the ring a hard jerk. The rider was still clasping the reins and with the combined efforts of Tulley and the badger the man was finally dislodged and plummeted to the ground. The man fairly landed on his head and though he still looked to be alive Tulley never got to confirm it, he watched as the badger fairly tackled the man and clamped his teeth on the man's head. Tulley didn't so much as flinch as he heard the man's skull crunch, the badger gave a jerk of its head and popped the man's head off like he would a dandelion head. The badger chewed twice and swallowed, then it clenched the man's torso in its teeth and picked him up, the man's arms and legs twitching as they hung from the jaws of the badger. Tulley still had not moved, the ring still clasped in his hands, the badger looked at him but it merely grunted and then turning, the dead man still in its mouth, it trundled away, the prominent black, white, and gray stripe running down its wide back and tail. Tulley still remained unmoving until even the sound of the animal had disappeared and the only thing left was a few drops of blood. Tulley dropped the ring and stood up, he glanced at the dead man and then turned to gather his cape and sabers, Tulley's right leg buckled and he fell to his hands and knees.

Tulley turned over to a sitting position and looked at his shin where a patch of his pants leg was blossoming blood.

Must've caught a tooth, Tulley thought as he pulled his pants leg up to look and sure enough, right in the middle of his shin was a round hole that leaked blood like a tiny spring. The fresh red blood flowed

The Black Sparrow

down his ankle and across the top of his foot, Tulley grimaced as he pulled off his pretty shirt to tie it around his lower leg. Slowly, gingerly Tulley rose to his feet to test his walking ability. He limped over to the cape and flung it back over his shoulders, then he picked up his sabers and after he slipped the spider silk back around his wrists he began the painful walk back toward the huge tree.

"You has a holes in the middles of yours shins!" Jessica exclaimed as she unwrapped the bloody shirt while Tulley sat in a chair, his injured leg propped up on another chair.

"Great," Lance commented. "The doctor can cut off your leg and then we would be a matching pair." Lance laughed softly to himself.

"Though that is a bit of a dark joke," Tulley commented in his usual monotone. "I am happy to hear you laugh again; however, I do hope I don't have to continuously injure myself to make you laugh."

"Bobo," Jessica called. "Go ands gets the salves Doctor lefts for Lance's leg, we shalls puts somes on Tulley's."

But to Jessica's astonishment Bobo did not step up to do as she had asked. Jessica turned to look over some of the children that had not gone to bed yet.

"Where's Bobo?" Jessica asked, a hint of a tremble behind her cheery voice. A few of the children looked down and back and forth at each other.

"Where's Bobo?" Jessica asked again, more firmly this time. Tulley sat up in the chair and began to scan the faces of the children in the flickering candlelight.

"She went outs to finds Hannie, Mims," one medium-sized child answered with head bowed and eyes gazing at the floor.

The earthen bowl Jessica held fell from her grasp, it shattered and water splashed out to mingle with the dirt on the floor. Tulley glanced down at the muddy spot at Jessica's feet and then jumped up to embrace her as a scream escaped her lips.

Chapter Five

Tulley flattened his body against Hannie's shoulder and neck as she surged forward, cutting through the tall grasses and breaking through leaves. He had found her footprints where she had followed Hannie into the brush behind the tree, Bobo had gone much farther than Jessica would have ever allowed, at first Bobo circled back but then the other footprints joined hers. There was a jumble of them, like the men had gathered around her and then Tulley found her short cloak, the clasp torn. Jessica buried her face in the auburn material and wept, the children gathering around her to comfort her; nobody noticed Tulley leave.

"Only what you can handle, old girl," Tulley called to Hannie as he watched the footprints of the four men stretch on ahead. The camp was not as far away as Tulley had thought it would be. He smelled the smoke from the fires first then he heard the sound of the brook just beyond. Hannie's body was becoming slick from her frothy sweat and her tongue lolled out the side of her mouth as she breathed hard. Tulley pointed her right for the center of the camp, gave her a pat on the neck and bailed off, tucking his body as he rolled and avoided her rear hooves. He knew they had heard Hannie coming and they were prepared, but when a riderless horse that didn't even have reins plummeted through camp and knocked down a tent, the men only cursed and mingled before they then began to look around for any other trouble.

Tulley pulled the hood of the squirrel hide over his face and then leapt forward toward the closest man. His body sailed straight toward the man's head, arms outstretched with a saber in each hand. The man looked up just at the last minute and flung up a piece of firewood. One saber glanced of the makeshift shield while the other one barely caught him in the shoulder. Tulley felt his hand that held the deflected saber tremble; something had cracked and it was not the piece of firewood the man held up. Tulley brought one foot down and managed to land a blow with that before he hit the ground. The man finally toppled but not before he let out a pained shout. Tulley spun on his heel and the saber bit into the man's throat instantly cutting off the alarm, but it was an instant too late.

Tulley had counted fourteen men when he had sneaked in and stolen Hannie and Gensieco away, since he had already killed two and released their badger he expected there to only be twelve. He glanced down at his left hand, the saber was cracked and would not last the night; the odds did not seem to be in Tulley's favor.

Bobo heard the commotion, the shouts, a sound like an animal screech, but she could see none of it. She was tied, gagged and blindfolded with a piece ripped from her own cloak. She did not know what time of day it was or where they had taken her. As soon as they had pounced on her and had her trussed up, one man tossed her over his shoulder, his large hand grasping the upper part of her thigh, and put her through a rough ride; her ribs still hurt from bouncing around on his shoulder. Bobo tried to wiggle around but only managed to roll onto her back, which would have been fine but now she was lying awkwardly on top of her tied hands.

"Where is she?!" Bobo heard someone yell; was that, Tulley? His usual quiet monotone was suddenly loud, full of anger and commanding.

It seemed fairly obvious he was looking for her. Bobo rolled back onto her side and since she could not call for help she began to wish he would find her. Someone let out a long and very loud scream, it seemed to be right on top of her and Bobo cringed as she expected a body to fall over her and probably smother her. There was the sound of a falling body as it landed next to her, the man's elbow did hit her in the face but she barely felt it, for a moment later she felt a pair of long thin arms grab her around the waist and lift her off the ground.

"Trust me!" Tulley's voice commanded in her ear. He was running, half dragging and half carrying her. Bobo managed to rub her face against his shoulder and uncover one of her eyes. She saw the camp steadily falling behind them as Tulley ran. Several of the tents were knocked down, one tent was on fire, as was a man running toward them, his body a flaming torch from head to foot. A handful of men were prone on the ground, blood staining the soil around them. A couple of men were just standing there, one of which was looking at his hands...or at least one hand, the other was gone just below the elbow. Two men were kneeling as they took aim with crude crossbows but both arrows went wide and they had to stop and reload. Bobo felt Tulley falter for a moment in mid-stride, Tulley gathered his body and then leapt through the air with Bobo draped over one shoulder. Bobo screamed through her gage as she saw the ground beneath them disappear and become water, she could not swim and she was still tied. In midair Tulley shifted her off his shoulder and for a moment they were plummeting separately, Bobo stared down at the oncoming water as she continued to scream through her gage. She felt Tulley's hands tightly grasp her shoulders and seemed to pull her up-right, she looked forward, the wind of their fall was causing her eye to water and everything looked blurry but she thought she could see the other side of the brook. Somehow, probably because it was a small brook and Tulley actually had very powerful legs, it seemed they were going to land on the other side of the water. Bobo pulled her feet up and tried to make herself into a ball as they continued to plummet forward. An arrow whistled by her ear so close that it scratched her check and ripped the gage still tied around her mouth. Tulley suddenly let go of her shoulders and like a stone they plummeted down, missing the other bank and landing in the water as it flowed around stones and washed away leaves, twigs and whatever else fell into its eddies, including the two little folk who had dared to jump from bank to bank.

"I am so sorry!" Tulley moaned over and over again as he walked toward the great tree, carrying Bobo's limp form in his arms. For the first time Lance could hear emotion in his voice, exhaustion, anger, sadness, regret....

Jessica rushed forward, a blanket in her arms, she wrapped it around Tulley's shoulders and across Bobo's body.

"I am so sorry! I had her, we were going to make it across but then we fell in the water and she was still tied up. I got her to breathe again but she won't awaken. I am so sorry!"

Jessica hushed Tulley as she guided him inside to a room that she kept just for sick children. There was a raised pallet that already had blankets and pillows and Jessica ran around the edges of the room lighting the half-dozen candles that was there. This room seemed to be in the heart of the tree, the walls were covered in the natural designs of the wood and the ceiling climbed up like a chimney and continued out of sight, though there was no windows Tulley could smell fresh air coming from the chimney like ceiling.

Jessica bent over Bobo as she listened to her shallow breathing, her clothes were torn, wet and muddy and her body had several scrapes and bruises.

"Outs, outs with yous," Jessica said as she turned upon Tulley and some of the worried children crowding at the door, Lance in behind them all. Tulley turned to leave and the children all took several hasty steps back, Lance could not move fast enough on his crutches and was knocked over by the throng.

"Gets some drys clothes ons, Tulleys," Jessica called as she shut the door. Tulley stopped and leaned against the door frame, his head bowed and his shoulders slumped as he stared at the floor, he suddenly looked like the old Tulley again, the shadow of a beard beginning to form on his face. Two of the bigger kids helped Lance back to a standing position but then they all mingled as they waited for Jessica to ask for anything.

"Tulley," Lance said as he came closer, his crutches making hollow sounds on the slats of the floor. "Are you hurt?"

"No," Tulley said as he stood straighter, the blanket falling from his shoulders. Lance noticed the two sabers tucked away at Tulley's hips, one on each side, but the one on the left was broken off just below the handle.

Tulley returned to the sick door sometime later, washed, shaved and in clean clothes. Lance was sitting in a chair that one of the children had brought for him, one arm folded across his chest while the other hand served as a resting place for his chin.

"Whats the news?" Tulley asked, back to his normal monotone.

"No news yet," Lance replied. They were silent for a time.

"Gensieco missed you," Lance said in an attempt at small talk. "She said if you didn't come back by nightfall she was going to go slaughter all those men, at least I think that's what she was saying. Her words are still pretty mixed between the languages. Jessica threatened to tie her to a chair."

"She is a fiery one, but don't under estimate her. A full-blooded Sprite will hold its own against a half-dozen men."

"I told them the story of how horses came to be, but that only upset her all the more. She said the history was all wrong and that horses are here for us because a Sprite caught a Pooka fairy in horse form and spared its life. Now Pookas don't exist anymore but horses do."

"It depends on what culture you are from. I have heard several different variations but they always seem to involve fairies of one sort or another."

They were silent again for a while and Tulley seemed to become lost in thought, Lance noticed his hand snake up to his shoulder where he would seem to twine a string around his fingers, but Lance could see no string. He watched Tulley make this gesture several times over the next ten minutes and still he could not see what Tulley was running between his fingers. They all nearly jumped when Jessica opened the door, her face was pinched and her eyes were red.

"I cans dos no mores, I am afraids shes wills be deads by mornings."

Several of the children made gasps and a few of them broke into tears, Jessica turned to go back into the room but Tulley caught her by the wrist and stopped her.

"Let me talk to her," he said softly.

"She is nots awakes," Jessica said, shaking her head.

"Please," Tulley said as he continued to hold her wrist. Jessica searched his eyes and after a quivering of her lower lip, she stepped aside.

"I'm sorry, I need to talk to her alone," Tulley said as he entered and quickly shut the door. Lance and Jessica exchanged looks and then Jessica turned to the children to calm them and send them to their rooms. Lance gently tucked his crutches under his arms and rose up. He managed to get to the door without making a sound and he pushed it open just enough to look into the room. He saw Tulley at the far side of the room, once again twining something through his fingers, Tulley then pressed his fingers to the wall in front of him as if he had stuck something to it. Lance watched in wonderment as Tulley then cupped his hands and leaned into the wall, his face nearly against it and resting in his hands. Was he speaking to the wall? What good did that do…?

Lance hit the floor with a crash and the door was pulled shut, he looked up to see who had knocked him down and saw Gensieco standing before the door, her little body guarding it as she held her arms outstretched. She had a fire in her eyes as she fussed at him but Lance immediately looked down before she could take hold of him with her stare.

"Gensieco, you know I can't understand you," Lance said as he braced himself on the chair and tried to stand up.

"You no look!" Gensieco snapped angrily. "Tulley speak magic. Tulley speak tree. You no look magic speak."

"How do you know that, Gensieco, only fairies possess magic anymore. Little Folk can't even transform anymore."

Gensieco knitted her brows at Lance and let out a long string of words in her own language. Lance shook his head and decided it was best he remain on the floor.

"Ordman, taus saico," Tulley whispered into the wall before his face. *Awaken, great spirit.*

"Why do you call me with those words?" came a voice into Tulley's head.

"Great spirit of this tree, I beg of you to tie yourself to this young lady and breathe some of your life into her."

"You have life left, and power it would seem. Why do you not do this thing?"

"My life is forfeit and this power is not my own, I do not wish to curse her with what I have. But you, great spirit, your life and your power is your own and can give it freely."

"And if I am not feeling so generous...?"

"It is your choice, great spirit, many do not wish to be generous anymore. They horde what they were gifted with rather than share their gifts."

Tulley felt a pressure upon his very being as the tree rumbled like an earthquake, its huge limbs swayed though there was no breeze and there was a groaning and squeaking as the great branches moved and rubbed together.

"How dare you insult me."

"Then prove me wrong."

"How dare you."

The pressure grew stronger and Tulley suddenly found he could not breathe anymore. Tulley remained frozen like that, unable to move, breathe or even blink. There was another rumble beneath his feet and then all was deathly still for a long moment.

"I have studied this girl and find her spirit worthy."

Lance and Gensieco stared at each other as the tree rumbled all around them but Gensieco did not show fear at this. The whole thing only took moments and once it was all done Lance had a brief thought that he had just imagined it all, but then Jessica came rushing forward, her eyes wide with fear. Gensieco stepped away from the door and Jessica flung it open just in time for them to see Tulley's body fall away from the wall where he had been standing. He hit the floor flat on his back, his arms and legs spread and his chest heaving as if he had been holding his breath. Jessica cried out when she saw Bobo sitting up in bed, with eyes wide, Jessica flew to the girl's side with tears in her own eyes.

Jessica wrapped her arms around Bobo and sobbed on her shoulder. Gensieco quietly stole into the room and kneeled down by Tulley, who now had his arm across his eyes.

"Bring me my satchel and pipe, I have such a headache," Tulley fairly whispered, Gensieco rushed out of the room nearly knocking Lance down on the way.

Bobo pushed Jessica away for a moment and looked at her, amazement on her face.

"Mims!" she fairly cooed with excitement, her voice sounding so much like a child's. "Mims, I think I was flying!"

Chapter Six

Tulley's hands shook as he stuffed his pipe, a few sprigs of the dry moss floated to the floor and Tulley scooped it back up lest one of the young ones found it later.

"Are you all right?" Lance asked as Tulley tried to light the pipe against one of the tallow candles, it took a few tries and he almost knocked the candle over but he managed it. Tulley grunted a little in answer and then leaned back against the wall as he drew in the smoke and held it.

"You sure you want to sleep on the floor?"

"Honestly I don't care right now," Tulley answered as he blew the smoke toward the window of their room and pinched the bridge of his nose. "My whole body hurts, I don't think I can stand up again, I'm lucky I made it to our room."

Lance studied him for a minute, his hands still trembled and dark circles were below his eyes. His face had suddenly looked gaunt and thin, his skin blotched and shiny from perspiration. Tulley had managed to stand and walk out of the sick room of his own accord but he didn't quite make it to their room still standing, the last few steps he dropped to his knees and crawled till he could sit against the wall just below the window.

"What did you do?" Lance finally ventured to ask. "Gensieco said you spoke magic to the tree."

"I did, at least to the druid spirit that resides in this tree. I asked it to give some of its abundant life to Bobo. I upset it a little though and now I am paying for that, have you ever broken a bone? My whole body feels like that right now."

"I don't understand, you actually talked to the tree?"

"Of course, everything living has a spirit, be it plant or animal, though one usually cannot talk to it unless it has a druid tied to it. When a druid dies it tends to tie itself in with the spirit of a plant and so it continues to live as that plant, trees being the most common. I guessed this tree had a druid spirit, it being so big and old, I just had to wake it up."

Tulley drew in on the pipe again and held it, his hands had steadied to a periodic tremble.

"So, if I had come any closer to death you would have just asked the tree to give me a bit of its life to revive me?" Lance asked.

"No," Tulley answered, his voice sounding heavy. "You are a stranger to this druid, it would have flatly told me no and probably killed me for waking it up. I took a chance for Bobo. I hoped the druid would consent and help her since he has watched her grow up beneath his branches. Luckily, I was right."

Jessica knocked on the door and entered without waiting for a reply, she had bandages tucked under one arm and a blanket under the other. She walked right up to Tulley, knelt down next to him and then threw her arms around his neck. Tulley held his pipe aloft and gently patted her on the back, Jessica held onto him for a little longer then pulled away and wiped her eyes.

"Bobo was thes firsts baby I evers birtheds, shes is very specials to mes. I don'ts understands whats you dids, buts shes is alives, thanks yous so muchs!"

Tulley nodded at her as he tucked the stem of his pipe back in the corner of his mouth, already his eyes were half closed and his shoulders were relaxed.

"Lets me sees yours shins," Jessica motioned to his bandaged shin that had a faded red blotch on the front. Jessica slowly unwrapped the injury, being careful of where the blood and bandage had dried to the skin, she gasped when she finally got it off. Tulley and Lance leaned in to look and saw a shin that was perfectly fine, uninjured and whole.

"You didn't have to do that," Tulley said as he placed his hand against the wall and patted it. Jessica and Lance each gave him confused looks.

"When the druid healed Bobo it must have decided to take care of my shin as well."

"And yet you can barely walk after upsetting it," Lance stated. Tulley shrugged.

"Fairies of any kind are fickle." Tulley let out a long sigh and reached for the blanket Jessica had brought in.

"I'm sorry," he murmured. "I am so exhausted." Tulley sprawled out on the floor and fell asleep hugging the wadded up blanket like a pillow. Jessica gently took the pipe from his lax fingers and dropped the smoldering thing into a bowl of water that sat on the table.

"You feeling better?" Lance asked late the next day as he twined a new string onto his guitar.

"Headache is still there," Tulley answered as he sat up. "Where did you find new string?"

"A couple of the boys killed a field mouse early this morning, I washed out one of the guts but I need to get it on my guitar before it starts to dry out. We will have fresh meat for dinner, are you hungry?" Lance looked toward Tulley and smiled.

"You seem awful cheery all the sudden." Tulley ran a hand through his uneven hair, it was starting to feel greasy, he would need a good washing soon.

"I think I found the story I have been looking for."

"Oh?" Tulley asked as he rose and went toward the door.

"Will you tell me of your adventures? I'm sure I can make up lyrics that will show how heroic you truly are."

Tulley paused for a moment at the door and then flatly answered, "No."

"Tulley, I made this for you," Bobo said as she brought him a small carved trinket on a string. Tulley held the trinket in his palm and turned it over a few times, the rough carving was of an oak leaf, much like the ones on the tree above them. Tulley tucked it around his neck and gently taking Bobo's hand in his, he kissed the back of it in thanks. Bobo giggled, an almost unnatural sound coming from a young lady that resembled a beautiful boy, and she ran off to be with the other children playing in the safe area. Tulley and Lance were both helping to watch the children while Jessica had went to help a pregnant mother who had gone into premature labor.

"Come on, Tulley," Lance poked at him. "What you did with the druid is unheard of now, tell me where you learned that."

"No."

Jessica came home the next morning riding on the back of a cart pulled by two fat old rabbits. She disembarked from the cart and the children gathered around to inspect the two large sacks the driver was handing down.

"Berries!" they began to exclaim when the fresh fruity scent reached them.

"How is the little mother?" Tulley asked as he came forward to take a sack.

"Shes is fines," Jessica said her eyes dancing. "Its was twins, boths is smalls but strongs. Bastian, hes is gratefuls and sends foods fors us alls."

"That's it!" Lance exclaimed from behind Tulley. "I can change your name so no one will ever know it was you, I can call you Bastian, a noble name."

"No."

Tulley held his head over the wooden trough and let Jessica douse it with the warm water, she then began to lather in the gritty soup making his scalp sting. Tulley could hear the tapping of Lance's crutches before the door slid open. Once again Lance marveled at Tulley's tattoos as he stood, with no shirt on, bent at the waist while Jessica thoroughly washed his hair.

"The king wants to hear stories of battle and saving pretty women, I'm sure you have done those things and I am sure he will pay you handsomely if he really likes it."

"No."

Tulley stuffed his pipe with wild tobacco he had found while scouting for the bandits, he leaned back on his cot as he puffed and looked at the stars through the small window. Lance rolled over in his soft bed and cleared his throat.

"I can...."

"No! Don't you ever give up?"

"No."

Tulley sighed and rose from his mat on the floor, he pulled his shirt on and picked up the squirrel hide from the back of a chair.

"Where are you going?" Lance asked as he watched Tulley grasp the unbroken saber and tuck it into his belt.

"I'm going to find Hannie back, I miss her quiet company."

"You're going in the dark?" Lance asked but there was no answer, not even the sound of footsteps as Tulley walked away.

Tulley returned late the next day leading Hannie and another horse, this one tall and black.

"Pooka!" Gensieco called when she saw the creature.

"Is that what you want to name it?" Tulley asked, he saw the knot of boys once again following Gensieco and he pushed the brim of her hat down. Two girls had joined the little group of followers but they merely stood next to Gensieco and cooed over the horses as well.

"Yes!" Gensieco laughed as she touched the nose of the black horse.

"Very well," Tulley said as he handed over the reins and walked toward the tree. Lance sat on the front porch and watched him come nearer. His clothes were dirty and stained, as was the saber. A smudge of red was on his forehead and some in his hair, his clothes were ruined.

"Ohs!" Jessica exclaimed as she came out the door. "Whats dids yous dos?"

"Are you injured? You are covered in blood!" Lance exclaimed.

Tulley untied the squirrel hide and pulled it off. "It's not mine," he answered. "I did what I had to," he said softly. "Those men won't be taking any more young girls ever again." Jessica's hands went to her mouth. "I'm sorry, Jessica, but could you wash my hair again?"

"Lance, remember that story you were trying to tell the children and I interrupted you?"

"*The Man Who Whispers Death*? What about it?"

"Will King Aiden really kick you and your mother out of his palace if you do not come back with a good story?"

Lance turned his head sideways a little and put down his guitar.

"How do you know that?" he asked. Tulley tapped the ash out of his pipe and dug in his hip pocket for another piece of the tobacco leaf.

"When you were sick, you spoke of such things. Finding a story for your young king weighs heavy on your mind, doesn't it?"

"Where are you going with all of this, Tulley?"

"I don't much care for all the stories about that man, the one they call the Black Sparrow. They are all so dark and make him out to be evil, they really don't know him at all."

"And you do?" Lance asked.

"Yes," Tulley answered in a matter-of-fact tone. Lance caught his breath and stared at Tulley, unbelieving.

"I didn't get these tattoos 'cause I was a huge fan of him, you know." Tulley spoke softly so he did not scare the children. "Everyone in our group had such tattoos."

Lance looked away, his eyes still wide, the hair on the back of his neck stood on end; he was suddenly scared of Tulley.

"I have thought about this for a long time now. I want you to write a story, the story of before this man became the Black Sparrow, I want people to see him as a good person, because that's what he was."

"But he killed so many," Lance whispered. "He killed the entire court of the Kingdom of the Rising Sun, they say that's what plunged all of the Little Folk and the spirits and fairies into such wars and unrest because they were the peacekeepers between all the clans of all the species." Lance's voice was rising in pitch and he was talking faster as he continued. Tulley held up his hand and shushed him.

"Lance, I have killed so many, I don't even know anymore. Does that make me evil? Does that make me like the Black Sparrow?"

"He killed generations for no reason. He hunted down entire clans of fairy folk and stole magic from spirits. You killed bandits, and saved Gensieco and Bobo."

"How do you know that the Black Sparrow wasn't also killing bandits? How do you know that this so-called Court of the Rising Sun wasn't corrupt?"

"They were the only ones keeping peace!"

"They used the Black Sparrow and his cursed men to kill, they hid behind them and used them as scapegoats. I know, I was there."

"You couldn't have been, it's been several generations since the Black Sparrow has even been seen, and even longer since the Court of the Rising Sun was killed."

"When one accrues this much magic over the years they tend to live longer than expected. I am much, much older than I look."

"You mean stolen!" Lance accused. "You killed fairy folk and spirits and stole their magic! You should be dead, you deserve to die!" Lance awkwardly got to his one foot and swung around on his crutches but Tulley caught his wrist.

"Why do you think I was in that cave?! I want to die! I thought it would be a suitable grave, to never see the sun again, to leave my spirit to wander for eternity in darkness. I was trying to kill myself when you literally fell into my lap, you were delirious from pain and begging for help. So I helped you…."

Lance froze, he had never heard such emotion in Tulley's voice before, it was pleading and sorrowful. Lance turned and looked at Tulley, undecided. After a moment Tulley released his wrist and sank back down in a sitting position, a moment later Lance followed.

"Is that why you have such a hard time sleeping?"

"Yes," Tulley said softly. "I can hear them, all of them. Screaming. When I am awake I can control it, but when I sleep the weeping enters in and I cannot help them. Because I did something very bad as a young man the Rising Sun cursed me, as long as these handprints on my back are still visible then the curse is still there and I have to do their bidding. That's why he killed them, in an attempt to save us and stop the killing. But it didn't exactly work out like he had planned because though they are gone the curse remains."

"So he committed a sin in an attempt to stop other sins?"

"Yes, you can look at it that way. But because people looked upon the Rising Sun as all powerful, God-like beings, he became the devil when he killed them. History doesn't even remember his real name."

Lance looked across the clearing before them and watched the children playing in the safe area, he sighed deeply and looked at Tulley. Tulley's brows were knitted a little and he had a pained look on his face.

Lance was so used to seeing Tulley's face as being blank and emotionless that his heart panged at the sight of him now.

"What was his real name?" Lance finally ventured to ask.

"Axel William Ramses."

Chapter Seven

Axel and his father stood in the doorway of their humble clay home with folded arms as they watched the new overseers move into the large house overlooking the modest town. For almost a year the town watched as the elaborate house was built, with large stables and gardens that went around it like a mote. Ever since their village had grown enough to be called a township people talked of how the Kingdom of the Rising Sun was going to send them an overseer. Someone from a foreign nation who understood military strategy and would protect them from invaders who deemed to steal what they grew and gathered.

Axel's keen eyes didn't miss a thing. He saw how rich they were by the fabrics and furniture that came in droves to the house. The servants who came were dressed in fine garments and some of them had horses of their own, a rarity for most people. The horses themselves were tall and black, their lean muscles making them swifter then any horse in the area. People began to wish for such things but very few could afford them and the ones who couldn't were left to watch with jealousy and longing. Slowly, and without people realizing it, the town became divided and people who had been friends their entire lives became enemies.

Today, as Axel and his father watched from their doorstep, a grand coach pulled by six prancing black steeds came to the front door of the grand new house. They could see the two tall figures with jet-black hair emerge from the coach, a man and a woman. A third figure rode upon another black steed and dismounted at the doorstep, throwing the reins to a waiting servant, this one was a young man. All three of them were dressed in deep blue with gems that sparkled in the light. Axel unfolded his arms and snorted loudly, showing his distaste as he turned around and entered their home. His father also turned and followed but he did not show weather he liked them or not.

Axel dropped the rough axe down for a short rest, he sighed as he turned to the wagon and the old dusty-colored horse that stood hitched to the front of it. The horse's eyes were half open as he dozed in the afternoon shade, a good sign that there was nothing dangerous lurking about. The wagon was only half full of chopped firewood pieces, he would have to work double-time if he was going to get it filled today, but he had come across a scene he could not pass up this morning as he was scouting for wood. Four young ladies were bathing in the very edge of the stream where the water was shallow and moved slowly. Though Axel was considered poor his family was rich in natural magic and he, like his father and his grandfather and many more before him, could change into a bird. Though his grandfather was an owl and his father was a hawk, Axel was a common sparrow. But he liked that better because it was easier to hide when you were not some large bird of prey. And so, Axel had flitted onto a branch high over the four ladies and he watched as they splashed in the water. They still had their underclothes on as they scrubbed their outer clothes on the rocks with the gritty homemade soap. Axel lay across the branch in his human form and watched their slender forms as they laughed and sang together. They tossed their outer clothes onto rocks in the sun to dry them and began to peel out of their under garments, Axel leaned over the edge of the

66

branch farther to watch. One young lady pulled her undershirt off and flung it at her nearest friend, her small white breast bouncing like her dark curls as she laughed and began to peel out of her shorts.

Axel let out a shout as he slid off the branch, the girls all screamed and immediately huddled around their bare-chested friend. They watched as the figure of a young man fell from a tree, but he changed into a brown sparrow and beat his wings as fast as he could to get away.

"Axel!" one of the girls screamed as she leapt up and changed into a barn swallow and pursued. Axel flew as fast as he could, dodging branches and weaving in and out of brush in an attempt to escape. But the blue and gold swallow was much faster; she caught him with her feet and gave him a good peck right in the center of his back. Axel fell from the air and managed to land on his feet, the swallow dived at him again. Axel rolled away in his human form and as he stood back up she throttled him.

"I'm sorry, Lisa," Axel said between choking breaths, but he was grinning.

"You better be sorry!" Lisa fairly shouted as she continued to shake him, her small hands tight around his neck.

"I just couldn't pass up the most beautiful girls in the town, all taking their clothes off."

Lisa shook him harder, then calmed to catch her own breath.

"Don't do it again!" she said savagely but Axel could tell she was hiding a smile. Axel gave his hat a slight raise in salute and bowed. Lisa straightened her undershirt and turned away to leave.

"Tell Aspin she has the most perfect breasts I have ever seen."

"And they will be the only breasts you shall see for a long time," Lisa sneered just before she jumped into the air and flew away on slender wings.

Axel grinned to himself as he remembered Aspin's perfect chest and lifted his water flask to his lips, he had not realized how parched he had become till the cool water hit his tongue.

Axel felt the tremor in the soil before her heard the pounding hoof beats. He looked over his right shoulder and saw a finely dressed young man riding hard toward him. The beautiful black steed was covered in foamy sweat and mud up to its belly. There was a shallow cut down its left flank and the young man was pulling on the bit so hard the poor creature was spitting blood.

"Stop! Stop, you damned beast!" the young man was shouting. Axel scowled as he watched the arrogant young man raise a riding crop and flog the horse's side in an attempt to beat it into submission but with every hit the animal would only leap forward again as it had been trained to do. Axel jumped out of the way as the horse pounded by and as it did so Axel reached out and grabbed the young man by the wrist. The man looked down at Axel for a brief moment, anger and surprise mingled on his pale face just before Axel yanked him from the saddle. The man hit the ground hard at Axel's feet and the horse bucked twice more before it came to a stop nearby, shaking legs splayed and head hung low as it coughed. Axel knew who this young man was the moment he saw his face, it was the overseers own son Harold Azsin.

Axel left Harold to roll around on the ground as he slowly walked up to the injured animal, speaking softly and deeply to sooth it. The horse flinched when Axel touched it but did not run, Axel ran his hands up and down the animal's wet neck and then proceeded to loosen the bridle.

"You should never ride a horse so hard. And throw away that riding crop, if you can't control an animal with just your voice and hands then you probably shouldn't be riding at all."

Axel slipped the bridle from the horse's head and the bit fell from its mouth, it landed in Axel's hand covered in blood.

"You monster," Axel felt the anger in him begin to rise. The horse raised his head slightly and pricked his ears forward, Axel heard the footstep behind him and instantly turned, his fist already aiming for Harold's face. Axel saw Harold's face in the direct path of his arching fist but just at the last second Harold ducked out of the way and came right back at Axel with a blow to his stomach that knocked the wind out of him and sent him sprawling. Axel spun around and landed on his hands and knees coughing.

"How dare you speak back to me, peasant! Do you know who I am?"

"An asshole," Axel wheezed as he stood back up to face Harold. Harold snarled and threw a punch for Axel's face but this time it was Axel's turn to duck. Axel tilted his head to the side and as Harold's arm went past his ear he reached up and grasped his wrist firmly and propelled him back to the ground where he landed face first. Harold spun around and was back up quickly, blood running down his face from a cut he now sported above his right eye. Harold wiped a hand across it and looked at the blood for a moment; Axel grinned and brought both hands up in a fighter's stance.

"Come on," he taunted. "I've wrestled baby weasels bigger than you."

Harold sneered. "I've been trained in many hand-to-hand techniques, I even killed a teacher once, you won't be a problem."

"Why are you just bragging about it? Show me!"

Both young men leapt at each other and each got one good hit in before they stumbled apart again.

"You deserve a good beating for what you did to that horse," Axel said as he spit blood onto the ground from a bloodied lip. Harold was breathing too hard to answer back right away, Axel smiled at the difficulty Harold was having.

"Come on," Axel said. "Let's do that again."

Harold shook his head and put a hand up. "No," he said. "I think you broke a rib." Axel took a step back and stood straight as he let his hands drop. "Good," he said. He studied Harold for a moment, the young man was bent at the waist, breathing heavily and holding one hand to his side. Axel grunted in distaste and turned toward the black horse again, he was happy to see the animal was standing a little steadier now.

"Ho now, easy, boy, it's all right now," Axel soothed as he ran his hand up and down the animal's noble face. He looked into the horse's deep brown eyes and felt another pang of anger as he saw all the fear and pain the animal felt. For a moment the horse's eyes flitted to something behind Axel but before Axel could turn and confront Harold again something sang through the air and caught him on the right cheekbone. Axel fell to the ground at the horse's feet and the last thing he saw was the animal rearing up above him, the muddy hooves hovering over his body.

Chapter Eight

Axel slowly opened his eyes, he could see a mesh of colors that slowly focused into the sunlight coming through the leaves. He started to sit up but immediately lay back down, his breath escaping between his clenched teeth in a sharp *tssk* sound. His fingers gently touched the right side of his face and he *tssked* again as he felt his swollen cheek and eye. He could still open his right eye but it felt gritty, like there was dirt in it, he wanted to rub it with his palm but he refrained from that action.

After several long minutes he was able to take hold of his situation and he finally managed to sit up without too many flashes of light in his skull. He could remember the horse and wondered if that's what had hit him, he looked at the ground where he had just been laying and saw two deep hoof imprints that had been on either side of his head. The animal had seen Axel below and spared Axel's life by spreading his front legs when he came back down. Axel looked around, he did not see Harold or the beaten black horse, even the bridal was gone; it seemed Harold had re-tacked the horse and fled leaving him on the ground. Axel leaned on one arm and his palm pressed into something on the ground, he picked it up and looked at it. It was the riding crop Harold had been using so mercilessly on the horse, the leather of the handle was braided around several fine smooth gems, but the slender wicked stem of the crop was snapped. Axel huffed a little as he came to the conclusion of what had hit him in the face with enough force to knock him to the ground.

"Sneaky cheating bastard," Axel said out loud as he forced himself to stand. His legs were wobbly and it took him a few unsteady steps to find his balance, now that he was standing his head began to pound and he was dizzy.

What time is it? Axel thought as he looked around. The old dusty-colored horse was still hooked to the cart and had not moved but he was not dozing anymore, he was looking intently at Axel and nickered softly. It was late, later then he should be out. His father would be home from the iron shop soon and would be worried.... And it was Axel's turn to make dinner. Axel groaned as he slowly walked toward the horse and cart. He picked up the axe on the way and had to lean against the side of the cart till the dizziness left him.

"All right, Old Boy," Axel said for the horse had no name and that's what they called him. "You're gonna have to help me, I'm not feeling so good right now." The cart was not made with a seat for the driver, the person was meant to sit on the horse's back as if he were merely riding him. Axel placed one foot in the stirrup and managed to pull himself up only to fall slumped over the animal's back. Old Boy stood patiently as Axel struggled to right himself, he nearly slipped off but after some swearing and bursts of pain in his head Axel finally managed to get settled on Old Boy's back.

"Home, Old Boy," Axel said softly, he clicked his tongue and immediately regretted it. Old Boy lumbered forward, his steps actually gentle for as big as he was, Axel tried to move with the sway of the animal to ease the throbbing in his head but it didn't seem to help.

Axel's father returned to their home at dusk as he usually did. The first thing he noticed was no Old Boy in the paddock, then no smell of smoke or food, his pace quickened as he neared their home. He burst through the door and called for Axel, when there was no reply he turned to the yard and barn; when he still did not find his son he turned back toward the town and on the powerful wings of a bird of prey he raced back to check with his son's best friend Eddie who was also the town's leather crafter.

"Ah, no, Mr. Ramses, Axel is not here. I haven't seen him all day, but you may want to ask Sam Haplin, I heard a rumor that Axel was caught peeping on some girls while they bathed, the Haplin boys might be giving him a stern lecture 'cause their little sister was part of the group."

Axel's father frowned deeply at this news and immediately turned in the direction of the Haplin's homestead.

"Thanks, Eddie," he called over his shoulder.

"Wait," Eddie called as he came from his doorway hopping around as he pulled on his boots. "I want to help."

Eddie reached the door first and banged on it with the side of his fist. They heard the clatter of silverware from inside as a chair scrapped across the floor. Sam Haplin was a large man with a speech impediment, six sons and one daughter, the daughter being the youngest.

"Julian, Eddie," Sam said slowly, sounding out each syllable so as not to slur his words. "How can I help you?" Eddie leaned to the side and looked around Sam to see each of his six boys slowly standing up to face them, his daughter was still sitting.

"We was looking for my son," Axel's father said. "Is he here?"

Sam turned and looked at his sons but they all shook their heads in unison, then he turned back to Julian and Eddie.

"I'm sorry," he continued in his slow speech, Eddie noticed Lisa was now standing behind her brothers; she had her fingers to her lips and was shaking her head.

"Well, if you see him, tell him to come home."

"Ah, he's probably out being sweet with a girl, you know how boys are," Sam laughed a little once he was done pronouncing the words and pointed a thumb over his shoulder to indicate his six boys.

"Not my son...thank you, Sam," Julian said as he turned away. Julian and Eddie walked around the corner of the house and as soon as they heard the front door closed they found themselves face to face with Lisa.

"Why are you here?" she demanded in a whisper. "We didn't tell our families what happened today, Eddie, I shouldn't have even told you that, now the whole town is gonna wanna hang Axel by his thumbs."

"No, they're not," Eddie said softly. "I only told Julian 'cause he came looking for Axel."

"I may still hang him by his thumbs," Julian said softly. "But we have to find him first. Miss Haplin, sorry to disturb your dinner with your family."

"A kiss for luck?" Eddie asked, holding his arms out for an embrace. Lisa slapped the back of his right hand and turned away. Eddie made a silent pout noise and quickly followed Julian but very softly he heard Lisa say, "Good luck, sweetie."

"We should check in with the doctor," Julian said as they fairly jogged across the small town. "Perhaps something happened and Axel is there."

The man who answered the door was dark skinned and wrinkled with a full head of white hair.

"Ah, I am sorry, Julian, he is not here. But look, I see a fire is in your hearth now."

Julian spun on his heel and looked down the gently sloping hill to where his modest house stood and sure enough there was a glow from one of the small windows and a wisp of smoke could be seen in the moonlight.

"Sorry to bother you," Julian said as he turned back to the doctor but he stopped when he saw the doctor had affixed the strap of his medical satchel to his shoulder.

"Well, come now," the doctor said as he pushed past Julian and Eddie. "I think I know what happened to him today."

The three of them walked all the way to Julian and Axel's home, Julian became uneasy when he saw Old Boy standing in the yard still hooked to the wagon. When they opened the door they found Axel sitting cross-legged on the floor in front of a freshly started fire, he had the water bucket next to him and had been dipping a piece of cloth into the cool water and placing it on his face, he did not turn when he heard the door open.

"Axel, what happened?" Julian admonished as he kneeled next to his son and saw the bruise and swelling. Axel could not open his right eye anymore and his head swam, he was surprised he had even gotten the fire going again.

"I'm sorry, Da," he said softly. "I will make dinner right away."

"Never mind dinner, what happened?" Julian asked again.

"Got into a scrap, didn't you," the doctor asked as he pushed a chair over and motioned for Axel to sit. Axel had to steady himself on the chair as he got up, Julian grasped his arm and grimaced as the fire light illuminated his swollen face better.

The doctor put his hand under Axel's chin and turned his face one way and then the other as he inspected the injury.

"Hmmmm, yep," he said as he turned away and picked out a wooden jar. He opened it and immediately the room was filled with a rancid odor that made everyone cringe, even the fire seemed to shrink. The doctor dipped his finger into the lime green salve and gently slathered it across Axel's swollen cheek.

"This will cool it and help the swelling go down, I cannot tell if your cheekbone is broken with all the swelling so I want to see you again tomorrow evening. And don't worry, the smell won't soak into your skin." The doctor studied his handy work and put the lid back onto the container. "Better hope it's not broken," he chided. "Pretty girls tend to avoid ugly boys."

"Well," Axel said with a faint smile. "I suppose I will have to find another way to woo the pretty girls."

"Cheeky kid," the doctor commented. "Now, are you pained anywhere else? The other lad had a cracked rib and more bruises than you."

"I'm fine," Axel said.

Julian and the doctor went to the door and stood outside for several long minutes, Axel could hear the hushed tones of their voices as they talked. Eddie spied the broken riding crop on the table and picked it up.

"That's what he hit me with," Axel commented as Julian reentered the house. Julian stood in the closed doorway for a long moment, his face cloudy and his arms crossed, the flickering firelight that danced across his features only made him look even more cross.

"Harold Azsin," Julian commented, Axel cringed, Eddie let out a quiet "Uh-oh."

"You got into a fight with Harold Azsin?! His father has been overseer for less than a month and you broke his son's ribs?"

Eddie took a step back, his wide eyes looking back and forth between father and son. Julian sighed and so did Axel a moment later for after that gesture he knew his father was not as angry as he seemed.

"Luckily, for whatever reason, Harold told his father and Hal that he got thrown by his horse, but you can't fool old Doc Hal, he's seen too many wounds. Now, tell me what made you decide to beat up Harold Azsin."

Axel recounted what happened between him and Harold in the woods while his father dumped some dried vegetables into a pot of water and set it over the fire to cook. Eddie pulled up a chair and sat on it backwards, his arms dangling over the back of the chair in front of him as he fiddled with the broken riding crop.

"If I ever see Harold again I'm going to beat the ever-living snot out of him," Axel finished. Eddie and his father had been quiet the entire time but now his father cut in.

"Axel William Ramses," he said, putting emphasis on his middle name as he did so. "Do not hate him just because he is mean, pity him that he is suffering inside."

"Pity?" Axel asked, Eddie perked up as well.

"I don't understand," Eddie said.

"I did not say I hated him."

"But I can tell you were thinking it," Julian continued. "Son, hate will eat away a person's heart and soul until there is nothing left but an empty shell. Do not hate Harold. I have seen the boy, I have looked into his eyes, they smolder. If you let hate eat away at your soul then you will be just like Harold Azsin, don't let that happen to you."

"Yes, Da," Axel said as he hung his head.

"Now," Julian said as he dished out some of the stew and handed each lad a bowl. "I heard you got caught spying today, remember what Grandda always told you about that?"

"That when he was a child men who were caught spying on women lost part of their finger as punishment."

"And?"

"That a man should revere women and never touch one unless it is his wife."

"Good," Julian said as he sat down with his own bowl. "Now, how did you get caught?" Axel could hear a faint smile in his father's voice.

"I fell out of the tree," Axel answered sheepishly.

Eddie burst out laughing.

Chapter Nine

"I think you got lucky, very lucky," Doctor Hal said as he once again held Axel's chin in his palm and turned his face from right to left. It had been nearly two weeks since Axel and Harold had gotten into a fight. Axel's face was back to normal except for a small bruise that ran just beneath his eye.

"Are you running in the races this year?" Doc Hal asked as he rummaged through some wooden containers on his shelf.

"Yes, sir," Axel answered. "I got Hindie from the nest in the middle of last summer, he was the biggest one of his litter and already had his eyes open. Boy, that was a close call with his mother though."

"Yes, I remember, she bit your friend Eddie on the ass."

Axel stifled a snicker as he remembered how Eddie was supposed to be the decoy while Axel sneaked into the nest of baby rabbits and grabbed one, Eddie wasn't quite fast enough.

"You sure that beast of yours is ready?"

"Of course, I have worked with Hindie nearly every day, and Eddie made a new riding harness for him. I traded that broken riding crop for it. Eddie took the stones out and made two matching jeweled riding crops, and Harold bought them!" Axel smiled smugly at what Eddie and he had accomplished.

"Ah, speaking of Harold, I want you to drop this off at his place on your way home, he says his ribs still hurt. It's actually just minced grass pills but he doesn't know that, so don't tell him." Doc Hal wagged a finger at Axel with one hand while he held out a container in the other. Axel's face fell as he looked at Doc Hal's waving finger right before his face.

"Why do I have to?" he asked.

"Perhaps you and Harold need to speak civilly, no better time than the present before those feelings you have toward each other can simmer and boil over." Doc Hal turned Axel's hand palm up and placed the wooden jar in it.

"Axel, what's in your coat pocket?" Julian asked that even when Axel came home and he saw the bulge, Axel grumbled softly to himself as he pulled the jar out.

"Doc Hal wanted me to deliver this to Harold, said I needed to be civil with him. Da, I really don't want to."

Julian nodded his head in agreement with the doctor. "He's right, son. Now, dinner is not finished yet so fly that over there right now and then come back, you can use being late for dinner as an excuse to get away."

"Yeah, okay."

Axel flew straight to the grand house and alighted right onto the front door step, a tiny feather floated down and landed in his golden blond hair as he reached out to knock on the door. He was sure a servant would answer and he could just leave it with one of them for Harold, but when no one answered right away he was tempted to leave it on the front step. He was just squatting down to set it on the top step when the door came open and he found himself looking up into the face of beauty incarnate.

She had a small childlike face, pale but with a rosy glow to her checks. Her nose was delicate as were her eyebrows and lashes and her painted lips were like two flower petals, one on top of the other. Her long black hair lay in thick waves across her shoulders and bosom, it framed her face like a picture and her large eyes were such a deep brown they were almost black. Axel could see himself reflected in those huge beautiful eyes, surrounded by tiny stars that danced when she smiled at him, then she blinked and the spell was broken.

Axel stood quickly and gave a bow, bending at the waist with one arm before his torso and one held behind it.

"Is the young master home?" Axel asked, then he faltered as his eyes fell on the elegant dress she was wearing. It was red and gold and pushed her bosom up and tapered her waist down to her hips and there it flared out softly and hung in loose folds around her ankles, her feet were tiny and though they were bare they were very clean. Was this a servant in such a splendid dress?

"Such manners," the young lady said and she laughed, her voice was soft and happy, and her accent was precious, something he had never heard before and he found himself wishing to hear more. Axel stood and the young lady held out her slender hand, Axel very gently took it in his and kissed it.

"I am Florence Azsin," the young lady said. "Just arrived back home from traveling. And what is your name, my fine gentleman?"

"Axel William Ramses, at your service."

"Three names, you must have nobility in your blood to be blessed with three names, I hear it is rare for that around here."

"Yes, Miss Azsin," Axel found himself saying as he was once again captivated by her large dark eyes. "My family has a strong noble line and strong ties to magic, for eight generations our magic ties have not faltered."

Florence smiled at him again and glanced at his old clothes, the stains on his coat, the rip in the cuff of his pants, the feather clinging to his hair. Axel was suddenly very conscious of his attire and began to feel very insignificant as he stood on the door step of this grand house.

Suddenly Florence reached out and grasped his hand.

"Come with me!" she said excitedly as she stepped out the door and began to lead Axel around the side of the house and straight into the dense wood beyond. She held her skirts off the ground with one hand as she ran, her tiny bare feet not making a sound, her other hand was tightly clasping Axel's hand as she pulled him behind. Axel could feel the warmth of her hand and how soft it was. Her black hair followed and swayed just above her hips as they also swayed with every delicate step. Axel swallowed back the feeling that was rising in his chest lest it over take him and he looked away.

Axel did not pay attention to how far they ran or even to where they were going, his eyes were constantly darting back to her nicely shaped bottom, sometimes her hair, once she looked back at him and he was lost in her eyes for a moment. Then, just as suddenly as she had started off, she stopped; Florence stepped to the side and Axel nearly fell headlong to the ground.

"Oh, I'm sorry!" Florence laughed, slightly out of breath from the sprint into the woods, Axel began to laugh as well but she suddenly hushed him. Florence stood against a tree and listened intently for several long moments, then she sighed and mischievously looked at Axel, her eyes dancing.

"Why are we here, Miss Azsin?" Axel ventured to ask.

"Oh," she said softly as she began to walk away from him, she slowly raised both arms into the air and stretched. "Just to get away. My brother's friends are here right now, but they aren't really his friends," she turned her head over her shoulder and made a scrunched-up face for a moment. "They are just pretending to be because they want to see me, and I am so tired of all the attention." Florence swung her hips as she walked and her skirts swayed with the rhythm; Axel found himself at a sudden loss for words.

"Do you want to see what I found?" she suddenly turned, her skirts and black hair seemed to arch around her. "Come!" she jumped toward

Axel and grasped his hand again. They did not run this time, Florence pressed a delicate finger to her painted lips as she led Axel a little farther into the woods. After a few minutes Axel could hear the sound of softly flowing water and he knew where he was. Florence pointed at a shallow pool at the edge of the wide stream, its surface was as still and reflective as a mirror.

"Do you see how it shines back the images with such clarity?" Florence whispered so softly that Axel almost didn't hear. "I think there is a snow fairy living in that pool. I have been coming here for the last three days trying to spy a glimpse of it, I have never seen a snow fairy before."

"There is one living there," Axel assured her just as softly. "But nobody has seen it for a couple of generations now, we believe it grew old and is taking a long rest."

"You mean it died?" Florence's hands flew to her mouth and her eyes grew wide.

"No, snow fairies don't exactly die...they just sorta sleep and build up magic energy until they are recovered. No one has ever found a dead snow fairy and there is no stories about them dying...however, not much is actually known about them... so...." Axel trailed off as he looked back down at Florence, he cleared his throat and continued. "We call this the Seeing Glass, and girls will sometimes come out here to look into the water and ask who they should marry."

"Really?" Florence said in a disbelieving tone, and then she laughed. "How barbaric."

"Why don't you ask it?" Axel poked fun at her.

"Does it ever answer?"

"If it does the girls never say," Axel shrugged.

"Probably because the girls don't want to marry the man it tells them to." Florence took a step closer and bent over the edge of the perfectly still water, it did seem unnatural for it to be so still while it was connected to a stream, and to be so clear and yet reflect so perfectly.

"Seeing Glass," Florence addressed the water with an air of high dignity. "Who should I marry?" Florence stared hard at her refection and then sat back with a quiet "humph," and folded her arms.

"It says it wants to speak to you," she said.

"What?" Axel asked totally bewildered.

"Yeah," Florence unfolded one delicate arm and pointed at the water. Axel leaned over the edge just as she had done, he could see himself even more clearly than in his mother's polished mirror his father had kept all these years. Beneath the surface of the water a minnow the size of his hand went darting by. Axel suddenly felt a foot on his thigh and he was pushed headfirst into the shallow water, he came up sputtering and stood in the waist deep pool, now rippling and muddy from his disturbance. Florence was on the ground laughing, her arms wrapped around her sides as she rolled back and forth.

"The look on your face!" she laughed. "Thank you, Axel, that just made my day!" Axel began to laugh as well despite the fact that now his only coat was muddy and soaked. Florence stopped for a moment and looked at him, then she began to laugh again all the harder, Axel started to splash her.

"You were gone for quite a while," Julian said as he sat by the fireplace and fiddled with a crossbow, there was a few tools laid out on the table and a couple of lit candles for added light. Julian was still wearing his hat in the house, a thing he rarely did, it was cocked to one side holding his mane of auburn hair down, a pipe was tucked in the corner of his mouth. "Did you and Harold have a good talk?"

"Harold wasn't there," Axel commented softly.

"Oh? Well, I know you were not with Eddie this evening, he and Miss Haplin went for a walk-about, alone. They took Sam's crossbow for protection but they say they slid down a ravine and broke it, I guess that's what the younger generation is calling it now, when I was young we just called it a romp...a walk-about.... Anyway, Eddie came crying to me a little while ago, begging me to fix this thing tonight before Sam realizes it's gone. Axel, sometimes I wander about your friends and where their brains are...Axel?" After a moment of silence, the only sound was the soft scraping of the tool, Julian took the pipe from his mouth and looked up.

"How did you get all dirty and wet, boy? You get into another fight and they dump water on you?" Julian tucked the pipe back in place and looked back at his work.

"What?" Axel looked at his father but he seemed to be looking right through him. "No, I um, I meet someone." Julian froze for a second and then continued working.

"Oh?"

"Yeah, it was Harold's sister, Florence."

"Hmmmmm."

There was no words for several minutes as Julian continued to study and carefully craft the broken handle of the crossbow, the sounds of the night seemed louder than usual and pressed into the quiet space.

"Da...?"

"Hmm...?"

"Tell me about Mum again."

Julian came to a stop and stared at the crossbow for a long moment, then he set the tool onto the table with the others and sitting up with the crossbow now laying in his lap he looked at Axel through the thin haze of fireplace and pipe smoke. Though he had told his son this many times, he knew Axel would never stop asking and in turn, he would never get tired of telling it, for it was his only work of art that could be spoken.

"A lass sits upon the flowers, covered in the morning dew,
Her face is soft with eyes abrite and hair of such a golden hue.

She holds a baby in her arms, and sings of far-off lands,
The baby giggles and laughs and wiggles as she holds his hands.

A beautiful mother this lady is, her voice so soft and so sweet,
Like tiny bells her laugh runs free, like fairies dancing on bare feet.

And she sang, I love you, child, oh, child of mine,
With eyes so blue, and hair so fine.
With the laughing and wiggling and giggling.
Watching the trees say hello, hello baby, and what do you know?
I love you, child, oh, child of mine.
With eyes so blue, and hair so fine.

A lass sits upon the flowers, covered in the morning dew,
Her heart was all she had to give, her skin now a porcelain hue.

Her lovely soul rises to the sun, her days of sorrowing is done,
But in the end there was a time, that her laughter would softly chime.
Sweet baby in her arms, she did protect from all harm.
Though they say she was beautiful, it was truly the care from her soul,
That made her lovely beyond as things, and saved the children in the spring.
And her voice still lingers here, if you are alone or in fear,
I love you, child, oh, child of mine, with eyes so blue and hair so fine."

Chapter Ten

Tulley's pipe had burnt out but he continued to hold the stem of it between his teeth as he spoke. He stopped for several minutes and looked at the grass stems he was tightly weaving into a new hat. His mouth was dry and tired from the entire afternoon of storytelling, one of the children had brought him a drink but the container was now empty. Lance looked as though he was far away in thought.

"So he really was just a man, like the rest of us."

"Yes, he was born a baby and grew to be a man, he is not a cursed spirit or a summoned demon of war as some stories call him. He is merely a man and that is what I hope this story will set right in people's minds."

Lance was lying flat on his back with his arms beneath his head, his leg bent at the knee with his bare foot rubbing gently back and forth in the soft dirt.

"What happened to Axel's mother? Do you know, Tulley?"

"I was told," Tulley began softly, "that there was a flash flood early one spring. Her, Axel and two other very young children were swept away in the water but she had managed to catch some floating debris and using her clothes, she lashed the children to it so they would not drown, after much struggling she had managed to swim and guide the children from the water but she was so exhausted and her body so battered from the rushing waters that she died that evening. Axel was barely a year old."

"How sad," Clover, one of the young girls, answered, she rubbed her sleeve across her dirty face and sniffled. Tulley slowly got up from his sitting position, his joints seemed stiff and he groaned a little as he straightened.

"Will you tell us more?" Kandid, one of the young boys, asked.

"Tomorrow," Tulley said as he knocked the cold ash from his pipe. He inspected his pipe a moment and then tucked it into his hip pocket, the pipe was on its last leg, another crack had shown itself in the white bone. Several of the children moaned and Lance sat up frowning.

"The day isn't over yet, you can't tease me with the little you have said so far."

"I have to take a little time to remember what happened next, I don't want to tell a falsehood, this is important to me, I want it to be truth.... Besides, I just talked more in one day than I have for several years, my mouth hurts." Tulley patted a few of the children on the head as he passed by them and walked toward the water barrel to the side of the great tree.

Tulley stood leaning against the window frame, the moon was not full but it was bright and he looked across the field of gently swaying grasses beneath them. He couldn't sleep, his head hurt and memories stirred in his mind from earlier. Lance sat at the small table behind him, Tulley could hear the rough scratching of the claw pen against the dry pressed leaves. The ink he was using was boiled blood and bark, it had a slightly tangy smell but not unpleasant. Tulley was mildly surprised but also relieved when Lance did not question him any further about the story.

"Someone is coming," Tulley commented, Lance stopped writing and perked up.

"Several someones are coming, fast," Tulley turned away from the window and quickly crossed their room.

"Jessica," he called as he quickly made his way down the wide hallway, dodging a few sleepy-eyed children here and there. Tulley got to the door and opened it before the visitors could even knock, there was four men, all rough from living out in the elements their whole lives, their thick beards covering their faces and making it hard to distinguish one from the other except for their clothing. At first the men seemed confused that a person other than Jessica answered the door but then it changed to relief when they heard Jessica call them to come inside.

"Whats yous doings outs and abouts, Arnish, don't yous knows the darks is dangerous."

"Sorry, Jessica, but it's an emergency," Arnish answered as they entered the doorway, the first two men carried makeshift weapons and the second two had a cloth held between them like a hammock, the sounds of a baby came from this hammock. Jessica gasped and flew forward as the men very gently laid it down and folded the edges back. A young women was curled up inside the hammock, her black hair stood out like tattoos against her pale face. She was drenched in sweat and her closed eyes were sunken and discolored as if she were sick. The men all stood back as Jessica bent over the woman and placed her hands on her face. Tulley glanced over his shoulder at some of the children who were beginning to gather at the bottom of the stairs, they saw him looking at them and instantly begin to silently trudge back up the stairs to their beds. Jessica very gently pulled the child from the woman's arms and stood up cradling the moaning infant, it was so tiny wrapped in the small blanket.

"She is dead," Jessica said softly, a pain in her voice that seemed to kill her accent. "What happened? Where is Bastian? Where is the other baby?"

Several of the men bowed their heads.

"It was a serpent, ma'am, a very large serpent. We believe the crying of the babies enticed it to enter their home. We cannot find the other baby and we cannot find Bastian, we fear they were eaten."

Jessica held the baby to her chest and gently rocked it back and forth.

"We are going after the creature, we heard about the man who brought Bobo back from the slavers," Arnish looked at Tulley with a judgmental air. Tulley folded his arms across his chest and leaned into the wall, his head slightly tilted and his auburn hair, grown out and thick, was once again laying over his eyes, his stair back was totally expressionless as usual.

"Are you the one?" Arnish asked.

"I'm not going," Tulley stated flatly. Arnish seemed taken aback for a moment and then shrugged.

"You look puny anyway," he muttered as he turned away. "We will go and kill the creature. Jessica, one of the family will be here at first light to tend to Aimee's body."

"It is best to find where it sleeps and post a guard, if it has just eaten it won't come out for days, even weeks. Don't go into its home seeking to kill it, it will just kill you," Tulley's voice had a hard edge that spoke of authority but Arnish shrugged off the advice and walked out the door.

Two of the men wrapped the woman back up and upon Jessica's request they picked up her body and laid it across two chairs against the wall. Lance had been standing at the top of the stairs and had heard most of what was said, Tulley brushed past him on his way back up to their room.

"You are not going to help them?" Lance inquired.

"I don't like snakes much and they certainly don't like me."

"You don't like much of anything though, and you are so grumpy at times that's it's no wonder they don't like you."

"I am not grumpy."

"You never smile, or laugh."

Tulley parted his lips in an attempt at smiling and said very dryly, "Ha, ha." Lance shook his head as he lit another candle and set the new one next to the nearly dead stub of the other.

"Poor Mother, Jessica just recently delivered her twins, how is she going to feed the baby?"

Tulley did not answer, Lance looked toward him and saw that he was on his mat, his back toward him with his knees curled up to his chest, a position he only took if his head was hurting and memories were bothering him, sometimes he dealt with the headaches and dreams and sometimes he took out his pipe and smoked some of the cave moss; however, he was now nearly out of the toxic stuff. Lance picked up another leaf and began to scratch out the story Tulley had recounted earlier while the words and images were still fresh in his mind, late in the night the candle finally burnt out and he fell asleep at the table. When Lance awoke the next morning, his neck and lower back achy from sleeping in such a position, he looked toward Tulley's sleeping mat and was just slightly surprised to see that Tulley was not there.

Tulley followed the tracks of the four men, they left a trail like a stampede of rodents had run through the underbrush. Tulley was barefoot and had left his shirt in the room but he did put on the vest to hide the handprint tattoos. His single saber was on his belt and he also had fashioned forearm guards with the sharpened claws of the squirrel sewn into the sides so he could rip through flesh. The trail wove its way through the surrounding woods and toward a rocky hillside that was visible from the top of the tree.

It figures, Tulley thought to himself. *Snakes love living underground.* Tulley finally came across three of the men surrounding a hole in the rocky ground that was large enough for one of them to enter, it was dark and a damp earthy smell rose up from it.

"Decided not to take my advice," Tulley said. Arnish spun around, his arm swinging for Tulley's head but Tulley half expected that and was already ducking down soon as he had spoken.

"Why are you here? Sneaking up on us?" Arnish demanded when he saw who it was.

"I had a hunch you wouldn't listen and thought you may need help."

"Well, we don't," Arnish said as he turned his back to Tulley.

"How long has he been down there?"

"We don't need your help."

"Since before sunup," one of the other men said, he was younger than the others and Tulley could hear deep concern in his voice.

"He a relative?" Tulley asked as he squatted down near the pit. The damp earthy smell was strong and seemed to come from deep beneath the surface, the air that wafted up was slightly cooler and it carried a scent that Tulley usually avoided; it was the musky scent of snake.

"Yes, he's my older brother, Hestian. Bastian was older brother to us both, I don't want to lose Hestian too but we couldn't stop him, he jumped right in."

"He will be just fine," Arnish said in a strong, commanding voice.

"Probably not," Tulley said and then dodged as Arnish swung at him again.

"He will be just fine," Arnish reinstated, only stronger this time.

"It smells like a very large snake and I can smell more than one, Hestian may have jumped into a hibernation pit that a few of the snakes are still using to sleep in during the summer. He may have been eaten or he has realized where he is and is hiding, if that's the case I will bring him back."

"You think you are going in there?" Arnish asked.

"If you were, you would have done it already, besides, I'm not afraid to die." Tulley dropped into the pit before Arnish could swing at him again.

The drop down was not as far as Tulley had thought but it was at an angle so the light that filtered through the opening was soon lost to the darkness below. Tulley crouched where he had landed for a short period as he let his eyes adjust. The stones and soil around him was worn smooth from the years of snakes slithering over them, and the tunnel before him forked a little farther down. Tulley sniffed and the musky smell made him want to gag, a small feeling of fear began to churn the pit of his stomach as he began to creep forward but he quelled it and continued. Tulley ran his hand along the smooth wall and had a fleeting thought that this would make a great underground stronghold but he shook his head and then wondered why he was still thinking like someone in battle. The darkness was stifling and though Tulley could see in the dark better than most he was startled when his hand came across the rough scales of a snake rather than the smooth stones of the wall. Tulley leapt back and landed in a crouch, one hand instantly going to the saber, the other held before him, the claws on his forearm pointed toward the enemy. Tulley held his breath as he waited but the snake had not moved at his touch, as Tulley listened he could hear the soft even breathing of the creature before him.

Sleeping...? Or did it think he was just one of the other snakes...? After what seemed an eternity Tulley slowly moved forward but dared not touch the snake again. This one was not huge, not big enough to swallow a man anyway. Tulley carefully continued to follow the path before him, he managed to avoid the snake's curled body and he emerged into what appeared to be a large room for he could hear the soft sounds of movement as scales slide across stone. Tulley felt a forked tongue tickle across his face and his skin instantly prickled, he ducked and rolled before the tongue could find him again. Tulley rolled over the curled body of another snake, this one only as big around as one of his thighs, the snake recoiled and Tulley could hear its sharp intake of breath as it smelled for him, he felt another tongue tickle his arm as he ducked again. Slowly the sounds of scales hissing over stone became louder and the musky smell became stronger as the snakes were woken and began to stir. Tulley pulled out his saber and held his breath as he began to walk backwards back in the direction he had come, he knew they sensed his body heat and he had no way of hiding that, but he quickly pulled off his vest and tossed it to the side in an attempt to throw his scent, several of the snakes followed but not all were fooled. Tulley could not fully tell how many there were, in the pitch black he could barely make out shapes and he couldn't distinguish between snake and rock unless one of them moved. Tulley lashed his saber out at a movement that got too close for his comfort and was satisfied to hear a sharp hiss as the snake pulled back from the danger. Tulley turned and ran just as a head the size of his chest struck out at him, he leapt over the coils of one snake and nearly ran into the coils of another.

"Stupid ass!" Tulley shouted as he swung his saber at another striking head. "You don't have to avenge your brother, he doesn't want you dead! Now I'm trying to find your ass and I probably won't!" Coils caught Tulley around the hips and yanked him across the floor, Tulley ripped his forearm claws into the snakes flesh and it loosened enough for him to jump upwards. "You have probably been eaten!" Tulley continued his monolog as he dodged and sliced at snakes all around him as if the floor had begun to boil. Tulley felt cold blood on his hands, it was probably a good thing it was cold, if the snakes were warmer they would be moving faster.

"Stupid ass!" Tulley shouted again as he felt a mouth clamp onto his bicep, the snake pulled back on his arm but Tulley cleanly severed its head from its body and continued his attempt at exiting the conclave of serpents. Tulley soon realized he was completely turned around and wasn't sure which way was the exit, he came against a wall and pressed his back into it, his eyes searching the blinding darkness, waiting for something to strike again. The snake's severed head was still clamped to his arm and he could feel the creature's jaw working back and forth as its muscles spasmed in death, he yanked the head from his arm and threw it into the roiling mass before him. Several of the snakes had exited, fleeing the danger after the first injuries they received, but the others only seemed to be enraged by the pain and they rose up against Tulley, striking from several different directions.

Tulley severed two more heads and sliced a third before he was caught by a large coil again, this time it knocked his feet out from under him and he went down hard, his head bouncing off the hard packed earth, sparks of white light lit up his vision for an instant and then he was back on his feet swinging his saber for all he was worth.

"Stupid ass!" Tulley shouted again and then he laughed hysterically as he felt the cool blood splash across his face. His arm throbbed and his head was beginning to feel as if it were not part of his body anymore, his breath came in shallow gasps between the laughter and his legs felt weak. Tulley bounded forward into the last few snakes before him and he felt the adrenaline course through him, he was so hyped up it made his head spin and his arms wanted to shake. He could only see one more snake with raised head as it slithered toward him over the writhing dead bodies of its comrades. With a shout he leapt toward it with saber raised and sliced through the snakes bottom jaw as it tried to strike him. The snake curled back on itself, its bottom jaw nearly severed from its head, it barely hung by a thread of flesh and it swung wildly back and forth as the creature retreated. Tulley landed on top of the slowly curling bodies and lost his footing, he fell across one large coil and felt it tremble beneath him from the impact.

"Stupid ass," Tulley said once more as he felt his right bicep, he could not move that arm and he lost all feeling from his shoulder to his fingertips. In the darkness he traced the tattoo with the fingertips of his left hand, this tattoo ran across the right side of his chest and up to the base of his neck where it forked and part of it continued over his shoulder and down his back. He could feel the scarring that was hidden in the black coloration and right at his neck, over his collarbone, he grasped what he was feeling for. As if he held a string between his fingers he twined them around and then wrapped the string around his bicep a couple of times. He felt the difference almost instantly as the natural magic around him flowed to the wound to slow down the poison. How many people, fairies, spirits had died by his hands for him to attain that tether he wandered absently...he shook his head a little. That was in the past.

Tulley rose up slowly and stumbling a little, he made his way off the dead snakes and attempted to point himself in the direction of the exit. He stopped when he heard the faint movement, it was not the twitching noises of the dead snakes but a deliberate slithering hiss of scales whispering over the floor. Tulley turned toward the sound and his eyes picked out the slow perfunctory movement. This snake was huge, its body was easily as tall as Tulley's hip as it moved around the edge of the room.

"There you are," Tulley fairly whispered as the enormous head rose up and its tongue slipped out to taste the blood on him. "The man eater."

Tulley gripped his saber tightly in his left hand, his right hand hung loosely at his side, the snake opened its mouth in a hushed breath and Tulley yelled as he leapt forward, his head spinning and his arm throbbing.

"They just started pouring out of the ground, there must have been twenty of them, and several had wounds from him. We could only get out of the way and watch as they were run out."

"The last one to come out had no bottom jaw, it had nearly bled to death already, it didn't make it very far before it curled up and died."

"We waited around for a while, sure he was dead, but then he come crawling out of that hole in the ground, covered in blood, laughing and swaying so badly it's a wonder he was able to get out. And he had this snake head with him, stuck to the end of some weapon, it was the biggest one we have ever seen!"

"He killed that man eater! It killed Bastian, Hestian and the wee baby but it couldn't kill him!"

Lance and Jessica were both looking back and forth between Arnish and Jim as they told what had happened, Neely had gone back home to grieve the loss of his two older brothers and left the other two to do something with the raving man who had crawled back out of the snake pit. Lance felt as though he would cry when Arnish appeared at their door that evening with Tulley hung over his shoulder like a sack of food. Tulley looked a sight, covered in dirt and the blood of the slain snakes; his hair was matted with it. But Arnish swung Tulley's body down and wrapping an arm around his torso, held him in a somewhat upright position.

"I'm not dead," Tulley moaned and Lance thought he would fall over from the shock of it all. Lance and Jessica cleaned Tulley up and got some suitable clothes on him and though they tried to get him to bed Tulley asked for some tea and sat at the table with a blanket around his shoulders. His right arm was still pretty useless and the punctures from the snake's teeth were swollen and turning dark colors. Tulley looked as though he had two black eyes and his face was gaunt, every once in a while a shiver would overtake his body and Jessica would insist on pressing a damp cloth to his head, the whole time fussing that he needed to be in bed.

"Let me finish my tea," was Tulley's only reply, even when Arnish and Jim began to press him about what had happened in the serpent's den.

"You have some nerves going in there like that," Jim stated, he was about to clap Tulley on the shoulder but thought better of it. "Nobody likes snakes, just the thought of being that close to one makes my skin crawl."

"Tulley," Arnish said. "We could use a man of your talents during the fall hunt, so don't die."

Tulley slowly sipped the tea and only replied, "I will think about it once I finish my tea."

Chapter Eleven

Axel clapped along with the rest of the people crowded at the gathering place. Eddie and Lisa swung each other around as several people strummed instruments and tapped out a quick stepping beat on a drum. Lisa's dress was light pink with white buttons down her back and a long feathery skirt, Eddie wore a dark green vest and trousers.

"Have some, son," Julian laughed and sloshed a cup of strong cider toward him. "It will help you fill out, strong shoulders and all."

"Da, I already have strong shoulders."

Julian laughed as he pressed the cup into Axel's hand, Axel held it for a time and then handed it to another when his father wasn't looking. Axel glanced over the people around him and caught sight of Florence; she was sitting amongst her family with a bored expression on her face. Axel glanced around and then began to make his way toward her. Florence sat slightly askew in her chair, her chin resting in one hand as she inspected the gold bracelet on her other wrist. She had one leg crossed over the other, her tiny foot sticking out from under her skirt and she was swinging it ever so slightly to the music.

"Florence, please sit up straight," Mrs. Azsin commented as she sat next to Florence, her back perfectly straight, her head erect and her hands folded in her lap. Florence merely shifted to rest her chin in her other hand and inspect the two gold rings on her now opposite hand. Harold and several of his well-dressed friends stood nearby, one of them exited their group and approached Florence, Axel stopped his approach when he saw the young man kneel down before her. They spoke for a moment and then Florence pushed her palm into his face, upsetting his balance and nearly toppling him. Mrs. Azsin nearly came out of her chair but before she could reprimand Florence for her actions, Florence had risen from her own chair and, holding her skirts up a little, she briskly walked away from the scene. Axel noted which way she went and quickly followed.

"Florence," Axel called softly. She paused for a moment and looked back, her eyes sparkled when she caught sight of him and after a quick wink she took off running, Axel grinned and followed in hot pursuit.

Florence rested her head on Axel's shoulder as they leaned back and looked at the pinks and purples of the sunset, she picked at the button on his sleeve and he moved his arm so she could grasp it.

"Axel, how old are you? Are you thirty yet?"

"No," Axel said softly. "I'm still very young, twenty-two, I think."

"How can you not know?"

"Da has it wrote down somewhere in a family book, he always said he would let me know when I turn thirty because then he will send me off into the world just as his Da did. Why do you ask?"

"Where I come from one is considered an adult at twenty six, I hear that in this area the age is thirty.... I was really just wondering if you had been married."

"No, have you?"

Florence was silent and held his arm closer as she buried her face into the inside of his elbow.

"Yes," she said softly and she felt Axel tense.

The Black Sparrow

"I am not married anymore, my husband died last year. That's why I came back to my father, but my stepmother is trying desperately to marry me off again."

"That's your stepmother?"

"Oh, yes, my mother passed in childbirth, so I never knew her. For so many years it was just my father and I, then my father married her twelve years ago and her and Harold have been with us ever since. Harold is a spoiled brat, I do not claim him as my brother. He is only a few months younger than I but because he is a boy and taller, he claims to be the older one, and he is so mean to me. Once, shortly after our parents were married Harold cut off my beautiful hair."

"That's terrible," Axel said as he ran his fingers through her ebony locks, it was soft and smelled like flowers.

"I married young so I could get away from them but it was a poorly arranged marriage, he was much older than me and drank all the time. It was the drink that did him in, he fell down the back stairs last winter and though he may have still been alive, nobody knew he was lying out there and he froze."

"Oh," Axel said, not sure what else to say to her story. "How long was you married?"

Florence took in a breath and sighed softly. "Nearly ten years, I am thirty-five years old, and a widow who lost everything her husband left her, though it was very little to begin with."

Axel leaned his head back to look at her, she certainly did not look like she was an adult, her face was still so young, her eyes full of wonder and innocence.

"I know what you are thinking," Florence whispered as she turned her face upwards and gently breathed on Axel's neck, Axel let out a tiny gasp as though he had just been hit in the gut.

"I am far from innocent, I am a woman, and I have needs," her lips brushed Axel's neck and he stood up so fast that Florence tumbled from her reclining position and got dirt on her skirts.

101

"I'm sorry, I'm sorry, I'm sorry," Axel blurted out as he tried to help her up.

"No," Florence said as she stood up and straightened her skirts. "I am sorry, I should not do such things, it will get us in trouble."

"Florence!" the shout startled them both and they turned to see Harold charging toward them like an angered animal.

"Get away from him," Harold grabbed Florence by the wrist and pulled her from Axel's side.

"You will disgrace us all."

"No, I won't, we did not do anything wrong," Florence spat as she yanked her arm free and stood her ground between Axel and Harold. "You will not get into another fight or I will tell Father."

Harold's brows came together and he fairly growled at her.

"Oh, yes, little brother, I know you have been getting into fights again, it is you who will disgrace us all yet again."

"You shut up," Harold said and he raised his hand as if to strike Florence.

"Don't you dare," Axel said in a deep, commanding voice as he reached around Florence and firmly grasped Harold's wrist. Axel heard footsteps behind him and the look on Harold's face changed as he relaxed his arm.

"Axel!" Julian called. "What are you doing?"

Axel released Harold's arm and after staring hard at him for another moment he turned to his father.

"Eddie? Sam?" Axel said when he saw not just Julian but Eddie and also Sam. Eddie folded his arms as Sam seemed to tower behind him.

"Always have to make things interesting, huh, even on my wedding day," Eddie looked disappointed but Axel knew him better than that, he liked to fight as much as any of Sam's sons and he was hoping something was going to happen.

"So sorry," Harold commented. "My sister was feeling a little glum and so Axel and I was trying to cheer her and get her to rejoin the festivities."

"Well, then," Julian said, Axel could tell by the tone of his voice that he was not believing a word of it. "The festivities are back this way."

Without a word the little group headed back in the direction of the music.

"Is Hindie ready for the races tomorrow?" Julian asked the next day.

"Yes," Axel said as he continued to rub beeswax up and down the straps of his riding harness.

"That's good," Julian moaned as he tried to put on his shoes.

"Too much, huh?"

"Oh, my head, I'm sure Eddie feels worse.... I think I'm going back to bed for a little while longer."

"I will bring you some water later," Axel said without looking up.

Early the next morning Axel harnessed Hindie and led him into town, his father following close behind with an old banner that bore the family name written in several different dialects and a very brief history of them.

"Oh!" Florence fairly coed when she saw Hindie. "He is so beautiful and graceful, has he ever raced before?"

"No, this is his first time, mine too."

"You will do wonderful! Oh, hello, Mr. Ramses."

Julian nodded to Florence and gently kissed her hand, then he turned away and walked toward the betting booth, the banner softly fluttering over his head.

"What does it say?" Florence asked as she stared at the green and gold.

"It has our family name on it, and a brief history, basically it says we traveled from a far-off place and settled here and founded this town, many generations ago. See that last name stitched in? That is my name."

"How intriguing," Florence said as she softly patted Hindie's head.

Harold suddenly rode over on his horse and sneered down at Axel from the top of a long-legged black steed. "So if you founded this dump, why are you and your family not the overseers?"

"Stop it, Harold," Florence fussed. "Don't make a scene here."

"I was not, I merely came over to tell you, Father is upset with you and wishes you to stay at the tent today."

"Very well," Florence said as she folded her arms. "I will be there shortly."

"Be sure you are," Harold said as he turned the horse around and walked him through the people, several of them had to jump out of the way before the horse knocked them down.

"Good luck, Axel," Florence said as she reached out and grasped his hand. "I will be watching from over there." She indicated a large dark blue and gold tent that already had her father and stepmother sitting beneath it. Florence fairly skipped away and Axel got a giddy feeling in the pit of his stomach as he watched her hips move and her delicate feet kick up the hem of her skirt.

"Did you get signed up?"

"What?"

"Did you get signed up?" Julian asked again from behind Axel.

"Not yet."

"You better get going, boy! The races are going to start soon."

"Right!" Axel said as he tossed the reins to his father and fairly jogged toward the sign up table.

"Thirty-three!?" Julian said in disbelief. "That's the last heap, we are going to be here all day before you even get to race, and if you win Hindie won't get much of a breather before the next heap."

"Sorry, Da, I guess I should have signed up soon as we got here."

"Don't worry about it," Julian said as he handed the reins back to Axel. "Just win, I bet about a year's worth on you."

"You worry too much," Axel said as he mounted Hindie and slowly made his way to the edge of the area. Axel looked up toward the blue and gold tent, he could see Mr. Azsin sitting with his wife on one side and Florence on the other. Axel envied him a little because he had a queen to his left and a goddess on his right. Florence seemed to catch sight of Axel and she waved a dainty white kerchief in the air, a slight breeze caught the thin cloth and it tore from her fingers, her hand went to her mouth as she watched the wind toy with the cloth. One of Harold's friends was nearby on a black steed and he turned toward the floating kerchief, he urged his horse forward and as the creature went up onto its hind legs, the young man reached upwards, his fingertips seemed to brush the kerchief but then the wind grabbed the delicate white cloth and blew it just a little higher.

Axel saw his opportunity and turned Hindie toward the scene, the large rabbit hopped gracefully with Axel astride him, barely jostling the young man. Axel pulled up on Hindie and urged him to stand, his own hand now reaching for the cloth just as the other young man had done a moment before, Hindie gave a tiny kick of his back legs and for a moment the two of them were floating as Axel was standing in the stirrups and reaching for the kerchief; he caught it in his fingers and Hindie landed back on his feet with barely a jerk. Axel turned Hindie and hopped him toward the Azsin's tent.

"My lady," Axel said as he handed the silky white cloth back to her. Florence smiled as she took it from him and grasping her hand, Axel bent down to kiss it. Florence then grasped his hand in return and she tied the white cloth to his wrist, Axel felt a little lightheaded as he turned Hindie and giving him a little more kick than normal, sped the rabbit away.

"Be careful," Julian said softly as Axel dismounted Hindie and then leaned against him stroking his soft fur. "Don't let your thoughts run today, I really need you on top of your opponents."

"No worries, Da."

Axel could barely remember the first few races. Hindie's tense body and the moment of weightlessness at the starting leap forward, the wind flying through his hair, the feel of Hindie's body bunching and stretching beneath him as he surged forward amongst the other racers; it was all just a indistinct set of events to him. Before and after every race Axel looked toward the Azsins' tent and each time was rewarded with Florence smiling down at him.

"Such a good show!" Julian said after the fourth run, he bear hugged Axel soon as he came off of Hindie's back.

"You are in the final race!" Eddie cried out as he also swooped in and hugged Axel.

"Get off me," Axel moaned. "I know I'm in the final race."

"You are guaranteed to win something even if you come in dead last this time," Julian affectionately rubbed the top of Axel's head with his palm and succeeded in messing up his hair.

"Da, lay off," Axel complained as he attempted to brush his hair back with his fingers.

"Ah," Julian laughed. "Your lady friend is watching, huh." Axel snorted and turned away, his ears felt hot.

"That's it, isn't it, son?" Julian and Eddie both laughed now. "Your ears are turning red."

Axel took Hindie's reins and began to walk away, leading his rabbit behind him.

Axel nosed Hindie up to the starting line, he could feel Hindie balancing and bunching his hind legs in preparation of that first exhilarating leap. Axel glanced up for Florence but his stomach suddenly dropped when he saw their tent was empty. Axel stood in the stirrups and looked over the crowd for her when suddenly Hindie surged forward and Axel was left floating in the air just above Hindie's body, the only thing he had a hold of was the reins.

"No! No! No!" Julian cried out as he watched his son nearly come unseated. There was a moment of heart-wrenching agony as Axel's feet left the stirrups completely and Hindie leapt forward nearly leaving Axel behind, but by some miracle Axel was able to grasp Hindie again and though he was not seated properly he was still on.

"What is he doing?!" Julian cried out as he grasped his hat on either side of his head in desperation.

"He's still on!" Eddie pointed out as Hindie skidded around the first sharp turn and Axel nearly rolled off.

"Is he holding him back?!" Julian bent the brim of his hat down over his ears.

"No," Eddie commented, his eyes still fixed on the racers. "It's all he can do to hold on, all he has is the reins, if he squeezes Hindie too tight with his legs he may injure Hindie."

"He's passing one, he's doing it!" Julian was nearly jumping up and down now.

Axel shut his eyes and dug his fingers into the fur just below Hindie's ears, he felt like he wanted to be sick and every turn Hindie skidded around nearly tore him from his perch.

"He's doing it, he's doing it!" Eddie was jumping up and down as Axel and Hindie was now in the middle of the group, three ahead and two behind.

"Oh, please, oh, please!" Julian was pleading out loud as he watched Axel come abreast of another racer. Axel dared a look up as Hindie's body flexed beneath him, he could see a few ahead of him and as he glanced to the side he once again saw the empty tent. At the last second Axel saw the slender body and jet-black hair as Florence leaned out over the window of her carriage and looked at him in wonder and that was all Axel needed. Hindie felt the elation run through Axel and it renewed him, he gave one powerful leap and passed the rider next to them, a second powerful leap brought him abreast of the next racer. Axel bent low over Hindie's shoulders and whispered in the rabbit's ear, encouraging him to go faster.

Julian was frozen on the sidelines as Axel suddenly passed up two more, one hand clutching the top of his head and the other pressed over his heart; there was only one more ahead of him now. The racer ahead of Axel was a small man from a neighboring town, he held a riding crop in one hand and was beating his rabbit's side mercilessly. Axel gritted his teeth as he neared this rider and he glanced at the rabbit next to him, the creature was angry, its eyes smoldered with every smack from the crop. Axel saw the movement before anybody else and the crowd gasped as he suddenly pulled Hindie back, the other rabbit lashed out at his rider and grabbing the man's boot in its teeth he yanked the man from his back. Axel had managed to get one foot back in the stirrup and with a slight kick he sent Hindie rocketing forward. Hindie passed the upset rider as the man tried to fight off his angered animal and passed the finish line with a leap and a twist. Axel could not hold onto Hindie any longer and his body flew sideways from the harness, he nearly landed on his feet but at the last second of his skidded landing his foot turned and he did a somersault that left him lying flat on his back with his head spinning.

There was utter silence for a full heartbeat as the people looked at Axel's prone form, then he slowly got to his feet and raised both arms into the air and everyone erupted.

Chapter Twelve

It seemed that the people would never end, everyone wanted to shake his hand or clap him on the back, Axel's head spun with it all. Hindie was lounging in a shady area with Sam and a couple of his son's standing guard so no one would disturb the resting beast.

"My boy!" Julian had cried out as he folded his arms around Axel, for a moment Axel went limp in his arms and Julian took a step back, his hands firmly grasping Axel's shoulders. "Are you hurt, son?" he asked but Axel only smiled in relief and shook his head.

"I was scared, Da," he said softly and then laughed. Axel looked for Florence but did not see her, the only one he saw was Harold sitting upon the long-legged black steed with several of his friends around him on identical horses.

Sometime later as Axel was standing at a table covered in lavish food Harold approached him and held out his hand in a friendly gesture. Axel glanced down at Harold's hand and then looked into the other's dark eyes.

"Come, shake. I congratulate you," Harold smiled at Axel and after a moment he took the offered hand, Harold clamped down on Axel's hand like a vice and Axel did the same in return.

"I know why your family dropped toward the bottom of this rotten little town, such terrible things your ancestors did, and I have the whole record of it, I found it buried in some library of the neighboring town, such terrible things. These people would despise you and your father now, I am very tempted to bring out the truth for those who do not know." Harold cocked his head at the look that crossed Axel's face.

"You don't even know, do you?" Harold squeezed tighter and Axel did the same, their fingers were losing feeling and beginning to turn dark red and purple. Harold reached up with his other hand and pulled out the end of an old piece of rolled leather from inside his jacket, the leather was thin and so old it was discolored and the ink had actually bleed through a little over the years.

"If you want it, you need to win another race, an expedition race you might say."

"When?" Axel asked with gritted teeth.

"Come back here, tomorrow night when the moon is at its apex and come alone." Harold tucked the rolled leather back and released Axel's hand, he then gave Axel a half-smile and turned away, the whole conversation happened so fast that hardly anyone noticed it.

"What was that all about?" Eddie asked softly as he sidled up next to Axel and picked up some dainty-looking piece of food.

"Tell you about it later," Axel said as he walked away.

"You can't!" Eddie hissed the next night as he and Axel stood in the shadows behind his leather shop, they could hear Lisa in the house to the rear singing ever so softly, her voice lilting with each breath. Hindie pressed his nose against Axel's arm and Axel could feel his warm breath through his shirt.

"He could be bluffing you," Eddie commented softly.

"I don't think so," Axel answered back. "Harold is right, if my ancestor was this town's founder then why are we not the overseers? And I have heard my father comment once, a long time ago, that there was terrible crimes commented by one of my ancestors but he didn't know what."

"Leave it be, Axel," Eddie said as he grasped Axel's shoulder in the dark. "You are young and...."

Axel swung his arm up and knocked Eddie's hand away.

"Don't," he hissed. "Don't start talking to me like I am a child. Just because you are nearly ten years my senior doesn't mean anything. I have been doing a man's work long before you have, my father has tried to raise me with honor and now that honor and my family name is at stake, I have to do something."

Eddie sighed and looked toward the half-moon as it splashed soft light down around them.

"All right," he said finally. "But I am going with you."

"You did not come alone," Harold commented as Axel and Eddie approached, Hindie between them. Harold smiled. "I see neither of us are fools." From out of the shadows stepped three of Harold's friends, each dressed in black with black scarves around their faces and each was leading a black horse.

"Meet your opponents," Harold raised his hand and one of the others placed a set of reins in his palm.

"You said I had to beat you," Axel said sternly.

"I said you had to win a race, I didn't say against whom. There are four of us and you make five, there is usually five in a heap so I just want to make this fair."

"Fair for who?" Eddie cut in. "We want to see this so-called document."

"It's here," Harold said, once again he pulled it out from his shirt but only long enough for them to tell it was indeed rolled leather with writing on it, then he tucked it back away and that smile was back on his face.

"Like I said, there is some terrible crimes recorded here, I'm afraid that if the people around here got word of it they would run you out, since it was committed by your father's grandfather, that was not very long ago at all, that bad blood may still be running through your veins."

"My father and I are noble gentlemen from a high-standing family. We possess the three names of high rank, while you only have two, Harold Azsin," Axel fairly spat when he said Harold's name.

"I am Axel William Ramses, from Julian William Ramses, of Andling William Ramses, of Bentrove William Ramses, of Dwayne William Ramses."

"Yeah, yeah, whatever," Harold cut in. "Honestly, I don't understand why people around here take such pride in family names, it's stupid and boring having to memorize such frivolous things."

Axel took in a sharp intake of breath and Eddie grasped his arm tightly.

"Come on," Eddie said softly. "He's just trying to make you mad, let's go back."

"No!" Axel pulled his arm away and turned, he took one step and was astride Hindie. "Let's do this," he called as he hopped Hindie to the starting line. Harold laughed softly to himself and he mounted, his friends following suit. They walked their snorting steeds to the line as well, two on each side of Axel and Hindie.

"Ready," one of the young men called. "Three, two, GO!" The horses all leapt forward just a second before Axel and Hindie, he had purposely skipped number one to throw Axel behind. Hindie's body stretched out as he leapt forward, still beside the horses but a full head behind. Axel was at their flanks and glanced to his left just in time to see a boot kick for his head, he ducked it and reaching up with his left hand he grasped the other's foot instead. Axel pulled on the foot and nearly unseated the rider but then he cried out as a pain shot through his knuckles and down his wrist, it was a sharp pain that he couldn't help but cry out and then it happened again. Axel released the foot and this time the other rider swung the riding crop at his head.

"Dirty bastard!" Eddie shouted so loudly that he was heard in the town. Axel ducked and felt the riding crop part his hair and then to his horror the riders on either side of him suddenly steered their horses together in an attempt to crush him. Axel pulled back on Hindie's reins so hard that the rabbit threatened to buck, the two horses came together and continued to run as if they were joined at the hip. Axel steered Hindie to the right and found the other rider blocking his way, he steered him back to the left and found the same thing. Eddie watched in amazement and horror as Axel let Hindie fall back a little bit and then leaning down low he gave Hindie an almost savage kick. Hindie leapt up and forward, his body stretched out with Axel clinging to his back like he had become one with the rabbit. Hindie's magnificent leap was taking him over the heads of the other riders and Eddie's heart suddenly swelled with pride as he saw that they were going to clear the daring jump. One of the riders on horseback looked up and saw Hindie and Axel over their heads, without hesitation he stood in the stirrups of his charging beast and reaching up he caught the fur of Hindie's back leg in his hand, Eddie cried out in alarm as he watched this rider give Hindie a savage jerk that seemed to rip them from the sky. Hindie and Axel came down nearly on top of the horses and their riders but only one of the riders was unseated as Axel and Hindie fell between them and was rolled beneath the pounding hooves.

"No!" Eddie cried out as he ran across the torn up soil toward Axel and Hindie. When Eddie reached him, Axel was on his hands and knees, his breath was coming in stuttering gasps, his whole body was shaking and blood was streaming from his nose and mouth.

"Axel! Axel! Say something!" Eddie grabbed Axel by the shoulders but Axel pushed him off and attempted to crawl toward Hindie, the rabbit was several feet away stumbling around the track as if he were drunk, after a moment Hindie finally fell onto his side panting heavily, his legs weakly kicking. Axel still tried to go to Hindie, every time Eddie tried to help him up he pushed Eddie away, but try as he might Axel couldn't get his feet under him. After several tries of this Axel finally fell prone and Eddie pulled him into his arms.

"Hey!" someone shouted and Eddie could hear several sets of running footsteps.

"Help!" Eddie called as he held Axel's shaking body. Two shadows fell across them and Eddie looked up to see two of his brother in laws towering over them.

"Help," Eddie said again. "He got trampled, he can't breathe."

The Haplin brothers looked at each other for a moment and then they reached down and grasped Axel, one picking up his legs and the other tucking his arms under Axel's arms. Axel cried out when they lifted him up but then they took off at a fast walk toward Doc Hal's place, a light was already burning in the window and Eddie could see Doc Hal standing in the doorway.

"Doc!" one of the brothers called. "It's Axel, he's bad off." Eddie followed as closely as he dared, he didn't want to get in the way but he was beside himself with worry and regret for not stopping Axel in the beginning. Doc Hal met them halfway and ordered the brothers to lay Axel down, Axel coughed and more blood ran from his nose and into his mouth staining his teeth pink in the lantern light. Hal pulled a knife from his belt and cut open Axel's shirt from neck to waist, one of the brothers took in a sharp gasp when the huge bruise blossoming on Axel's side was revealed, it ran from his collarbone to his hip in multicolors of reds, purples, blues and even black, blood seemed to be leaking from his very pores in a few places.

Hal glanced at the injury and then gently placed his hands on either side of Axel's head.

"Look at me, Axel," he said as he gently bent his head forward to catch the light. "Keep breathing, stay with me, I don't want you to pass out just yet."

Hal placed his hand over Axel's eyes for a moment and then removed it, he studied the reaction of Axel's pupils to the light, he did it a second time and a third.

"Where all does it hurt, Axel?" he asked once he was satisfied with looking at Axel's eyes.

"Can't...breathe...," Axel managed between pained gasps.

"I know, but can you tell me if there's any place that hurts worse than others?"

Axel did not answer, he took one long labored breath and Hal watched as his eyes rolled back, for a brief moment they were white in the lantern light and then his body went limp and Axel was still except for the ever-so-soft breaths that emitted from his battered body.

Eddie caught sight of the knife Hal had dropped next to Axel's body, reaching out with a bloodied hand he scooped it up and rose. Hal suddenly rose as well and wrapped one hand around Eddie's throat and the other around Eddie's wrist.

"Leave it be," Doc Hal commanded. "Tend to Axel first and then you can seek revenge on whoever did this." Eddie dropped the knife and fell back to his knees beside Axel's still form.

"Doc," a voice called from the track. "There's someone laying over here, he's all dressed in black. I think he's dead, Doc."

Chapter Thirteen

"He needs rest, and you make too much noise."

"Please just let me sit next to the bed," Eddie pleaded with Doc Hal. Hal narrowed his eyes at Eddie but then turned his head when a hand gently grasped his shoulder from behind.

"Let him come in, Hal, he can watch while I get some sleep, but if he makes so much as a squeak I will break his jaw," Julian said softly. Hal nodded slightly and removed his arm from barring the doorway. Eddie slowly entered the dim room, his head was bowed and his eyes were downcast, he looked like a child who was about to be thoroughly scolded. There were three beds in the room, Julian stopped before one and lay prone on it while Axel lay on another, the third was being used like a table, on it sat rolled linen, an extra blanket and a bowl of water with several strips of cloth resting in the water, there was also a whole array of different jars of medicines and elixirs. Eddie looked around the room and took the wooden stool next to Axel's bed, it had no back and one leg was slightly shorter than the other so it was actually very uncomfortable to sit on. Julian looked at Eddie for a long time, Eddie tried to shrink smaller as he felt Julian's eyes boring into the back of his head. The room was deathly quiet and Eddie was beginning to regret his visit, Axel moaned a little and Eddie nearly jumped off the stole.

"A bit jumpy, Eddie?" Julian said softly.

"Yes, sir," Eddie answered.

"Why so formal? You scared of something?"

"Um, yes, sir."

Julian took in a long breath and let out a quiet and exasperated sigh.

"What were you all doing on the track at night, Eddie?"

"Well, Mr. Ramses, I don't know the exact details, sir."

"Then tell me what you do know, and don't lie to me, Eddie, I have known you long enough, I can tell when you are lying."

"He was racing Hindie with some other guys."

"No shit," Julian said softly and matter-of-factly, Eddie's heart sank even lower, Julian was beyond mad at him. Eddie began to fear that Julian would kill him over this. Eddie turned toward Julian, his eyes still downcast and began to softly recite everything Axel had told him before the exhibition race. Julian lay on the bed with his arms behind his head, propping him up a little, he stared straight at the ceiling as he knitted his brows in anger.

"You know you both could have died," Julian said softly. "Harold does not fear consequences, he was never held to them. Men like that are reckless and will continue to wreak havoc and do as they please until the day they do kill someone, and then they continue to kill. I heard rumors that Harold has already killed, it is one reason they are so far from their native homelands. And now Harold is wreaking havoc in our little town but so far it seems Axel is the one suffering the consequences, more than once now. Doc Hal wasn't even sure if he would make it through yesterday. Broken ribs all down his right side, an injured lung, two broken knuckles, some serious abrasions and a lot of blood loss, not to mention the fact that he still hasn't woke up."

Eddie cringed as Julian spoke and looked down toward Axel. A damp cloth was across his forehead, crusty dried blood was still in the corner of one nostril and his thick golden locks were now clinging to his sweating pale face. His right hand was swollen and bruised as was his shoulder. The blankets were pulled up enough to only cover half of his torso so Eddie could clearly see all the thick bandages wrapped around his chest with some spots of red bleeding through. There was a cut across Axel's jaw and another, deeper one across his left forearm.

"Eddie," Julian said softly. "Periodically change that damp cloth and wipe the blood from his mouth if he starts coughing again."

"Yes, sir," Eddie answered, he then heard Julian roll over in the bed and a short while later the heavier uneven breathing of one in a fitful sleep.

Eddie remained on the uncomfortable stool all day watching Axel, Doc Hal periodically came in and looked over the bandages and checked the fever, once he leaned over Julian and gently laid a hand on his forehead for a brief time, Julian was so exhausted that he didn't even stir at the touch. Toward the evening Eddie himself fell asleep on the stool, his arms folded across his chest and his head bent so low that his chin was also on his chest. Eddie twitched as he dreamed of Axel's body rolling under the pounding hooves, he could see every hoof strike on his body and blood seemed to coat the air like a mist. Eddie cried out in his sleep and fell from the stool. Julian leapt up from dead sleep and looked wide eyed at Axel, Doc Hal was almost instantly in the doorway also looking at Axel, then they both looked at Eddie on the floor.

"I think it's time for you to go home," Doc Hal commented as Julian ran his fingers through his hair in frustration.

"I am sorry," Eddie said with a slight tremble in his voice. "I had a nightmare."

"So did I," Julian said and Eddie could hear the anger behind his quiet tones. Eddie got up and softly walked out of Hal's quiet home, Julian followed. Doc Hal placed a hand on Julian's shoulder and stopped him in the doorway, they spoke a few brief hushed words and then Julian continued right behind Eddie.

"Eddie," Julian said quietly, though they were now standing in the front yard. "I cannot express just how stupid you two were to go through with all that the other night."

"And I can't express just how sorry I am," Eddie began. Julian pulled his fist back and punched Eddie so fast and hard that Eddie fell flat on his back, arms spread wide, Julian stood over Eddie for a moment, saw that he was still alive and turned to walk away. Doc Hal knelt next to Eddie and helped him to sit up. Eddie's head was reeling and his jaw ached, he ran his tongue over his teeth and felt several of them wiggle painfully. Julian stopped just before he shut the door and glanced over his shoulder.

"Did I break it?" he asked.

"No," Hal answered.

"Damn, maybe next time," Julian said as he shut the door behind himself.

Julian had one arm tucked beneath Axel's neck as he slowly, almost painstakingly dripped honey into Axel's open mouth. It was now day five and though the fever was gone and his breathing was more normal, Axel still had not woken. As much as he wanted to, Julian could not stay with Axel the entire time because on the third day three men took him away to question him about what had happened.

"Someone was killed that night?" Julian asked completely blindsided by the news.

"Knocked off his horse, it seems, broke his neck when he hit the ground."

"My condolences to his family," Julian answered. One of the men shrugged.

"He was not from around here, a friend to Harold Azsin from their old home come to visit for a while. The family does not wish to seek punishment, to their understanding it was a complete accident, they just want closure."

Julian sighed inwardly, he had not noticed but he had been barely breathing the entire conversation up until then.

"Relax," one of the men said. "To be honest with you, he wasn't a good kid and we would rather not be here questioning about his death, but we are employed by his family and they are paying us to do so. Give me something good to tell them, it doesn't have to be the truth."

"But the truth is all I have to give," Julian answered, holding his hands out in a gesture of honesty.

"Don't worry about it then," another of the three said. "We already got the eyewitness account from your son's friend. Harold and another boy gave us a different story but one of Harold's friends who was riding one of the horses that night is pretty shook up over this, his story matched the other guy."

"Eddie?"

"Yeah, I think that was his name. Well, anyway, sorry to keep you from your son, it sounds like he got pretty roughed up, I hope he heals quickly."

"Thank you," Julian answered. Julian blinked a few times as he thought over the whole conversation with the three men and he almost wanted to start crying at how lucky they were, if the family of that dead boy wished for punishment to avenge his death, Axel and Eddie would both be dead by now. Julian used the damp cloth to wipe a drop of honey from Axel's lower lip, Axel's mouth twitched like a sleeping child. He coughed a little as the honey in his mouth began to drip down his throat, then he finally swallowed and Julian began the process all over again.

"Is he swallowing better?" Hal asked as he came into the dim room.

"Yes," Julian said. "Should we try some broth again today?"

"If you wish to." Doc Hal went to the one small window in the room and pulled the heavy cloth away to let in the sunlight and fresh air, Axel flinched a little at the sudden brightness and Julian looked down to see his eyes flutter open for a moment.

"Doc!" Julian said excitedly. Hal turned and kneeled next to the bed as Julian continued to cradle Axel's head in his arm, he pulled a tiny canister from his pocket, opened it and waved it beneath Axel's nose once. Julian cringed at the smell, he could not imagine how bad it must smell to Axel. Axel turned his head away a little and softly coughed twice, then his eyes came half open and remained that way.

"Axel!" Julian said, his voice almost cracking.

"How do you feel?" Hal asked as he tucked the vile smelling canister back in his pocket. Axel continued to stare blankly upwards until Julian nervously looked at Hal, deep concern and fear registering on his face. But then Axel blinked a few times and tried to speak, his voice was so soft and raspy that they almost could not hear him.

"Please, give me some of that broth, I am so hungry."

Chapter Fourteen

Axel sat propped up in bed, a thin polished wood board in one hand and a piece of charcoal from the fireplace in the other.

"What are you doing?" Eddie asked as he let himself in. Axel glanced up but continued to scratch on the board.

"I brought you lunch, your father says he will be home late again so Lisa made you something." Eddie set the wooden bowl down next to Axel's bed, he could smell the meat and spices that floated in the thick golden broth, Eddie leaned in briefly and looked at what Axel was writing.

"Your spelling is terrible," he said softly. Axel stopped what he was doing and then hurled the thin wood tablet across the room.

"Woah!" Eddie said as he stepped back. "What did I say?" Axel rubbed his hands over his face and through his hair.

"I'm sorry, Eddie," he said with a sigh. "I'm just so tired of sitting here all day, it's been almost three weeks. And every night Da gets home later and later, he needs my help. It's almost gathering season and people need their things fixed for the hunt."

"It will be all right," Eddie said as he offered Axel another pillow, Axel shook his head and began to peel back the covers.

"Where are you going?" Eddie asked with some desperation. "I was going to teach you some more letters so you can read and write better."

"I need to get out for a little while, I'm going for a walk," Axel took in a sharp breath as he pulled on his boots.

"What about your lunch?" Eddie asked. "I just walked it here all the way from my house and I didn't spill a drop."

"I will eat it when I get back," Axel said as he slowly stood up and gingerly tucked his arm into one sleeve of his shirt.

"I will go with you," Eddie said as he stood up out of his chair, Axel turned to him and pushed a finger against Eddie's forehead causing him to sit back down.

"I would like some alone time," Axel stated. "You, Hal, my Da, Lisa, even Sam's boys, there has always been someone watching me these last three weeks, it's getting a little creepy." Axel tucked the other arm in his sleeve with less difficulty. "You know, I woke up the other morning and…. What's Sam's youngest named?"

"Jep."

"Yeah, Jep was sleeping in bed next to me, that's not exactly who I want in bed next to me, Eddie."

Eddie stifled a laugh and Axel gave him a crooked look.

"Don't worry, I will be back, I am just going for a short walk."

Axel stepped out into the yard and stopped for a moment to look at his surroundings and take in the warmth and beauty of the sun. He put his arms out as though to embrace the warm glow and took in a deep breath, which he immediately regretted as a sudden pain stabbed him in the side. Axel gently patted his ribs and then reaching over he grasped the long walking cane his father had made for him a week ago when he first was allowed out of bed, it was a sturdy oak branch that he had stripped the bark off of and rubbed with beeswax to give it a smooth polish, Axel decided he would use it as a fighting staff once he was well enough again. Axel looked around for a moment and then looked toward the woods in the direction of the Seeing Glass, after a moment of thought he started walking that way.

The world around him had changed over the month he was confined to his room, the air had the smell of fall and cold coming, it was a sharp almost crisp smell that tingled in his nose as he breathed. Axel thought it was a beautiful smell because it heralded the changing of the seasons and the rebirth that came every spring. Axel looked down mostly, watching where he stepped so as not to trip, his father and Doc Hal would want to skin his hide if he upset his half-healed ribs. Every now and then there was a dead leaf that had fallen from one of the trees, its edges brown and dry, sometimes its middle still green and yellow, Axel would stop and stab his walking stick into these a few times and the smell of fall would waft up around him as the leaf was crushed.

By the time Axel got to the Seeing Glass he was out of breath and his whole right side was beginning to ache, he slowly sat down next to the edge to catch his breath. Axel looked at the soft dirt next to him and noticed a tiny footprint as if someone had leaned over to look into the glass, the soil here was light brown and so fine it was almost silky to the touch, Axel pulled his boots off and pressed his feet into the softness, wiggling his toes back and forth. After a minute of this Axel leaned over to look into the water just as the previous person had, it was as still and reflective as ever. He could see how his skin had grown pale and his hair, cut shorter during his time in bed, was sticking up in odd angles and looked messy. Axel dipped his hand into the water and began to run his fingers through his hair in an attempt to tame it. Axel stopped for a moment when he heard the humming, he sat up and looked across the still pool to the other corner and his heart leapt.

She was barefoot and leading a midnight mare behind her, her skirt was a little shorter than usual, ending at her calves and her hair was trussed up in a large messy bun at the nape of her neck, a gold belt ran around her slender waist and rested on her hips. Florence stopped when she caught sight of Axel and for a brief moment a look of fear came across her face, then she smiled and dropping the reins, she raced forward to embrace him.

Axel groaned a little when she wrapped her arms around him but he folded his arms over her and refused to let go.

"I'm sorry," Florence said, her face against his chest. "Did I hurt you?"

"No, it's okay, the pain is well worth this," Axel said softly as he felt the warmth in the pit of his stomach begin to blossom, he fought it down because he didn't want to embarrass himself but Florence began to giggle when she pressed her body closer to his.

"No, no," Axel said as he pushed her away a little. "I'm sorry, I can't."

"Why not?" Florence asked. "We are both adults and we are alone here."

"I was raised to be a gentleman, it's my morals, I'm sorry, as much as I want to, I can't...not yet."

Florence released him and smiled broadly. "So, it will happen sometime?"

"Oh, yes! Just, not now."

"I applaud your strength of will," Florence said and Axel let out a breath because if she had asked one more time at that moment he would have not been able to stop again.

"I tried to visit you a few times but your father kept turning me away."

Axel frowned a little but then shrugged it off. "I was pretty sick for the first couple of weeks, Doc Hal practically lived at my house for a while."

"Axel, I am sorry for what Harold did, it was foolish of him, but I am so happy you are all right."

"Yeah, me too," Axel said softly as he thought about the young man who had gotten killed, his father had recently told him about that and how the young man's family was not seeking revenge.

"How is Hindie?" Florence asked suddenly. Axel frowned and a feeling of despair quickly replaced the happy warmth.

"Da had to put him down," Axel said softly.

"Oh, Axel, I am so sorry, I didn't know."

"He had a broken back and wouldn't eat, but it's okay because now he is not in any more pain."

They were silent for a time and Florence reached over to grasp his hand.

"Let us met here every few days," she said. "It's so nice and quiet and I am still hoping to catch a peek at a snow fairy."

"Every day," Axel said softly.

"Every three days, it's hard for me to sneak away, my father does not want me to wander on my own, keeps saying an animal will eat me."

"It's not the dangerous time of the year yet," Axel said. "It gets really dangerous in the winter time because animals get hungry and then they get bold and venture farther to find food, but it's been a few years since anyone in our town has been eaten by an animal."

"That's good to know, but I am sure I will be fine with you protecting me."

"I will give my life for you," he said as he looked down at her. They were both reclining next to the Seeing Glass now while the black mare took bites out of some still green leaves nearby.

"Axel, do you know any poetry? I was told that this region has some great poets."

"I don't know anything by heart," Axel said as he gently rubbed his fingertips across the back of Florence's hand.

"Do you write any poetry?"

"I have never tried, but if I think about it I may be able to come up with something."

"Oh, please do," Florence said with a small laugh. Axel looked up and studied the leaves and sky, Florence watched him as he subconsciously chewed his lower lip in thought.

"Shall I compare thee to a sunbeam, floating and laughing on the air, Dazzling upon a waking dream, but thou is far more fair."

"Oh, Axel, I love it," Florence fairly cooed as she placed a hand over her heart. "Tell me more."

"Thou eyes twinkle brighter than the stars, thou face outshines the moon,

Thou lips as a rose in blossom, thou voice as majestic as the loon's."

"Beautiful," Florence said as she leaned over to place her head on his shoulder, that warm feeling began to fill Axel again.

"Axel, what's a loon?" Florence asked.

"I think it's a large bird that has a beautiful singing voice, it lives near water."

"So you have never heard one? What if it has a terrible singing voice?" Then Florence began to laugh and Axel joined in.

"Where have you been?" Julian asked when Axel returned later that day, he had been gone much longer then he planned, Florence and he talked for a long time, just about anything and everything. Axel smiled and looked down at his hand, he could still feel the warmth and smallness of hers as he held it.

"I just went for a walk, I was getting so tired of sitting in bed."

"How are your ribs?"

"A little sore but I'm all right, Da."

"Good," Julian said as he squeezed Axel's shoulder. "Now do me a favor, next time you want to take a walk, walk into town and visit me so I know you are okay." Julian looked more tired than usual and he had dark areas forming beneath his eyes.

"Sorry, Da," Axel said softly. "Why don't you sit down, I can make something to eat."

"Do I look that bad?"

"Yeah."

"Well, don't worry about food, Lisa brought some to the shop in town."

"Oh, yeah, Eddie brought me something to eat earlier too," Axel said as he remembered the bowl sitting in his room, it was surely cold now but he was still going to eat it anyway.

"I think I will go to bed early," Julian said as he turned toward the bedroom.

The next morning Axel was awakened to a crash from inside their room, he sat up quite startled and looked down to see his father on his hands and knees next to his own bed.

"Da!" Axel said as he kicked back the covers and rolled out. Julian clasped the side of his bed and pulled himself up, Axel took hold of his arm in an attempt to help.

"I'm all right," Julian said. "I just got a little dizzy, that's all."

"Da, you're burning up, you need to get back in bed, I will go get Doc Hal."

"I'm all right," Julian said again but he sank back to the floor, nearly pulling Axel down as well.

"Just wait, don't move," Axel said, he pulled a blanket down and dropped it over his father, Julian clutched at the still warm cloth and held it close.

"I will be right back."

"Axel is right," Hal said as he checked Julian's pulse. "You need to stay in bed for a day or two. When was the last time you had a good meal?"

"No time, I got a lot of work at the shop."

"I forbid it." Hal flared out another blanket over Julian's bed and let it settle down over him.

"How old are you now, Julian?"

"In my one hundred and sixtieth year, I think," Julian said slowly as he thought about it.

"You should have great-grandchildren by now," Hal stated. "I never asked before but I always wondered, I am nosy like that, but I came here right after Axel was born, why didn't you and Kelsey have more children, before Axel?"

"We did," Julian said softly. "There was two before Axel but they were not alive when they were born."

"I am sorry, that is a hard thing to face."

"Kelsey was heartbroken and we didn't try for any more children for a long time. When Axel was born she was so worried that he was going to die that she would not let anyone hold him, he was nearly three months old before I was able to hold him in my own arms."

"Well, you got yourself a good son out there," Doc Hal indicated toward the front of the house where Axel was sitting so as not to disturb them.

"He is, I have done my best by him."

Doc Hal nodded and then frowned. "But I hate to tell you this, Julian," Doc Hal suddenly became somber and Julian's heart began to sink.

"What is it?"

"You are getting gray hair," Hal said, a quirky smile suddenly appeared. Julian sighed and then laughed a little.

Chapter Fifteen

Julian only stayed in bed for a day, Axel could not keep him there but he was at least able to keep him home for another day.

"Just have Eddie bring me a few small things from the shop that I can work on here," Julian said as Axel barred the door.

"You know I am your elder, you should listen to me."

"And you are still sick, you look like an old man," Axel stated. "And you can't push me out of the way, you might break my ribs again."

"I don't think I have the strength to anyway."

"That's good," Axel said with humor. "I was hoping you wouldn't even try."

Axel and Julian both worked on a few of the damaged weapons, the ones that had cracks and needed leather binding or just needed a sharpening stone run across their edge for a little while.

"How is the firewood doing for the forge?" Axel asked absentmindedly as he weaved a few strips of leather around the handle of a large carving knife.

"We still have plenty left," Julian lied, Axel glanced up at him, he knew his father had lied, he knew the reason he was getting home so late was because he was going out to cut his own wood to keep the forge going; it was a chore that Axel had been doing for years now but he could not swing an axe with his ribs as they were.

Axel continued to go for his walks every day, usually he did go into town to visit his father and help with the smaller tasks, but every three days, as promised, he went to the Seeing Glass and waited for Florence, and true to her word, she came. This went on well into the winter and even in the cold and snow they continued to meet.

"It's so cold but so beautiful," Florence said as she looked at the whiteness around them. Their light bodies and wide shoes made it possible for them to walk on top of the snow. As the weeks went by the cold and snow eventually turned to slush and mud and then finally, with a scent like fresh rain and earth the spring came.

"It's so amazing just how fast the flowers grow here," Florence said as she ran her hand across the petals of a wild pink rose.

"Do you miss where you came from?"

"No," Florence said dryly. "There is nothing left for me or my family there."

"I'm sorry," Axel said.

"You say sorry a lot," Florence chided. "But that's okay, I like that about you."

"And I like this about you," Axel said as he reached out and pinched her butt.

"Unhand me, you fiend!" Florence said with a laugh and then she began to run. This was a fun pastime for them, Axel thoroughly enjoyed the chase and Florence enjoyed being chased. Axel reached forward and grabbed her by the hips, he lifted her up over his head and held her like that, her feet kicking and her small fists swinging, Axel wiggling his fingers back and forth on her sides as he held her and her laughing scream filled the woods.

"You are terrible!" Florence said as Axel set her back on her feet, she pushed him away and turned to run again.

"Florence!" an angered voice called out. Florence stopped so suddenly that she nearly fell over, they both looked up to see a man on a midnight steed riding right for them.

"No!" Florence shouted as she threw herself in front of Axel with her arms wide. The rider pulled back his steed but the running animal fought at the bit and though its head was turned to the side it still charged straight ahead.

"Watch out!" Axel shouted as he pushed Florence away, he tried to turn away himself but was a little too slow, the horse's broad chest slammed into his shoulder and sent him reeling.

"Reese!" Florence screamed as she leapt up and though the horse was still bucking around, she grabbed Reese by the arm and using all the strength in her tiny body she unseated him and sent him crashing to the ground. Reese landed on his shoulder and cried out in pain, the thin helmet he wore, more for show then for protection, flew from his head from the impact. The black horse took off again, bucking and prancing the whole way and after a moment it was gone.

Axel got to his feet and slowly approached the crumpled form of the guard, he had long thick hair that was just as jet black as Florence's.

"My father has been getting upset over my disappearances, I guess he sent his head guard to follow. Damn bastard." Florence kicked Reese and the man groaned, Axel looked at her in wide-eyed amazement.

"Get up, Reese," Florence nearly spat. "Or I'm going to kick you again!"

"Please don't, miss," Reese moaned. "I think my shoulder is dislocated." Florence suddenly softened at this and even helped Reese to stand up.

"Are you all right?" she asked Axel. "You have dirt all over your face."

"Yes," Axel said as he began to wipe away the dirt. "I am fine."

"Reese!" she immediately turned back to the guard. "Why did you charge at us like that?"

"I heard you scream, miss," Reese said with bowed head. "I was coming to save you from the heathen."

"He is not a heathen, nor is he a thief or a rapist. Now get back home and tell my father to butt out of my business."

"I'm sorry, miss, but I just can't do that, your father said he would punish me if I did not return with you safe."

Florence folded her arms and scowled.

"And if that runaway stallion of yours goes back without a rider my father will burn down the forest. All right, Reese, I will go back with you." Florence reached out and took Axel's hand in hers.

"I'm sorry," she said softly, then she leaned in and whispered. "See you in three days." She ever so gently pressed her lips against his cheek; it sent shivers through his body as he felt just how warm and soft they were. Reese was holding one arm pressed to his side and the other he offered to Florence, which she took with some hesitation. Axel watched them walk away for a moment as he cherished the feeling of her lips on his cheek, he should be used to it by now, she had been kissing him on the cheek whenever they parted for months now, but it still gave him a thrill.

Once Axel could not see them anymore he turned and sprinted all the way home, leaping over obstacles and dodging one way and then another as he saw images of himself fending his beautiful lady in some heroic battle. Axel burst through the front door and nearly upset his father as he was coming out.

"Ah! Thordin!" Julian said as he dropped the newly finished crossbow.

"Sorry, Da," Axel said as he scooped it up, he looked it over in a second and handed it back to his father. "No harm done."

Julian took it from Axel with one eyebrow raised, then he turned away to sit down and thoroughly inspect it.

"Where have you been again?"

"Just out and about," Axel said as he seemed to dance around the room.

"Went to see her again, huh? No grandchildren on the way, right?"

"Da, when are you going to stop asking me that? No, no grandchildren for you, don't you know me? You raised me better than that."

"I know I did," Julian said without looking up. "But I also know those urges, I was young once too, you know."

"You got more gray hair, Da," Axel teased in an attempt to steer the conversation away from how to make babies, a conversation that they seemed to be repeating every week now.

"Yeah, and it's all because of you, I don't need any miniatures of you running around just yet."

"Yeah, then you would probably start to go bald." Axel began to laugh but Julian rose and gently cuffed him on the ear.

"By the way, son, how did you get mud on your chin?"

"I have something to show you," Florence said, her eyes shining. "Come on! It's at my stables."

Axel was slightly taken aback when Florence ran up to him in the middle of town right in front of his father's shop, he looked back at his father in a pleading way.

"Go ahead, son," Julian said without looking up from the handle he was carving out of a block of wood. "It's not like the whole town doesn't know you two are always together so just show them."

"Huh?" Axel began but Florence grabbed his hand and started leading him toward her grand house on the rise overlooking the town.

"What is it?" Axel asked a short time later as they stood around the huge wooden crate and looked in at the large bird. The bird's back was mostly black and speckled with a pattern of white. Its entire head was black with a long wicked-looking bill and the black ran down its neck where it changed to a band of black and white, then a band of greenish blue that seemed to change tint as it moved. The bird's breast was large and white and it stood on two black webbed feet, but what caught Axel's attention the most was its eyes, not just because they were red but because they showed a broken soul.

"It's a loon," Florence said. "I asked my father to get me a loon because I wanted to hear it sing, but it won't sing, and it won't eat."

"You have to let it go," Axel said.

"I don't want to, it's mine, I waited all winter for the men to return with it."

"You have to let it go," Axel said again. "It's going to die."

"It will be all right," Florence said. "I will take care of it." The loon was backed into a corner and she reached in to touch its feathers, Axel saw the minuet change in the creature and reached in as well just as the loon's large bill came down to break Florence's arm. Axel's arm shoot forward and covered Florence's, the wicked bill clamped down on both of their arms but Axel's took the brunt of the attack. The bird only held their arms for a moment and then let go as it squished itself into the corner even tighter.

"I will have it killed!" Florence shouted as she held her injured arm, it was already beginning to bruise. Axel's arm was loose at his side, warm blood was beginning to seep out of the shallow cut he received but he didn't even notice.

"Are you okay?" Axel asked as he tried to hold her shoulders. Florence shrugged him off and turned her back to him, she was crying.

"How could an animal like that possess a beautiful voice, it is an evil creature, just look at its eyes! Look at them! They are red. I want it killed, right now!" Florence continued to shout as she walked away, two stable workers were standing off to the side and merely watched her storm off with bored expressions on their faces, Axel turned to one of them.

"Is she really going to have it killed?" he asked.

"Yes," one of the workers answered as if it was no big deal. Axel turned and looked around for a moment, then he grasped a shovel from the hands of one of the workers and he immediately began to hack at the corner of the crate where it was sealed. The loon turned its head sideways and watched him, after several good hits the lock was broken and Axel flung the door wide for the loon to escape. The bird stared hard at Axel for a moment and then it fled the crate and out the door of the stables, knocking Axel down in the process. Axel watched as the large bird flapped its wings as it ran, knocking a few people over in its path, then with one powerful leap it took to the sky and after circling once it was gone.

"You let it go!" Florence fairly screamed at him as she beat her small fists against his chest.

Axel sat next to the Seeing Glass and waited, his heart ached with each passing hour, this was now the fourth time that Florence did not appear at their customary meeting place on every third day.

"I will go to her home today and knock until I get an answer," he said to himself. Axel turned and put his arms out, his change was so sudden and beautiful that people who could not change would wonder if it were real. Axel flew toward the Azsins' home and circled it once, he had done this just three days prior, landing on the balcony of Florence's room he had found the doors locked then and though he had heard movement inside she did not answer to his knocking, today the doors were open. Axel landed in the doorway with a flurry of wings that made Florence's hair flutter and her skirts swish. By the first step Axel was a young man again and by the second he was embracing Florence.

"I was getting so worried," he said as he draped his head over her shoulder, then he realized she was not hugging him back and he stepped away from her.

"Florence?" he asked softly. "What is wrong?"

"You," Florence said flatly as she turned away. Axel felt a stab of pain at the very being of his soul.

"You released that evil creature."

"I'm sorry, but it wasn't evil, it was just scared."

"You disobeyed my wishes, I wanted it killed. Why would you go against anything I want?"

Axel stood with his hands held palm up, he wasn't sure what to do or say, the pain he felt inside was beginning to eat away at him.

"I don't know what to do to fix this," he finally said. Florence turned back to him, her arms folded across her bosom and a dark look on her face.

"Get on your knees," she commanded and Axel instantly went to his knees before her.

"Do you swear, to always be by my side and to immediately do whatever I ask?"

"Yes!" Axel answered as the pain he felt subsided for a moment.

"Do you swear it?"

"Yes!" Axel said again. Florence pulled a tiny knife from her sleeve and handed it to Axel, Axel looked at it for a moment then he pulled his collar down and cut a small X over his heart. Blood instantly sprang forth from his bronze skin and began to leave tiny rivulets down his chest. Florence suddenly smiled at him and in an instant she had her arms wrapped around him, pushing his face into her breasts. Axel felt elation immediately and he put his arms around her to keep his face there as he deeply breathed in her scent.

Florence pushed him away and as he looked up at her he suddenly found her lips against his but then just as suddenly they were gone.

"Now," she said softly as she returned his face to her bosom. "I want you to go steal a horse."

Axel was so dazzled by all the sudden affection that at first he had not realized what she had said, then the pain suddenly returned to his soul with a vengeance as he finally understood what just happened.

Chapter Sixteen

"What?" Axel said slowly.

"Why do you ask 'What'?" Florence said as she folded her arms over her bosom again.

"You just swore yourself to me, and I want a white horse. If you want me then you must do as I say, unless that swear you just took means nothing to you, a gentleman, a nobleman.... I can't handle a life of hardship, you are poor. I want to help you become like me, but you have to do just as I say."

Axel looked at Florence, searching her beautiful face for a long time, she was suddenly different and he was not sure of what happened, what had changed her...or was she always like this and he had just never noticed?

"The guards told me of a poor family that lives on the edge of the Calm Sea, and they have a huge white horse. They called it a draft horse and said it is as white as freshly fallen snow, with long silver main and tail, and as large as two of our own horses standing side by side. They tried to buy the horse but the man would not sell, so I want you to steal it for me. I am tired of these lean long-legged black horses, I want a giant white horse, I want that giant white horse."

"But, Florence," Axel began to plead but stopped when her eyes clouded over in anger and she turned away.

"You swore."

Axel stood and placed his hands on her shoulders, he gently turned her back around to face him but she would not look at him. Florence reached a hand out and pressed it against his shirt where he had cut the X into his flesh, it was still bleeding a little and the blood seeped through his shirt leaving an X-shaped stain. Axel's chest hurt, not from the cut but from within, something inside of him was finding it hard to continue and he suddenly felt as though he wanted to crawl into a dark corner and hide there for the rest of his life. A few drops of his blood stained Florence's palm and she held it up for him to see, Axel looked at it and he slowly turned away and walked back to her balcony. Axel continued to slowly walk forward, he placed one foot onto the low rail and let his body drop over the edge, for a moment Florence rushed forward thinking he had killed himself but before she even got to the edge to look, a sparrow flew up past the balcony and headed in the direction of Axel's home. Florence watched as the common-looking brown bird with the black throat and gray chest flew away, and slowly she felt an anger well up inside of her because she could not fly and she became envious every time she saw Axel change and take to the air. She clenched her fists and gritted her teeth as she walked back into her room and locked the balcony door behind her.

Julian's heart sank when he came home and found the fireplace cold and Axel nowhere in sight. After a moment of thought he came to the conclusion that it was the third day, so he was probably with Florence.

"He's going to get into trouble with her," he said to himself as he found the striking stone that was always on the stone ledge over the fireplace. He struck it a few times and managed to light a candle, then he noticed the thin polished writing tablet that was perched on the ledge next to the candle. Julian picked it up and held it sideways to catch the small flickering flame.

"Da, I hav to go an get something for Florants, I do not kno how long I will be gone but please do not worre."

Julian's hands began to shake as he read over the tablet several times, Axel's spelling was not the greatest, nor was his penmanship but Julian could read it. Julian dropped the tablet to the floor and stood in the flickering shadows for a long time.

Axel's stomach twisted with hunger. He was starving and utterly exhausted but he had managed to fly all the way to the Calm Sea without stopping, it had taken him over a day flying over the trees. The Calm Sea was in fact a large lake, so vast that one could not see over it to the other side, but with it being just a lake there was no tide to go in and out and so it was calm and peaceful. Axel sat in a tree, his legs hanging down as he looked toward several houses near the water's edge. They were small but well kept and several of them were actually a house and stable combined so the heat from the animals and the fireplaces could be shared in the winter time. Only one house and stable stood separate from each other, it was farthest away from the shore and the paddock connected to the stable was large with a tall strong fence of small tree logs. Axel watched as a very young boy, maybe six years old, led a large white horse from the stable.

The horse was indeed beautiful, its body was startling white and its mane and tail was gray which looked silver against the white. It had a thick muscular neck which curved from its shoulders to its ears. Its chest and hind quarters were large and well rounded with divots and dimples that pronounced its sheer strength. Its body was wide and its legs thick, it was well proportioned for its size, no part of it looked too large or no small, everything was in harmony.

Axel watched as the young boy led the huge horse around the paddock, then the animal stopped and lowered its head, it allowed the boy to entangle his tiny hands into its mane, then the beast lifted its head and fairly swung the boy onto its back. The boy steered the huge horse around without saddle or reins, a man, the boy's father no doubt, opened the gate to the paddock and the boy rode the horse out. Axel watched in amazement as the boy, with just a touch of his hand, backed the horse up to a cart that looked too small for such a large animal. The horse stood stock still as the little boy walked up and down its back, setting the harness in place as the father handed the pieces up to him.

Axel ignored his complaining belly and curled himself up in the crock of the branch and dozed until darkness overtook the area. The smell of food from the little house awoke him, he moved down the tree a little lower and continued to watch until, much later, the firelight in the window began to die down and all was quiet. Axel looked toward the moon as it peeked in and out of wispy clouds, it was not very bright and that was what he was hoping for.

Very silently Axel dropped from the tree and crouched on the ground in the shadows until he was sure no one knew of his presence. Slowly and on bare feet he made his way toward the stable where they had shut the horse up for the night. Axel softly placed his hands against the thick rough door of the stable, after a moment of blindly feeling in the shadows he was able to find the latch and ever so gently he opened it.

The man in the house was awoken by a gently tinkle of a bell, he sat up in bed and immediately looked toward the stable. He knew how beautiful his horse was and it was not uncommon for people to ask him to sell it but the creature was more valuable to him than any of his other possessions. In the very dim light of the moon the man could just make out the edge of the stable door, it was open, the alarm cable he had placed on the door had worked yet again; this was certainly not the first time someone had tried to steal the white horse.

The man leapt out of bed and grasped the crossbow he kept on hand, he did not stop to put on his shoes or shirt but quickly crept out the door in only his trousers.

Axel stood before the magnificent horse for a moment and marveled at his sheer size and strength. Reaching out slowly he placed a hand on the horse's nose, it sniffed and twitched as it rumbled deep in its chest, it did not know who Axel was and it could sense the nervousness and fear that emanated from Axel's very being; this made the horse fidget and snort with anxiety. Axel softly ran his hand up the horse's nose and stopped with his palm pressed into the horse's forehead.

"Easy, big guy, easy," Axel said softly in deep tones to calm the horse. The horse began to step from side to side as Axel moved to his shoulder and grasped his long mane.

"Halt!" a commanding voice cried out so suddenly that it frightened Axel and the horse, the horse's front feet came off the ground a little and it tossed its huge head several times nearly knocking Axel over. Axel looked toward the open door to see the silhouette of a man pointing a crossbow at him, Axel tried to pull the horse around so he could hide behind him but with a twang and a whistle the man released the arrow and his aim was true. Axel cried out as he felt the burning bite of the arrow, it ripped through the flesh high on his shoulder, near his neck. A sick feeling welled up from the pit of his stomach as his mind slowly replayed the feeling of the arrowhead piercing his skin and the shift going through the wound; the end of it lodged in his shoulder, only a splash of blue feathers before him, the rest of the arrow protruding from his body behind. Axel instantly reached back with his other hand and yanked the arrow free, doing more harm to the wound than good. The man only had a single-fire crossbow and he charged forward now with a sturdy rod in his hand, Axel still had one hand tangled in the silvery mane of the horse and all he could do was turn with the horse and try to steer clear of the striking hooves. The man reached forward for the horse's mane as well but just before he grasped it Axel brought his knee up hard into the animal's side and the horse bolted forward with Axel doing all he could to cling to the animal's side.

"No! Kenja!" the man shouted and Axel looked toward the door to see the tiny boy attempting to shut it on him.

"No!" Axel screamed out at the boy. The boy looked up at the stampeding animal and froze in place as fear instantly took hold of him, Axel tried to reach forward to push him out of the way but he found it impossible with the horse jostling him so badly. The little boy's huge brown eyes looked right into Axel's at the last second before the frightened animal plowed him under and disappeared into the night with Axel still half clinging, half being dragged at its side.

Axel could only let the animal run itself out and finally, with the horse breathing heavily and still stamping its large hooves, he got him to stop on a rise some distance from the small home. Axel stood with his fingers still grasping the silver mane and his face pressed into the animal's sweaty neck. From below a woman's screams split the night like a banshee announcing someone's death, Axel's body shook and he could not help the burning tears that ran down his face and mingled with the sweat of the horse he had just stolen.

Axel rode the great white horse back to Florence. He did not eat, he did not sleep, he barely even gave the horse enough time to do these things as he fled with the stolen animal. Axel rode the horse straight across the front of the Azsins' property and into the stable. The two stable workers stopped what they were doing and stared in wonder at the great white animal before them. Axel slid from the horse's back and just leaned against him for a time, he leaned his forehead into the horse's shoulder and breathed in the strong horse scent. His heart was heavy and he wanted to start crying again but his tears were all gone and his eyes were gritty. He could not get the child out of his head, over and over again he saw that terrified wide-eyed face and heard the wailing of the mother.

"Axel!" Florence fairly squealed as she came running into the stable. "You did it, you brought me the white horse! He is so magnificent, even more so than I imagined!"

"Florence," Axel said softly with such a sadness that he could have made a laughing person stop and weep.

"Oh, your shoulder, it's bleeding. Come with me and I will take care of it," Florence said as she grasped his hand and began to lead him toward the house.

"Such a creature," she continued to bubble over while they walked.

"Florence," Axel said again but she seemed to not hear.

"My servants will wash him and brush him till he shines, and we will have a feast in his honor, tonight! I will tell the servants to make the feast for tonight, and I will ride him through town so everyone can see the beauty he holds."

"Florence."

"Oh, hush," Florence scolded as she took him to her room. "Sit and take off your shirt so I can see to your shoulder." Axel did as she bid but his heart felt heavier than before.

"You are so beautiful," Axel said softly. "But Florence, I just killed a boy."

Florence froze for a second at these words, then she continued to gently rub a damp cloth over the angry wound.

"He was just right there, I couldn't stop the horse, I tried to reach out and push him out of the way, but, I just, couldn't," Axel's voice cracked at these final words and he buried his face in his hands. Florence put the damp cloth down and placed both hands onto his bare chest.

"Shhhhhhhhhh," she said softly as she leaned into him. "It's all right, everything will be all right. You did exactly as I asked you to do and that's all that matters. My father will protect you, I will see to that."

"But Florence," Axel suddenly pushed her away. "I stole and killed, and all you can think about is parading this white horse around and having a feast! I just killed a boy!"

Florence was suddenly embracing him with her lips pressed against his; her lips parted and her tongue pressed in between his teeth. A sudden and wide array of emotions hit Axel then and he suddenly wanted to pull Florence's clothes off. He was angry and yet he wanted to make love to her. He felt sick to his stomach with grief and yet he felt the hardness in his groin and suddenly Florence's hand was there too, untying the front of his trousers. Florence pushed him into the bedpost as she held their lips locked, pain ran through Axel's shoulder and he was suddenly overcome by the grief again and he pushed her away.

"No," he panted. "We can't do this, not now. I have to return the horse."

"Shhhhhh," Florence said again as she pushed him into a sitting position on the bed and brought her slender leg up to hug her knee against his bare side, she pulled her skirt up and pressed the skin of her inner thigh against his bare skin and without a second thought he wrapped his arms around her again and pulled her close.

One of Florence's hands went around his shoulders while the other one reached behind her to grasp the heavy vase that sat on her night-stand, the flowers still fresh and looked full of life as they fell to the floor. Florence raised the vase in her slender hand and just as she bit Axel on the lip she brought the vase down onto the back of his head.

Axel's body went lax in her arms and she dropped the broken vase where the last pieces shattered against the polished floor. Axel slumped forward against her and she took a step back to let his body fall face first onto the floor, then she looked into her polished mirror and ripped the front of her dress open. She made sure it was enough to expose one breast, then she quickly pulled her hair out of sorts and began to scream as she also pulled the sheets half off the bed.

After her second scream loud foot falls came from the hall and without even knocking Harold burst into the room, Florence stood in the middle of the room swaying, the front of her dress ripped open and her room in disarray. Harold reached out to grasp her with one hand while the other pulled up the blanket to cover her.

"What happened!?" he demanded. "Who is this?"

"He tried to rape me," Florence sobbed. "He touched me and ripped my dress." Harold put an arm around Florence and held her as several guards also entered the room. The guards fell upon Axel's prone form and carried him out as Florence continued to sway though Harold had his arm around her.

"Are you hurt?" he asked.

"Of course I'm hurt," Florence sobbed, then with a tiny hiccup her knees gave way and Harold had to catch her lest she fell to the floor.

Chapter Seventeen

Axel awoke to a heavy and damp darkness that smelled of earth and stone. He was lying on his back and he could feel cold wet stone beneath his shoulders. His head hurt as did his jawline, he ran his fingers across his face and found a long cut that was still bleeding. He was still gently stroking the cut with his fingertips when a sound like wood scraping across stone came to him and a moment later there was a feeble light. Axel squinted in the darkness and as the light came nearer he saw it was a woman backing down a set of very steep wooden stairs with a tray and lantern in one hand while the other reached forward to hold the edge of each step in front of her.

"Ah, you are awaken," she said when she saw him sitting up and looking at her. "The guards said they could not wake you, not even throwing a bucket of water down on you worked, so they sent me down but I see I am not needed now."

"I'm very confused," Axel said as he reached out a hand and grasped the hem of her skirt. "Where am I? What happened?"

"You are in the pit for the attempted rape and murder of the overseer's daughter."

Axel took in a quick breath as he suddenly felt like his heart was ripped away from him.

"But I didn't, I mean, why would they think such a thing, I love her," Axel stumbled over his words and the woman turned to look at him.

"Oh dear, dear, dear boy. She has done it again, she has you. But don't worry, she is just testing the water, things will get better once she settles down again."

Axel looked up at the woman as hot tears began to leak from the corners of his eyes, the woman looked at Axel with a pitiful stare, then she went to him with open arms and gathering him closer to her she gently rocked him like a child.

"Shhhh," she said softly. "It's all right to cry, it makes a strong man."

After a few deep breaths Axel managed to take control of his emotions and he just sat there with head bowed.

"Let me tend to your wounds," the woman said as she picked up some thin rolls of cloth from the tray she had brought down.

"They will be wanting you in court soon so you will want to look your best," the woman said softly, then she pressed a small loaf of bread into his hands. "You should eat something as well."

Axe did not answer, he could not, his body hurt and he was in shock as he tried to sort out what had gone wrong. But the more he thought about it the more vivid those last few moments were, her bare leg against his side, her lips on his and then her teeth biting into his lip and the taste of blood in his mouth.

They came for him some time later and bolted a set of cuffs to his wrists. Axel hung his head as they walked him toward the gathering place in the near center of town. People lined the windy street and stood nearly ankle deep in mud in a few places to get a good look at him.

"Where is his shirt?"

"Axel is a good lad, why are they doing all this?"

"Look at his shoulder, she must've fought him off."

"They should have at least given him a shirt."

Axel could hear what some of the people were saying but most of the voices were merely mumbles between the people that he could not make out. Axel glanced up a few times and caught the eye of several people, they all looked away, except for one man. Axel looked again and his heart stuttered, he knew that face, from far away; it was the man he had stolen the horse from. The man was following them through the crowd and he had a murderous look in his eye, one hand was tucked beneath his shirt.

I am already condemned, Axel thought to himself. *And will surely be dead on the morrow; however, if this man wishes to take my life to ease his pain then perhaps I can at least grant him that.*

Axel turned toward the man soon as there was a break in the crowd, he lowered his hands to leave his chest bare and he looked at the man pleadingly. The man did not hesitate an instant, he burst forth from between two people and now his hidden hand was raised and he was grasping a dagger. He cried out as his arm swung downward right for Axel's heart, Axel stood still and shut his eyes hoping for a clean kill.

Suddenly Axel was knocked off his feet as two of the guards stepped in to apprehend the man with the dagger. One guard grasped his arm and bent it back until he dropped the wicked-looking dagger, soon as he did the other guard landed him a firm blow to his abdomen, the man instantly doubled over in a painful coughing fit.

"He," the man was trying to speak between gasps and coughs. "He, he killed, he killed my son!" the man finally managed to shout. The guards helped the man to stand but held a firm grip to his arms.

"He came and stole my horse and killed my son. My only son! My poor wife was so grief stricken that she was dead by morning, now I am utterly alone. Everything dear to me has been ripped away, and he was the one who did it!"

Several gasps and many whispers ran through the people gathered around.

"Bring them both forward," Mr. Azsin seemed to boom over the noise. "You, stranger, you will have your say. I can understand why you wish to kill him but it will not be done by your hand."

Axel was lying on his back staring blankly into the sun, the guards helped Axel to his feet and pushed him forward again.

"Is it true," Mr. Azsin said before Axel and everyone gathered. "That you have killed and stolen?"

Axel felt the heaviness in his chest again and he felt as though he could not speak for the heavy feeling was spreading up to his throat. After several minutes of silence with the people watching one of the guards slapped his hand against the back of Axel's head. Axel grimaced from the blow and then looked up and the first person he laid eyes on was his own father, Julian looked at Axel for a moment and then looked away. Axel's heart felt as though it fell to the ground before him and was laid open for all to see. His breath stopped and there was a few moments of panic when he could not get his lungs to start working again. Axel looked toward Mr. Azsin and saw Florence seated behind her father, a dark veil covering her face, her hands were gripping the arms of her chair as though she wished to break them; Axel suddenly felt a spark of rage against Florence.

"Yes," he suddenly said firmly and loudly. "I went and stole a white horse from the man seated over there," he indicated the stranger with a tilt of his head. "And in the process his young son was trampled beneath the horse as it bolted. I am truly sorry for that, my only intention was to steal the horse. But, I am asking for help now, for I was bid to steal that horse, it was against my will. I was merely taking orders from someone I love with all my being...." Axel looked toward Florence again and she was looking back at him, the corner of her veil lifted. The words on Axel's lips froze and his shoulders slumped as his heart suddenly went to her, a tear rolled down her cheek as she gave him a pleading look.

Axel looked away and became silent, no matter what Mr. Azsin said he would not answer. The guard back handed him several more times but then the people began to call out that the guard needed to stop. Mr. Azsin stood and calmed everyone with gentle waves of his hands.

"Since he has gone silent I will now speak of other happenings by this young man," Mr. Azsin took up several pieces of rolled leather and began to read.

"Several seasons ago a lad by the name of Marcus Birdly was killed during illegal night racing, Axel William Ramses was present and racing these boys when his animal knocked Marcus down and broke his neck."

So that was his name, Axel thought to himself, nobody had ever told him the young man's name. *Marcus, I am sorry.*

"And this," Mr. Azsin held up a roll of leather that was so old the ink was bleeding through, Axel instantly recognized it.

"This has evidence that further proves that this young man also tried to rape and kill my daughter. It is said that it takes seven generations to wipe out the bad blood of a family," Mr. Azsin looked at the people for confirmation, many of them were nodding in agreement. Mr. Azsin unrolled the leather and continued to speak.

"According to the date and the information we have on the William Ramses family history, four generations ago, Bentrove William Ramses was thrown from the overseers position and had one hand cut off as punishment for the rape of four young girls, none over the age of ten."

There were gasps and one scream from the crowd, Axel suddenly began to feel sick, of course Harold would hold onto that info and hand it over at a time like this. Axel looked toward his father and saw that he had his face in his hands, did he know what had happened so many years ago...? Axel looked away from his distraught father and looked back toward Mr. Azsin, Florence was standing now, her mouth close to her father's ear as she spoke softly to him.

"Father, are you going to kill him?" she whispered.

"Well, Florence, my dear, just look at all the terrible things he has done recently. For the stealing and the rape he would lose one hand but he would also lose the other for the killing, he will just be a burden to others without his hands. And besides, his blood should be cleansed from our town, it has only been four generations, he needs to be killed, my dear."

"Oh, Father," Florence nearly wept as she put her arms around him. "Please don't kill him, I have a better idea."

"Hmmm," Mr. Azsin said. "He still needs to pay for the crimes he has committed, I know with your good heart you have already forgiven him but what about that man who lost his son and wife?"

"Don't kill him, Father," Florence said again, her voice tight with emotion. "Instead, let him serve out his punishment in the east, on the battlefield. Send him to the slavers right away and if he survives several years of fighting and returns then I feel it was meant to be and his bloodline will be closer to being cleansed without the need to kill off the family, Axel is the last one to carry on the William Ramses name, would you really want to be the one to kill off a once noble family?"

"No, I would not," Mr. Azsin said softly as he put one arm around his daughter and hugged her gently, then he motioned for her to sit back down and he stood with his arms raised.

"I have decided to show kindness upon this young lad," Mr. Azsin called out over the hushed people. "Instead of killing him he is to be sent far east where there is still much war, he will go with the slavers and sent to the front where he will have to fight, I know it sounds harsh, but, he does have a chance to survive and return here and continue to live among the people he knows and be near the magic of his native wood."

Axel looked up at Mr. Azsin with unbelieving eyes, Florence was once again seated behind her father and she looked toward Axel and smiled beneath her veil.

They did not take Axel back to the pit, instead they also bolted cuffs to his feet and put him into a large cage much like the one the loon was in. Axel sat in the corner with his knees drawn up and his head bowed.

"Here, son."

Axel's head shot up at the sound of that voice and he saw his father with his arm thrust through the narrow slats holding a folded shirt in his hand.

"Da!" Axel leapt up and tried to reach through the bars but his cuffed wrists prevented it.

"I am so sorry, Da," Axel said as he felt a tightness growing in his chest.

"Escape, son, and I will hide you," Julian said softly and urgently, he shoved the folded shirt in Axel's hand and was gone.

Florence walked briskly toward the area where Axel was being held, there was only a few guards and she had already dismissed them for a short while. Julian and her met at the corner, they nearly walked right into each other and they each took a step back, looks of disgust on their faces.

"You little bitch," Julian fairly spat at her. "I have never hit a woman in my life, until now." Julian's hand came across her face, though half-heartedly. Florence fell to the ground with a gasp of surprise, it was the first time she had ever been struck by a man and though it did not hurt the action shook her to her very soul. She looked up but Julian was already gone, not even his footsteps could be heard. Florence rose up and lifting her skirts a little she ran, Axel saw her coming and went to the side of the cage closest to her, but Florence had a look of rage on her face and she reached through the bars and gave Axel a stinging smack.

"You evil boy," she fairly screamed. "I saved you from certain death and your father strikes me, calling me a bitch. Do you think of me like that as well?"

Axel looked up at her, a purely hurt look on his face.

"No," he pleaded. "I would never say such things to you, if I did then I should die for such a terrible thing."

"I think I will forget what I heard, though it hurt me terribly."

Florence and Axel regarded each other for a long moment, then she reached through the slats and embraced him.

"I am sorry if I ever hurt you," he said softly. "I am just so confused, I love you so much and I just don't know what is best right now."

"I am best," Florence said softly. "Don't ever forget me."

Axel felt Florence's fingers tuck themselves into the waistline of his trousers, then they were gone, leaving something cold and metallic behind.

Axel studied the tiny key and found that it not only undid the cuffs but the door as well. He had to quickly duck down and he curled himself up in the corner when he heard the guard coming.

"Dinner," the guard said. He merely looked down at Axel's curled form, he did not notice how the cuffs were not properly attached anymore, he merely placed the food within reach of the cage and left again. Axel crept forward sometime later and exited his confined quarters, he walked in the shadows as silently as he could and went through several doors completely unnoticed.

Axel stopped at the last door and leaned into it, he could hear the soft chatting of the two on the other side. Axel closed his eyes and ran a hand over his face for a moment, this was the last door he needed to go through. Axel silently crouched down beside the door and scratched at it with his fingernail. The guards stopped talking as they listened but then continued with their conversation when they didn't hear any more noise. Axel scratched again but this time in a different spot. Once again the guards stopped and he heard them shuffle their feet from the other side. There was a moment of silence as the door suddenly flew open and the two guards rushed through the open doorway. Axel leapt up and swinging his arm out, he caught one guard in the face, the guard went down with a groan. The other guard spun on Axel but Axel's other arm was already swinging around, he slammed his hand into the side of the guard's head and bounced his forehead off the door frame, this guard crumpled on top of his comrade without a sound.

Axel ran through the streets now, heading for his home, he had to find his father first and then flee as fast as he could. He saw the shadow of a person ahead of him in the street and flitted upward upon wings of gray silence. Axel flew to his home and alighted into the yard, then he froze as he looked at the front door, broken off its hinges. He felt a tingle run down his spine and with a cry for his father he rushed forward only to stop at the door and fall to his knees.

The coals in the fireplace barely glowed and several had been swept from their bed of ash, the table was overturned and one chair was broken, broken pottery scattered throughout the place. Julian lay amongst the ruin of their home, several deep cuts across his body, one of his arms bent at a terrible angle and blood smeared across several areas of the floor. In the thin moonlight filtering through the small window Axel could see that his father's eyes were open and for the briefest of moments his heart jumped.

"Da!" He crawled forward and grasped his father's shirt, tugging gently. Julian did not move and Axel stared at him in disbelief for a time, then as his heart once again felt as though it was ripped from his chest, a cry of such anguish came from his mouth that the night creatures all around them suddenly became still and an eerie silence settled upon the small town.

Axel sat next to his father silently sobbing, one hand upon the once warm and smiling face, the other hand clasping Julian's clenched fist; he had grasped something during the fight and held onto it even in death. Axel eventually had to use two hands to pry open his father's cold fingers. Clasped in his hand was the tooth of some large serpent, so long that it spanned across his palm and looked like the broken blade of some translucent dagger. Axel took up a piece of leather off the floor and wrapped the tooth in it, it had to be poisonous if it was that large. Also next to Axel upon the floor was the hat that Julian wore for many years, it was a little worn and the wide brim that went all the way around was a little misshapen but it had been Julian's and he had sewn tiny pieces of bark, leaves and dirt into the inside of it so no matter where he may have traveled he would always feel close to his native wood. Axel tucked the wrapped up tooth into the inside of his father's hat, then he firmly placed it on his head, it was a perfect fit.

Several men suddenly appeared at the door and were ready to charge in but stopped short at the sight of the place, the overturned and broken items, the dead man upon the floor and Axel sitting next to him, softly crying.

"Get up," one guard finally said. "You vile little vermin."

Axel looked up at them, he had pulled the brim of the hat down over his eyes and he was crying just hard enough that he had not even heard them come in. The guards and Axel stared at each other for a moment and then Axel rose and walked toward them with his hands held forward in an unresisting gesture. Axel turned back to his father for just a moment and instantly wished he had not, seeing his father laying there among all the broken memories of their home, it made his heart ache. Axel closed his eyes, that last image of his dear father now forever burned into his memory.

"Goodbye, Da."

Chapter Eighteen

Tulley sat with his chin resting in his palm, the stem of his bone pipe tucked between his teeth. The pipe was unlit; the cracks had grown to the point of making the pipe useless but he sucked on it all the same. He was watching Lance with a slightly proud eye. Tulley could not sleep through the night and had stayed up all night finishing something he had been working on for Lance, and that morning he presented it to the baffled young man.

"What is it?" Lance asked as he looked at the piece of carved wood with the leather weaved through the top to form something that looked like a harness.

"Give me your leg," Tulley said. Lance was sitting in a chair and he held up his good leg, Tulley shook his head, an almost bemused look on his face.

"No, your other leg."

"My stump?"

"It's still a leg, isn't it?"

Tulley fit the wooden piece to Lance's thigh and tightened the straps. The leather pinched and felt uncomfortable but after a moment of tugging and readjusting it Tulley stood up and held his hand out to Lance. Lance looked at the apparatus in wide-eyed wonderment like a child. Lance took Tulley's hand and with a little help he stood up out of the chair without the use of his crutches. Lance felt sudden elation in the pit of his stomach and he couldn't stop the smile that came across his face. Jessica clapped her hands approvingly and Lance looked over his shoulder at her laughing, then suddenly Tulley let go of Lance's hands and he had to swing his arms for balance on the strange new leg. Tulley stepped away as Lance stumbled forward and fell, Tulley didn't even try to catch him. Lance caught himself with his hands and immediately tried to get back up, Tulley stepped aside to give Lance room and walked toward Jessica.

"You nots goings to helps hims?" Jessica asked as she watched Lance struggle.

"No," Tulley said as he folded his arms and watched from beneath his unruly hair. "This is good for him, his spirits have been down for far too long."

Now, much later in the day, Tulley watched Lance as he sucked on his empty pipe. Lance was attempting to walk with the children, the younger ones all wanting to touch his new limb, the older ones poking fun at him and challenging him to races, Tulley smiled for a moment and then let the smile slip away. Jessica came up behind him and pulled the broken pipe from his mouth.

"Heres," she said as she pulled her own pipe from her mouth. "I don'ts uses it muches at alls, yous cans has it." Jessica tucked the pipe in the corner of Tulley's mouth and pocketed the broken one, then she began to pick at his hair.

"Whys don'ts yous lets me cuts this agains?" she asked as she began to massage Tulley's scalp, Tulley relaxed a little as her fingers ran through his hair.

"It helps to keep the sun out of my eyes."

"Buts, yous has a hats for thats. Lets me cuts it, Tulleys, you has such prettys eyes. Are theys greens?" Jessica bent her face down in front of Tulley's and searched for his eyes, Tulley looked up and stared into hers.

"I don't know, I never asked what color my eyes are."

"Yes," Jessica replied. "I woulds calls thems greens. Lets me cuts its. Yous ares so handsomes when yours hairs is cuts and yours faces is shaveds, especiallys sinces yous puts a littles meats backs on yours bones."

"It's all thanks to your cooking over these several seasons," Tulley said.

"Yous is so handsomes, I woulds likes to kisses yous, you makes this olds ladys feels happy."

"You are not old," Tulley commented as he put his hands on her hips and pulled her in to sit on his lap. "I'm old, you are just a baby compared to me. And you are a wonderful woman, with a heart of gold; however, I will never kiss another woman as long as I live."

"Ahs, it's alls rights. Yous has hads a great loves in yours life and its is a wonderfuls things thats yous respects her memory."

"Thank you for understanding."

Jessica leaned her head against his shoulder and embraced him for a moment.

"Ouch!" she suddenly said as she jumped up. A rock had come flying out of nowhere and struck Jessica in the back of her shoulder. Tulley instantly stood up and his eyes immediately went to Gensieco, who stood on the far side of the safe area with a rock sling in one hand.

"Gensieco," Tulley called out in a deep voice. Gensieco instantly put the sling behind her back and dropped it to the ground. "Come here now."

Gensieco did not move for a long moment, then she very slowly began to walk toward Tulley and Jessica.

"It was an accident," she said softly. Tulley folded his arms as he looked down at her and she cringed.

"I know better than that, I taught you how to use that, I know your aim is spot on. Now apologize, young lady."

Gensieco looked down and smoothed out her short skirt, Jessica had made the outfit with a skirt that went to her ankles but Gensieco complained that it was too restricting and trimmed the skirt to her knees.

"I am sorry, Miss Jessica," Gensieco said in her childlike voice with the accent that added a slight lilt to each word.

"Ohs, I'm sures its was an accidents," Jessica said as she smoothed her own skirts and then turned away.

"I has to feeds baby Bastian nows," Jessica called and was suddenly swarmed by five of the teenage girls who wished to help. They had been lucky enough to find a close neighbor who had a calm old rabbit that was nursing a litter at the time and every morning one of the boys would ride one of the horses to this neighbor and bring home fresh milk. It was certainly not mother's milk and at first the tiny baby would not eat but now the infant was thriving and could almost sit up on his own. The baby's given name was Tifus, but most everyone who looked at him said he did not seem like a Tifus, so they changed his name to Bastian, to keep the memory of his parents alive.

Jessica stopped for a moment and looked up at the branches of the tree, they groaned as though a great wind was blowing but there was hardly a breeze to stir the leaves. Tulley looked up as well and let a large plume of smoke escape from his mouth, he knew what was happening but he did not know how much time they had left. He watched as the tree groaned again and suddenly Lance was at his side.

"What does it mean?" Lance asked.

"Nothing to worry about right now," Tulley said as he let out another plume.

"Oh, come on, Tulley, I saw the look on your face when the tree first groaned like that a few days ago, I think it's the first time I saw real emotion, though I don't know what kind it was."

"Fear," Tulley answered, then he turned to Lance and put a hand onto his shoulder. "But we have nothing to fear."

"That, doesn't really make any sense," Lance said slowly.

"Just don't fear what is bound to happen next," Tulley said through another plume of smoke, then he let his hand drop from Lance's shoulder and walked away.

"Hey," Lance called back. "When are you going to tell us more about Axel? You can't keep me on edge like this, it's been two days now."

Tulley did not answer as he walked away, he merely waved one hand at his side in recognition that Lance had spoken.

"Crabby old man!" Lance called after him.

"Impatient young one," Tulley called back.

"Whats do yous means?" Jessica asked as she bathed Bastian.

"It would seem we are going to have visitors soon, it may be pretty scary for a little while, but the best thing to do is stay calm, do as you are asked and above all do not fight."

Jessica was looking hard at Tulley for several minutes.

"How does yous knows this?"

"The druid that lives in this tree is calling them, it is calling his family. Something has happened to the tree they were living in and now they are calling to each other until they find each other."

"This is my homes, has beens my wholes life. Theys can'ts takes it aways."

"Jessica, do you know anything about Druids?"

"A littles, very littles, actuallys."

"Druids have dark skin, almost black, actually. They have long limbs and are very thin, much like the creature the children call a walking stick. They live in the tops of the trees, preferably a tree that houses an ancestor from their clan. Males actually outnumber females ten to one so whatever you do, respect a female druid. They not only have great power over magic of the forests but they are protected by all the males of the clan. So please, Jessica, I know this is your home, but I am begging you, do not provoke them."

Jessica sighed heavily and then lifted Bastian from the shallow basin of water.

"Holds hims for a moments," she said as she handed the naked infant over to Tulley. Tulley and the child regarded each other for a long moment and then the baby began to screw up his face as a cry welled up in his throat.

"Oh, shhhhh," Tulley said softly as he cradled the child in his arms. Baby Bastian reached up and grasped the front of Tulley's shirt, leaving little damp handprints. Jessica smiled as she held the towel out and Tulley gently handed Bastian over.

"Yous is goods ats thats," she commented.

"I have handled a baby or two over the years."

Tulley had constructed a hammock from spider's web and hung it in some of the upper branches of the tree. The night was cool and there was no clouds to blot out the stars, Tulley rubbed the bridge of his nose in an attempt to ease the headache, it was so bad he actually wanted to shed tears. He had run out of moss and though the cave was only a full day's walk away he had not gone back for any more. The tree still groaned periodically but not nearly as loud anymore, Tulley wondered if that meant the Druid clan was nearly there, he had only witnessed a Druid clan moving once before. Druids could jump very well and on windy days they tended to grasp leaves and ride them, their bodies were so thin and lightweight that it was possible for them to do so.

Tulley looked up at the sky and listened to the soft noises of the night, the stars overhead were a decoration of white dots on a black canvas. As Tulley looked up something momentarily blocked out his sight of the stars and Tulley felt the hair on the back of his neck rise. He began to sit up out of the hammock but before he could fully exit it something cut one end and the hammock swung loose, nearly dumping Tulley out. Tulley's ankle caught in the hammock strings and he tried to bend his body upwards to grasp something before he fell, he could not see the Druids around him, their bodies blended in with the darkness and branches of the tree perfectly. Tulley's fingers had just grasped a nearby branch when something came down on the back of his head and filled his skull with a wicked cracking sound.

Chapter Nineteen

Lance rolled over on his pallet and rubbed his face, it was hot in his room. He had taken off all his clothes except for his pants, something he rarely did. He was not tall and muscular like Tulley, he had a hairy chest that he was self-conscious of and though he was lean he did not have the build. Now that Tulley didn't look like a skeleton with skin and sinew stretched over the bones, he was actually a good-looking guy, someone Lance wished he could someday own up to.

Lance blinked and suddenly sat up, for a moment he thought he had seen a figure in the small square of their window. He swung his leg over and hopped to the small opening.

"Tulley?" he called as he looked out. A thin hand with long fingers suddenly wrapped around Lance's neck and threatened to yank him out of the window. Lance swung his arms out and caught himself on the window frame. He looked upwards with his eyes and saw only blackness from where the long dark arm came. The hand tightened around his neck and Lance began to see spots flash and bounce around before his eyes. He strained at the edges of the window, digging his nails in, the pain in his fingertips cleared his head just a little but it wasn't enough to keep him there. His arms began to tremble and he felt his fingers lose their grip just as a roaring blackness engulfed him.

Jessica was awake immediately, some sixth sense alerting her to the danger. She rolled out of bed, her dagger in her hand, and crept forward. Her room also had a tiny window, this one overlooked the front door. The moon cast a weak light into the safe area around the tree and she caught her breath when she saw the unfamiliar shapes. They were tall, at least a full head taller than even Tulley, and they had long thin limbs. At first Jessica wasn't even sure if they were human, but then they moved and soft words were carried upon the gentle breeze to her ear; they were words she had never heard before.

The four Druids were standing in a circle looking down at something on the ground. One Druid reached out a long leg and poked the object with his long narrow foot, nothing happened so the Druid did it again. When nothing happened a second time the Druid turned away and Jessica saw what the object was. Tulley lay on the ground in a heap, his arms and legs tangled beneath him as he lay on his face. One of Jessica's hands flew to her mouth as the other tightened around the dagger. Then she saw another dark creature emerge from the shadows, she squinted as she tried to make out what it was. It was indeed another Druid, but this one was dragging Lance by the wrist as though he weighed nothing. The newcomer stopped near the others and held up his prize, Lance's head hung forward and another Druid cupped his chin in his hand and lifted Lance's head so he could look closely at his face. Jessica was so intent upon watching Tulley and Lance that she nearly screamed when a dark face suddenly appeared right before hers. Jessica fell back but continued to hold the knife behind her back. The Druid had a pointed chin and pointy ears, his yellow eyes seemed to have an inner flame that made them even more frightening.

Jessica began to pull her weapon forward to strike at the Druid that was coming through her window when she froze as she remembered how Tulley pleaded that she not fight them, the knife fell from her grasp and thudded as the tip of the blade sunk into the floorboards. The Druid had to stand slightly hunched in her room and it seemed to smile at her as it retrieved the knife. It regarded the weapon for a moment and then tucked it into the waistline of his skimpy tattered-looking shorts, it tilted its head a little motioning toward the door; without turning away from the Druid Jessica exited her room. The Druid watched Jessica with a bemused expression as she walked sideways with her back against the wall so she could see him at all times.

Lance was awake by the time Jessica was herded into the circle of Druids, but Tulley still lay on his face with his arms and legs folded beneath him.

"Help me," Jessica urged softly as she straightened Tulley's body and tried to wake him but Tulley still would not stir and when Jessica tucked her hand beneath his head she felt the wet slick blood behind one of his ears. Jessica held her hand up and Lance stared at it in the feeble moonlight.

"Is that blood?" he asked.

"Lance," Jessica said softly. "What about the children?" As if to answer her question a scream split the night and everyone turned toward the tree, Jessica's hands went to her face and she began to rise but Tulley grasped her arm.

"They didn't kill us, they won't kill the children either."

"Tulley!" Jessica gasped as she fairly fell on top of him and held him.

"I'm all right," Tulley said as he struggled to sit up with Jessica grasping him so. Tulley looked at the Druids standing around them and then looking up his eyes roamed the darkness of the tree overhead.

"Eh," Tulley called, several of the Druids turned toward him. "Moha kekan maleasian keys." *You didn't have to do that.*

The Druids quickly looked back and forth at each other when they heard Tulley reprimand them in their own language, they looked shocked, angered and frightened all at the same time. One of the Druids wore several thick woven necklaces that hung across his chest, he stepped forward and slapped Tulley across the face, Tulley barely flinched and his expression did not change in the least.

"Moha Kekan maleasian keys flavis." *You didn't have to do that either.* The Druid slapped Tulley again, this time it was harder and the sound echoed back to them through the darkness, Tulley closed his eyes for a moment in a grimace.

"You," the druid said in a very deep voice. "Are not worthy to speak our words. You will not violate our words with your filthy tongue."

"And you think you are worthy to speak our language," Tulley said without hesitation. "I am not the filthy one here, your tribe stinks."

The Druid reached forward and grasped the air just above Tulley's shoulder, Tulley's expressionless face took on a hardness that Lance had never seen before and for a moment the look caused the Druid to stop, but only for a moment. The Druid yanked his fist back and Tulley gasped in pain as he nearly doubled over with Jessica still holding onto him.

"That is a deep one," the Druid said as he relaxed his fist. The Druid pulled out a knife and slit the front of Tulley's shirt open enough to see the lightning tattoos that ran over his shoulders and across his chest.

"Looks like the work of Vataris, be thankful you had such a talented Shaman to do it…Gartanging."

"Do not call me Gartanging," Tulley said softly but fiercely. "I am not that man."

"I am mistaken then," the Druid said as he stood back up, he then turned and spoke rapidly to the others around him and several of them nodded and left the circle. Lance, Tulley and Jessica all watched as the Druids herded the children from their home and knotted them all together but still separate from the three adults. A handful of the younger ones were crying and Jessica tried to go to them, crawling as fast as she could on her hands and knees, Tulley grasped her around the waist and hauled her back where he then wrapped his arms around her and shushed her.

"It is good that you did not fight them," Tulley said softly. "Now, please continue to keep peace."

"Keep peace," Jessica said into his chest. "And who was it that told them they stink?"

"Words do not bother Druids, most of the time they make name calling amid enemies into a game. It's the physical violence that will cause them to kill us all, they can hit us all they want but we must not raise a hand to them, now calm down or I will not let you go."

"I am calm," Jessica said as she tried to push away from Tulley.

"No, you're not," Tulley said as he loosened his arms a little. "You lose your accent when you are upset."

"Tulley, look," Lance whispered as he motioned toward the door. Two Druids had just emerged escorting Gensieco, one on either side of her, each had a hand on her shoulders. Almost as soon as they exited Druids from all sides flocked to them and converged around Gensieco, speaking rapidly to her in their language and reaching out to gently touch her as if they thought she wasn't real. Gensieco shrank down before the tall Druids and fearfully looked back and forth at each one. Tulley released Jessica and stood up so he could see better, but more Druids crowded around Gensieco and Tulley completely lost sight of her.

"Tulley!" she screamed as she tried to push through the Druids that were swarming her. Tulley rushed forward past the two who were left guarding them, the guards shouted but none of the others seemed to take notice. Tulley saw Gensieco's small white hand reach out from amid the black bodies of the Druids and he grasped it and roughly pulled her free. Tulley fell to his knees and held Gensieco to his chest as he tried to shield her from the crowding Druids, Gensieco's tiny body was shaking with fright in his embrace; they began hitting Tulley and pulling at his arms as they tried to take Gensieco back.

"Leave her be," came a deep female voice and the crowd of Druids suddenly fell away; they silently began to melt back into the surrounding shadows. From out of the darkness came six Druids carrying a large woven mat of grass between them and on this woven mat sat a very slender, nearly naked female Druid. Her eyes were bright red, unlike the yellow eyes of all the males. She sat cross-legged with a toddler cradled on her knees, in one arm she held an infant that suckled on one of her small bare breasts and at her shoulder, hugging her neck, was another child who was just slightly older than the toddler in her lap; the toddler shifted and the female's swollen pregnant belly was exposed. All of the children with the female Druid were completely naked and had yellow eyes just like the rest of the male Druids. Jessica gasped slightly at the sight of her and she grasped Lance's arm.

"She looks unwell," Jessica whispered so softly that only Lance heard her. Tulley turned toward this Druid and bowed his head, Gensieco was still against his chest, her little arms locked around his body so tightly that he would not have gotten her to let go even if he tried.

"I am Supae," the Druid said as the six carrying the mat gently set her down.

"I am Tulley."

"Why are you here, Tulley?" Supae asked as she shifted the nursing infant to the other side. "You seem out of place here. Why do you hide? My magic is strong and I can see the shroud that you have covered yourself with."

"It is my meager attempt to block out what haunts me from my past."

"I see," Supae said, she turned her head toward the child hugging her neck and spoke softly into his ear, the child released her neck and sat down beside her, also cross-legged.

"Why are you living in our ancestor? Our tribe has never encountered something like this before."

"This kind woman lives here and cares for the lost and orphaned children from the area. We are merely taking a rest here from when my friend was ill."

"Yes, I see," Supae said softly as she looked over toward Jessica and Lance. "Come forward."

Lance and Jessica hesitated for a moment, then they rose and came nearer, Supae narrowed her eyes a little when she saw how Lance had to hop. One of the other Druids noticed her look and stepped forward, he came up behind Lance and tucking his hands beneath Lance's arms he lifted Lance up as though he were a child, for a moment a look of horror came over Lance's face but he composed himself quickly. The Druid set Lance down next to Tulley and before Lance could really get a good look at Supae, Tulley reached over and pushed his head down in a bow like his own. Jessica kneeled down on the other side of Tulley and bowed her head immediately.

"This is Jessica and Lance," Tulley said softly, his head still bowed.

"Why do you live in our ancestor?" Supae addressed Jessica.

"I am sorry," Jessica said softly. "Your ancestor has been my home since I was a very young child. My father came across this tree and made it into the home we have now. It has protected us for a very long time and we wish to remain here where it is safe."

"No," Supae said. "This is our ancestor and we have come to live with him, you and all your children must leave."

Jessica fell forward onto her belly before Supae, her hands stretched out before her and her forehead resting on the ground.

"Please," Jessica said as calmly as she could. "Please reconsider. The next season will be winter and we will have nowhere to go, there are so many young children who will be left with nothing."

"No," Supae said. "This is our home now and we are the stronger. If you do not leave then we will kill you, it is simple to see what you must do."

"You can't!" Jessica suddenly blurted out as she rose up onto her knees staring at Supae, a Druid stepped forward to backhand her but Tulley flung his arm out and blocked the blow. Suddenly two Druids jumped forward with daggers drawn, Tulley pushed Lance and Jessica down hard and reached out to grasp the wrists of the two Druids, stopping the knives before they could cut him, but as soon as he did that, four more Druids converged upon him with daggers drawn. Tulley was still on his knees with Gensieco still hugging his chest, the four other Druids came from all sides and placed their knife tips against Tulley's throat as he continued to hold the first two at bay, but the Druids stopped and waited for orders from Supae, one Druid had placed his foot onto Lance's back as he lay on the ground so he could not rise up and help Tulley.

"That is enough," Supae said sounding bored. The four Druids leaned back a little but remained circling Tulley with their daggers at the ready.

"Supae," Tulley said softly with head bowed again but still holding the wrists of the first two Druids, they strained at Tulley's grip but could not pull their arms free.

"Please speak to your ancestor and ask him what you should do about Jessica and the children."

"Our ancestor is sleeping now, he is exhausted from calling to us for so long, I will not wake him."

"Then can we speak together, there are things I must tell you. Grant me council with you Supae, alone." The four Druids suddenly stepped forward again with their daggers around Tulley's neck when he asked this, Supae shook her head slowly.

"I cannot grant you council with me alone, I am the last female of our tribe, if you kill me then this tribe will die. I am young, I am sure to have many more children and I may be able to save my tribe if I can give birth to a girl. Even if I consent to have council with you alone they will not allow it."

"Then render me motionless, tie my hands and feet so I cannot move, blindfold me so I cannot see, just so long as I can hear and speak to you. This council must only be between us."

"Why do you seek council with me, can you not have a council with one of the males?"

"I seek council with you because they will listen to you."

"You are a smart man, how do you know they will listen to me when some Druid tribes are governed by the males."

"Because I have recently spoken with your ancestor and he told me that a female governed his tribe."

A fleeting look of surprise crossed Supae's face and an uneasiness ran through the Druids who stood around the clearing guarding them.

"I will grant you council."

Lance and Jessica were taken to stand with the group of guarded children, Jessica quickly walked through them all hugging them and calming them while Lance sat on the ground, now he was holding Gensieco but not because she was scared anymore, she struggled against him as she tried to go and defend Tulley.

"Don't," Lance kept saying in her ear over and over again. "Tulley told you not to fight."

"But they are tying him up," Gensieco pleaded in her childlike voice.

"But if you fight, then they will kill us all."

"Tulley and I will defeat them."

"Gensieco, look around, more and more of them keep appearing from out of the shadows, there are too many even for Tulley and you to fight."

Gensieco glanced around and saw that Lance was right, she settled down in his arms and began to mumble in her language so Lance could not understand her.

Three Druids had converged upon Tulley and yanked Gensieco from him, they deposited her in Lance's arms, all the while she was kicking and screaming until Tulley sternly spoke to her in her language. They then tied and blindfolded Tulley so securely that Tulley couldn't even kneel anymore, he fell onto his side and upon the orders of Supae Tulley was dragged a short distance away. Supae handed over the children she was holding and with a helping hand she stood up and walked to Tulley. The Druid with her set a pillow down and held her arm as she sat upon it, her huge belly made her balance unstable and she looked so thin and malnourished that Jessica feared she would collapse. The Druid walked back to the others and stood with them with his dagger drawn, they were all tense and ready to jump to Supae's rescue at any moment.

Supae and Tulley spoke long into the night and did not conclude their conversation until the early hours of morning, when the sun began to cast the pink and orange into the sky. Their voices were hushed so that even when the night breeze blew across them it did not carry their words to the others. Supae finally motioned for her Druids to come and get her, they brought the mat forward and helped her to sit back down, leaving Tulley behind still tied and laying on his side. Supae spoke to her tribe in their language and they all began to walk away, jumping into trees where they disappeared among the leaves and branches. One Druid handed Jessica back her dagger and pointed at Tulley, then he too melted into the surrounding foliage. Jessica ran forward without hesitation and began to unbind Tulley.

"What happened?" she said. "What did you say?"

Tulley groaned as he attempted to sit up. "Bastards," he said softly. "They tied me so tight all my limbs went to sleep."

"Tulley, what's going on?"

"Supae agreed to wait for her ancestor to awaken and they will ask him what to do about you and the children living here, so until then, continue like nothing happened. They have gone to the tops of the trees, they will not bother you or the children."

"Are you sure?"

"Druids are a very proud and honest race, they will keep their word even if someone else doesn't."

Four days later the Druids reappeared and Supae asked for Jessica to come before her.

"We have spoken to our ancestor and he told us many things about you and your family. Your father found our ancestor many years ago, he had been struck by lightning, his trunk was hollow and fungus and bugs were killing him. Your father cleared away the fungus and killed the bugs. He took out the dead burnt insides of our ancestor and helped him to heal, without your father's help out ancestor would have died a long time ago. He says you are good people, and he enjoys seeing the children play beneath his branches and grow up into more good people. He has been shrouding you and the children from danger for many years now, as long as you are beneath the shadows of his branches then you are safe. He does not wish you to be run from your home inside of him, but asks that we all live together in peace. You and the children here beneath his branches, our tribe up above in the branches, so I extend a friendly hand to you. We will live together in peace, helping each other and protecting each other, if you wish to do so as well, then take my hand."

Supae had extended her long thin arm forward and Jessica took it without hesitation, almost immediately she felt something flow between them as Supae held firmly to her hand. Jessica looked down and for a fleeting moment she saw silvery strands like hair twining themselves around their clasped hands. The strands tightened and disappeared and Supae released Jessica's hand, Jessica looked at her hand for moment in surprise and then they smiled at each other.

Chapter Twenty

"You did very good," Tulley commented later that evening as Jessica recounted what Supae had offered her. "Making a pack with a tribe of Druids is a very good thing, what Supae did, binding her magic tie and your magic tie together, is no easy feat. Supae will become a very powerful shaman someday."

"I ams worrieds abouts her," Jessica said as she sat mending the cut in the front of Tulley's shirt. "She's so thins, and she's nursings an infants whiles she's is pregnants."

"Druids have very few females and if they do not have as many children as they can, then their tribe will die out. The remaining males will scatter, the very young will go to other tribes, some of the young adults will fight another tribe in an attempt to steal a female and make up their own tribe, and the older males do whatever they want. There is several things about them you should know. With the lack of females, most male Druids pair up with other males. Also, once this baby is born and Supae is ready for another, which could be mere days after, they will have an orgy that will last several days."

"A what?!" Lance suddenly looked up from the table where he was still scratching out more about Axel.

"They make babies," Gensieco said as she hopped up onto a stool next to Lance and looked at what he was doing. Lance's face began to burn, Jessica had a sly and yet somehow horrified grin and Tulley glanced up toward the ceiling as though Gensieco had said nothing at all.

"I want to make babies someday," Gensieco said as she took the claw pen from Lance's hand, he did not notice for it seemed he had frozen in place.

"Gensieco, you are too young, and Lance, I am surprised at you. Surely you have had a sweet heart and romped around the woods with her," Tulley said.

"Um, well, ah," Lance stammered out.

"Oh, leaves hims alones," Jessica said as she shook out Tulley's newly mended shirt and held it out to him.

"It's just, they um, they do it in the tree, like right above our heads?" Lance managed to ask.

"Usually, but since Jessica and the children are down here, they will most likely find a more secluded place," Tulley answered as he pulled his shirt over his head. "But, if you want, I will say something to Supae and see to it that they don't do it in this tree."

"That would be good," Lance said as he looked down at what Gensieco was doing with his claw pen, she had drawn a picture of Tulley with his shirt off, it showed the contour of his muscles and the lighting tattoos stood out boldly.

"Gensieco, that's my notes and you...wow! That's actually really good," Lance said as he leaned over to get a closer look. Tulley glanced at the paper and then looked up at Gensieco, she met his eyes with a sly smile. For a moment her eyes danced and memories of happier times suddenly surfaced for Tulley to grasp at but then Tulley's face changed and he held her gaze as he forced the memories to fade. The sly smile on Gensieco's face slowly disappeared and a little bit of anger surfaced instead as she watched Tulley shake his head slightly in disappointment, then he turned away and walked off. Gensieco handed the claw pen back to Lance, nearly stabbing him in the hand with it, she rose up from the stool and grasping the picture in her little hands she balled it up and tossed it into the fireplace before Lance could stop her. Gensieco then also turned and walked away, leaving Lance upon his knee before the fire as he tried to pull out the wad before the small flames devoured it.

A man's cry of anguish broke the soft noises of the night and instantly caused Lance to roll off his bed with his heart racing. He heard an audible thumping noise, slow and rhythmic coming from the wall near the window, he could hear a heavy breathing and soft words in another language.

"Tulley?" Lance asked, concern lacing every word; he could barely make out Tulley's figure near the wall. Lance crawled to the small table and struck the lighting stones until he lit the candle, he could hear feet running down the hall and a moment later the quick knocking of Jessica's fist.

"Come in," Lance called as he held the candle and hopped to Tulley. Jessica opened the door and saw Lance kneeling next to Tulley, Tulley was kneeling as well, facing the wall with his palms pressed against it so firmly that the muscles in his shoulders were straining. Tulley was softly banging his forehead against the wall as he spoke words that they did not understand; however, between the words, three kept coming up that they did understand.

"Damn you, Gensieco."

"Tulley? What is wrong?" Jessica asked as she gently placed a hand on his shoulder, she felt the muscles tighten and she could feel the perspiration that blanketed his body, tiny circles of wet droplets speckled the floor around him. Tulley stopped what he was doing and became silent as he just pressed his forehead into the wall now.

"She tried to use her magic on me, she knew what she was doing when she looked me in the eye. All the memories that she made surface, I'm not going to be able to sleep for days. Damn you, Gensieco, damn you," Tulley said through gritted teeth.

"Why don't you just face them?" a voice asked from the window, they looked up and saw two Druids hanging to the bark of the tree just outside, looking in on them through the window with curious concern.

"I can't," Tulley said. "I have worked too hard to keep them away."

"You look rough," the other Druid said. "Supae can make you a tonic."

Tulley took in a few deep breaths as he tried to compose himself before he answered.

"No."

"It will help you sleep."

"No!" Tulley said loudly as he pushed himself onto his feet, he knocked over the candle and they were momentarily blinded by the sudden dark.

"Where are you going?" Jessica called as Tulley unsteadily walked toward the door.

"I don't know yet," Tulley answered.

"Wills yous pleases tell Supae thats I ams concerneds for Tulley?" Jessica called up to one of the Druids that was hanging on a low branch watching the children play. "He has beens gones for twos days nows."

The Druid nodded at Jessica and then swiftly climbed up the branch to the top of the tree where Supae resided with her youngest children. Supae took Jessica's concerns to heart and sent out several Druids to search for Tulley.

"He was to the west, I believe he ate some fungus," Jarsic, the Druid with the braided necklaces, said as he half carried Tulley back. Tulley was awake but not very coherent, sweat ran down his face and body on tiny rivulets and his hands were shaking. Jarsic deposited Tulley on the ground, Tulley sat for a moment, his shoulders slouched and his head bowed, Jessica reached for him but was not fast enough, Tulley slumped to the side and laid motionless on the ground, his eyes staring at nothing. Jessica and Lance crowded over him and Jessica lightly slapped his cheek in an attempt to rouse him.

Tulley blinked slowly and looked up at her.

"I'm sorry," he said softly. "My head hurts so much."

"Shhhh, its is goings to bes alrights," Jessica said as her and Lance tried to help him sit back up. Jarsic returned with a small bowl in his hand, there was a thick liquid in it that was slightly orange in color and smelled sweet.

"No," Tulley said softly and he feebly pushed the bowl away when Jarsic offered it to him.

"You need it," Jarsic said as he held the bowl out again. "That fungus you ate is making you sick. This will make you better."

"No," Tulley said again. Jarsic suddenly moved so fast that Tulley could not protest, he wrapped one long arm around Tulley's head and forced the brim of the bowl between his teeth. Tulley tried to push Jarsic away but could not and all he could do was sputter and choke as the liquid filled his mouth and ran down his chin and neck. Jarsic dropped the empty bowl and firmly put one large, long fingered hand over Tulley's mouth and nose.

"Stop being a child," Jarsic said as he waited for Tulley to swallow, Tulley finally did and Jarsic immediately let go of him, his body fell back and Tulley lay on the ground breathing heavily. Lance and Jessica leaned over him again, his eyes were wide and a slight look of fear crossed his face for a moment.

"Jessica, Lance," he stated softly. "I want to apologize now for anything I might do or say in the near future."

"What did you give him?" Lance asked Jarsic a short time later as they watched Tulley chasing things they could not see.

"Tonic," Jarsic answered, then winced when Tulley leapt up in the air only to come straight down and land on his face. "Perhaps it was too strong for him."

"You don't say," Lance commented. "I have never heard him laugh before, and now he has laughed so much and so loudly that he is probably going to lose his voice. He also keeps saying he is looking for a lady but he does not know her name, but she does fly."

Jarsic grinned a little as Tulley suddenly came to a stop and then began to spin around waving his hands over his head as if he was fending off a mad insect. The children were all gathered around in little knots as they watched Tulley and his antics, they were confused and kept asking Jessica and Lance what was wrong with him.

"He is a little bit sick right now," Lance told Bobo when she finally ventured over to ask.

"Then shouldn't he be in bed?"

Lance bit his lip for a second. "Maybe if we tied him to the bed."

Tulley suddenly came running toward them and Bobo ducked behind Jarsic, Tulley grasped Lance by the shoulders and brought his face very close to Lance's, he was grinning and his eyes were wide like an excited child.

"Have you seen her, that beauty? Her legs, hmmmm, and her breast, did you see her breasts?!"

"No," Lance said as he pulled his head back, but Tulley just pulled him closer.

"Why don't you tell us about them?" Jarsic said with an evil tone and grin.

"No, you don't have to," Lance quickly said but Tulley did not seem to hear.

"They were huge, as big as a robin's eggs, and soft, so soft...by the way, man, did you know you are missing a leg?"

"Yes...yes, I did know."

"Don't worry," Tulley said excitably as he waved his hands in the air. "I will find it for you!" Tulley then turned on his heel and went racing away, Jarsic made a motion with his hand and a Druid that was hanging on a branch nearby dropped down to follow.

"How long will he be like this?" Lance asked as he ran a hand through his hair in desperation.

"Not long, I think," Jarsic answered. "It affects your kind much stronger than ours, he should be asleep soon."

"A half-dose would have been great."

Jarsic turned his head and looked down at Lance. "That was a half-dose."

The young Druid who had followed Tulley came running back.

"Where's Tulley?" Lance asked as he looked around.

"He climbed to the top of a tree, claiming he could fly and he jumped. I caught him with web and left him hanging in the tree, over there."

"Is he getting tired yet?"

"I don't know, sir; he wouldn't stop talking when I left him."

"I will go get him," Jarsic said and strode forward in the direction the young Druid had just come.

Tulley was hanging upside-down from a small tree, his legs wrapped in a spider web and his arms hanging free, his body softly swayed in the breeze. Jarsic caught one of his wrists and looked at him for a moment, then he let go of Tulley's wrist with a twist and Tulley's body spun franticly.

"The tonic finally put him to sleep," Jarsic said when he returned, dragging Tulley by the collar behind him. "Put him to bed, give him water if he doesn't wake soon or he is going to be screaming for water when he does."

"Are you feeling better?"

Tulley rolled over in the fetal position and curled one arm over his head. Tulley spoke but his words were so laden with sleep that Lance could not understand him, Tulley cleared his throat and tried again.

"How long have I been asleep?"

"Two days now, are you thirsty?"

"Very."

Lance handed over a cup and Tulley sat up enough to drink it, then he let himself fall back onto his mat and curled his arm over his head again.

"Did I shame myself?"

"Not really, you mostly just ran around looking for some woman with big breasts and chasing things we could not see. Oh, Supae had her baby early this morning, it's a boy."

"Butterflies," Tulley mumbled.

"Butterflies?"

"They were everywhere, such bright colors. But there was one, it was huge and black and did not like me. Last time I drank something a Druid gave me, I thought I was underwater and kept holding my breath and trying to swim across the ground."

Lance stifled a laugh, Tulley raised one hand and pointed upwards at nothing in particular.

"Don't ever accept food, drink or smoke from a Druid. Almost everything they consume will give one hallucinations, it's just a way of life for them." Tulley's hand fell back down and his knuckles thudded on the floor.

"I'm going back to sleep, that tonic is still making me see things," he now pointed at the wall just above the small window. "There's a snake on the wall watching me."

Chapter Twenty-one

"That is not how you throw a punch," Tulley said, he took Bobo's fist in his and placed her fingers properly, then he placed her arms close to her sides, tucked in with fist held ready in front of her. Tulley had taken it upon himself to start teaching the boys basic fighting skills; however, the girls felt left out.

"I don'ts sees why yous can'ts alsos teachs the girls," Jessica had commented. "Its woulds bes goods fors thems, they cans protects themselves." Tulley completely agreed and was glad Jessica had consented.

Tulley held his hands up in front of Bobo and she began to punch his palms.

"Follow through, that's it, good job."

Lance sat off to the side and watched, strumming his guitar leisurely as he worked on a little ditty about children chasing grasshoppers.

"And in the spring, when the crickets sing, and the fledgling takes to wing...."

"You have been singing that one verse for a half-hour now," Tulley called.

"Well, I could work on something else but a certain crabby old man has yet to tell me more about Axel," Lance looked over and saw the almost nonexistent change of Tulley's features. It had taken a long time but Lance had learned to pick out Tulley's expressions from the minute changes of not only his face but his body language as well; at this time Tulley was smiling without moving his lips.

"Oh, yes."

"Please more."

"Tell us more."

All the children suddenly began to chatter all at once, Tulley put up his hands in mock surrender.

"The deal was if Lance could best me then I would tell more," Tulley said as he took several steps back from the crowding children. The children then simultaneously turned upon Lance and began to poke at him to get up.

"All right, all right," Lance said as he stood up. He had gotten so good at walking on the wooden leg that it just looked like he was an old man with a stiff knee. Tulley and Lance each stood upon a pedestal that was just big enough for their feet, they faced each other and where just far enough apart that they couldn't touch each other with outstretched hands; fighting staffs were handed to them.

"Do you want me to stand on one leg?" Tulley called out, some of the children snickered.

"Nah, but you may want to get that hair out of your eyes, honestly it's starting to look like a dead animal curled around your head." The children laughed again and Tulley took a moment to swipe his hair back and tie a strip of cloth around his head like a headband.

"Now you just look like a girl, get a haircut."

"Stop stalling," Tulley struck at Lance and was blocked, Lance looked at Tulley with a grin. The sounds of their staffs hitting together made solid thunking sounds throughout the area, every once in a while one of them would shout to help reinforce a blow. Tulley landed a good blow to Lance's wooden leg, nearly toppling him and Lance got a solid hit on the back of Tulley's hand. Tulley let go of his staff with that hand for a moment to wave it through the air as if it were on fire.

"You okay, old man?"

"Yes, are you?"

"Of course." Tulley jabbed his staff forward one handedly and nailed Lance in the abdomen.

"How about now?" Tulley asked as Lance doubled over wheezing. Lance hugged his staff to his chest as he coughed and tried to regain his breath.

"Why are you waiting?" he wheezed. "Just finish me off already."

"But we have only been at this for a few minutes, how are you going to get better if you give up so quickly?"

"It's all for fun," Lance said as he hopped off the pedestal and handed the staff over to an older boy named Ryejin. Tulley shook his head as he stepped down as well.

"Two things," he said as he held up two fingers to emphasize his words. "One, if you are fighting for your life, it's not all that fun, and two, I'm not telling you any more of Axel today."

"So you are never going to tell us more about Axel, huh?" asked one of the youngsters.

"I will, even without Lance besting me, but in my own time. I have to make sure the story is straight in my head before I pass it along to someone else." Tulley handed his staff off as well and tucking his thumbs into the waist of his pants he walked away. Gensieco ran up to him and placing her hand on his arm she followed him, Tulley let Gensieco hold onto his arm for a short while then he shrugged her off. Gensieco placed her hand in the same spot. Tulley stopped for a moment and looked down at her, she smiled at him with her childlike features and her eyes seemed to sparkle. Lance watched as Tulley stared her down for a few long moments then he placed his other hand over hers and held onto it so she now had to follow as he continued to walk away.

Lance wandered if Tulley was going to awaken in the middle of the night screaming and relapse again.

Tulley walked Gensieco away from the great tree and continued to hold onto her hand as they walked out of the safe area and into the tall grasses to the east. Gensieco looked around her and tried to pull away but Tulley only squeezed her hand against his arm tighter and continued to walk, all the while looking straight ahead.

"Tulley," Gensieco finally spoke up. "Where are we going?"

"Not much farther," Tulley answered. "I want this conversation to be between us." Gensieco fell silent and bowed her head as Tulley walked her a little farther before he stopped and motioned for her to sit down; they both sat on the ground across from each other.

"Do you know why I need to speak to you?" Tulley said, his voice low and level with a tone that spoke volumes, Gensieco winced.

"Is it about last week, when I looked you in the eye?"

"Yes." Gensieco found that she could not look at Tulley when he was so disappointed in her.

"I am sorry, Tulley," she said softly. "It's just that I don't understand what I can do yet."

"I don't believe that is the problem," Tulley said, his voice still hard. "Do you know what you did to me?"

"I was trying to make you happy," Gensieco finally looked up at him and she raised her arms for an embrace. Tulley did not move.

"I know that," Gensieco continued slowly. "When I look men in the eye, they smile. They notice me. They follow me around and ask me if I need help with anything. They laugh. Tulley, I have never heard you laugh except when you had drank that tonic." Since Tulley had not moved, Gensieco went to him and put her arms around his neck. Tulley was like stone, cold and unmoving.

"I just want to see you happy, I did not know you had such sad memories tied in with the happy ones." Gensieco nuzzled her face into the side of his neck just below his ear, she took a deep breath in and sighed.

"I love you," she whispered and her lips began to caress his neck. Tulley pushed her away then and stood up.

"You do not yet know what love is, child."

"I am not a child!" Gensieco nearly cried out. "I am nearly one hundred years old, I did not ask to look like a Sprite and be so young. I wish I looked like my father! Then maybe people would give me the respect I deserve!" Gensieco suddenly jumped up and stared hard into Tulley's eyes. She felt her powers swirl within her as her anger mounted and she directed that power straight toward Tulley. Tulley's hands clenched and his face changed a little, he was frowning now but he continued to stare right back at Gensieco. Gensieco's heart ached for him, so many emotions swirled within her all at once, love, jealousy, anger, wanting, envy; she squeezed all the emotions together deep inside of her and she felt something pop and all the compressed emotion suddenly flew through her body. They continued to stand face to face, their eyes locked, Gensieco slowly began to raise her hands back up as though she wanted an embrace. Tulley stood stock still, his clenched fists at his sides, his eyes wide; the dark green seemed to swirl and mix, slowly becoming lighter. It seemed that in an instant, he ran through his entire life as Gensieco's magic awoke the memories once more. So many people that were gone now surfaced in his mind's eye. Fallen comrades, enemies he had been sent out to kill, his own little band of companions who also bore the handprint tattoos on their backs. Faces of children, all dirty and half starved, faces of the very old, their skin dark and wrinkled. Faces of so many people, and then there was the face that he had once loved with such a strong desire that it pained him to see her again; his wife's image flashed before him. She was smiling, she was sleeping, she was holding an infant on her lap, then a toddler and another infant. She was laughing, she was eating, she was crying, she was old, she was dead.

A tear suddenly rolled down Tulley's right cheek and his eyes stopped swirling as he held on to that image of his wife's dead face, so peaceful, her face aged but still so beautiful, her brown and gray hair framing her still features; she had died with a smile on her face, it was a small smile but full of happiness. An echo of her voice came to his mind.

"Thank you, for taking care of me and continuing to love me even when I grew old, thank you."

Gensieco saw the change that came over Tulley and the single tear that rolled down his cheek, she felt her hold over him breaking and though she forced more power toward him the hold only crumbled all the faster. Gensieco placed one hand on Tulley's chest and reached up toward his face with the other, Tulley struck it down before she could touch him. Gensieco took a sudden step back, shocked at the stinging pain on the back of her hand and even more shocked that she had been stared down.

"I have broken the power you hold over me, you can never again control me," Tulley was breathing heavily and he unclenched his fists, stretching out his fingers until some of them made popping noises. Gensieco gasped and looked at Tulley with terror and disgust, her eyes flashed red as she tried to take hold of him again but Tulley shook his head at her. Gensieco suddenly began to cry, hot tears flooded down her cheeks and she turned away and ran. Tulley watched her go and then fell onto his knees, his shoulders slumped, his head pounding; he covered his face with his hands and wept.

"We were getting worried about you, Supae was about to send out some scouts."

"I'm fine," Tulley said as he sat down next to Lance. Lance picked up on the hidden pain in his voice.

"Are you okay? Where is Gensieco?"

"She ran away," Tulley said softly as he brought his knees up, wrapped his arms around them and bowed his head. Lance had seen him sit like this many times now but he only did when something pained him, be it emotional or physical pain.

"Why?" Lance asked suddenly. "It's sunset, she shouldn't be out there all alone."

"She has a full grasp of her powers now, she may even be able to turn animals away now, she will be fine. I broke the hold of her powers over me and it upset her terribly."

"You can do that? I thought a Sprite's power was omnipotent."

"It can be broken, by a very strong will, though it can be very painful." Lance could clearly hear the exhaustion in Tulley's voice now.

"You have a headache?" Lance asked softly.

"Not right now," Tulley answered back just as softly.

"Oh," Lance said, then he fidgeted a little and looked back up at the sunset. They were sitting at the very edge of the safe area, the children would all have eaten by now and Jessica would be chasing them to bed. The Druids were in the branches overhead and a few in the surrounding trees, they too were watching the sunset as they did every night, sitting silently as they soaked in the last rays; they believed that the sun died each evening and all the color was the sun releasing its powers to the world.

"You have something on your mind, you have been wanting to ask me something but have yet to ask," Tulley said, his face still against his knees.

"Is it that obvious?"

"Yes, you constantly stare at my tattoos every time I have my shirt off."

"Sorry, they fascinate me. I asked Jarsic about them and he only said they are your magic tethers, and when I asked him what that was he said they were invisible threads that are imbedded in your tattoos but they stick out at the end of each tattoo and look like snakes swirling in water."

"That is correct, but it seems you are still curious about them."

"Yeah, what are they exactly, I have only heard of them, never seen one, that's why I stare at your tattoos."

"I thought that was why. You will never see a magic tether, only two beings can see them, Huldras and Druids. Every being, man, animal or plant, has a life thread or magic tie. A magic tie is an invisible string that protrudes from one's body somewhere, near the heart usually, and it keeps them tied to the magic of the forests around them. A magic tie can be taken and given to another, thus becoming magic tethers. Only shamans are able to do this, they cut open the flesh and weave the tethers into the body of the other, then they fill the cuts with ash and let the wounds heal leaving tattoos so the being who cannot see the tether, can find it. Some shamans make this their life's work, weaving magic tethers into the flesh of warriors to aid them on the battlefield. A magic tether does not give one magical powers, it merely strengthens what that being already possess, if they do have magic in their blood then that will be strengthened; otherwise, the being will just be stronger, faster, can see better and farther. They are much more in tune with the natural magic around them and can speak to other spirits who are usually silent. If I did not have my magic tethers I would not have been able to speak to the Druid in this tree and ask him to save Bobo. The tethers tend to make people live longer and they can go for long periods of not eating or drinking. They can also withstand mortal wounds better and they can use the tether to bind a wound on their body, when that snake bit me on the arm, I bound my arm with a tether to slow down the poison. I have had these tethers for a long time, though they have aided me many times I do regret having them because I killed the people they came from, I will not get anymore." Tulley was silent for a moment and then as an afterthought he continued. "Some of the men in our group had so many woven into their flesh that they looked like striped animals."

Lance took in all the info with some amazement.

"Here, give me your hand," Tulley said as he pulled his collar to the side to reveal the tattoo that curled over that shoulder. Tulley directed Lance's fingers over the tattoo and for a fleeting moment

Lance felt something like a long curling hair brush his fingertips, there was a power to this invisible thread and it made Lance's arm prickle in gooseflesh.

"So I have one of these?"

"Yes, you have one, your original life thread that you were born with, we are all born with one." Tulley straightened and pulled his shirt back in place, the sun was set now and the Druids were slowly making their ways to their hammocks in the top of the tree.

"Come on, I am tired."

"Will you be all right sleeping tonight?"

Tulley shrugged and attempted to run his fingers through his mess of hair.

"I don't know, but I am ready to tell you more about Axel and it is best to do it without the children, Axel is about to be thrown into the horrors of battle."

Chapter Twenty-two

Axel's boots were stolen by the third day, one of the other prisoners in the group tackled him through the night and though Axel cried out and fought back, kicking and punching and even biting, none of the guards came to help and when the larger man finally backed down and ran off, Axel was left with a black eye and bare feet. By the fifth day Axel's feet were so swollen and bruised that his ankles and lower legs were scuffed and cut up from all the times he stumbled and fell, it was also on the fifth day that he was attacked again and this time they took his shirt. The next night as Axel sat slumped near the camp fire one of the guards came to him.

"I am Malik, head guard of this convoy. I am sworn to get every single prisoner to the battle alive, they can't care less if you can't walk, they just want extra bodies to put out front, but if you die of starvation then I will get in trouble." Malik held forth a small wooden plank that had a soupy pile of old vegetables with one roasted grub. Axel looked at it, only moving his eyes, his body was too exhausted to do anything else.

"I will be back shortly and if you have not eaten this then I will make you eat it," Malik said as he roughly shoved the plank into Axel's hands, once Malik walked away Axel let the plank slip from his lap and the soggy mess made an audible splat on the ground.

"I would have eaten that," a small voice said to Axel's left.

"Sorry, Bryan," Axel said softly. Bryan was young, half the age of Axel, his small build and baby face made him look even younger. The convoy of prisoners marching to the battle had stopped in a town three days prior and waited there while Malik had spoken to the overseer, when he returned he was towing a very scared young man behind him. Bryan had neglected his work in the small town and one of the other men had been accidentally killed because of his negligence, so the townspeople placed a murder charge on Bryan and though they had at first decided they would just leave him in the tiny underground jail cell for a few years, Malik changed their minds and they sent Bryan away with him instead. Bryan was shunned by the other prisoners, most of these were hard men who had murdered many times, but when Bryan spotted Axel and saw how quiet and downcast he was, Bryan decided that Axel would be the least dangerous to stick around.

Axel gingerly inspected his feet, they were black and blue in places and one of his toes was swollen and red from an infected cut. He had open sores on the bottom of his feet that also looked like they were becoming infected, Axel picked at one with his finger and winced in pain.

"We can try to wrap your feet again," Bryan ventured. The last several nights Bryan had picked leaves and moss from some of the nearby plants and together they had attempted to bind Axel's feet, but every day they had walked so much that the makeshift boots had worn through and Axel was left walking barefoot again.

"Why bother," Axel said as he laid flat on the ground, his body covered in dirty smudges and a few scrapes ran across his bare chest. Axel pulled his father's hat over his eyes and breathed in the scent of his home, he heard Bryan moving away from their tiny fire, the manacles around his ankles made tiny chinking noises as he walked. Many of the prisoners were not bound, but for each single prisoner there was three guards, every night the guards took turns to stand in a circle around the fourteen prisoners, there was so many of them that they were almost shoulder to shoulder, and they actually were not armed, but though they carried no weapons the prisoners did not attempt to overpower them and flee.

"You have to be a master of hand-to-hand fighting to be a guard like that." Axel had overheard one of the other prisoners speaking on the first night he had been handed over to Malik.

A tiny shiver ran through Axel's body, his feet had so many red cuts that he would not have been surprised if he was running a low fever. Just as Axel was beginning to drift off to sleep he heard a noise near his head and suddenly his hat was plucked away and disappeared into the darkness. Axel rolled over and was on his feet in an instant, his sudden rage overpowering the pain he felt. Axel cried out profanities as he rushed and tackled the man who had dared to steal his hat. The man had not expected Axel to get so angry over a hat but when he was plowed over by the furious young man and he felt blow after blow upon his face and body, the man tried to give it back.

Two guards had to come forward and pull Axel off of the man who was now unconscious, Malik had witnessed the whole scene and Axel watched as Malik came forward and picked up the hat; Axel cursed at Malik and struggled against the guards holding him back.

"Give it back," Axel panted as the guards at each of his arms kept him immobile.

"What's so special about it?" Malik asked as he inspected the old, dirty and misshapen hat.

"It's the last thing I have of my father's, he is dead."

Malik began to hold the hat out for Axel but then thought better of it.

"Is that your food on the ground? I told you to eat it." Malik motioned for the guards to release Axel.

"I am going to hang on to this for a little bit, until you eat that food I had brought you."

Axel stared hard at Malik, his face red from anger and the exertion of the fight. Slowly Axel reached down to the plank and the food that now sat in the dirt, he picked up the roasted grub, its fat body curled tightly and the size of his fist. Though it was covered in dirt he held it up and took a large bite, the inner juices squelched out and ran down his chin, Malik watched him until he swallowed then he handed the hat back to Axel.

It took nearly three weeks of solid everyday marching to reach the battle camp, along the way they had picked up eight more prisoners and a handful of new guards. Axel had stolen a shirt from some other poor prisoner, this one was thread bare and had a bloodstain on the side but it was better than being left bare to the elements. His feet were nearly black from the dirt and still had several open sores but he could walk without stumbling too badly now. He had lost weight, the entire band had, he would have lost more but Malik continued to threaten taking his hat if he stopped eating again. They had survived on bugs mostly, once a guard managed to capture a fledging hawk that had fallen from the nest, the guards ate their fill of the tender meat and left the rest to the prisoners. Axel could not bring himself to eat any of it.

They heard the camp before they saw it, they came upon it at dusk and the slight glow from all the campfires blended in with the sunset. The smell of food and fresh water made some of the prisoners run forward but they were met by border guards with long staffs that knocked them down. Axel stopped walking for a minute and looked upon the camp, it was tents and fires for as far as he could see. Men and horses roamed the area freely, there was singing and dancing, along with fighting and some couples were savagely embracing each other in the open. A guard pushed Axel forward and as they walked into the camp, Axel immediately noticed a lot of young girls, they barely looked to be teenagers. They were scantily clad and had jewels woven into their hair. Most of them had dark makeup around their eyes that made them look all the more stunning. Axel stopped again as he watched one of these young girls dancing around a fire, she had no shirt on, only a few flower petals tied around her small chest, for a brief moment she caught his eye as she swirled her skirt around and Axel couldn't help but smile at her.

"Keep moving," Malik said. "You have plenty of time to watch the Sprites later."

"What are Sprites?" Bryan asked from behind Axel, the smaller figure was nearly lost just in Axel's shadow; Bryan had a knack for hiding.

"I don't know," Axel said as the guards continued to herd the prisoners forward. They were brought before a tent that was twice the size of the others, it had two guards posted on each of the four sides and another guard standing in the front holding the reins of a huge gray horse that wore battle armor. Axel felt a ping in his chest when he saw the large muscled beast, he vaguely wandered if it would survive to old age and be able to live peacefully in some lush pasture for once. They stood before the tent for a long time before a tall woman wearing armor finally emerged. She had a helmet tucked under one arm and a manacled hand rested on the hilt of a large sword that was strapped to her waist. She wore makeup around her eyes just like the Sprites and her thick black hair was trussed up in a long ponytail that hung nearly to her waist.

"Your majesty," Malik said as he bowed deeply before her.

"You took your time coming back, Malik," the woman said, her voice rich and deep.

"My apologies, we took the long way back and picked up a few extra prisoners for you."

The queen tilted her head back a little and glanced at the line of men before her.

"Very well, go talk to my son for payment, the little bastard needs to do something to contribute."

"Yes, your majesty," Malik said with another deep bow. The queen took the reins of the horse and leapt into the saddle with the agility of a cat despite the armor she wore.

"All hail Queen Charlotte," the guards around the tent suddenly chorused at once as she wheeled her horse around with a vicious jab to its flanks. The horse snorted as it spun then leapt forward and the tall queen was soon gone.

"Take them to the eastern side," Malik ordered as he strode away.

The eastern side of the camp was a rank place, there was a deep ravine that bordered the camp with thick forest beyond. The ravine was muddy at the bottom and Axel could smell decaying flesh coming from it.

"What's down there?" Axel asked one of the guards.

"There is nothing directly down there, but farther up they throw the bodies in the ravine and burn them, when it rains heavy it washes down rotten pieces that didn't burn." Axel turned away and put a hand over his nose, Bryan vomited at the guard's feet.

"Hey now!" the guard said roughly and shoved Bryan to the ground. Axel looked at the dirty tents and even dirtier men around the small fires. There was hardly anyone speaking and very few eating, they all appeared to be prisoners and the guards around the area only made Axel sure of his conclusion.

"Where do we go?" Bryan asked. Axel shrugged and went toward a firepit that only had embers left and one old man lying next to it, curled up and sleeping. Axel sat down across from the old man and studied him, his face was scared and wrinkled, he was missing two fingers on one hand and after a moment Axel noticed that he was not sleeping but was actually dead. Without saying a word to Bryan, Axel rose up and left the burning embers and the old man, Bryan followed and they went to a quiet shadowy place and sat down.

"Oh, Da," Axel said softly as he sat hugging his knees to his chest. "What am I going to do?"

Axel fell asleep with his head resting on his knees, his hat pulled down to block out any light from the fires, he awoke when Bryan poked him in the side and looking up he saw that several Sprites had come into the area and were dancing around a large fire. Their bare feet kicked up their skirts as they spun and gracefully moved their arms through the air. Several times they moved away from the fire to come face to face with one of the other prisoners, their small childlike faces smiling as they would brush their lips against the men's stunned features. A few men had come with the Sprites and had drums and lutes, Axel watched and listened as the men began to beat out a tune and their voices rose in a frolicking chant.

"Uncharted days a marching, forever this day of my misery,
The dead and the rats and the fighting cats, my only company.

I used to be a poor man, but with a lovely and loving wife,
But one night she came and I fell in desire and it changed my life.

Now to wield a sword I'm paid by the blood I shed,
Assassins we are and we all love the color red.

We know our fate and we will reap what we will sow,
As arrows fly through the night the blood does ever flow.

The cries of my salvation is always just away,
And as screams of the night fear the light, I fall down and pray.

Oh, why did she go, she meant my life to me,
But what I did she cannot forgive and I'm now in a bloody sea.

I'm killing, till my soul turns to black,
But I swear, by the blood I shed I'll never sin again if she'll just come back.

From the midst of death we continue on as the blood does flow,
And we beat our shields and shout, shout to the dead down below.

Now my trade is shield and blade and blood forevermore,
And as the eyes of the dead follow us we count out our score.

In my dreams she's always there, singing our babies lullaby,
And my heart does ache as that song will haunt me till I die.

Oh, where did she go now, she meant my life to me,
But I was tempted in the night made her turn and flee.

Now as I kill all those around me I raise my sword and yell,
"You won't be seeing me today, you won't be seeing me in hell!"

Axel listened to the eerie song as the men's deep voices broadcast it through the camp and the Sprites danced. The words struck a tender spot in his chest and he once more laid his head down on his knees, hot tears began to run from his eyes as his body shook with sobs.

A small warm hand was on his shoulder and Axel looked up, not ashamed at the tears streaming down his cheeks. A Sprite lifted the brim of his hat just enough so she could look at his face, their eyes met and she smiled at him, a warm feeling began to form in Axel's chest.

"Don't cry," she said softly, her voice sweet to his ears. "We are very happy you are here, we need good strong men to protect us. Will you protect me, my handsome, strong man?"

Axel stared into her eyes and he felt a strange euphonium come over him, though he knew where he was, he was suddenly happy to be there.

"Of course," he said slowly. The Sprite smiled at him as her bright blue eyes stared into his eyes for a moment longer, then she pulled his face forward and kissed him.

Axel dreamed of Florence that night, she was dancing around the fire with the Sprites, scantily clad as they were and laughing as she also kicked up her bare feet. Repeatedly she came to Axel to put her hands on his face and kissed him, Axel would reach out to grab her waist but just as he got his hands around her she would spin away and dance once more.

"Get up, boy!"

The shout was nearly in Axel's left ear, startled out of his sleep he immediately rolled away from the danger only to be almost trampled by the hooves of a galloping horse. Axel scrambled to his feet, the camp was suddenly alive with fire. Screams of men and horses were mixed with the metallic din of sword fighting and Axel could smell the almost sweet aroma of burning flesh. Axel looked to his left and saw Malik and another guard pushing weapons into the hands of prisoners, Bryan's young face was frozen with fear as Malik tried to shove a sword into his small hands, the sword fell to the ground as Bryan's wide eyes darted in all different directions.

"Insolence!" Malik shouted as he backhanded Bryan across the face, the boy's body spun around and he fell face first to the ground where he remained motionless. Axel rushed forward with his hands outstretched for a weapon but Malik was already turning away and he disappeared into a knot of fighting men, swinging his sword savagely. The weight of a body slammed into Axel's back and propelled him forward into another man, they both went down in a heap and Axel felt the point of a weapon graze his forearm. Axel leapt back up and fled only to run into another, but this man was larger and they did not fall together. Malik turned upon Axel and raised his sword, Axel put one hand up and cried out in terror as Malik's sword began its descent but at the last moment Malik seemed to recognize him and stayed his hand. Axel had never before seen such raw beastly anger in a man's eyes, they thirsted for blood and struck fear deep in Axel's very being.

"Out of my way!" Malik shouted as he shoved Axel to the side.

"I need a weapon!" Axel cried out, but once again Malik had disappeared into the throngs of fighting men. Axel felt a small weight land against his chest and upon instinct he grasped it, the object was soft and warm and Axel froze in shock as he realized it was someone's severed arm; the limb leaked blood down the front of his body. Axel let the arm roll out of his fingers and he turned away, his stomach knotting instantly; he fell to his knees and vomited. The world around him suddenly seemed to slow, he looked down at the puddle of vomit he had just expelled and he wiped his mouth off with the back of his hand, not caring that it was covered in someone else's blood and that now the blood was on his face. Axel saw the glint of a dropped weapon several steps away, he got back to his feet but was instantly back down on the ground again; something had tripped him. Bryan was prone on the ground but with a terrified scream he lashed out at Axel, his hands frantically groping for Axel's face and eyes. Axel felt Bryan's nails leave four cuts across the side of his neck, he grabbed at Bryan's flailing hands and tried to fend him off without injuring him. The youth's eyes were mad with terror and though he was looking right at Axel, he did not recognize him; he seemed to be looking right through him as he screamed and kicked.

Axel screamed as well and finally managing to get onto his hands and knees he scuttled away from Bryan as fast as he could, leaving the weapon he had spotted behind for someone else to find. Axel finally got to his feet and looked around, everything still seemed to be moving slower than normal. The entire camp had a hazy glow from burning tents and campfires and the occasional flaming person. The noise was deafening, shouts of rage, the screams of the dying, the thundering of hooves, the clanging of metal. A man near Axel spun around and faced him after a long sword nearly cleaved him in half, the man fell to his knees, his face not yet registering what had just happened but as his hands felt his intestines spilling from his sliced abdomen he screamed and fell forward right at Axel's feet. An ache began to swell in Axel's chest and the icy fingers of terror began to tighten their hold. Everywhere he turned he saw men dying, he tripped over the dead and more than once was almost trampled. Axel began to run, he did not know which direction just so long as he kept moving. He tripped over bodies, dodged spears and swords and somehow managed to not get hit. A small figure suddenly appeared before Axel, she was covered in blood and her skirts were ripped revealing her slender white legs beneath. She fell into Axel and then fell to the ground, Axel looked at her for a moment, she only had one eye, the left side of her face was gone, cleanly cut away by a sword. Axel turned away from the Sprite only to run into another small figure, this time it was Bryan. They collided and both fell to the ground, but Bryan was not screaming in terror anymore. He lay on the ground beneath Axel writhing in pain and gurgling on his own blood, Axel leapt up with a cry as the terror fully took hold of him, from the side of Bryan's neck, just below his ear, was the shaft and feathered end of an arrow.

Everything around Axel seemed to suddenly stand still as he watched the life fade from the young man's eyes, once so full of life, they were now just voids in his soul. Axel had never seen a man die before, had never looked into his eyes and saw the light fade to black.

What am I doing here? Axel's mind raced as he looked at the frozen figures around him. *I have to get out of here, these are men, and I am still just a boy. What am I doing here?!*

Suddenly time snapped back to normal and Axel found himself running again, but this time it was in blind terror. He made a straight line toward what he thought was the ravine, not bothering to dodge weapons or people, he plowed into them and either knocked them down or deflected off of them and continued. A sword left a shallow gash in his thigh, a war club glanced off his shoulder, he even ran into the flank of a running horse and was knocked down, but he noticed none of this as the terror he felt chased him. Then suddenly, he stopped.

Axel stood in the dark trembling, he did not know why he stopped. He was breathing so heavily and his heart was pounding so hard that it took him a moment to realize he was not amongst the fighting anymore. Axel looked down and as his spinning head cleared a little he saw that he was standing on the very edge of the ravine, the darkness below was ominous and yet welcoming, the stench that came up to him suddenly did not seem so bad. Axel looked across the ravine and could see the darkness and security of the woods beyond, all he had to do was fly there. Of course, flying would make everything so much easier but he had momentarily forgotten that in the middle of all the death and terror.

Axel took in a deep breath, his tortured lungs accepted the chilly night air, he raised his arms but then he stopped; something was wrong. A pain was blossoming in his right side, he suddenly became aware of a slippery warmth running down his side and hip. Slowly he reached his left hand across his body and felt his ribs beneath his right arm, and there, just below his right elbow, he felt the shaft of an arrow lodged between his ribs. Axel gasped in pain as he grasped the shaft but it was deep and he was beginning to get lightheaded. He looked across the ravine once more and saw the darkness just ahead of him, he was so close. Axel took one faltering step forward and slipped into the ravine where the shallow stinking mud seemed to be waiting for him; he had finally made it to the darkness.

Chapter Twenty-three

They came with the darkness just before the dawn. Walking softly and blending with the shadows, they slinked through the battle-torn camp, the sounds of the wounded still lingered on the still night air. They stripped the bodies in the cover of the darkness, boots were pulled from the feet of the remaining bodies, pockets were turned out and clothes that were not too torn were stuffed into sacks. Occasionally the cry of a wounded man was stifled as the looters even took from them. Their dark forms moved from body to body until they had all they could carry and then just as they had come, they melted back into the darkness and were gone.

Landrew walked with long strides, his feet finding sure footing even in the dark. He knew the man was still following him but he could not see him due to the patch of fog that he had entered. Landrew stopped and slowly turned his head from side to side, the fog making the noises muffled and distorted.

Suddenly Max came from out of the darkness and landed a blow to Landrew's jaw, Landrew took a step back but did not fall; instead, just as Max's fist met his face he grabbed Max's arm and swung him around. As soon as he let go of Max's hand he leapt into the air and the powerful wings of a large red-headed woodpecker beat the fog into swirls around them. Max saw the woodpecker disappear and instantly followed as a regal cardinal with a murderous gleam in his black eyes. The two birds flew straight up and the cardinal managed to catch up to the woodpecker, he slammed into the woodpecker's back and ripped feathers out with his small taloned feet. The two birds turned upon each other and beat their wings into each other's heads, pecking and clawing, the feathers flew as the two birds plummeted back toward the ground. The woodpecker spun the cardinal around and gave him a vicious kick to aid him in his descent, the woodpecker turned upwards again and at the last moment the cardinal righted himself before he hit the ground, and once again was following. The woodpecker dodged as the cardinal again caught up and tried for another midair tackle; swooping low the woodpecker spied what appeared to be a battlefield, and though the dead had already been carried off there was still a few weapons strewn about. Diving down to the ground Landrew changed and ran as fast as his feet could carry him, he spied a shield and he slid across the ground to grasp it, he saw Max closing in and in one fluid motion he stood back up with the shield before him as he faced his opponent. Max hefted a broken battle axe, half of the sharpened axe head was broken away but it still made for a formidable weapon.

"A battlefield, no wonder you are in the area, my dear Max, I see you are still a worm in this never-ending war."

"Shut up, Landrew, you have no idea just how many times I have wished you were dead. You keep stealing away the prisoners, my Queen Charlotte is not pleased and has ordered you captured and executed."

"Oh, I know, I have heard the proclamation on the breezes...but tell me, dear cousin Max, are you going to turn me in?"

"Shut up," Max cried out as he swung the axe, Landrew brought up the shield and felt the heavy blow reverberate through his arm. "I will kill you and turn in your corpse."

"Such terrible words coming from a family member," Landrew seemed to tease as he blocked another blow.

"You are no family of mine," Max said. "You are cowardly."

Landrew spun away from the next blow and let Max bury the axe into the soft earth, he grasped the hilt of a sword he had spied and turned back to Max.

"You always were a disappointment, Max," Landrew said with a shake of his head.

"Don't play your mind games with me," Max growled as he wretched the axe free. Landrew turned the sword in his hand and using the flat edge he gave Max a stinging smack against his thigh, Max cried out and swung the large axe but Landrew had already leapt back. The tip of the axe caught his chin, it was just enough to make it bleed and Landrew sneered as Max was nearly knocked over by the weight of the axe and the momentum of his swing.

"I already shaved this morning, Max," Landrew commented as he wiped the blood away with his sleeve. Max swung the axe back around and Landrew blocked the blow with his shield, the solid thump rang out and the heavy blow made Landrew's arm tingle. Landrew swiped at Max but was dodged. Max leapt back with the axe raised over his head and fell flat on his back, Landrew suddenly began to laugh.

"Don't laugh at me!" Max cried out as he leapt to his feet without the axe. Landrew saw a flash leave Max's hand and a sudden pain shot through his right leg all the way down to his toes and back up that side of his back. Max had grasped a dagger that was on the ground and threw it. Landrew dropped the sword and grasped the dagger's hilt that now protruded from his right hip, he yanked it out and gasped when he felt the blade grate against bone. It was a small knife, one that would easily be hidden in a boot, it had jewels up and down the hilt and on the very end of the hilt was a royal mark. Landrew vaguely wondered if this dagger belonged to the queen herself, the Bloody Bitch Charlotte.

"So the red bird has a fang," Landrew said as a dizziness washed over him for a moment, he looked back to Max just as Max leapt at him. With a screech the red feathers appeared and Max used his wings to beat Landrew about the head. He pecked and scratched at his face with his beak and feet, Landrew put his arms around his head and struck out with the dagger. For a moment the bird fell back and seemed puzzled, then as the pain came to Max he cried out savagely and flew upwards, Landrew looked at the blood on his hands and grinned.

Landrew turned away and ran, his hip bleeding and sending pain through his leg with each step. He knew the camp must be near and beyond that was the safety of the woods, he hoped to steal bandages in the camp and then let his woman take care of the wound when he got back. The camp was silent when he entered, he pulled the hood of his short cloak over his head to hide his flaming-red hair, he loved the fact that he did not have the common black or brown hair but the red was always a dead giveaway. Landrew walked through the camp as if he belonged there and nobody took notice of him, he stayed to the shadows and walked along the back of the tents, he came to a sudden stop when he heard his name spoken from the inside of the tent.

"Are you sure about this?" a deeper and tired voice was saying.

"Yes, yes, I am," he heard Max answer. "I followed him this way, he is here somewhere. You have a traitor in your midst, sir, and I am determined to find him."

"Very well," the other man said. "We will silently alert the men so this Landrew will not suspect anything, I will personally place a reward on him, these men listen to me better than the queen."

"That's treason," Max said savagely as he smacked his hand onto a table.

"You want to cry out treason in a camp full of mercenaries and thieves, they will kill you for following the Bloody Bitch so loyally. The queen herself knows they despise her, which is why she has me leading these rogues and not herself."

Landrew was crouching near the entrance of the tent and he leaned into the shadows more as the two men exited, they stood at the doorway for a moment and conversed silently, Landrew reached out and grasped the general's cloak. He smiled as he felt the heavy fabric in his hand, then he released it as the general and Max walked away, neither of them knowing just how close to death they had just been.

Landrew quietly continued on until he came to the far edge of the camp, he could see the remnants of a battle that must have happened that very evening for bodies were still strewn about. Landrew forged an injury as he walked to blend in with the wandering wounded better, it was an easy feat for his hip ached and he could feel the blood still slowly running down his leg. There were several guards about trying to round up the prisoners that were still alive, Landrew kept his head bowed as he walked toward the edge of what looked to be a large ditch that separated the camp from the dark safety of the woods. Landrew glanced around but with so many guards near he knew he couldn't change and fly away without notice. He saw another man come running into the area and stop to speak to a guard, carefully Landrew stepped over the edge of the ravine and slid into the deep ditch. The mud at the bottom was ankle deep and had the stench of death and decay, Landrew gagged for a moment and then composed himself. He tried to take a step forward and was tripped by a body, he fell into the mud and silently cursed as the foul earth splashed onto his face. Landrew suddenly froze when he felt a cold hand grasp at his face, he smacked it away and a cry of terror rose up from the mud before him. A young man lay in the ditch just before Landrew, his pale face visible in the darkness.

"No, shush!" Landrew hissed as the young man cried out again but the boy's eyes were unseeing and he was delirious with pain. Landrew tried to cover his mouth with a muddied hand but the boy still wheezed screams through his fingers. Landrew's other hand grasped something heavy in the mud, he picked up the rock and with one swift blow he knocked the lad out. Landrew heard shouts from above and instantly he laid himself flat in the putrid mud and held his breath as he buried his face in it. He could hear the soft labored breathing of the boy next to him and he prayed they overlooked this area. Landrew held his breath for as long as he could, then he dared to raise his head enough to get some air. Someone came sloshing through the mud and he froze as he watched the light come closer from beneath his hood, the figure stopped for a moment and stood over Landrew.

"Poor kid," he heard the man say. Once it seemed that the man had moved on Landrew slowly turned his head and took a breath. The stench wasn't as bad now and the coolness of the mud felt good on his hip. He continued to lay at the bottom of the ditch for another hour until he could not hear any movement from above. Landrew slowly sat up and began to smear handfuls of mud into his hair, though he wore a hood, the sun was just beginning to peek over the hills and it would be easier for someone to recognize him now. Landrew climbed out of the ditch and looked toward the woods, he glanced back at the young man still laying in the mud and apologized. Landrew took two steps forward and stopped as his heart gave him a vicious twinge, he couldn't just leave this lad to his death, the poor boy must have been a prisoner and shouldn't be there anyway.

Landrew turned back and slid into the ditch once again. He looked at the lad for a moment and noted the arrow lodged in his side, carefully he lifted the young man up and cradled him like a child. His body was thin and light, covered in mud and blood.

"What are you doing in a man's war, kid?" Landrew said softly as he ignored the pain in his hip and slowly climbed back out of the ditch. Landrew walked toward the woods, the young man's limbs hanging and his head lolled back, his eyes remained closed though he groaned loudly several times.

"Nearly there," Landrew said silently as he gritted his teeth.

"Halt!" a voice cried out as a guard detached himself from the shadows of a tree. Landrew stopped and turned to the man. "Where are you going?"

"Please let me pass," Landrew fairly sobbed. "My son is badly hurt, I must get him home immediately!" The guard came forward and looked at the young man's pale face and how the stinking mud covered them both.

"Very well, but I don't think he is going to make it home," the man said as he stepped aside.

"Thank you, sir," Landrew sobbed as he almost jogged forward, hugging the young man as though he really was holding his son. Landrew entered the woods and as soon as he felt it was safe to stop he knelt down and gently deposited the boy on the ground. The young man was still breathing, his face young and pale.

"Thank you," Landrew said softly. "Because of you that guard didn't even look at me, I will take you with me and do the best I can to save you."

Landrew inspected the arrow and then taking out his knife he cut the end off near the boy's flesh. Landrew unclasped his cloak and laid it on the ground, though it was a short length he was able to lay the boy in it and gather the corners to himself.

A moment later a large red-headed woodpecker took to the air carrying the makeshift hammock and the wounded boy.

Chapter Twenty-four

Landrew flew through the morning, keeping a tight hold on the corners of the cloak, though the lad was young and thin the burden became heavy on the long flight and Landrew stopped several times to rest and check the boy's condition. Finally, about midday, the woodpecker came to a hidden clearing deep in the woods and screeched his arrival as he descended. Several people ran forward to take the burden from Landrew's grasp.

"Good to see you back, sir."

"Ah, Kalim," Landrew addressed his second-in-command as he awkwardly landed, Kalim immediately noticed the blood on his hip and thigh and he wrinkled his large nose at the smell.

"Kalim," Landrew said as he grasped his friend's shoulder. "That boy is not to die, he saved my life, though he didn't do a damn thing, so, don't let him die, I command it," Landrew added the last part as if it were an afterthought.

"I will do my best, sir, but don't you need a doctor as well?"

"Naw, it's nothing my Amy can't fix. Don't worry about me, take care of him, I don't even know his name." Landrew waved Kalim off as he limped away heading toward his humble home. Kalim watched Landrew walk away for a moment, then he turned his attention to the young man that was lying on the ground with several men crouched around him, he stepped forward to join them.

"He doesn't look so good," one man said as he held the boy's wrist trying to find a pulse. "Kalim, did he say why he brought a half-dead boy back?"

"He looks more than half dead," one of the others commented. "And he's filthy and reeks."

"Landrew reeked as well, Allen, but he commanded that this young man was to be saved, so we better get him inside somewhere and see what all is wrong with him."

"I think he is already dead," the man holding the boy's wrist said. Kalim immediately bent down and gently placed his ear on the boy's chest, the others held their breath as they waited.

"No, he still lives, get him inside," Kalim stood up and wiped the stinking mud from the side of his face, then he helped the others to lift the lad up and carefully carry him toward a low squat building that served as the infirmary.

"Amy, my beautiful, sexy wife, where are you?" Landrew called as he entered the small two-room house.

"In the backyard washing your lovely dirty clothes," Amy called back. Landrew went to the small door that was ajar and looked into the tiny clearing behind their small home; he smiled and leaned against the doorframe for a moment.

Amy was tall for a woman and so slender that if she bound her hair back she could pass for a man. Though her body did not have much form and she hardly ever wore skirts he found such beauty in her general way of life that he fell in love with her after their first conversation.

"That's so sexy how you beat my shirts to get those stains out," Landrew commented from the doorway.

"And it's even more sexy how you get the stains there in the first place," Amy said as she turned and smiled at her tall redheaded husband, Landrew was standing with his hip hidden behind the doorframe so she wouldn't be startled. Amy went to Landrew and was about to put her arms around his neck but stopped when she got close enough to smell him.

"Just stand there," Landrew said softly as he put his hands behind his back and leaned down to kiss her. Landrew kissed the scar that ran across her cheekbone below her right eye, then he tenderly worked his way down till the scar ran across her lips. Amy had a lisp to her speech because of the disfigurement but nobody ever seemed to notice.

"I am so happy you are back in one piece this time," Amy said between a kiss.

"Oh, right, well," Landrew said between another kiss. Amy pulled her head back and looked at him with a raised eyebrow.

"I did, kinda meet Max...."

"Oh, Landrew...."

"And I did, kinda get stabbed."

"Landrew!" Amy began to inspect him and instantly noticed his hip as he leaned away from the doorway.

"Get those nasty clothes off and take a bath, I will go and get some herbs."

"You are so sexy when you are angry," Landrew commented as he turned away to do as she commanded.

Landrew hurriedly took a bath in the cool waters of the tiny stream near their home. The water was from a spring, as fresh and sweet as early morning dew, but it was also icy cold. Landrew left his muddy clothes in a stinking pile on the ground and holding a large leaf over his nether regions he walked bare butt back home.

Amy had not returned yet so Landrew crawled beneath the blanket on their cot-like bed, he was so exhausted that he was almost instantly asleep. Amy arrived some minutes later with bandages and some sprigs of dried and fresh plants, she yanked the blanket away and Landrew was instantly awake as he felt the cooler air touch his bare skin.

"Ah, you already got some blood on the blanket," Amy sighed a little.

"I will help you wash it," Landrew said as Amy began to clean the injury.

"It doesn't look too bad," Amy said as she worked. "But it is angry from the filth, if you start having a fever I will have to cut away the bad flesh."

"I did try to wash after I got away from the ditch."

Amy stopped for a moment and looked at him. "You went to the Bloody Bitch's camp, and fell in the death ditch?"

"It's how I escaped, I pretended to be dead and had to lay there for some time."

Amy sighed and Landrew winced as she pressed some of the herbs into the wound.

"Now, you sleep. I do not want to see you out of this bed, do you understand me, Landrew?" Amy placed her hand on Landrew's chest and made him lay back down.

"I will, but Amy, I really need you to look after the boy I brought back with me. He was in the ditch as well but he had been shot, the shaft was still in his body when I brought him back, I feared if I pulled it out he would bleed to death. But I owe my life to him, the guard who stopped me didn't even look at my face because he was looking at him, I told Kalim that I forbid this boy to die. Please help him, you have the most gentle hands when it comes to wounds and making the injured feel safe."

"I will go, right away," Amy said as she clasped his hand for a moment before she left to find the boy Landrew spoke of.

"Kalim," Amy called. Kalim was carrying a small container of water toward the infirmary.

"Where is he? This boy Landrew forbids to die?"

"He is here, Miss Amy, but it's not good."

Amy followed Kalim into the small building and found several men standing around the dirty pale boy. They had cut away his shirt and one of them was holding the bloody piece of arrow while another was pressing a cloth firmly against the boy's side.

"You barbarians!" Amy suddenly cried out. "He is filthy, you pull the arrow out but don't clean him up any! Out! All of you out! I will take care of him…. Wait! Allen and Kalim, you stay and help. Start heating water, he needs a good scrub." Amy looked over the young man for a moment and quickly assessed all the other scrapes and bruises.

"And I want to put him in a herbal soak for a while."

"Yes, miss," Allen and Kalim answered in unison as they ran out to prepare what she requested. Allen and Kalim helped Amy to undress the young man and they used cloths and warm water to wipe as much filth off as they could. After some time the stench dissipated and everyone, including the young man, seemed to breathe easier. Amy covered him in a couple of blankets as she continued to prepare the herbal bath. She had already stuffed the wound with smashed herbs that would not only help to clean it but numb it as well. Once the bath was ready they gently lowered his body into the warm water that was cloudy with crushed leaves and healing spices. Amy began to work on gently scrubbing his entire body to encourage the healing waters to work better.

"He is so young, not even thirty, I would say," Amy commented as she gently rubbed his face. Amy turned away for a moment and when she looked back at him she gasped loudly, he was looking at her. His eyes were half open and a blue glint like she had never seen before was shining out from his pale face.

"How do you feel?" Amy asked gently. At first the young man was silent and just continued to stare at her, he moved one arm and his hand came from the water for a moment to touch her face.

"Are you real?" he breathed out so softly that Amy almost missed it.

"I am real," Amy said just as softly as she grasped his hand before it slipped beneath the water again, he smiled weakly at her.

"What is your name?" Amy asked. The boy's eyes wandered for a moment and then he slowly looked back at her.

"Axel," he said softly, then his eyes closed and he laid his head back in pure exhaustion.

The pain came first, a pounding in his head and an ache in his limbs. Axel tried to move his arms but felt as though they had no strength; his legs felt the same. His eyes seemed to be the only things he could move, so he slowly opened them and as his vision came into focus he saw a tall redheaded man sitting on a chair next to him. The man held strips of sapling bark between his fingers and he was expertly weaving them together to make what looked like a vase. The man was concentrating so hard on the vase that Axel watched him till he nearly finished it before he realized Axel was awake.

"Hello," he said cheerily with a large smile. Axel winced as the noise echoed in his skull.

"Oh, sorry," the man said but much softer. "Are you hungry? If you have a headache Amy can put some medicine in a stew that will help ease it."

"Not really," Axel fairly croaked, his throat was dry and his lips felt chapped.

"Here, take a drink, though," the man said as he held up a small cup to Axel's lips. Axel took a drink and coughed a little, the water was fresh and icy cold, it felt good as it soothed his throat.

"Who are you?" Axel managed to rasp.

"Hold that thought for a moment, if I do not send for Amy to let her know you are awake she will be furious with me." The man stood, he was tall and well built, with broad shoulders and narrow hips. He went to the door which was open to let in the light and fresh air. A figure appeared in the door way and they conversed for several minutes, the second man looked in at Axel, he had well-tanned skin and a large nose.

"Thank you, Kalim," the redheaded man said as he turned back toward Axel.

"Now then," the man said as he clasped his hands together in glee and returned to his chair. "I am Landrew, just Landrew. I was born of slaves during the early years of Queen Charlotte and have no claim to a family name. I believe you are Axel, is it just Axel?"

"Axel William Ramses," Axel said softly, his headache was slowly easing.

"Two family names," Landrew said with a soft chuckle. "That speaks of nobility, my boy, how did you come to be where I found you?"

Axel blinked several times. "It's a long and painful story."

Landrew put his hands up and softly shook his head. "Say no more, I am a patient man, if you wish to tell me then you may tell me when you are ready.... My wife was right about you, your eyes are stunning."

"Um, thank you."

"You have a face of old, my boy. It is uncommon to find one of our kind with anything other than dark eyes and dark hair anymore."

"But you are a redhead."

"Yes, my brother and I are an exception like yourself, rare ones we are," Landrew chuckled again. A figure was suddenly standing in the open door and it took a moment for Axel to realize that it was a woman clad in men's clothing. She came forward, a woven basket tucked under one arm brimming with fresh leaves of several different scents.

"I am Amy, how do you feel?" the woman asked, but her speech was slurred and Axel looked at her quizzically so the woman repeated herself with slightly better pronunciation.

"Weak, I have a headache and I can't seem to move my limbs."

"That is understandable, you have been here for eight days now."

Axel blinked as he tried to comprehend, where had those eight days gone...? Swallowed up by fever and exhaustion, no doubt.

"Are you hungry? You have gotten quite thin, I can bring you something to ease the headache, are you in any other pain?"

Axel thought for a moment as he took better stock of his body. "My side feels strange, not painful but tingly, like someone is trying to tickle me."

"That too is understandable and perfectly fine," Amy said with a nod of her head. "I will bring you a little something to eat, but not much, you are still weak and you don't want to over tax yourself with too much food, will you please eat some?"

Axel nodded slightly and Amy smiled. "I am so happy to finally see you awake and talking," she said. Amy looked at Axel for a moment longer and cooed like a proud mother, then she turned away to fetch some food.

"My wife has grown quite fond of you, my boy, it is good you did not die."

Axel looked down as he searched his memories for what had happened. The screams and the fighting came back to him, the stench and the heat of fires, then the pain and chill of mud as even more stench filled him.

"I wanted to die," he said softly. "But then when the opportunity came, I fought it. I did not know death could be so terrifying. I can still see their faces, so many faces of men dying all around me. I fell into that ditch, I don't know for how long I laid there but I have never known a worse time. Somebody came and I thought he would save me but instead he slapped me and stole everything he could; he emptied my pockets and he took my hat... that was the only thing I had left of my father's."

"I am sorry, lad," Landrew said. "Was that also your tie to your home?" Axel nodded slightly.

"Well, you are young, you may still be able to pull on that magic, though you are so far away. When you are better we will try, huh?"

"All right," Axel said. Amy returned then and Landrew helped Axel to sit up as Amy helped him to eat, his arms were so weak he had a hard time getting the spoon to his mouth.

"Thank you, but no more, please," Axel said after only a few bites.

"I will leave it here for you, the gravy will keep most all day. It has herbs and spices cooked in that will give you strength," Amy commented as she set the bowl aside. Axel blinked several times, suddenly very tired, Amy and Landrew both smiled at him.

"Just like a baby," Landrew commented with another chuckle. "Eat something and go to sleep."

Axel had not realized his eyes were almost closed.

"I'm sorry," he said softly, he wanted to say more but was asleep a moment later.

The next day Axel was sitting up in bed studying the rough woven threads of his blanket when Amy came in to see him.

"Did you sleep well?" she asked, Axel nodded. Amy had linens under one arm and a small clay jar in her hand. "You still look a little feverish," she commented as she set the items down and placed her hand on his forehead.

"I can still smell the blood," Axel commented softly. "I had a dream I was back in that ditch and when I woke up I could smell blood."

"I am sorry," Amy frowned at him. "That may be something to haunt you for a while longer, but you will overcome it, with time. Now, I need to change the bandage on your side."

Amy's hands were warm and gentle as she unwrapped the bandage that covered the arrow wound, it still felt as though the wound tingled and once she removed the bandage Axel saw why. Amy cupped three fat white maggots in her hand, they were so large that they were wiggling out of her grasp.

"Were those inside of me?" Axel asked as he shied away from the creatures.

"No," Amy said as she dropped them into the clay jar. "You had dead flesh around the wound and a bad infection. These maggots only eat the dead and infected, leaving the good living flesh clean, look for yourself."

Axel timidly raised his arm and looked at his side, he felt a little sick when he saw the hole in his flesh, but it was not weeping blood and the flesh was clean and slightly red as it was showing signs of healing.

"They helped save your life," Amy said as she held up the jar for Axel to once again see the fat white maggots wiggling around each other.

Chapter Twenty-five

"My dear cousin Max, it grieves me that you are still so blind to the actions of your so-called beloved Queen Charlotte, there is a good reason for her being called the Bloody Bitch and I wish you would come to see it...."

"Landrew, what are you doing? It's well after dark," Amy rolled over beneath the blanket and looked at her husband as he sat with a single candle and scratched letters on a piece of parchment.

"Just writing a letter to Max."

"Again, why do you keep all this anger toward each other alive?"

"Because if I can change this land by changing the mind of just one man, then I want Max to be that one man. He has done much evil and I wish he would realize that."

"You are a patient man," Amy said softly as she rolled back over. "Perhaps Max needs love and acceptance instead of scolding."

"We all used to love and accept him," Landrew began, but Amy sighed audibly.

"Yes, I know, my dear, I am going back to sleep."

Axel sat in the sun, his shirt off and the bandages long gone, his side sported the circular scar just below his elbow and the small X was barely visible on his chest. He basked in the warmth of the sun and dozed off and on with an afternoon breeze licking his pale skin.

"How about a haircut?"

Axel opened his eyes and looked up through the tangle of hair that was threatening to cover his eyes. Landrew stood over him with a blanket tucked under one arm and the customary grin on his face, his eyes fairly danced and Axel knew he was up to something.

"I don't know if I trust you, Landrew," Axel answered with a half-grin. "What are you up to?"

"I wanted to take you around to my other camp to meet a few more of my righthand men, but I don't want you to look like a wild man, that mane is worse than a mouse nest."

Axel eyed the knife on Landrew's hip and quickly tied his hair back instead, Landrew shrugged and laughed.

"Do you feel up to a little traveling? I know we have not tried your wings yet, you may not be able to fly at all but you should try anyway, I came prepared," Landrew indicated the blanket tucked under his arm.

"What's that for?" Axel asked. Landrew looked at him for a moment and laughed loudly when he realized Axel really did not know what he planned on doing with the blanket.

"You have never been far from home before, have you?"

"No," Axel said slowly.

"You have so much to learn, my boy. Sometimes if the magic for change is weak in a person because they are far from their home, then they cannot change their clothes with them, so even if you can change into your animal, you may change back into a man and have no clothes on."

A look of shock and awe came over Axel's face for a moment and then his cheeks began to turn red from the thought of how embarrassing that would be.

"Don't worry about it, lad, you are young. And some day I am sure you will return to your home to gather some items and keep them close so the magic stays strong with you."

"I wish I had my father's hat," Axel commented, Landrew nodded in understanding but then urged him to get up.

"Go ahead and try."

"Well," Axel began. "You know how I told you my father was a hawk…."

"Hmmm, yes, a great bird of prey, a rarity to be such an animal."

"Well," Axel continued almost timidly. "My grandfather was an owl, and his grandfather was also a hawk."

"That is impressive, no wonder your family was noble."

"Well, there is more to it; one of my distant grandfathers was an eagle and a general for a king."

Landrew's jaw dropped. "You're joking!" he blurted out. Axel timidly shook his head. "We don't talk about him much because he tried to overthrow the king and take over the kingdom and the only reason our whole bloodline wasn't wiped out was because the queen secretly loved him, so he was placed as an overseer to a small town far from the middle of the kingdom, and his name was changed."

"So you are actually a descendant of General Reyes?"

"Yeah," Axel said quietly. "But I am embarrassed, so I don't talk about it much."

"Why are you embarrassed lad, out here people will look at you like a hero if they knew."

"Well, it's because there is a long line of prey animals in my family, which is rare, and, I am not a prey animal."

"Oh," Landrew said with a chuckle. "What are you then? A hummingbird?"

"Of course not," Axel scoffed.

"Then let's see it, boy, hop hop," Landrew said as he clapped his hands a few times. Axel sighed and looking up toward the sky he concentrated on wings and wind and flight; he pulled on a feeling that was always deep within himself and spooled out the magic that was there. Landrew watched as Axel suddenly leapt upwards and in an instant a plain brown sparrow, twice the size of a normal sparrow, was streaking through the air, straight up to circle around the top of a tree and then straight back down to land again as Axel right before Landrew. Axel looked down at himself to make sure his pants were still there and then laughed a little sheepishly with relief.

"Good show," Landrew said. "I think you are well enough to take a little trip, get yourself a shirt, we are going to check on Hector in the northern camp."

Landrew flew in a straight line while Axel played through the clouds and did loop-de-loops around him. The great redheaded woodpecker looked uninterested even when the sparrow dived down to hit him in the back a few times, but once Axel saw Landrew was not taking the bait he stopped pestering him.

"Such a nuisance," Landrew commented once they landed. "How are you feeling?"

"Really good," Axel answered, his blue eyes were flashing and his face was flushed from the exercise. "But I don't think I am completely mended."

They had come to another well-hidden glen that had a nearby spring of fresh water, Landrew walked through the area waving and shaking hands and stopping briefly to chat and introduce Axel. Axel scanned the area and couldn't help but notice that almost every single man was injured somehow, and they were all men. Many were fresh injuries and some were old and already healed. Some men were missing limbs and had some form of makeshift hand or foot attached to the end of the arm or leg. One area had several men cooking, another area had men weaving or carving, yet another had men sitting around making and repairing weapons. Axel's eyes lit up for a moment when he saw this area and he began to move toward them but stopped as the image of his father lying dead on their floor came back to him; Landrew immediately noticed the change and went to Axel.

"What is wrong?" he asked.

"My father used to repair weapons, I helped many times. He was an iron worker, had been his whole life. But he is dead now."

"Ah, maybe we will pass this group of people up, I don't have to talk to everyone," Landrew said as he placed a hand on Axel's shoulder and began to turn away, Axel shrugged off the weight of Landrew's hand and went toward the group anyway, he kneeled down and struck up a conversation with a man that had an eyepatch on.

"Who is your new friend? He is quite handsome."

"Ah, Hect," Landrew said, turning toward the man who spoke. "I think you have been hanging out with the Druids again."

"So what, at least they understand me better than most." Hector was a good-looking man with dark brown eyes and a hard nature about him, he didn't like women in his camp and that posed a problem between him and Amy, but Landrew had been friends with Hector for a long time so he asked him to be head of a camp and aid slaves and prisoners that were stolen away from battle.

"I like him, may I keep him?" Hect commented as they watched Axel show one of the others a better way of repairing the hilt of a dagger.

"I don't think he's into what you like, Hector," Landrew chuckled. Hector suddenly turned away and Landrew shook his head as he watched him leave, Hect didn't like not getting his way much.

Landrew and Axel continued to stroll through the camp, Landrew was like a celebrity, most everyone knew him and they were all so thankful to him, shaking his hand and calling out to him with laughter in their voices. Axel suddenly stopped and stared hard at a group of men not far away.

"What is wrong?" Landrew asked again when he saw the hardness suddenly cloud Axel's eyes.

"Who is that man, over there in the hat?"

"I'm not sure, there is three men wearing hats and they all have their backs turned to us," Landrew said as he tried to identify the men.

"The one with the wide-brim hat," Axel commented as he strode forward with fists clenched, the anger seemed to radiate off of him like smoke from a fire, Landrew took an involuntary step back.

"Excuse me, sir, but where did you come by your hat?" Axel asked as he grasped the man's shoulder and spun him around. Landrew jumped a little when he saw it was Hect that Axel seemed about to pick a fight with.

"Aw, shit," Landrew said under his breath. Hector looked at Axel for a moment and a shocked look passed his eyes as he tried to read the anger on Axel's face.

"I found it," he said. "Some worm had lost it in the mud."

"You stole it!" Axel immediately accused. "You stole it from me and left me for dead! You slapped me across the face and took what little I had, you said you were going to help me and you left me to die!"

"Come on now," Hector said as he shoved Axel back. "I didn't want to drag a stinking grub back to camp, you would have been dead by the time we got there."

"Then you should have killed me! Rather than leave me there."

"You can't be the one that was in the death ditch, that boy was dead," Hector protested as he clenched his fists and a small crowd of people began to gather around, Landrew included.

"Calm down," Landrew tried to catch their attention.

"Give back what you stole!" Axel demanded again. Hector leaned forward, his nose nearly touching Axel's, and said flatly, "No."

Axel suddenly leapt at the man, his hands reaching for Hector's throat but with a sudden laugh and a speed that Axel could not follow a chickadee flew upwards and Axel was left holding Hect's tan jacket. Landrew reached forward to grasp Axel by the shoulder but was just a little too late, his hand closed over air as a flurry of feathers brushed his face and Axel took to the air in pursuit of the speedy chickadee. The chickadee turned not expecting Axel to have followed and was caught off guard, the two birds collided in midair and began to whirl in a circle as they beat their wings at each other and clawed and bit; their bodies plummeted and several people jumped out of the way as the birds hit the ground with a sickening thud. Landrew leapt forward to grasp them but once again was not fast enough, he barely caught the chickadee but the small bird turned toward him and bit his forearm leaving Landrew holding a handful of feathers. The two birds took to the air again, chasing each other back and forth.

"Get your asses back down here!" Landrew yelled as he shook his fists at them, when neither bird complied he cried out in anger and suddenly a redheaded woodpecker was chasing them both down. Landrew screeched as he caught each one by their heads in his feet, he kept a good grip on them and spun them around a few times, the two smaller birds screamed in fear, then Landrew bashed them together and released them. Hector and Axel fell the short distance to the ground, their human bodies limp with shock, and Landrew followed right behind. All three landed in a heap with Landrew on top pinning them both down. Axel was pale and grimacing, he had some blood on his mouth and nose while Hect already had an impressive black eye.

"Damn it, you two, be adults and listen to each other," Landrew growled, then he wrapped his hands around Hector's neck and propped him up.

"Damn you, Hect, why did you bite me when I was not a part of the fight, you know I can easily kill you just as well as anybody else. I do not tolerate insolence very well."

"Sorry, sir," Hect managed to gasp out as Landrew applied more pressure.

"You are both in trouble!" Landrew continued to seethed, then he took a few deep breaths and just as fast as his anger had mounted it suddenly abated. Landrew released Hector's neck and stood up allowing both men to catch their breaths. Landrew pulled both of them to their feet a little roughly and though his face was calm, his voice spoke volumes.

"Now, shake hands before I knock your heads together again."

Hector and Axel awkwardly shook hands, not daring to look each other in the eye.

"I am Axel William Ramses."

"Hector Prigget, but I prefer Hect.... You know you should think about training to fight, you already have a pretty good jab." Hect indicated his eye, which was steadily swelling.

"Only if I can use you as a punching bag," Axel said as he gripped Hect's hand tighter; Hect laughed a little and then looked at Landrew.

"You going to teach him or what?" Hect asked.

"Only if I don't kill him before we get back home, stupid picking a fight with someone you don't know.... Now Hect, give back whatever you took from Axel."

"I'm sorry," Hect said softly as he flipped the hat from his head. "It's just that I could see death in your eyes."

"I begged you to kill me back there," Axel commented with gritted teeth.

"Perhaps I should have killed you, then I wouldn't be getting my skull bashed by my boss," Hect answered as he glanced at Landrew. Landrew stood with arms folded and a dark look in his eyes.

"I will be more than happy to bash it in for him," Axel commented.

"Just you try!"

"That is enough," Landrew swung around and slapped them both upside the head at the same time.

"Here's your stuff and a few other things," Hect said as he emptied his pockets and gave Axel a belt, a necklace and ring, some coins and a small dagger. "Don't lose them on your way home."

"Get out of here," Landrew said as he gave Hect a kick in the butt that sent him forward at a brisk pace, then he turned upon Axel.

"I should make you walk all the way back without directions," Landrew began but he stopped when he saw how pale Axel had become, the blood on his face standing out even brighter than before. Landrew rubbed a hand across his face and sighed.

"Come on, Amy will be upset if we are not home soon, she is going to be furious if she sees your face so you better wash up before we leave." Landrew shook his head as he now ran his hand through his hair.

"You either have way too much confidence in yourself or do really stupid things when you get angry."

Chapter Twenty-six

"Why is it still dark?" Axel moaned as Landrew yanked the blanket off of him the next morning.

"Because if you wish to learn from me then the first lesson is to wake up early to meet the new day."

Axel sat up and rubbed his face vigorously. "I'm up," he moaned. "I'm so sore," he continued to moan a moment later as he finally rose up from his sleeping area in the corner.

"Let him sleep a little longer," Amy said softly as she exited their bedroom still tying her shirt around her waist. Axel immediately looked away when he saw the smooth pale flesh of her exposed shoulder.

"Even in battle the soldiers do not rest because they are weary," Landrew said as he gave Amy a quick peck on the check. "But he will just watch today, maybe he will do some exercises tomorrow, so do not worry, my dear."

"Will I get to train him as well?" Amy asked. A mischievous grin came across Landrew's face as he looked at Axel, Axel was in the process of picking at his back teeth with his little finger, he stopped, finger still in mouth, and looked back at Landrew with a raised eyebrow.

"What?" Axel asked, his word muffled by his hand, Landrew looked back at Amy and winked.

"No," Landrew said, boredom etched in his voice. "You are not holding the staff correctly, it's been nearly two weeks and you still can't flip the staff from one hand to the other properly. What will you do if you are injured and loss the use of your right hand?" Landrew rapped the stick he was holding across Axel's knuckles, making them sting fiercely.

"I just won't let my right hand get injured," Axel answered.

"Wrong," Landrew said, this time the stick knocked Axel's hat off, the one thing that Landrew knew would piss him off. Axel spun and lashed his hand out to catch the hat, at that very moment Landrew gave his right forearm a hard blow. Axel felt the pain throb all the way to his fingertips and then his hand went numb. Axel watched in stunned silence as the hat fell from his fingers, he could not grasp it tight enough to hold onto it.

"Now!" Landrew suddenly cried out as he leapt at Axel, his much shorter stick raised. Axel yanked his staff up awkwardly in his left hand as he tried to fend off Landrew's onslaught, he fumbled the staff with his right hand several times before he dropped it completely and received a stinging blow across his cheek from Landrew.

"Won't let your right hand get injured, huh," Landrew commented. "How's that working out for ya?"

Axel glared at Landrew with tears rimming his eyes as he rubbed the burning welt on his cheek, he shook his head and stood up.

"Let's try again, shall we?" Landrew said as he fell into a fighting stance, brandishing his stick like a sword.

"Landrew!" Kalim's deep voice rang out a moment before someone began to strike the warning gong. Without hesitation Landrew spun on his heel and raced toward Kalim, several others right behind him, Axel included. Kalim was waving a piece of leaf, on it was a hurried message that appeared to have been written in blood: "War cat."

"Shit," Landrew said as he glanced at the two words. "When did it come?"

"The south wind just brought it," Kalim said. Landrew glanced at his men, no words were needed, he looked in the eyes of the ones he wanted to follow and then with one leapt straight up, a powerful wind swept through the area as nearly every man standing there changed into a creature of flight. Landrew had not looked into Axel's eyes and Axel knew it was a sign to stay there but after a moment of looking at the small flock of different-sized birds all following the redheaded wood-pecker, he too leapt up and left the ground far below as he beat his smaller wings as hard as he could to keep up. The woodpecker glanced back for a moment and screamed in annoyance at seeing the sparrow behind them but when the sparrow showed no sign of turning back the woodpecker then sped up the pace in hopes of leaving the small bird behind. Axel knew they must be heading toward Hector's camp and after some time of hard flying they finally came to the area, all of them out of breath but ready to fight. Axel followed and landed in a tree just as the others had done, he looked around himself and saw that there were several of the people from Hector's camp in the trees as well. They were frightened and a few were bleeding as they clung to each other like baby opossums clinging to their mother.

Landrew flitted from one tree to another, stopping only for a mo-ment to speak to the people who were hiding, each one of them would point down toward the camp below. Axel dared to land on the same branch as Landrew and ask what was going on but before he could even get the words out Landrew suddenly had him by the collar.

"Why did you follow?" he demanded.

"I want to help," Axel pleaded as he gripped Landrew's wrists.

"You are going to get hurt, if this is what I think it is, we already have dead to deal with and I do not want you to be added to the total."

"But what is it?" Axel asked as Landrew released him and Axel had to scamper to keep from falling out of the tree.

"It's a war cat, sometimes Queen Charlotte will send them out to hunt deserters, Hect's camp is full of deserters. Anyone who was able to wander away from the battlefield on their own was usually found by Hect and brought back here."

Axel looked around at all the people hiding in the trees. "Where is Hect?" he asked.

"He is down there somewhere," Landrew answered as he scanned the area below. "He is hiding with several others, war cats are sneaky little bastards."

"There he is," Kalim called out as they saw a chickadee suddenly swoop into the area, the bird seemed distressed and a moment later Axel saw why. A large well-muscled bobcat crashed through some underbrush as it chased after the chickadee, it nearly landed a large paw on top of Hect as it bounded after him. Axel could see wounds on the animal, several deep ones and a long war spear was protruding from its side, a line of crimson leaked from the wound and stained the cat's yellow fur to red. There was a harness around the cat's head and shoulders, several of the thick woven straps were broken and flailing about as the cat bounded in pursuit, the wounds did not seem to slow it down at all.

"Sprite powers?" Kalim called to Landrew as the cat continued though its blood was slowly seeping from its body.

"Perhaps, if it is, then it won't stop till it's dead," Landrew called back, then he leapt from the branches and hurtled straight for the creature below. Hect saw Landrew falling toward them and he immediately circled the cat to keep it in one place, the cat spun around and with a movement faster than the eye could follow its large paw swiped through the air and the flying chickadee was gone with only a puff of feathers. Landrew managed to land on the cat's shoulders and take hold of the harness that circled its head, he hauled back on the straps causing them to tighten around the cat's face. The bobcat froze for a moment when it felt the tension, then it suddenly exploded in a ball of yellow fur, claws and fangs as it spun and rolled in an attempt to buck Landrew off. Its large paws swiped at him repeatedly but Landrew dodged them for a short while. The men who had followed Landrew began to dive from the trees, one after another the birds attacked with their beaks and claws, a couple of the larger birds went for the bobcat's face and beat it about the head with their wings. The bobcat bit into one bird's wing and the bird screamed out as it crunched through the brittle bone. The bird changed back and Axel could recognize Frandling, his arm caught between the cat's teeth as he cried out in pain, the cat slinging his body around with each swing of its head. The large cat spun around and released Frandling as though he were just a rag doll. Axel leapt up as Frandling came flying through the air right toward him, Axel changed into a sparrow and caught Frandling in his feet but the force of the throw and the weight of his body was too much, though Axel beat his wings furiously they both spun and plummeted to the ground, hitting hard enough to knock the wind out of Axel and leave Frandling unconscious. Axel struggled to a kneeling position, wheezing heavily as he tried to catch his breath and clear the spots from his vision. He looked at Frandling's arm, it was bleeding in many places and no doubt broken in several. Axel peeled off his shirt and hurriedly wrapped the man's arm as tight as he dared. Hect suddenly appeared beside him and grasped his shoulder, Axel nearly cried out in fright. Hect held onto Axel's shoulder for balance, he was disheveled and had blood all over his chest, he clutched a small clay jar in one hand and Axel noticed his body periodically shook.

"Are you…."

Hect looked down at Axel and cut him off with just his glare. "I got to get this inside that beast, its poison. The creature is terribly injured and under the spell of a Sprite, there is no other way to save it. But every time I attempt to get it into the creature's mouth it pummels me."

There was a cry of pain as the bobcat struck down two of the birds and then began to go after Landrew again.

"Let me help," Axel said. The cat swiped a foot over its head again as he continued to try and knock Landrew from its back, this time a claw caught Landrew's shirt and flung him away. Landrew's body did several summersaults through the air and he landed on his hands and feet, as soon as he stopped sliding he ran forward again, pulling the two short daggers from his belt as he flung himself at the spinning beast. The cat had not seen him coming as it continued to ward off the onslaught of attacking birds. Landrew landed on the cat's face this time, one dagger sinking into the creature's eye, as soon as he hit his mark Landrew kicked off of the cat and flew upwards with a flash of wings only to dive right back down. The cat's mouth flew open in a scream and before it could turn away Hect was suddenly there shoving his arm deep into the cat's throat, Hect fell backwards before the cat realized what had happened but he wasn't fast enough, the cat's front teeth clamped down on his hand and Hect came away with a fierce cry of pain. Hect fell to the ground just beneath the cat's front paws, he was looking at his bleeding hand, shock and pain covered his face. Axel saw the cat look down at Hect with its one good eye and one bleeding eye, he saw the paw slowly raise and suddenly he knew Hect wasn't going to move in time. Axel leapt forward and with a determination he had never felt before he dived at the cat's other eye. The cat fell back when the sparrow's beak pierced its other eye. Axel flipped backwards and changed back into a man just before he landed on his feet beside Hect, he grabbed Hect's arm and hoisted him to his feet then propelled him away from the enraged animal.

"We have to keep fighting for a little longer," Hect said as he stumbled forward. "It will take a little time for the poison to work."

"Hect, your hand!" Axel said as he noticed the damage, Hect was missing his two small fingers on his right hand and blood leaked out leaving a line of red on the ground.

"Forget about my hand," Hect said as he grasped a sword that was on the ground, he gritted his teeth because he had picked it up with his right hand, Axel had only ever seen him fight right handed but as Axel watched, Hect tossed the sword to his left and then ran forward swinging the weapon with expert ease.

The cat had either pinned or tossed almost everyone by now, Landrew lay on the ground some feet away unmoving, the only one left attacking the beast was Kalim, he was a royal-looking blue jay, his crown of blue feathers was ruffled as he continued to dive and then fly away again and again, his white breast had some red smeared across it but though the cat tried, it had not gotten the better of him yet. Hect ran forward and slashed at the cat's leg as it looked up at Kalim, the cat screamed, it was breathing heavily and stumbling a little now. It looked down at Hect and as Hect swung his sword back for another strike the cat swung its own paw and sent Hect cartwheeling across the ground straight toward Axel. Axel turned toward Hect just as his body slammed into him and they both went down in a tangle of limbs, something hard hit the back of Axel's head and he lay on the ground, vision coming and going as he watched the cat come bounding toward them. Hect lay unconscious across Axel's body and was too heavy for Axel to shove off right away, Axel managed to sit up and pulling the small dagger from Hect's belt he thrust his arm upwards just as the cat's open jaws were descending upon them. The dagger tip pierced the animal's nose and the cat fell back with a scream of pain and rage, it was stumbling worse now, barely able to stay on its feet, it turned its side to Axel and Hect and with one deep-throated growl it fell on top of them, the weight of its suddenly limp body was heavy and threatening to suffocate them, Axel could see no more.

"Get away from me, woman! Leave my hand alone!"

"Shut up, Hector, you need help." The squabbling continued and Axel vaguely wondered why it was still so dark, then he noticed the flickering fires and realized it was actually after dark.

"Hey, how's your head doing this time? Does your chest hurt?"

Axel was lying on his back and Landrew was next to him lying on his side, a bowl of food sitting between them as Landrew spooned it into his mouth.

"I'm okay, really groggy. What happened?"

"That cat fell on top of you and Hect, nearly smothered you both, you actually weren't breathing when we got the cat pulled off, and your face was blue, literally blue. I may have been a little hard beating on your chest, how does it feel?"

Axel slowly sat up and took a few deep breaths. "Really sore," he coughed. Axel and Landrew were silent for a while and Axel watched with some wonderment as Amy continually grabbed the back of Hect's shirt to keep him where he was as she bandaged his hand.

"Why does Hect do that? Amy is a good healer." Landrew glanced at them and sighed a little.

"That is a long story, but I will at least give you the details now. I know you are aware that Hect prefers men over women." Axel made a gag noise. "My boy," Landrew continued. "You came from a very sheltered little town. Many years ago Amy came into camp disguised as a man, she is as strong as a man and could fight as a man, she is the youngest of eight children, all her siblings are boys. She came to the war areas looking for them. Hect, thinking she was a man, fell in love with her. Amy, thinking that Hect somehow figured out she was a woman, went along with it. You can only imagine the surprise when Hect found out she was a woman and Amy found out he did not like women. So, Hect's hatred toward women only grew stronger and though they were very professional toward each other I could see the strain between them, especially after Amy and I decided to be together. But Hect is a good man, a very good man. I trust him with my life and if I asked him to protect Amy he would lay down his life for her as well, but I won't ask him to do that. So to relieve the strain between them I asked Hect to form his own camp. He does have his vices, like going to the battlefield and stealing from the wounded and dead. He will not carry people back to his camp, they have to get up and do it on their own, which is why he left you in the ditch, if you are still sore about that."

Hect finally got away from Amy and came toward them, he was limping and held a bowl of strong liquid in his undamaged hand.

"Want some, little worm?" Hect asked as he held the bowl out toward Axel.

"Go away," Axel moaned. Hect took a drink and sat down next to Axel instead, he was drunk and Landrew watched a bit bemused as Hect put one arm around Axel's shoulders.

"You know what, little dirt mole," Hect said as he put his cheek against Axel's, Axel tried to squirm away but Hect held him in place. "I am glad I didn't kill you in that ditch, because look at what happened today, that cat probably would have eaten me…like it ate a couple of the others," Hect released Axel for a moment and he got a faraway look in his eyes as he stared at the fire.

"For what it's worth," Landrew chimed in. "I am glad Hect didn't kill you as well."

"Yeah," Hect said as he came back to his senses. "Then I wouldn't be able to do this." Hect's hand snaked down Axel's back and he firmly grabbed Axel's butt. Axel gasped as he jumped up and Landrew couldn't stifle his laughter, Hect was still reaching for him when Axel spun around and his fist caught Hect squarely in the nose, knocking him backwards and spilling his drink all over himself.

Chapter Twenty-seven

The time Axel spent with Landrew and his men went by quickly. The training was vigorous and the chores even harder. Landrew was a harsh teacher but Amy was even more so. Axel grew in knowledge and stature as the years passed, three winters went by and a third summer was coming. It was early spring when Landrew amazed Axel yet again with his knowledge of the world. They were foraging for food and a new place to make a camp for the coming year when they came upon the wounded deer. It was a young buck, its antlers small and still in the fuzzy growth of spring. The deer was limping badly and had the savage marks of a wild cat or some other large creature with claws, the slashes were across its shoulders and right side. Landrew slowly approached the deer and they all watched as he held a hand up and the deer slowly lowered its head to place its large black nose in his palm.

"What's he saying?" Axel asked Kalim as he watched Landrew's lips move but could not hear him.

"He speaks Druid, some animals understand it. I have seen him do this before, tame a wild animal with just a few words. If the deer understands him then he will help it and have an ally in the forest, if the deer does not, it will probably try to kill him."

"How often does it work?" Axel asked as he noticed the others holding their weapons at the ready.

"It worked once before, with a lost starving bear cub."

The deer breathed deeply as Landrew continued to hold his hand on its nose, it was as if the deer was trying to smell Landrew's honesty, finally after several long minutes the deer slowly laid down and Landrew motioned for the others to come near and help with his wounds; they would now have an ally that was both powerful and majestic.

"Here, read this to me," Landrew said as he handed Axel a piece of parchment that had been brought by an east wind. Axel looked over the writing for a minute before he began to read it out loud, he was still unsure of some of the writing from their area.

"It is decreed that upon the first day of summer, the Pond Island Meeting will take place." Axel looked over the parchment again, there was other writing but it was all unknown to him.

"They have it written in different languages so the message can be passed on to others," Amy told him as she looked over his shoulder.

"What does it mean?" he asked.

"The Pond Island Meeting happens once every eight years, it is a way for the king to look over his subjects, or in this case the queen, the Bloody Bitch. But she herself will not be there, she never is, instead she sends some of her trusted men to look over it and listen in on any gossip about herself. There is much to do there but the only reason I ever went was for the fighting sports. Great fighters from all over this region will be there and it is a grand spectacle. I myself and my brother used to be their champions. So, since I have trained you so well, Axel, would you like to go and become the new champion? Many people still remember me and my brother, I would love to show up there and give them a piece of my skill again, through you, that is."

"It sounds great," Axel said as Amy took the parchment from him and sent it on with the wind to be dropped to other people in the area. "I have never been to such a place before."

"Oh, my boy, you are in for a treat!" Landrew said as he clapped Axel on the shoulder. "By and by, though, you do need a haircut...and is that a beard showing up on your chin?!"

Landrew trained Axel even harder in preparation for the first day of summer. His fighting skills continued to improve but Landrew began to be picky with Axel's actions as well.

"You need more patience," he scolded Axel. "Tolerance, persistence, endurance. It's all the same thing and yet each one has different principles that you need to strive to live by. It's not just how you act inside the ring that counts but how you act when you think no one is looking."

"But I thought I was already good at all those," Axel pleaded but Landrew only folded his arms and shook his head.

"I have a mission for you, we are going to Hect's camp shortly." Axel bristled at the mention of Hector. "I want you," Landrew continued. "To totally ignore him."

"But he is constantly putting his hands on me!"

"And what do you do when he does that?"

"Punch him."

"Exactly! Hect loves it when you pick a fight with him, it gives him even more of a chance to get his hands on you. You are a very handsome young man, blame your parents for that. But, if you ignore him he will not do it as often, and over time he may even stop completely. Now, let's go."

"No dinner for you tonight!" Landrew seethed at Axel when they had made it back home. "You should not have knocked Hect out, he was not trying to pull your shirt off, you had a spider on your back, I saw it."

"Yeah, sure, whatever."

"Time to go!" Landrew cried out before daybreak on the first day of summer. "The moon and night creatures say this is the day, you can smell it on the air! It is summer!"

Axel sat up in bed and glared at Landrew for a moment, then he laughed and rose up from his small cot.

It took three days for their little group to fly to the small island in the middle of the pond. Axel was amazed at how many people were already there. Small boats were lined up as people who could not fly rowed to the island, a constant stream of birds and butterflies were going to and from the island. Their little group landed on the sandy shores and walked, taking in all the sights and sounds and smells. Axel was nearly overwhelmed by all the new things that was suddenly before him.

"Here, try this," Landrew said as he traded a bag of herbs Amy had prepared for a cut of meat from over a fire, the old man tending the fire only had two teeth left and he smiled largely at them. Axel took the slice of meat and tried it, it was juicy and pungent with a flavor he had never tasted before.

"What is it?" he asked.

"Really big bat," Landrew answered as he ate his own piece. "A delicacy for us but something his village eats every day."

"Oh, it is good."

"Here, hang on to these herb pouches Amy made for us, use them for trade but don't get swindled. We will try to stay together but it is easy to get separated here."

"No kidding," Axel said as he made several turns in place to look at everything around him. "What are we going to look at first?"

"The fighting, of course!" Landrew said gleefully. They finally found the fighting arena, a large circle surrounded by crowds upon crowds of people. Axel was more interested in the spectators than the fight that was going on right in front of him.

"Who are they?" he was constantly asking Landrew.

"Fairies. Druids. Sprites." Each time Landrew answered he grew more and more aggravated. "For the goodness of Thorndin! You are so sheltered, my boy."

"I'm sorry," Axel said sounding rather sassy. "I only know what my teacher has taught me."

"Come on," Landrew scoffed as he made his way to a large table covered with parchments. Landrew studied the writings for a short while and then cried out as he jabbed a finger at a name.

"Martin the Able! He was the only one who was ever able to best me in the ring. But he will be no match for Axel of the Might!"

"That's the name you are giving me? Can't we discuss this?"

"No, you will be Axel of the Might, and that is final," Landrew said as he scratched out Axel's name on a piece of parchment, Landrew then nodded at the man standing behind the table and handed him two bags of herbs, the man held the bags up to his nose and smelled the freshness, then he nodded and tucked the bags into a satchel at his hip.

"Was that bribery?" Axel asked as they walked away.

"No, not at all," Landrew laughed. "Now, let's go and find Martin so you can watch him and learn some of his best moves."

Axel watched as two men carried another between them, the man looked dead as his limbs hung loosely and his head lolled from side to side, covered in blood; a heavy feeling began to form in Axel's chest.

"Landrew," Axel called out as he nearly lost him in the crowd. "Are these fights to the death?"

"No, of course not, but men have died from them, it is just something that happens, but don't worry about it."

Axel stopped in his tracks and Landrew had to go back and grab him by the shirt front to make him follow, Axel did not protest as Landrew pulled him through the crowd.

"There he is!" Landrew pointed out a tall broad-shouldered man who was in the ring. The man had no hair on his head, which only made him look even tougher, his large muscled shoulders had a few tattoos

251

and scars, one forearm was wrapped as though he were injured and his fists were clenched so tightly his knuckles were white.

"Oh, good," Landrew said. "It is a round for hand-to-hand combat, your specialty. I hope we did not miss him fighting a weapons round...." Axel ignored Landrew as he watched the two men square off and he involuntarily gasped when Martin landed one hit to the side of his opponent's head, the other man went down and did not move.

"Landrew," Axel said, his eyes glued to the gloating Martin. "I don't wanna play anymore."

"Of course not, boy," Landrew said as he booed Martin with some of the others. "This is real, if you thought I was hard on you, and you thought Amy was cruel, just wait, we will look like a big sloppy puppy compared to all this."

When Axel did not answer Landrew sensed something was wrong, he turned to the young man and softly exhaled in surprise.

"Axel, are you all right? You are suddenly very pale, come on, let's go find a place to sit down."

"I'm sorry, Landrew," Axel said as they walked away. "My stomach is churning."

"Here, sit down, you want a drink?" Landrew asked as they found a small table near a large fire pit surrounded by other small tables and people. Landrew left Axel sitting at the table while he went to find something to drink, when he returned Axel had his forehead against the table as he softly talked to himself.

Landrew bent his head down over Axel's and spoke softly to him. "No one is forcing you to fight. We can just watch it this first year."

"No," Axel answered, his face still against the table. "I want to fight, I just have to get control of myself." Axel turned his head and looked at the two wooden cups Landrew held, he grabbed one from his hands and drank it without stopping for breath.

"Yeah, that's taking control," Landrew said with a laugh, he held his own cup up and was about to drink from it when Axel grabbed that one as well.

"Well," Landrew said in an amused tone. "I guess, I will, um…go get some more." Landrew once again left Axel at the table and when he came back a second time Axel had his head down again but this time he was groaning.

"Drank it too fast," Landrew said as he sat down across from him. "But that's all right, give it a little bit and your head will stop spinning. Want another while you are waiting?" Landrew chuckled as he held out another cup, Axel turned his head enough to look at him with one eye. Landrew shrugged goodheartedly and then drank both the cups just as Axel had a moment ago. Landrew belched and laughed and he slammed the two cups down.

"You old drunk," Axel moaned from the tabletop.

"You inexperienced one," Landrew said. They both laughed.

They returned to watch the fighting some time later, both feeling giddy they laughed at each other and made snide remarks to each other as they walked between the other people.

A fairy suddenly stepping into Axel's path and bowed to him. "Greetings to you, young man," the fairy said, then he turned and walked away. Axel was stunned for a moment, he had never had a fairy speak to him before, he stood still for several long moments after the fairy had already walked away and stared after him.

"Well, that was good," Landrew said as he put his arm around Axel's shoulders. "He must have seen something good in you, my boy. Only good things come from fairies' speech, so come on, let's go watch the fights."

"He was so lovely to look at, Landrew, a very handsome fairy," Axel said as Landrew pulled him along.

"Of course, all fairies are the most lovely things you will see, it is why they are called the Fair Folk…Fairies, Fair Folk…you get it?"

"Yeah, yeah, I get it," Axel said as they found a place to stand and see the ring. Two men were sizing each other up, they were both of medium build, both shorter than Axel and both held a short sword.

"Ah, swords can be entertaining. These must be some who have hopes of joining a royal guard, the royal guard have to be masters at swords."

"What if they know a little bit of everything, like I do?" Axel asked as he watched one man take a hit to his shoulder.

"Those are people who wish to join an elite team of assassins that work under the shadows of the royal guards. The kingdoms claim such men do not exist but that is because they want them to remain secretive and in the shadows, but they are there, believe me, my brother was one for a very short time."

"Oh, yeah, you mentioned that before. Didn't he leave because they wouldn't let you become one?"

"Yes, it is because at the time a bow was my least favorite weapon, I couldn't hit a deer that was standing still."

Axel suddenly laughed at that as he imagined Landrew standing just below the deer shooting arrows at it and cursing as each one missed the large creature.

"I am sorry, I should not laugh."

"Oh, go right ahead and laugh," Landrew said as he laughed too. "Why do you think I had Amy teach you how to shoot, and teach you kickboxing. I will admit that there are a few things I am not good at, but I embrace it, like this!" Landrew wrapped an arm around Axel's neck and took him down in one fluid movement, Axel laughed as he hit the ground, people suddenly moved out of the way and the attention was drawn away from the sword fighters. Axel hooked one foot around Landrew's ankle and yanked him down as well but they were both back up in seconds.

"Come on," Landrew said as he held up his fists and began to bounce in the balls of his feet. Axel shrugged and held up his hands in the defensive. Landrew jabbed at Axel several times and Axel either dodged or deflected, the two sword fighters stopped as the crowd around them began to filter onto the field to make room for Axel and Landrew. Landrew suddenly jumped back and grabbed a sword from the hand of one of the fighters.

"Hey!" the man cried out with a dumbfounded look on his face. Landrew swung at Axel and Axel did a backbend without the use of his hands so he wouldn't get cut in half, the crowd awed when Axel immediately popped back up and dodged another swing. Axel looked toward the other fighter and held out his hand, the man understood the gesture and tossed his sword. Axel caught it and spun away just as Landrew swung again, as he completed the turn he swung on Landrew and the two swords hit with such force it hurt their forearms. The crowd could see how they were not playing around and they backed up to give even more room as Axel and Landrew danced around each other, their swords continuously clanging. Axel kicked out with his foot and Landrew was barely able to dodge the strike. Landrew slide his sword blade along Axel's until their pommels met, they were now face to face.

"I never showed you this move yet," Landrew said with a grin, they were both already breathing heavily from their efforts.

"What's that?" Axel asked. Landrew tilted his head back and then slammed his forehead so hard into Axel's that it rattled Axel's teeth. Axel took several steps back and shook his head, he turned back to Landrew and raised his sword when a man's deep voice boomed over them.

"That is enough, save your fighting till later, give them their swords back and go sober up."

"That's a good idea," Landrew said as he flipped his sword back toward the man he had taken it from. He took hold of Axel's arm and began to walk him away.

"Smile and wave at the judges, you just gave them a taste of what you're made of," Landrew told him, he had that evil mischievous grin all over his face.

Axel looked at Landrew with knitted brows. "I don't like you anymore."

Chapter Twenty-eight

"Kalim!" Axel urgently whispered over breakfast, he kept looking back at the lone woman who was walking through the crowd, though her body was scantily dressed, her head from the shoulders up was covered and the people parted giving her a wide berth when they noticed her.

"Does she really have a tail?" Axel whispered as he stared.

"Yes, young Master Ramses," Kalim answered, his voice muffled for he was holding a cup to his lips. "That is a Huldra and I highly suggest you look away."

"I thought Huldras were ugly old hags," Axel whispered again as he looked down at his breakfast plate.

"Not all the time, it is believed they can change from a beautiful goddess to an ugly old woman at will, it all depends on if they wish to seduce you and eat you or just scare the life out of you and then eat you. Huldras are actually very rare, she must have some business with someone here, they almost never leave their forest... unless...." Kalim became silent for a moment as a look of deep thought came over his face.

"Unless?" Axel asked, his head still bowed over his plate. A knife was suddenly struck into the table next to Axel's plate, Axel fell from his chair as the knife wielder behind him growled.

"My home forest recently burned to the ground." The voice belonged to a female but it was a deep, gravely female voice and slightly muffled from the wrappings of fine silk that was around her head. Kalim had barely flinched but Axel could see that his fingers were trembling as he continued to hold his cup close to his lips, Axel looked up the long bare legs that were now standing over him.

"Teach this child to respect the ones who can eat his heart while he watches," the Huldra directed at Kalim, her head turned back toward Axel and she looked down at him, Axel could not see her eyes through the wrappings; her tail lashed around and struck him across the face, then she pulled her knife from the tabletop and walked away. Everything around them was silent as the Huldra continued down the path the others made for her, even the chirping insects had gone silent. The cup fell from Kalim's fingertips and spilled across the table as he finally took in a breath, he pressed the palm of his hand into his face as he took control of himself, then he looked down at Axel from between his fingers.

"You have a cut on your cheek from her knife," Kalim said softly. "Luckily for you it wasn't poisoned or you would be choking on your own vomit right now." Axel slowly ran two fingers across his check, there was indeed a cut but it was so small and thin that it barely bled. Axel sat on the ground for a while longer as he tried to absorb what had just happened.

"Axel! Axel, my boy!" Landrew cried out as he made his way through the crowd toward the table. "The judges all agree with me, you have been put on the list of fighters for today, that little show we did yesterday really piqued their interest in you...why are you sitting on the ground?"

"I will tell you about it later," Kalim said as he got up from the table and walked away. Axel suddenly seemed to come to his senses and he looked up at Landrew.

"What do you mean?" he asked as Landrew grabbed his arm and yanked him to his feet. "I can't fight Martin right now."

"No, no, no," Landrew laughed. "They are going to put you up against a few other first time fighters like yourself, but if you beat these today then tomorrow they will pit you against more experienced ones." Landrew clasped his hands together in his excitement. "And then you can beat the snot out of Martin!"

"Can I get a few drinks first?" Axel asked timidly.

Axel sat on the edge of his seat most all morning as they waited and watched one match after another. Landrew either did not notice Axel's nervousness or was ignoring it as he booed some and cheered for others after each fight.

"Are you studying the winners?" Landrew asked several times. "You may be matched against one of them."

"Yes, I am," Axel always answered but he was more worried about keeping his breakfast where it belonged. It was nearly midday before the judges called his name, at first Axel had not noticed but when he did not stand up Landrew grabbed his arm and propelled him forward.

"Simply hand to hand, my boy," Landrew called as Axel found himself face to face with a man that was his height but older and with more build. The man had a large dark beard that still had food stains on his chin from his breakfast, Axel's stomach bucked and twisted even more when he caught a whiff of the man's breath, one hand automatically went to cover his nose. The man looked at the hand covering Axel's face and was suddenly enraged, he charged Axel with an animal-like cry but Axel coolly sidestepped and struck him on the back of the head as he simultaneously tripped him with his foot. The man went into the dirt face first and made no attempts to rise back up.

"Record time!" one of the judges at the large table cried out. Landrew leapt forward and bear hugged Axel in his glee, Axel stood there and dumbly looked down at the man on the ground.

"That was it?" he asked Landrew.

"See, easy!" Landrew said with a laugh as they went back to their seat but Axel didn't even get to sit down as the judges called for him again. The second man was tall and thin with long meaty arms, it made him look top heavy as he threw a few jabs toward Axel in preparation of the fight, Axel glanced at Landrew and the man saw his opening, he took a quick step toward Axel as he jabbed at him with his long right arm, Axel grasped the man's wrist and turning his back to him completely he bent his body forward and took the weight of the man over his shoulder. Axel stood back up in one unfaltering movement, the man was lifted off his feet and Axel easily swung him over his shoulder and onto the ground. The man hit the ground hard, the air squeaked from his body and he lay there utterly stunned and gasping for breath.

"Maybe slow down a little," Landrew said as Axel came back to his seat and managed to sit down that time. "You need to become a crowd favorite as well as a first-place fighter, play with them a little."

"I think I can manage that," Axel said with a grin, his confidence suddenly back after just two fights.

Axel was called several more times that afternoon, each time he defeated his opponent with a grin on his face, as he continued to proceed to the next round he became more and more confident and was having fun at the same time.

"Don't get cocky," Landrew warned after each fight for he could see it in Axel's eyes, though Axel continually assured him he was not.

"Your opponents may lack experience but they are not dumb, they are all standing around studying the other fights so don't underestimate anyone."

"I will do my best," Axel said, sounding slightly annoyed.

"Good lad, that's all I ask you to do," Landrew said as he clapped him on the shoulder. That night Axel celebrated with a few of the other winning fighters from that day, though they had been throwing punches and making mean comments about each other in the fighting ring, Axel discovered that they were actually a pretty good group of men. Landrew found him later in the night, drunk and dancing with a couple of Sprites that were hanging all over him.

"Get to bed, Axel," Landrew scolded and he grabbed each Sprite by the back of the neck and pulled them off of him. Landrew kept a firm hold on the Sprites and kept them facing forward as he walked them away.

"Who is paying you?" he asked them. The Sprites giggled as they playfully struggled against Landrew's grasp.

"Oh, you big strong man," one of them cooed. "You are hurting us, we didn't do anything wrong."

"You know the rules while on the island," Landrew said roughly. "No controlling anybody, now who is paying you to control the young fighters?" The Sprites merely giggled and continued to speak in their sweet seductive tones.

"Are you going to throw us in a cage now because we have been bad?"

"I like being in a cage, as long as you are there with me."

"No, you can't have him, he is going to be in my cage with me."

Landrew tightened the grip on the backs of their necks and fairly carried their small childlike bodies as he walked them straight to a guard's tent.

"More, huh," the guard said when he saw Landrew coming. "Somebody is working hard to win, I have four others caught controlling the fighters." Landrew watched for a moment as the guard bound the Sprites' hands and feet and blindfolded them, there were indeed four others in the tent already, they lounged around on pillows and blankets though they too were bound and blind. Landrew turned back and found Axel sitting by himself at a table, he was slouched down so far his chin was resting on the table edge.

"Landrew," he said in a questioning tone. "What happened? I don't remember drinking anything."

"Well, sometimes drinks will do that to you, come on. You need to go to bed."

"Yeah," Axel said as he tried to stand but fell over instead, Landrew pinched the bridge of his nose for a moment before he helped Axel back to his feet, the boy had a long day ahead of him.

Axel had troubling dreams that night, he tossed and turned and got up once to vomit, Landrew gave him a tonic to settle his stomach and watched over him as he continued to twitch and roll under his blankets. Axel saw a slender but well-shaped woman before him, she was wearing a maroon dress that tapered her waist and flared out around her ankles. Her long wavy black hair bounced as she danced before him, spinning and laughing, her arms and hips moving gracefully. Every time Axel reached for her, she would dance away from him, he could see her lovely smile but the rest of her face was covered by the black hair, Axel so wanted to put his arms around her hips and smell her hair as he kissed her, but no matter how far he reached she was always just past his fingertips.

"What is wrong with you?" Landrew asked later that morning as Axel was nearly bested by a man shorter and smaller than he was. "Was it the drink last night?"

"No, not really," Axel said as he sat down heavily, he put his head in his hands. "I had a troubling dream last night, I do not know why I dreamed of her but it was indeed Florence, she is haunting me…she must be a witch."

"Perhaps," Landrew said as his thoughts instead turned to the Sprites who had him in their grasp last night.

"Put her out of your mind for a bit, Axel, don't let it ruin your day. I have been hearing gossip, you are steadily becoming the favorite, it may not be long and you will fight Martin."

"I hope it is not today," Axel answered. "I feel terrible."

"Just a few hits caught you, sore ribs, nothing broken. Tonight I will make a poultice and rub your back, Amy had made it just for you so you know it will work wonders for bruises."

"That sounds good," Axel said with a little groan from between his palms.

"Next round," one of the judges called out.

"Axel of the Might."

Axel groaned again as he stood up.

"Martin the Able."

Axel's knees trembled and he fell back to his seat in disbelief.

Chapter Twenty-nine

"Landrew, this is not right," Axel fairly spat as the people began to cheer, some of them cried out his name while others cried out the name of Martin. "I have fought four others today and Martin has only fought with one, and now they place us in a fight?"

"He is scared," Landrew said softly as he glanced at Martin walking toward them, his shoulders squared and his bald head tilted as he glared at Axel with a malicious grin.

"He don't look scared," Axel said as he stood up in preparation.

"He must have bribed the judges, but two people can play that game. Sit down and don't move even if he comes face to face with you," Landrew pushed Axel back down and then turned and quickly made his way through the crowd. Axel watched as Martin stopped in the middle of the crowd, he raised one hand and motioned for Axel to come forward, when Axel did not move from his seat Martin scowled and took a step toward him.

"Are you scared?" Martin taunted. "Get up and face me, I will show you how a real man fights."

Axel remained silent and did not move but he continued to stare right back at Martin, his face only showing a cool determination. Martin took several more steps toward Axel, now he was within arm's reach, he bent down so they were nearly nose to nose.

"You smell like a pile of shit," Martin said. "You reek of fear. My mother was half your size and never smelled of fear." Martin raised a hand and gently tapped Axel's cheek, Axel didn't even blink, the second time he hit it hard enough to make Axel's head turn. Landrew's hand suddenly snaked out from beside Axel and hit Martin so hard in the face that Martin almost stumbled, the look of surprise and confusion overcame his features as he looked at Axel's hands and saw that they were still resting on his lap, then he noticed Landrew.

"You!" Martin said as he raised his hand.

"That's enough!" one of the judges called out, he was standing directly behind Landrew. "We will postpone this until after the zenith of the day; however, since you have struck your opponent while he was submissive then I give permission of him to do the same, and you cannot raise your hand against him Martin the Able."

Axel suddenly stood up directly in front of Martin, he had to look up a little to glare into Martin's eyes.

"You are not worth my time, scum," Axel said just loud enough for Martin to hear but with such a vicious tone that Martin blinked a few times. Axel turned away from him and followed Landrew into the parting crowd, several people began to chant Axel's name as Landrew and him exited the area, the judge following close behind.

As soon as they entered the tent Axel felt his knees give way, he reached out and grabbed the back of Landrew's shirt, the judge who was still following jumped forward and caught Axel under the arms.

"Good show, lad," the judge said. "You can breathe now, it is not good to hold your breath like that."

Axel had not noticed he was holding his breath, he took in several deep draws as Landrew and the judge helped him to sit down, Axel dropped his head in his hands and Landrew's heart went out to him when he saw how they shook.

"You are right, Landrew, he is exhausted," the judge said softly. "I will try to sway their decision but I am not sure what Martin has bribed them with."

"If you can hold this off till tomorrow I will give you the matching one," Landrew said as he indicated the finely made dagger that now hung at the judge's hip, the judge nodded with a grin and left the tent.

"Here," Landrew said a few minutes later as he brought Axel a bowl with some sweet-smelling herbs mixed in. "Drink this, it will calm you."

Axel was still sitting with his head in his hands, he slowly raised his head and took the bowl but he did not drink right away.

"You gave him your dagger?" Axel asked.

"Of course, it is the most valuable thing I brought with me. Kalim has the other one, but we knew if something happened they would be our best bet for trade. Now drink that and lay down for a little while if you want. I was very impressed when you stood up to face Martin, and then you didn't even hit him."

"Honestly," Axel said as he stopped drinking for a moment. "I was too scared to hit him."

Kalim came with the news that the fight would be postponed till morning, Axel had been sitting on the edge of his seat the entire time and when he got the news he rose up, walked to his sleeping spot and let himself fall into the jumble of soft ferns and blankets. Landrew roused him long enough to rub ointment onto his bruises and sore muscles, then he let him rest.

"We will still get up early and do some training in the morning," Landrew said, Axel moaned in acknowledgement.

Axel dumped the water bucket over his head, the fresh cool liquid slipped and splashed down his bare back and washed away the sweat from his vigorous morning training with Landrew and Kalim, he glanced up squinting against the water on his eyelashes and looked at the gaggle of young ladies who were watching him.

"I wish they wouldn't crowd around and stare so," he said to Landrew, who was splashing water into his own face.

"Perhaps you should put your shirt back on," Landrew said with a grin.

"I can't, you ruined it with that sword practice."

"Perhaps you should have moved faster," Landrew said with the same grin. "Or at least blocked better."

Axel grumbled as he dumped more water over his head.

"Are you ready for this?" Landrew asked.

"As ready as I will ever be," Axel answered.

"Just do your best, I'm sure you will win."

"But what if I don't win? Landrew, every time I think of Martin I get a sour feeling in my stomach. I heard rumors that two men Martin fought are now dead."

"We will not speak of that here," Landrew cautioned. "I do not know if they are true, so we will not speak of it. But don't worry, you have worked very hard, you will achieve your goals and be all the stronger for it, but the ones who cheat, their achievements will not last long because they are weak."

"Wise words," a voice came to them, it was rough and yet velvety in a strange way, Landrew and Axel turned around to face the man behind them. "My son has described all your fights to me," a very old fairy said as he held onto the arm of a younger version of himself. They both had long delicate faces with auburn hair, the old one wore his hair long and loose while the younger one had his cut short except for one thin braid that was tucked behind his left ear. He had bright green eyes that didn't miss a thing but his father's eyes were dim and cloudy, Axel noticed right away how they clung tightly to each other's arms.

"I hear that you bear three names, young man, I understand that for Little Folk that speaks of nobility, and from what my son tells me, you fight noble. It has been a long time since someone with such skill has been here, continue in your noble ways, young man, but I feel I must warn you, Martin is not noble and he has not fought in such a way for many years. Beware of him, young man, beware."

Axel's heart plummeted when he heard those words, the fairies began to turn away and Landrew bowed deeply, Axel noticed and quickly did the same.

"Thank you very much for your words of concern and guidance," Landrew said solemnly. Axel looked at Landrew from his bowed position with a worried stare.

"Don't worry," Landrew said in a jesting tone once the fairies had left. "Do like you have been doing, look Martin in the eyes and then punch him so hard that you knock one of them out of his head, I know you can do it." Landrew made a punch motion and then slapped one hand over an eye as he made an exaggerated look of shock.

"I think I am going to take a quick nap," Axel said slowly, not laughing at Landrew's attempt at being funny.

Axel's nap was very short and rather disturbing, he saw a black-haired beauty but she held her hands over her face and turned away from him, her slender shoulders shaking as she cried.

"Whoa! What happened to you?" Landrew asked when Axel rose up and dressed. "You look worse now than you did before you lay down."

"I saw her again, she was in my dreams. Why now? I have put her from my mind for so long, and seeing her again, even in my dreams, makes my chest ache."

"Put her from your mind if you can, you have come this far, I am sure you can make it all the way," Landrew said as he gestured for Axel to give him an arm. Axel held his arms out and Landrew massaged the muscles from the shoulders down, then he massaged Axel's hands and carefully wrapped a thin strip of cloth around his wrists and knuckles.

Landrew and Axel made their way toward the fighting area, people were already crowded around waiting and Landrew had to push people aside so they could pass. Axel had many hands reach out and touch him, mostly on his arms, shoulders and chest but there were a few that patted him on the head like he were a child and some that grabbed his butt; those made him take quicker steps and constantly look behind himself until they reached their destination.

"You got this," Landrew said as he gave Axel a quick shoulder massage. "Just clear your mind, focus on the fight, ignore his jeers and knock one of his eyeballs out…or one of the others if that doesn't work."

Axel grinned at that. "Right," he said. "Because he doesn't need to make any offspring."

"That's right," Landrew said with a laugh as he gave Axel a little shove forward.

Axel and Martin both stepped forward, Martin merely squared his shoulders and rotated his neck, Axel bounced around on his toes and threw a few punches in the space between them. Axel saw Martin begin to rotate his neck once more and he sprang forward with a kick to the side of Martin's thigh. Martin took a tiny step back and grunted, he looked at Axel and raised his fist with a smile, Axel's stomach was suddenly in knots.

Martin was larger than Axel and a little slower with his moves but he had good blocking abilities and long arms. Though Axel landed several good punches and kicks Martin did not go down and would return the hit full force. Axel barely dodged a fast-moving punch for his face, he felt Martin's knuckles graze his ear, Martin took several more kicks to his thigh and side but still did not fall. The two fighters continued on, each looking for an opening in the other's defense. Axel could feel the knots in his stomach as Martin stared at him, a stupid mean smile on his face, but though he felt shaky and uncertain on the inside he kept that hard and determined look on his face and did not let the fear show. Martin and Axel were both winded and sweating heavily as the midmorning sun beat down on them, Axel blinked a bead of sweat from his eye and Martin rushed him just as he closed them, Axel felt the kick to his side and the force lifted his feet off the ground, the air whooshed from his body painfully and Axel came plummeting back down; he managed to land on his feet and one hand, the other arm he threw up to fend off another kick. Martin's second kick hit Axel so hard in the forearm that he felt the force of it all the way to his toes. Axel gritted his teeth and just as Martin was pulling his foot away to aim another blow Axel's other hand shot upwards and he grabbed Martin's foot. Axel quickly stood upright taking Martin's foot with him forcing the man to nearly flip over backwards. Martin stumbled and Axel immediately jumped inside of Martin's swing, right against his body, and he began to pummel the large man as hard as he could. Martin grunted as Axel managed to land several good blows to his ribs and abdomen but the big man still did not go down. Martin raised both arms above his head and was beginning to swing them down upon Axel's head, the crowd gasped and without even looking to see what was about to happen Axel ducked down and backwards away from the deadly blow that was coming for him. He landed on his feet and one hand again, crouched down low to ground, he was about to jump up and rush Martin when he heard one of the judges cry out and strike the small metal plate against the table to signal a break between the fighting. Axel remained where he was for a moment, watching Martin to make sure he did not try to hit him again, Martin looked down at Axel and then with a sniff of disgust he turned away. Axel watched Martin walk away for several steps before he finally stood and went to Landrew.

"You are amazing!" Landrew said as he took hold of Axel's shoulders. "How do you feel? That was a pretty hard blow to the ribs, my boy, but you took it well, the people are loving you!"

"I actually feel pretty good," Axel said with a big grin but Landrew could see the tremble at the corner of his mouth.

"Just keep it up," Landrew coached. "Your blocking is top notch, Martin is bigger, you have watched him fight, you know his weaknesses, play on those and keep him moving, he will wear out faster than you."

Two rounds later and in the middle of the day both Axel and Martin were beginning to show the wear and tear. Each had taken hard hits, Axel had gone down several times but was always back on his feet immediately, Martin finally went down and Axel was able to jump on top of him and pummel his face until Martin clamped his hands down upon Axel's shoulders and threw him into the crowd, several people went down with Axel but they pushed him back to his feet and sent him reeling back toward Martin. Martin and Axel sat on their chairs across from each other and continued to stare at each other as they caught their breaths between fights. Landrew gently wiped the blood from Axel's face and applied ointment to a cut over his eye so it would stop bleeding and not blind him. Martin had several women hanging on to him, one sat on his lap and massaged his hands while another was draped over his shoulder, a third was sponging the sweat from his body.

"I feel terrible," Axel said just loud enough for Landrew to hear.

"You are starting to look terrible, how could you let him hit you in the face?"

"It just happened, I guess."

"Well, you are going into the fourth round, not very many have made it this far and none of them have made it past the fifth round with Martin, but you will, in fact you will beat him in the fourth and not even give him the chance to get to the fifth. I have faith in you, I trained you, I know you can do this."

"I can, and I will," Axel said more to reassure himself than Landrew.

"That's the spirit!" Landrew said as the judges called out the next round, Landrew pushed Axel up and watched with pride and some concern as Axel walked forward to face Martin yet again. The strikes were coming less and slower now, they were both worn thin but had a determination not to stop, Martin had resorted to calling Axel names and degrading his skills.

"You are not shit, you are worse than shit, you are the maggots that climb on the shit and eat the shit," Martin called out. "Your mother ate shit when she carried you and fed you shit when you were a baby."

Axel gritted his teeth behind his split lips and ignored the taunts. He managed to land several hard blows but so did Martin, they seemed to circle each other more than fight right now, some of the crowd began to boo and taunt them.

"My sisters fighting is more entertaining!" one loud-mouthed person called out. For a moment Axel let his eye wander over the crowd, he knew he should not have but a dress of royal blue caught his eye, it was so out of place amongst all the browns, greens, and tans of the common people. Axel saw the blue again and as his mind took in the figure of the woman wearing it, her shapely body with the thick black hair that hung to her waist in lazy waves and the haughty way she held her head up as she looked back at him, her dark eyes blazing. Axel suddenly froze, his heart seemed to stop within his chest and he nearly reached a hand up to clutch at it. They stared at each other for what seemed such a long time, everything around Axel suddenly slowed and he drank in her beauty, but her face had a strange look on it and as soon as they made eye contact she turned away so that what seemed such a long time was barely a second, but that second was all that Martin needed. Axel was just turning his eyes back to Martin when he felt the blow to his cheek, Martin's huge fist seemed to cover Axel's face and as Axel began to spin away from the force of the blow Martin caught him from the other side. Axel threw his arms up to cover his head as Martin suddenly rained down with a renewed energy, Axel had to take several steps back but Martin followed. Axel's ears rang, he felt blood flowing freely from his nose and his head began to spin as his vision started to fade in and out, then he heard the sound of his salvation, the judges banged on the table and cried out, Martin landed one more blow and then turned away with an angry growl. The last blow rocked Axel to his core, he gasped and tried to right himself but he couldn't, he felt himself falling, mentally and physically. His body hit the ground and jarred his mind back to focus for a moment, he saw Landrew rushing forward, reaching for him and he forced his faltering mind to stay awake. Landrew's hands were on his shoulders, gently shaking him and calling out his name, Axel pushed his hands under him and slowly pushed himself up, Landrew grasped his arm from one side and Kalim grasped him from the other.

"I can do it, I can do it," Axel gasped as he shrugged them off and limped to his chair on his own, Axel sat down hard and Landrew was immediately by his side offering him water while Kalim inspected some of the damage.

"What happened?" Landrew asked, he tried to mask the worry but Axel could hear it in his voice anyway.

"I saw her, I really did. Florence was there just now, wearing a dress of royal blue. I did not know she was watching, she looked into my eyes and I just could not move anymore," Axel's voice sounded hoarse, he bent forward in his seat and spit a mouthful of blood on the ground. Landrew looked up at Kalim but he did not even need to speak a word, Kalim merely nodded and leapt to his feet.

"Kalim will find her, he will get the others to help and they will keep her away from you so you can continue without distraction. Are you all right? Any places that hurt more than they should?"

"I think I am fine," Axel said. "I am so mad at myself now for doing that, I know I can't take my eyes off of him, and he got one hit in after the match, I don't think anybody noticed."

"I noticed," Landrew said with an angry oath. "That fat bastard is getting scared so he is going to do whatever he can to get the upper hand." Landrew then suddenly became somber as he wiped some blood from Axel's knuckles.

"Do you want to continue?"

Axel's head snapped up and he looked hard at Landrew.

"Yes."

"Are you sure? Because you don't have to, I know I boasted of how you are going to win but people do die in these fights, and I feared the worst when you froze like that. I saw you go down and the first thing I thought of was Amy, actually. She will never forgive me if you die because of something I pushed you too do."

"You are not pushing me to do anything," Axel said. "Was you really that worried about me?"

"Yes, and I will never forgive myself if something happened to you. I have grown rather fond of you, the whole camp has, and you know Amy loves you as her son...I do, too," Landrew got the last words out with a little difficulty. Axel grinned though his lips hurt and his head was pounding.

"That really makes me feel good," Axel said. "To know that you care about me so much. But don't worry, I am going to win this thing. I have already come this far, I have to knock his balls out, remember, one kind or the other."

They both laughed a little. "Or both," Axel added as an afterthought.

"You have come such a long way since I first found you almost dead in that ditch, please be careful, and think about this for a moment, it's okay to lose sometimes."

"I will think about it, but you know just how stubborn I can be," Axel said as he stood up, he gave Landrew a gentle hit to the shoulder. "I looked into Martin's eyes when he was pummeling me, they are different now than when we started, he knows he can't win."

Landrew watched as Axel walked forward to face Martin once again, though he was hurting and exhausted he held his head high and straightened his shoulders, he walked with purpose, he walked like a man and Landrew suddenly felt like he wanted to cry out with pride for that young man he had helped raise and train over the past several years.

Axel came before Martin and looked him in the eye, Martin's face was blank and void of everything, even his eyes did not show the fear that Axel had seen before, Martin clenched his fists and held them up, flexing his fingers so the new wrappings his women had bound around his knuckles fit more comfortable. Axel flexed his own hands and felt the same cloth that had been bound around his hands for the entire time so far, it was frayed and stained with blood now, some of it Martin's and some of it his own. They waited, their bodies tense as their ears strained for the sound of the metal plate to bang on the tabletop; the sound came and Martin's eyes suddenly sparked as a wild grin split his face.

Axel was taken aback for a moment when he saw the sudden smile crease Martin's face, then Martin rushed forward and though Axel landed several hard nearly fatal blows upon his body, Martin fairly bear hugged Axel and got in several good hits of his own. Martin got one arm around Axel's head and began to squeeze, Axel found he could not breathe and though he punched at Martin the big man was not easing up, then finally after several seconds of suffocation that had been stretched out for Axel, he managed to get a leg between their bodies and he struck out as hard as he could. Axel actually felt his bare foot connect with Martin's groin. The big man seemed to freeze for a moment and then he fell away to his hands and knees as he coughed and nearly threw up from the pain Axel had inflicted upon his nether region. Axel felt Martin release his head and he tried to take in a breath but suddenly found it difficult, he stumbled on his feet as he fairly turned in a circle where he stood. He felt something burning on his chest like hot embers had touched his skin, he swiped his hands across his chest but the embers were still there, he looked down and saw no fire on his skin, only four fresh scratches that were slowly seeping blood across his chest and belly. Axel could see Martin kneeling before him and he took a faltering step forward to swing on him, Martin reached up and grabbed Axel's fist, stopping it in midair, both fighters groaned from the pain, then Martin raised his other fist and punched Axel in the middle of the chest, sending him reeling backwards till he lost his footing and fell flat on his back.

Martin did not even wait to see that Axel stayed down, he raised both arms in the air with a savage cry of victory, some of the crowd copied his cry. Axel was barely down for a moment, he got back to his feet and stumbled around as though he were drunk, his head was spinning and his chest felt as though he had broken ribs now, he wheezed and bloody froth came from his mouth and nose. Axel looked toward Martin, who continued to cry out with the crowd.

"No," Axel said, his voice barely a whisper. "I have come too far!" Axel took in a labored breath, the heat he felt in his chest was quickly spreading, the fire ran down his limbs and was covering his face now, for a moment he feared his hair was actually aflame; he ran a hand over his head just to make sure. Axel stumbled forward, he had seen Landrew from the corner of his eye take several quick steps toward him but Axel put his hand up to stop him. Axel blinked a few times and shook his head, "One more hit," he said, and he made his move. The charge was fast and true, in two strong steps Axel was upon Martin and with one leap his leg was swinging right for Martin's head. Martin was halfway standing when he saw the movement, he barely had time to turn his eyes to look when Axel's foot struck him on the temple. There was an audible crack upon impact and the crowd suddenly became silent as they watched Martin's body flip sideways from the force, he landed heavily on his face and did not move, not even a twitch. Axel stood over him, his feet planted wide as he tried to hold his balance, he swayed and looked toward the judges, they were all nodding at him and he smiled though his face was mangled from the fight. Axel suddenly fell to his knees, his hands went to his chest as he vomited onto the ground in front of him, Landrew rushed forward and grabbed Axel before he fell into the stinking bloody puddle. He grasped Axel's shoulders and pulled him backwards into his arms, Axel saw the ground and then the sky and then Landrew's face as everything spun around him. He choked a little and a small amount of bloody vomit trickled down his chin, then his eyes rolled upwards till only bloodshot white could be seen and he began to convulse in Landrew's arms.

Chapter Thirty

"His skin is on fire," Kalim said as he also knelt over Axel and tried to aid Landrew in some way. Axel had stopped convulsing after several long heart-wrenching minutes, Landrew had held him against his chest doing his best to keep his arms pinned and not let his head strike the ground, but Axel's whole body seemed to fight him and Landrew felt utterly exhausted by the time Axel stilled. Kalim immediately noticed the fresh marks across Axel's chest, the blood still oozing sluggishly from them.

"The blood is very dark there," Kalim pointed out as he dumped out the satchel he wore, an assortment of small bags and wooden jars tumbled out. "It has to be poison." Kalim smeared an ointment across the fresh cuts and then with Landrew's help they tilted Axel's head back and Kalim slowly dripped a brown liquid down his throat, Axel's breathing was heavy and he coughed as the medicine tickled the back of his throat but his eyes remained closed. Landrew had been so engrossed with Axel that he had not noticed any of the commotion around him, he glanced up and saw the other men from his camp who had followed, they had surrounded Martin and were pummeling him from all sides.

"Watch him," Landrew said to Kalim as he gently laid Axel's body flat on the ground. Landrew went to his men who were in the process of kicking Martin as he lay on the ground, several of the judges and guards were trying to pull the five men away but they either shoved them away or punched them as well. Landrew did not even need to speak, he merely placed a hand upon the shoulder of his closest man and they all stopped and gave him access to their little ring around Martin. Landrew bent down over the motionless form and took hold of one of Martin's hands, he began to unwrap the thin cloth that bound his arms from the elbows to the knuckles, it took a moment for it was a long strip of cloth but as he unwrapped Martin's knuckles he found what he suspected. With a cry of rage Landrew dragged Martin toward the judges, who were standing near and nursing the bruises that Landrew's men had just inflicted upon them, Landrew's anger was so deep that he dragged Martin around as though he were a rag doll.

"There!" Landrew shouted so more than just the judges could hear. "That is how your champion fights, poisoned spikes across his knuckles."

Martin was beginning to awaken from his beating as Landrew said this, the words slowly registered to him but as realization hit he suddenly stood and shoved Landrew down. Landrew hit the ground hard and Martin turned to run but Landrew's men had been there the whole time just waiting for another reason to hit him again. The two closest to Martin tackled him and as one bound his arms behind his back the other pushed his face into the dirt so hard that Martin screamed when he felt his nose break. They yanked Martin back to his feet and Landrew stood before him, his eyes blazing and his jaw set. Landrew raised his hand then to strike Martin, the other shut his eyes and turned his face away from the blow but it didn't come, instead Landrew lowered his arm and spit into Martin's face.

Landrew turned away and left Martin to the fate of his men, the guards were already demanding they hand Martin over but they merely began to march Martin away as they continued to either punch or push the guards back. Landrew looked to where Axel was and saw the ground bare, even all of Kalim's medicines and herbs had been gathered up.

"Landrew," Kalim called. The crowd was parting as Kalim and another man carried Axel on a blanket between them, one of Axel's arms was dragging across the ground, his battered knuckles leaving smears of blood. Landrew rushed forward and gently laid his arm across his chest as they moved, then he also took hold of the blanket and helped to carry him. They found a doctor on the island who had claimed to know all about poisons and antidotes but he was young and stuttered when he spoke, Landrew fairly towered over him as he checked over Axel and that just made his stuttering worse.

"N-N-N-N-Not go-go-go-go-go...."

"Good?" Landrew cut him off, the young man nodded.

"Do you have an antidote?" Landrew's tone was sharp, his face hard, Kalim kept his head down and stayed silent, it had been many years since he had seen Landrew angry like this. The young man opened his mouth to speak but then he shut it and shrugged instead. Landrew lashed out then, he grasped the doctor by his collar and looked him straight in the eyes.

"I tell you this, if he dies then you will also."

The young doctor gasped and Landrew released him, for a moment the doctor just stood there, his face pale, then he suddenly exploded into action; gathering up different dried herbs and ointments he began to mix items together.

Landrew looked toward the men who were slowly gathering around Axel's bed, he knew them all, fought side by side with nearly every single one, shared many meals with them all and knew each of their life's stories, and yet for knowing them for so long they had never seen him cry. Landrew sucked on his lips for a moment as he looked down at Axel's still form, his eyes were beginning to burn and he blinked them several times.

"Take care of him," Landrew said with a tightness in his voice as he turned away and exited the tent. Landrew pulled his hood up over his head and walked quickly through the gathering crowd with head bowed, in minutes he was exiting the rows of tents and heading toward the dense woods, upon the edge of the festivities area he came across the body, Martin had been tied to a tree, blood had spilled down the front of his body from the deep slash that ran across his neck from ear to ear. A guard was there tacking a sign to the tree above Martin's head, Landrew did not stop to read it. As soon as Landrew came into the shadows of the woods he began to run, he knew he had to save Axel and he had a plan but he knew he had little time left to put that plan into action. Landrew came to a small stream and looked at the water, he had to find a secluded area with water that was as clear and smooth as the sky on an early summer day. Landrew jumped into the air and began to follow the stream from above, the water moved fast for the most part and the stream was wide, it caressed the roots of trees and washed over rocks and boulders as it quickly moved along. Landrew followed it for some time and was beginning to get discouraged, he was about to turn around when he came to a small clear patch near the water's edge. Here the fast water swirled into a small nook on the edge of the stream, Landrew immediately knew it was what he was looking for because though the water swirled into the small pool with speed and force, the pool was still as ice, not a ripple on the surface and nothing so much as stirred beneath. Landrew fell upon his knees next to the water, he leaned over the edge and slowly swirled his fingers over the surface of the water. Landrew felt the coolness of the water, it struck his fingers and seemed to creep up his arm, he felt the skin of his forearm prickle and a shiver ran up and down his back. For a long moment nothing happened and Landrew remained leaning over the water, his arm outstretched, he was still breathing hard from his hurried search and he squeezed his eyes shut as the burning in them became too much; a single tear fell from the corner of his left eye and silently slipped into the water. A tiny hand suddenly grasped Landrew's fingers as they touched the water, Landrew gasped and tried to pull his hand away but the strength of the being who now held him was much stronger than he was. Landrew could see the small face beneath the water, it was white, not a blemish or mark upon it except for a small nose, red delicate lips and a pair of very large vibrant blue eyes. The Snow Fairy was staring at him from just beneath the surface of its home but then Landrew blinked and the being was gone, the grip upon his fingers disappeared without even leaving a ripple in the water.

"No!" Landrew suddenly cried out. "Come back! I need you!" Landrew thrust both hands into the water and grabbed at nothing, he looked at his wet dripping hands for a moment and then he unclasped his short cloak and let it fall to the ground, he looked into the water once more and swallowed his fear as he dived in.

The water was cold and enveloped him immediately, Landrew kicked and struck at the water as he struggled to get his head above the surface again but like most all the other Little Folk, Landrew could not swim and was quickly sinking to the bottom of the still pool. Landrew could feel the current from the stream take hold of him, it was pulling him from the snow fairy's quiet little home, he struggled against the moving water and managed to get his head above the surface for one quick breath before he went under again. He struggled to keep his stinging eyes open as his lungs began to burn, after a short time he felt himself touch the bottom of the stream, he grasped a root he found amongst the rocks and he held on to it so the current would not take him. He squinted in the water looking for the Snow Fairy, he could not see the creature. Landrew began to pull himself along the bottom of the stream by grasping anything he could, he slowly crawled back to the inner safety of the Snow Fairy's home, his chest hurt and his mind raced; he wanted to scream but knew he had to hold onto the little bit of air he had. The fairy suddenly appeared before him, its white face taking up Landrew's view. Its small nostrils were now flared as it took in the water, the gills on its chest slowly opened and closed with each breath, its huge eyes blinked at him once and Landrew thought he saw a look of annoyance. Landrew reached for the small being just in front of him but the little creature spun around in the water and kicked Landrew in the chest with such strength that Landrew lost his grip and the air suddenly exited his tortured lungs in a burst of bubbles that rocketed to the surface. Landrew's body sailed backwards through the water and into the fast-moving current of the stream, the water hit Landrew and flung his body around as it dragged him along, Landrew felt himself bounce off of rocks and other debris in the water; his mind began to flash red and black and his last thoughts was that image of Axel convulsing in his arms.

Landrew was sprawled across the ground, his arms spread wide and his legs still in the water. He tried to take in a breath and couldn't, he was just coming to consciousness when the weight on his chest hit again and he spewed water from his mouth. He coughed and choked and struggled to breathe as the weight on his chest hit him a second time, he forced his eyes open a little and saw the Snow Fairy standing on his chest, it bent down a little and jumped, Landrew gasped as he saw the fairy coming back down to land on top of him again, he tried to roll out of the way but his limbs did not respond very well.

"Stop," Landrew gasped once the fairy landed, it looked at him and then flopped down to sit on his chest. The fairy was small, the size of a four-year-old, he was naked and had little patches of green and brown hair in odd places all over his body but his face was clean and smooth, or was that moss growing on him…. Landrew's vision was still blurry. The Snow Fairy reached out one webbed hand and poked Landrew in the face, he noticed that the creature only had three fingers and three toes on each limb.

"Why do you search for me, Landrew Woodpecker?" the fairy's voice was soft and gaspy and it took Landrew a moment to realize it was speaking Druid to him.

Landrew searched his hazy mind for the answer but though he understood the fairy he found he could not answer in Druid so he spoke normally.

"How do you know me?" Landrew asked. The fairy smiled, the smile covered most of his face and showed off a row of tiny pointed teeth; the fairy answered back in Landrew's own language.

"We have our ways, we know most everything there is to know."

"So then you know why I am looking for you."

"I do, but I so like it when people beg, so Landrew, ask of me, beg of me, worship me and perhaps I will grant what you ask."

"Please," Landrew said immediately. "Please, I beg of you to save the life of someone very dear to me. He is like a son to me now and it is my fault he is dying. He was inflicted with the evil doings of others and does not deserve a death like this."

The Snow Fairy slowly nodded his head but then looked away.

"No, I will not," he said. Landrew blinked a few times.

"Please!" Landrew said as he started the rise up even though the fairy still sat upon his chest, the fairy bounced a little and Landrew stopped.

"Why should I help you? I have so many others I can help, so many others with less wishes than you, easier wishes, wishes of beauty and wealth. Wishes of their spouse to worship them, wishes of silly little things. It amazes me what you folk deem important to you. So, no, I think I will not help you, Landrew Woodpecker." The fairy turned away and rolled off of Landrew's chest, he was descending into the water when Landrew grasped his small arm and held on to him.

"No, please, you must help me!" Landrew begged. The Snow Fairy turned its large eyes back to Landrew and glared at him, it suddenly looked like storm clouds were swirling within them.

"Why?" he asked again. "Many people receive their wish and are still very unhappy with it, many of them come back to complain, and then I usually eat them." The fairy had said the last few words with an excited malicious tone.

"You will never see me again, I will not come back to complain. I will honor your name and keep this place sacred in my heart. If Axel ever dies I just would not be able to handle it. My wife would be heartbroken as well, we have both been through so many hardships, please grant me this one wish so we can continue to be happy."

"If he ever dies," the fairy said softly. "Are you sure you want this? I can cure him of everything and he will remain that way. No sickness or poison will ever lay him low in such a way again. But think on it, you may come to regret this day, he may come to regret this day."

"Yes, please!" Landrew fairly sobbed as he fell to his knees before the fairy. "Just so long as he continues to live!"

"Oh, he will live," the small creature said with another toothy grin. "Go back to this young man, Landrew Woodpecker, and hold his hand for a time, I give life to him, in great abundance."

The Snow Fairy then pulled his arm free, Landrew watched him descend back to the depths of his watery home and disappear amongst the rocks and roots. He continued to kneel for a moment as he processed what the fairy had said, then he leapt into the air and beat his wings as fast as he could back to camp.

Landrew came back as the sun was setting and he hurried into the tent, his men were still there standing or sitting around as they waited. Kalim was beside Axel who was still in the bed, deathly pale and sweating, Landrew's heart sank and he rushed forward.

"The young doctor has fled, he fears for his life, says Axel will be dead by morning. I have been doing all I can but I have no knowledge of this type of poison, I am sorry, Landrew," Kalim said as he stood up from his chair so Landrew could sit down. Landrew slowly took the chair and moved it closer to the bed, he sat down, his eyes never leaving Axel's face as he looked for any sign of change; there was none. Landrew reached out and took one of Axel's hands in his, it was clammy and limp, he gently squeezed it as he held it. Landrew listened to Axel's shallow breathing and vaguely wandered if the Snow Fairy was just bluffing to get him to leave.

"Kalim," he said softly. "Send someone to fetch Amy."

"I already have, sir," Kalim answered softly.

"Thank you," Landrew breathed as he laid his head down on one arm on the edge of the bed, his other hand still grasping Axel's. Landrew felt a tremble in Axel's fingers and a slight pressure as Axel squeezed back, Landrew's heart ached.

"Thank you," he whispered again. "Thank you."

Chapter Thirty-one

Amy gently put her hands on Landrew's shoulders, he was slouched awkwardly in his chair as he dozed next to Axel's bed. Landrew suddenly came awake and immediately looked at Axel, when he saw that Axel was still there he then looked over his shoulder to see who had placed their hands on him.

"Amy," Landrew said softly, his voice full of exhaustion. Amy came around to face Landrew, they looked at each other for several long moments then they kissed.

"I am so sorry," Landrew said when they pulled apart, he ran his thumb over the scar on her face.

"It's okay," Amy said softly. "When they told me Axel was dying I expected to come to a funeral, but here he is, still living. You should not apologize."

Landrew bit his lower lip, how had he been so lucky to find someone who understood him so well.

"He won't wake up," Landrew said softly. "He has no fever anymore, it's just like he is asleep and doesn't want to wake up."

"Give him time," Amy said softly.

"But it's been days…."

"Shhhhhh," Amy said softly as she placed her fingertip on his lips. "Give him time."

Axel rolled over and pulled his arm up over his face, the sun was bright and shining right through his eyelids; a hand suddenly grasped his arm.

"Axel!" Landrew's voice was strained.

"What?" Axel moaned out slowly.

"Wake up, boy, please wake up."

"Why? I am still tired."

"Just get up, please!"

Axel pulled his arm down and squinted up at Landrew.

"What happened to you? You look terrible," Axel commented when he noticed the dark circles around Landrew's eyes, then he noticed all the others leaning in from behind Landrew. Axel slowly sat up as he looked from one face to the next.

"Did something happen?" he asked.

"Look at him," one of the men said softly and in wonderment. "Not a bruise or scratch on him, anywhere."

Axel ran a searching hand across his face, then he looked at his knuckles and down at his chest.

"How do you feel?" Landrew asked.

"I feel great," Axel said as he put his hands onto his chest. "Should I not?"

"Forget that I asked," Landrew said as he put a hand on Axel's shoulder. "So good to see you up, my boy."

"We should go inform the judges so Axel still receives his prize," Kalim commented. "Before they pass it along to someone else."

"You mean, I did beat Martin? I can't really remember what happened."

"Don't try too hard, to remember, I mean," Landrew said. "Just know that you did beat Martin, fair and square."

"That is awesome!" Axel said as he pushed the blanket back and got up without hesitation.

"See, I told you to give him time," Amy's voice came over the men that were gathered around Axel, she pushed through them and hugged Axel without warning.

"I think something very bad must have happened," Axel said as he put his arms around Amy.

"Why do you say that?"

"Because you are here, and you don't go traveling much anymore."

"You are such a smart boy," Amy said as she pulled away from the embrace, she reached up and lovingly patted him on the cheeks.

"Landrew!" Allen suddenly burst into the tent and skidded to a stop when he saw Axel standing.

"Axel!" he blurted out next, then he shook his head and continued in such a hurried spiel of words that it was a little difficult to understand him. "I just came across some men going through the area, they are searching everywhere, I overheard two of them talking. They work for some family of overseers who apparently have a very spoiled brat of a daughter named Florence."

Landrew and Axel both looked at each other.

"They really don't seem to like her," Allen continued. "But they have been ordered to find Axel, they know he is here somewhere, they know he is dying, they were told to speed it up. Axel, they are going to kill you!"

"Now I am positive I saw her," Axel said as he searched for his shirt and cloak.

"What are you going to do?" Landrew asked.

"I don't know yet," Axel said as he strapped on his belt and slid his small dagger to the side where it was more comfortable. "Where is my hat?"

"Here it is," Amy said as she held it out for him.

"Axel," Landrew said as he placed his hands on his shoulders. "You are a man, it is your decision what happens next, you can stay and fight or you can flee, we do not know why they wish you dead, but it does not make you less of a man if you leave now."

"I know why they want me dead," Axel answered. "She is seeking some kind of revenge. I think I will find her instead, I feel that a talk is long overdue for her and I."

Axel had taken an old cloak with a large hood and a staff in his hand, he kept his eyes half closed and his head deeply bowed as he slowly walked, the staff held before him as he went searching for Florence on the island.

"We will distract them as best we can," Landrew had told him as he suggested Axel dress as a blind man. Several times the guards searching for him ran past but they did not stop him, one of them nearly ran right into Axel but he merely cursed him for his stupidity and continued on his way, grumbling about having to find Axel of the Might. Axel grinned to himself as he listened to the guards passing him up to ask others where Axel of the Might was.

It did not take long for him to find the splendid tent that was set up just for Florence, he went to the side of it and listened. He could hear Florence singing to herself inside. Axel slowly leaned against the corner of the tent as he took in her words, it was an old love song that was popular in his small town many years ago, as he listened he began to feel a small ache in his chest.

"And you sleep tonight, upon my breasts,
Our hearts are one, beating in our chests.
And you sleep tonight, with your fingertips,
Gently touching, my soft round lips.
And you sleep tonight, dreaming so sweet,
Do you remember, how we used to meet...well, do you remember, Axel?"

Axel straightened from his position but did not move for a time, Florence moved toward him and struck at him from the other side of the fabric, her small fist billowed the fabric out and caught him in the shoulder.

"How did you know it was me?" Axel asked as he raised the bottom of the tent up and rolled into Florence's well-furnished room.

"I have been expecting you, ever since you saw me while you were fighting, such a barbaric thing to do." Axel looked at Florence and as she turned, her dress flared out from her finely shaped waist and her long black hair followed suit, Axel began to feel his knees tremble.

"Oh, I have missed you so much," Axel said softly as he slowly reached for her, Florence turned to look at him and her eyes wandered up and down his body several times before they settled on his face.

"My, oh, my, you have grown to be even more handsome." Florence turned away and delicately sat on the edge of her bed, bringing one leg over the other and exposing her bare feet and lower legs. "Come now, sit on the bed with me," Florence said as she patted the area right next to her. "We have so much to talk about."

"You are still so beautiful," Axel said softly as he moved forward but he did not sit next to her, instead he planted a hand on either side of her and leaned into her, pressing their lips together. Florence raised her hands to embrace Axel but he pulled away and stepped out of her reach.

"So many nights I had wished you were with me," Florence said as she fell back onto the bed, arching her back and pulling her collar down a little to expose the tops of her fleshy white breasts. "Come here, Axel, be with me," she fairly moaned.

"I cannot," Axel said softly though he felt the fluttering in his stomach and his very being wanted her. "I just wanted to see you, to know if it were still true between us, before I went on my way, it would seem that someone wants me dead."

"My brother," Florence scoffed. "I told him not to send the guards after you, he had no idea you were here, I did not tell him that I had seen you, he just found out this morning. But now you have seen me, so get away before the guards catch you and kill you."

"I just wanted to know, do you still love me? Will you still wait for me though it has been so long already, look, the scar is still there," Axel pulled down his shirt front to show the small X he had carved into his flesh, it was faded and nearly invisible but one could still see it once Axel had pointed it out.

Florence folded her arms as she sat up on her bed. "Many men want me," she said with a bit of anger. "My father wishes to marry me off as soon as possible but I keep refusing, you may have to wait even longer than you already have."

"I will make you mine, Florence."

"You have nothing to your name, you are still as poor as you were before…more so now for you do not even have a home anymore. Perhaps I do not love you anymore."

Axel wrapped an arm around her waist and brought her close, she trembled in his strong embrace, much stronger now than she had memories of, the blood rushed to her face and an involuntary moan escaped her lips.

"You still want me," Axel said and then they began to kiss each other. On the lips, on the face, on the neck, Florence leaned her head back and let out a giggling moan as Axel's lips made their way down her neck and to space between her breasts. Florence brought her legs up to wrap around Axel's waist and Axel took a step forward and laid her on the bed before him, still bent over her as he kissed her.

Light suddenly fell across them as someone pulled open the tent flap, Florence gasped as she scrambled to cover her exposure and Axel immediately fell to a defensive fighting position.

"You!" Harold growled deeply as his hand went to the dagger at his belt. "So you have come back to finish what you started, but I will finish you instead!"

"I don't want to hurt you," Axel said as he eyed the knife Harold had pulled out but he could see that Harold was not playing around as he leapt at Axel and nearly buried the knife into his flesh. Axel dodged just fast enough for the blade to miss his skin but not his clothing, a large cut appeared in the side of Axel's shirt that revealed his muscled flesh beneath.

"I will kill you," Harold spat as he leapt again. Axel dodged to the side and his hands shot out like lightning as he disarmed Harold.

"I don't want to hurt you," Axel said again as he held firmly to Harold's arm and spun him around to pin his arm to his back.

"Then I have the advantage," Harold said through gritted teeth. Harold swung his head back and smashed it into Axel's nose, Axel stumbled back as the pain radiated through his face, when he looked back up a moment later Harold was now holding a short sword.

"You have no honor," Axel said. "Killing an unarmed man."

"You should have thought of honor a long time ago when you tried to rape my sister." Harold took a step forward and made a wide exaggerated swing at Axel's head, it was easy for Axel to duck. A look of surprise came across Harold's face when he saw Axel drop down and then step forward to come back up inside of his swing, Axel looked Harold in the eye for a moment before he punched him squarely in the jaw. Harold reeled backwards, the sword fell to the ground with a heavy thud and a second later there was an even heavier sound as Harold hit the ground and lay still.

"I will be back," Axel said as he straightened his hat and raced out the tent door without a second look.

"What happened?" Landrew asked harshly when Axel and him met later that day in a secluded area. "You really are a dead man now, there is word all over that you killed Harold Azsin."

"Oh, no," Axel said under his breath. "I did not mean to, he came at me with a dagger and then a sword, I had to defend myself."

"Shhhh," Landrew pushed Axel into some thick brush and quickly followed suit, Axel gritted his teeth as he felt several thorns pierce his skin.

"There are guards all over looking for you," Landrew said a few minutes later after they watched several people pass. "They are employing others just to help look, you are to be killed on sight, Axel."

"I should have never went to see her," Axel seethed at himself. "Landrew, what should I do now, we are fairly trapped here."

"If we leave now we might be able to make it. There is no moon tonight and it is cloudy, everything is going to be pitch black. We would be flying blind but long as we get away I will be able to figure out where we are come daylight."

Landrew stopped and held his breath as several people came near again, they were looking intently on the ground and come straight for their hiding spot in the thorny underbrush. Axel and Landrew both held their breaths and studied the three guards, they were armed but they were also very young, probably inexperienced. Landrew motioned upwards and they both glanced up to see the brambles were thickly woven over their heads, Axel gave Landrew a look that said, "Greatest hiding place ever, you moron," and Landrew answered back with an apologetic shrug. They waited for the guards to come almost upon them when they burst out of the thorny brush and bowled them over. All three of the young guards went down hard and an arrow was loosed from a crossbow, it sang past Landrew's ear but he did not stop to check for injuries as they both rushed forward and upwards, their short traveling capes billowed behind them as they made their leaps and spread their arms, which were now graceful wings. The guards jumped back up, they may have been young but they had been trained well as they quickly brought their weapons about. One threw a spear at Axel and barely missed him, Axel dived to the left as the spear flew past between the two birds, Landrew screeched out in anger but they did not turn back to fight the young lads, they continued upwards and onwards into the gathering dusk.

"Landrew, I keep going over this in my head and I just don't see how I killed Harold. You taught me how to fight and I did not land a killing blow, I just knocked him out and left."

Landrew looked up at Axel from across the tiny mound of coals. They had flown all night and into the morning, they were both exhausted and frustrated for though Landrew had said he would figure out where they were, he did not recognize the horizon when the sun came up. Landrew poked a stick at the blue robin's egg that sat amongst the hot coals, he carefully rolled it over to its other side, now the scorched side was face up and Landrew studied the black against the blue for a moment.

"Then perhaps you did not kill him," Landrew said softly.

"Great, we can stop hiding."

"No," Landrew continued. "He is dead, I went and saw the body myself. But it was not from a fisted blow, he had a dagger in his back. And that beautiful woman that you are so in love with still, she was sitting there, holding his body and crying that a man with bright hair had done this. Axel, I think you were the only blonde man on the whole island, are you still so in love with that woman now?"

Axel could not answer, he only stared with wide concerned eyes into the fire as he took in what Landrew had just told him.

"Axel, from my understandings and what you have told me of Florence and her family, they are powerful and she is very spoiled and set in her ways. She is worse than a Sprite, the way she plays with your mind has you so twisted to worship her like this. I normally do not give advice on these matters because when it comes to one person loving another they will see their loved one as a god, or goddess in your case. But Axel, my boy, I urge you to forget about this woman, move far away, change your name, dye your hair if you have to and turn your back on her. So far nothing good has come from her and I feel that nothing ever will."

Axel still did not answer as he continued to look into the fire, after some time Landrew shoved the egg out with the stick and then tossed the stick on top of the coals, the stick flared up and then died down. Axel turned away from Landrew and lay down like a small child, his short cloak laid on the ground behind him like a pair of broken wings.

Chapter Thirty-two

"So, Axel had a bit of a rough life," Lance said as he put down his pen and looked up at Tulley.

"Indeeds," Jessica also commented as she sucked on the stem of her pipe. Tulley looked at the dead coals in the fireplace and then glanced toward the tiny window, the sun was beginning to rise and it bleached the sky with color.

"You should get to bed," Tulley said softly as he turned and stood up. "We have been up all night, the children will be awake soon and none of us has slept."

"It does not seem like we have been up this long," Lance said. "This story of Axel is fascinating, I wish you would continue."

"I'm sorry," Tulley said as he opened the door to get a better look at the sunrise. Lance and Jessica looked at him for a moment as he stood there, his figure framed in the doorway; he looked old and tired with his strong shoulders now slumped down. Tulley slowly raised one hand to his head and held his palm over one eye for a moment, then his knees buckled and he fell to the ground.

"I'm fine, I'm sorry I worried you so," Tulley told Jessica as she bustled around the room.

"You was shaking like a leaf, I will worry about you, Tulley," Jessica grumped as she wrung out another cloth and pressed it to the cut Tulley had received on the side of his head when he passed out.

"But I really am fine, it's just the after-effects of breaking the hold Gensieco had on me, and I probably should not have stayed up all night like that."

"And you tell me not to worry," Jessica said as she put her hands on her hips. "Men, you just can't take care of yourselves."

Tulley sighed and submitted to Jessica's banter, she was not satisfied until the bleeding had stopped, then she ordered Tulley to sleep and not leave his bed until she told him he could. Jessica pulled the heavy cloth curtain over the window and the room became dark, she then picked up her bowl and washcloth and shuffled silently out the door.

Tulley could hear Lance's soft breathing from the other side of the room, he had flopped down and fallen asleep as soon as Tulley had come around and told them he would be just fine. Tulley hunkered down on his small cot and was almost asleep when he heard the hoarse whisper.

"Tulley, are you awake?"

"Yes, Jarsic," Tulley said, rubbing his eyes. "What is it?" The curtain shifted a little and Jarsic's long fingered hand clasped the corner of the window from the outside, slowly he drew the curtain back and Tulley watched as he ducked into the room, pulling his long-limbed body through the small window like some sort of magic trick.

"Some of the younger ones have returned from gathering, they say there is smoke far to the east, much smoke, like a forest fire."

"Well, let us hope that is not what it is."

"They said the air is sweet with the smoke, like bodies burning."

Tulley bowed his head for a moment and tightly closed his eyes. "Has anyone gone to look?" he said softly, Lance grunted in his sleep and rolled over.

"No, it is of no concern to us, if it were Druids being killed then our ancestor would have told us so, but perhaps it is concern to you, that is why I tell you."

"Thank you, Jarsic," Tulley said as he ran a hand through his thick hair, he grimaced when his fingers touched the cut.

"Also," Jarsic continued. "They saw Gensieco traveling alone, she was going east."

Tulley hung outwards from the thin swaying branch far above the ground. Once Jarsic had left he rose and prepared for a journey without waking Lance, he scratched a note onto the parchment that Lance had been writing on through the night and then sneaked away. Hannie was happy to see him and she softly nickered as she trotted toward him, Tulley clucked his tongue at her and pressed his palm into her nose, she happily crunched on the piece of shelled acorn he had brought for her.

"All right, old girl," Tulley said softly as he slipped a bridal over her head. "I have a long journey and would like your company." Together they headed east and every evening Tulley would climb a tree as high as he dared to search for the smoke. It was the third day now and the smoke was barely a thin wisp rising up, the wind scattering it to nothing.

"One more day, I think," Tulley said to himself, then he looked down and descended back to where Hannie waited patiently for him. Hannie did not look at him as he descended, instead her eyes were fixed upon some shadows to their left, her ears pricked forward as she stood with her legs locked. Tulley stopped and clung to the tree bark still far above her, he knew if she had taken notice of something then it was something he should take notice of as well. As Tulley watched he saw movement from the shadows and ever so slowly a small hooded figure came forward, a small hand outstretched toward Hannie's nose.

"What is this?" Tulley said very quietly to himself for the figure below was a Sprite but it was not Gensieco. The Sprite very slowly rubbed Hannie's nose as she spoke softly to her, then she took hold of the reins and looked around searching for the rider. Tulley did not move, he merely watched as the Sprite leapt up upon Hannie's back and turned her to go east. Tulley finally came to the ground sometime later and looked at the tracks Hannie had left, he looked toward the east and then began to walk at a brisk pace following the prints.

Tulley came to the end of the tracks late in the evening, the sun was just descending and he climbed a tree to look over the carnage, it was as he feared. There had been a village here, a small one, but now it was only burned houses, butchered animals and several piles of thick black ash with bones sticking out of it here and there. There were still people wandering about but they were large rough men and each carried a weapon of some kind. Tulley closed his eyes tight when he heard a woman scream, of course they would kill all the men and keep most of the women and some of the younger boys alive; slavers did that. Tulley caught sight of the Sprite who had taken Hannie, she was now leading the horse through the burning rubble toward one large house that had not been burned, as she neared a woman who still had her hands bound, rushed out of the house, she was bare from the waist up and her skirts were terribly torn. A large man burst from the same house, he was enraged and had blood on his face, in just a few steps he was upon the poor woman and fairly laid on top of her as he took hold of her again, then he dragged her back to the house, all the while she was screaming at the top of her lungs. Tulley pressed his face into the bark of the tree as he tried to block out the tortured woman's cries.

Tulley stayed late into the night and attempted to count how many there were, it was difficult to do in the dark but his best guess was a little over thirty. It was well past midnight when the camp finally became silent and the fires had begun to die down. Tulley slowly began to descend from the tree, keeping his head on a constant swivel and stealthily walked through the quiet area, his bare feet kicked up tiny puffs of ash as he went. Tulley backed into the shadows against the wall of the large house and slowly snaked around to the back where he found a door, but upon trying the latch he found it bared on the inside by a man sleeping across the floor in front of it; the man made a growl in his sleep when the door softly bumped his back and Tulley shut it as quickly and quietly as he could. Just above the door was an uncovered window, Tulley bent his knees a little and jumped straight up, he barely got his fingers over the edge of the sill. Gritting his teeth he pulled himself up enough to peek over the edge and hung thus as he squinted into the darkness inside. He could hear breathing, some of it gentle and even and some of it was accompanied by whispers that he could not quite make out. Tulley strained his ears as he tried to pick through the soft muffled voices. His arms were beginning to shake when he realized they were speaking a language from the far south and suddenly everything clicked into place.

"I will help you," Tulley whispered and the voice from inside suddenly hushed. "Let me help you," Tulley whispered again as he strained to pull his body up farther and get his elbows onto the windowsill.

"Who are you?" a woman asked ever so softly.

"Someone passing through, they do not know I am here yet. How many of you are there?"

"Sixteen," the woman answered. "Mostly children. They killed all our men." There was a catch in the woman's voice and she became silent, then a different voice spoke.

"There are two men on the other side of the door, and we are all bound, including the children. There is nothing we can use to make a rope out the window except the clothes we are wearing."

"Let me figure that out," Tulley said as he managed to finally pull himself into the room, still just as silent as a shadow. "Are there any boys here?"

"No, not here. Something strange happened to them, and some of the men, they just put down their weapons and surrendered."

"They have a Sprite in camp, she is controlling them," Tulley whispered as he began to cut their bonds. Some of the girls were quite young, maybe four years old, Tulley's heart went out to them as they immediately wrapped their arms around their mothers or big sisters. He came across the woman who had been chased down and beaten by the man, she had tried to pull pieces off her skirt to cover herself, Tulley respectfully kept his eyes downcast as he took off his cape and shirt, he handed her the later to dress with.

Tulley held his cape up and began to carefully cut it into strips with his dagger, he did not wish to rip it for the harsh tearing noise of the heavy fabric would carry through the night.

"If I tell you which way to go can you all reach safety on your own?"

"Yes, of course," one of the adults answered.

"Good, I am going to lower you out of the window, stay in the shadows and if you notice someone just stop and do not move, cast your eyes down and keep your teeth covered if they have a torch. They will notice movement before anything else so that is the most important, do not move."

Tulley then slowly and painstakingly began to lower the women and children out of the window, once a few of the adults were down the children were next, then the remaining adults were last, then Tulley himself went through the window.

"What about the ones they did not kill?" one of the women spoke up. "I cannot leave without my son, he is still alive."

"I will go and look but you will have to leave," Tulley answered, the woman suddenly became defiant.

"There are far too many here for me to fight with just a dagger," Tulley hissed. "And if I run into the Sprite then I am as good as caught, I do not have the strength to withstand her magic right now. So move or be left behind."

Tulley began to walk away and the woman followed without question, they were nearly to what Tulley deemed was safe when one of the women stopped.

"Manjin," she said under her breath, then she began to run. Tulley wanted to cry out but knew he could not, so he raced after her. There was a young boy walking that the woman had seen and she instantly embraced him when she reached him.

"Manjin, we have to go," the woman said as she then stood with his hand clasped in hers, but he would not move. The woman was just looking back at her son with a questioning look when Tulley's hand clamped over his open mouth and instantly stifled the cry of alarm the boy was about to release. The boy struggled in Tulley's arms and the mother struck Tulley on the side of the head as Tulley very gently choked the boy. The boy went limp in his arms and Tulley turned to look at the woman.

"You," the woman began, her voice was louder than a whisper but Tulley immediately cut her off.

"He is not dead but we almost were, now take him and don't try to wake him just yet, not until I say so."

"Yes," the woman said with a trembling voice as she held the small limp child against her and fled back to the others.

"Do you see those two stars," Tulley said pointing into the sky. "Follow them at night, hide during the day. You will come across a tree that is king over the others, you will come across Druids. I will try to release the ones who are left but just in case I am delayed, ask for a Druid named Jarsic, tell him Tulley sent you. And once the sun comes up, if he is not awake yet," Tulley pointed to the boy he had knocked out, "you may wake him then and he should be just fine." The women were nodding but not moving as they looked at Tulley in the darkness, their sad eyes like hollow pits in their faces.

"Go," Tulley said urgently and they suddenly turned to leave. Tulley waited until he could not see or hear them, though they were silent as they could be he could still pick out the faint footsteps. Tulley turned back and ducked down, he took the dagger from his belt and looked at it for a moment, even in the darkness he could see just how sharp the blade was; this was not going to be easy. Slowly he made his way back into the area of ash piles, carefully searching for any signs of movement among the men who were sleeping near the beds of coals. Tulley stopped for a moment and lifted a jug that was sitting near the hand of a sleeping man, he sniffed the contents and found it to be a strong honey drink; he took a gulp and set the jug back down. Slowly he came back to the house that was not burnt and using two sticks, he raked a few coals from a nearby fire bed and carried them to the side of the house. He set the hot coals down and laid the sticks over them, then he cut a piece from the hem of his pants and gently blew on the tiny glowing lumps until he caught the rough woven fabric on fire.

Tulley stood back in the shadows and watched as the home quickly became engulfed, the men that were left inside came out shouting and cursing that the women were gone. A small handful of young men slowly filed out as well, they were not hurried and many of them just stood before the burning house and watched it as though they were in a daze.

Oh, come on, Tulley thought to himself as he searched for the one person he needed now, then he saw her. She was so small compared to the others that he had almost missed her flitting about in the flickering light, he watched as she gathered together the small knot of young men and boys they were keeping prisoner and marched them away from the blaze. The slavers did not seem to care that the house was a light, they ran about searching for any clues of the women's whereabouts; one of them did venture right to Tulley's hiding place and he couldn't resist wrapping his arms around the man's face and running the sharp edge of the dagger across his throat. The man fell at Tulley's feet, his body convulsing as his hands wrapped around his throat and the blood poured between his fingers. Tulley quickly moved to a different spot and continued to watch the Sprite that was still leading the boys away, after some time she stopped at the edge of what was left of the tiny town and they all turned as one and watched the men running around and the flames of the home licking across the walls and roof. Tulley stopped for a moment to take a deep breath, then he rushed forward and snatched the Sprite off her feet and disappeared back to the shadows, the strong little being fighting against the grasp Tulley had on her and trying to bite the hand that was over her mouth. Tulley stopped for a very short period and wrapped both arms around the Sprite as he whispered in her ear.

"I will not kill you," he said softly in her own language. "If you release them from your power."

"If I release them then they will kill me, she will kill me," the Sprite fairly spat at him once he loosened his hand enough for her to speak. Tulley heard the footstep before he felt the small fist hit him on the back of the head, it did not hurt, merely surprised him. Tulley looked up just as the small group of young men converged upon him, they kicked and punched at him as he kneeled on the ground still holding the Sprite in his arms. The punches and kicks did not hurt at first and Tulley curled his body around the Sprite as he tried to crawl forward with the tangle of angry boys around him.

"Tell them to stop," he told the Sprite as one young man grasped a rock and began to pound it against Tulley's shoulder.

"Never," the Sprite managed to say through his hand. Tulley shoved his way through the boys and ran with the struggling Sprite still held in his arms, she managed to bite his hand but he ignored her sharp little teeth and kept going with the boys following right behind. Luckily they were not shouting as they continued to chase him, if they were not under her spell of control then they would be yelling and whooping, but instead they ran madly after him like some sort of phantoms slowly but surely catching up with their prey. Tulley dodged around a few things but he could not step around the small figure that suddenly loomed up just before him; he fairly ran into the childlike figure and tripped in his attempt to avoid the collision. As Tulley went down he felt the Sprite pulled from his grasp, he hit the ground hard as the Sprite was yanked into the arms of the other still standing. Tulley heard one frightened cry come from the Sprite and then her body hit the ground next to him, blood blossoming out of a wound on her chest. Tulley looked at it in wonder for a moment before he looked up at the small figure before him; Gensieco stood over him with a bloodied knife in her hand.

"I will help you," she said softly as she respectfully cast her eyes downward.

"Are you sure we can trust her?" Jarsic said softly several days later when they had finally made it back at the great tree. Tulley looked at Gensieco and watched her as she was greeted by some of her friends upon her return.

"She has hardly spoken," Tulley commented. "And she has yet to look up from the ground. But if you are leery of her I will not stop you from watching her closely."

"I believe I will," Jarsic slowly answered back.

Chapter Thirty-three

Lance regarded Tulley and Gensieco for a few minutes as they stood side by side, they were both wearing brown and green clothes, they were both standing with arms crossed and they both had their hats pulled down so far that one could not see their eyes.

"They look like they could be older brother and younger sister," Lance commented softly to Jessica. "Or maybe even father and daughter." Jessica glanced up from her sewing and also regarded them, then she looked back to the needle that she expertly threaded through a new pair of pants for baby Bastian. Ever since Tulley brought Gensieco back with him she stayed by his side, she never tried to touch him or hug him anymore but she did not stray from him, and she always had her eyes downcast with her hat pulled down low, the way Tulley used to always place it on her head. Gensieco was silent for the first few days, it was not until the fourth day that Lance had heard her speak and then it was only a few words in her own tongue so only Tulley understood her.

"Why do you suppose she is so changed?" Lance asked Jessica, Jessica answered without looking up.

"Shes is brokens and lost. Shes has discovereds thats the mans she loves does nots loves her in thes sames ways. And shes dids somethings very bads to thes mans she loves ands is remorsefuls."

"I did not notice that she loved him so," Lance said as he looked back down at his writings.

"Because yous ares a mans," Jessica said with a slight huff.

"Right," Lance said as he gently rolled up his work and left Jessica sitting at the table. "I think I will go check the traps."

"Takes someones withs yous."

"I'll be fine," Lance answered.

"Why did he go by himself?" Tulley asked that night when Lance had not returned. "He knows that we have to be extra careful now with those slavers only a few days' journey away. I'm sure they are looking for the women and children still."

"I tolds him nots to gos alones," Jessica said. One of the women that Tulley had saved from the slavers spoke up and Tulley translated.

"My little one said she saw him going north, toward the water."

Tulley looked at Jarsic who was leisurely lounging on a chair, his long limbs folded in ways he found to be comfortable. "Are there still snares by the stream?"

Jarsic scratched at one of his tiny ears as he thought. "Yes," he finally answered.

"That's fantastic," Tulley said with his normal monotone voice. "He probably got snared by one of our own traps, I'm going to go find him."

"Should I go as well?" Jarsic asked without any sign of getting up.

"No," Tulley answered, but he stopped for a moment at the door and pointed a finger at Gensieco, motioning for her to follow. Gensieco jumped up from her seat in the corner and quickly fell in step behind Tulley as though she was trying to replace his shadow.

"Gensico," Tulley said some time later as they walked through the dark, the thin moon barely giving them enough light to see the way ahead. "Why did you kill that other Sprite?"

"She would have never let those boys go otherwise," Gensieco answered as if she had been expecting the question from day one.

"It was not for some other purpose?" Tulley noticed the hesitation in her step.

"No," she answered softly.

"Those are part of the same slavers I stole you from," Tulley continued, Gensieco stopped walking and after a few steps Tulley stopped as well and looked back at her.

"I had to free her," Gensieco said, a tiny hint of sorrow in her voice. "If I did not kill her they would have beaten her and raped her and starved her for losing the boys, I freed her."

"Like how you were starved and naked when I saved you?"

"Yes," Gensieco said softly. "They are very cruel men."

"You killed one of them recently," Tulley said it as a statement.

"How did you know that?" Gensieco asked with a slight tremble in her voice.

"I have seen far too much death to not know someone has killed, especially for their first time. It bothers you, I can see it when you look at nothing in the distance and remember, the emotion shows on your face."

Gensieco suddenly fell to her knees and began to cry.

"He was hitting me, with a split reed, it cut the shirt on my back and was beginning to cut my skin, and I looked at him, I was so angry, I looked at him and commanded him to die. He stopped, he took his own knife from his belt and slit his own throat. He was the first I have ever killed, I did not know my powers could do that to a man. And then the Sprite, it was so easy to do, the knife slid between her ribs so easily and I did not even realize exactly what I had done until we were walking back with the boys. But I keep telling myself that I released her, I saved her from a worse fate. Her spirit will wander a little and then settle and be reborn." Gensieco covered her face with her hands and her thin childlike frame shook as she silently sobbed. "I don't ever want to look a man in the eye again."

"It will be all right, Gensieco," Tulley said softly as he set his hand on her shoulder, her body stilled and she tried to stop sobbing. "There are times were you can help someone by looking them in the eye, if they are scared or in pain you can calm them. You will have to look them in the eye again eventually, but only when you are ready."

"I know," she said softly. "I do not want to but I have to." Tulley let her compose herself and as she slowly got back to her feet he squeezed her shoulder a little to reassure her that everything would be all right.

"Better now?" he asked softly.

"Yes," she sniffled a little.

"Good, now let's go and find this dunce."

"Oh! Thank Thorndin!" Lance called from the pit.

"I told you before, do not thank Thorndin, he was a controlling greedy bastard."

"Yeah, yeah, just get me out of here."

"Maybe," Tulley said as he and Gensieco both stood on the edge of the pit looking down at Lance.

"What do you mean maybe?" Lance called back up, frustration clearly heard in his voice. "Do you know how hard it is for a one-legged man to climb out of a pit? I have dirt in places it don't belong."

Tulley suddenly shushed Lance loudly and his head snapped up as he looked into the branches of a nearby tree, Gensieco swiveled her head around as well.

"I think there is something there," Tulley said softly a minute later.

"Can you see it?" Gensieco asked.

"No, I just have a feeling." Tulley let his eyes wander over the branches of the tree as his body remained motionless, after another minute of searching he slowly moved.

"I'm going to drop a few large sticks down to you, try to use them to climb high enough to grab my hand," Tulley said softly as he moved, his eyes still on the tree. A few minutes later Lance was struggling to climb the debris Tulley had dropped into the hole, it was hard for him to get a hold with his wooden leg and he fell back down several times but finally he was able to grab Tulley's hand and with a slight grunt Tulley pulled him from the pit. Lance crawled across the ground for a moment panting from the effort, he really was covered in dirt and his voice was hoarse from him calling for help.

"I am so thirsty," he fairly croaked.

"We shouldn't stay," Tulley said softly as he continued to study the nearby tree, Gensieco was beginning to be spooked by Tulley's behavior. Tulley pulled Lance to his feet and pushed them both forward; however, they had barely taken two steps when the shadows overhead moved.

"Down!" Tulley shouted as the huge owl swooped over them, its large taloned feet outstretched for the grab. Gensieco and Tulley both jumped in either direction and hit the ground but Lance merely fell forward and the owl was on top of him in a heartbeat, Tulley felt the air rush around him as the powerful wings of the night creature carried it back up into the tree. Lance was screaming in pure terror from the clutches of the large bird. The owl's foot was not big enough to completely encircle Lance's torso but its talons sank into his flesh and ensured he was not going anywhere. Lance felt the strength of the foot as it squeezed him and the sharp biting pain as his flesh was pierced, his own voice pierced the darkness as his body left the ground and he heard the whooshing of air on his ears; that sound was familiar to him and struck another fear into him. The darkness of the night and the whistling of the wind in his ears reminded him of the long fall in the darkness of that cave, the fall that was the cause of him losing his leg, the fall that changed his life forever; he shut his eyes and continued to scream as he waited for his body to hit bottom. The owl landed back in the tree and Lance's body was pinned beneath its foot, it knocked the air from his lungs and the talons only dug in deeper, Lance felt his head become light from the pain, he looked up and could see the huge globes of the owl's eyes looking back at him, the creature blinked slowly and then its sharp beak struck at him. Lance tried to move as best he could while being pinned down, the beak glanced off his shoulder and left a large tear in his flesh. Lance managed to find his voice again and cried out in pain and anger. The owl's head went up and it readjusted its foot, its talons cut through Lance's flesh in new places and it pressed him harder into the tree branch, this time making him completely immobile. Lance could not even turn his head to see the owl's beak coming down for another strike.

Tulley was suddenly standing over him, a sizable rock in his hand, the owl's beak was already coming for Lance and Tulley struck at it as it descended. The owl pulled its head back in surprise, its huge eyes blinked shut in pain and snapped back open as the owl screeched.

"Come on!" Tulley shouted as he threw the rock fast and hard right into one of the large eyes. The owl screeched again and spreading its huge wings it tried to fly backwards and away from Tulley but as it began to leave the branch Tulley yanked the dagger from his hip and leapt at the joint of the owl's wing where it joined to the body. The owl's wing fell limp and instead of taking flight from the tree branch the owl plummeted toward the ground with Lance still clutched in its foot and Tulley still stabbing and slicing at the wing joint. The owl's other wing flailed frantically as it tried to save itself from the fall, in the process it released its feet and Lance found himself in freefall just above the other two. Tulley looked up and saw Lance's limp form just above him, he knew they were going to hit the ground and Lance did not need to be injured further. Leaving his knife wedged between two bones in the owl's wing Tulley leapt upwards, his arms outstretched to grab Lance in the air. Lance felt Tulley's hands grab him and pull him closer, then they hit the ground. Tulley landed awkwardly and tumbled, Lance's added weight throwing him off. They both rolled a couple of times and finally stopped with Lance lying flat on the ground and Tulley kneeling over him.

Lance was gasping for breath as Tulley ran his hands over the numerous bleeding spots in his torso, Lance was covered in blood and it quickly stained Tulley's hands.

"Hey, it's okay now," Tulley was telling him. "I got you, you're okay." Lance finally managed to take one good breath and cried out in pain, then he clamped his teeth shut as Tulley pulled him to a sitting position to inspect his back. Lance had nearly a dozen spots were his skin had been cleanly sliced by the talons but they were not bleeding as bad as the rent in his shoulder. Tulley pulled off his new shirt that Jessica had just made for him and began to rip it, he glanced up at the owl, just a short distance away, as it continued to hop and stumble around, one wing flapping and the other hanging limp; Tulley would have to kill it before they left because he had sliced all the tendons in that wing and left the owl maimed for the rest of its life.

"Jessica is going to be upset," Lance managed to mumble as he laid on the ground and watched Tulley rip the shirt.

"She will be okay with me using the shirt for this," Tulley said as he ripped another strip.

"I wish I had muscles like you," Lance continued as he looked at Tulley's bare chest, his voice a little slurred.

"You're delirious, you don't want muscles like me," Tulley said as he leaned down and began to expertly bandage Lance's shoulder. "Now, be quite and concentrate on your body, tell me where it all hurts, does anything inside hurt?"

"No, actually nothing hurts right now, I am just so tired all the sudden. I think…I'm going…to sleep…." Lance's breathing became shallow. Gensieco finally came out of hiding and stood next to Tulley looking down at the bloody mess of Lance's body.

"Try to stay with me," Tulley said as he gently slapped Lance's cheek, Lance opened his eyes wide for a moment but they slowly began to close again.

"Hey!" Gensieco said as she pushed Tulley aside. "Tulley said to stay awake, so you have to stay awake."

Tulley leaned away as he watched Gensieco push her hat up and look down at Lance, their eyes met and Lance's eyes suddenly opened and his mouth went slack, his tongue slowly licked his lips.

"All right," Lance said, his voice suddenly clear. Gensieco stared at him for a few more long moments, then she stood back up and glanced toward Tulley.

"Thank you," Tulley whispered.

"Thank you, again," Lance said weakly the next day as he was propped up in bed and Tulley was helping him to eat some soup.

"You can't die now," Tulley said. "You still have to relay the history of Axel and let the world know that he is not an evil person."

"Yeah," Lance said slowly, he sat silently for a minute, his face in thought. "Hey, where is Axel now? He must be out there somewhere."

"I don't know," Tulley said softly. "He had a really rough time the last few generations, he doesn't want to be what he is anymore."

"What if he used his strength to help people, he might be able to end all the wars, he could even become an icon of hope to the people."

"He tried that for a time, but his image was already so blackened by what the council forced him to do, or blamed on him, that he is now a scary person that grown men fear and parents tell their children about to make them behave. If he were to appear now people would still be trying to kill him."

"But times are different, they might not be trying to kill him now. People are too busy trying to survive and avoid being forced into service by the young king."

"But people do not forget very easily, especially when it is something bad about a person, it is natural for people to gossip about all the bad someone has done but for some reason it is hard for them to talk about all the good."

"You are right," Lance answered. "I can understand why he is hiding, if I was the enemy of several kingdoms and feared by so many I would probably hide for several generations as well."

They did not speak for several minutes as Tulley continued to help Lance eat and drink.

"Do you miss him?" Lance suddenly asked. Tulley looked at him and was silent, Lance could see the tiny changes in his features that spook of a deep sadness, then his features hardened and he put the bowl down.

"No," he finally answered. "In the end, before he disappeared, he had become cruel and angry, he drank night and day and was constantly trying to kill himself. He killed others easily, even children, and he was finding that he liked to kill. So no, I do not miss him as he was then, I only miss him as he was before, before all the killing and hatred had corrupted him. I miss Axel, but not what he had eventually become, not the Black Sparrow."

Chapter Thirty-four

"He has been terribly quiet the last few days," Amy said softly as she scrubbed a dish in the slowly flowing waters before her, Landrew also held a dish and was rinsing out the remains of the food that had been cooked in it.

"He is still trying to figure out what path to take in his life," Landrew answered solemnly.

"Still no word back from your brother?"

"No, but I don't think we should wait around, he and his men are constantly traveling so the wind may not even know where he is from one day to the next," Landrew looked out over the slowly flowing water as it sparkled in the afternoon sun, he narrowed his eyes as he watched two small snakes, about the length of his arms, slowly glide with the water on the far side. One of the snakes stopped for a moment as its body curled around a submerged rock, then it continued on and Landrew stood up to watch until they were far down the stream and out of sight.

"I think I will just tell him where to go and what signs to watch for," Landrew continued as he knelt back down and finished washing out the pot. "Lando usually stays within a certain area depending on what time of the year it is, I believe Axel will find him eventually."

"That is probably for the best, the men reported some guards searching and asking about Axel just yesterday, they are getting closer each day; we may have to move our camp."

"I have thought of that, just never expressed my thoughts to the men yet," Landrew took the two clean pots in one arm and he held out his other hand to Amy, she took it and they both walked hand in hand back to their small home. Axel was sitting on the roof staring at nothing, a look of deep contemplation on his young face.

"I packed you some food, and here is some jars of medicine, for bites and sickness of the stomach," Amy held up the satchel for Axel to take. Axel looked at the leather bag and halfheartedly smiled at Amy as he put the strap over his shoulder and across his chest.

"And here is a new staff, no knots or weak spots, good for fighting," Kalim said as he held out a strong and smoothly carved staff that was about Axel's height.

"And this is actually from Hect but he couldn't be here, kinda sick at heart that you are leaving," Landrew said as he held out a cape that was made of supple mole skin, the soft silky fur on the inside for comfort and warmth. "He said he made it himself and this upper piece," Landrew indicated the piece that looked like a short cloak that was sewn over the mole skin from shoulders to waist. "It is squirrel hide for extra protection since mole skin is actually kinda soft and thin, it won't deflect a sword." Axel looked at the long cloak for a moment and he felt a tug in his chest, he was actually going to miss Hect.

"Tell him I said thank you," Axel said as he settled it onto his shoulders and connected the clasp.

"And I want you to take this," Landrew held out a plain dagger. "My brother should have one just like it so you two can recognize each other."

Axel deftly attached the dagger to his hip next to his own smaller one, he looked at the faces of everyone gathered around him for a moment and then he pulled his hat down over his eyes. Amy suddenly embraced him and so did Landrew, pinning them both in his arms.

"Now get out of here before you make me cry in front of my men," Landrew fairly laughed. Axel could not answer as the tightness of his throat made it hard to breathe, Landrew and Amy both stepped away and after a quick nod to them Axel looked up and jumped, his arms gracefully spreading outwards as the long cape waved a little behind him. The wind from Axel's wings stirred everyone's hair as they watched him rise up, as soon as he was gone a tear slipped down Amy's face, she glanced at Landrew and saw that he and a few of the others were silently but shamelessly crying as well; they all knew they may never see him again.

Axel flew for several days, not stopping to rest and doing his best to keep in the direction Landrew had instructed him to go. Far beneath him he watched the landscape change, different trees came and went, a large part of grassland passed below him and still he continued on without stopping; it was not until the fourth day that he decided he should probably stop and at least drink some water. Axel found a small swampy area and as he hung from a low-hanging tree branch he scooped up a little water in his hand and tasted it, it was brackish and silty, he spit the water back out and sighed heavily; now that he had stopped he was terribly thirsty.

Axel's heart suddenly jumped in his chest when he saw the pale woman swim by just beneath the surface of the water, she had nothing covering her well-shaped body and her skin was as pale as the inside of an oyster shell. The woman, for it truly was a woman and not some young undeveloped girl, slowly rose out of the water and looked at Axel with her large brown eyes. Axel stared at her for the longest time, his mouth slightly agape as he took in her beauty. She tilted her head a little, tiny rivulets of water ran from her wet hair down her face and naked body.

"I'm sorry," Axel finally managed. "I was just getting a drink but the water does not taste very good so I spat it out. I am sorry I spit in your pool."

The woman tilted her head the other way and blinked slowly a few times as she looked at Axel, then she gracefully raised her arm, her hand still hanging limp, once her arm reached the apex of the movement, she slowly raised her hand as well and pointed at something on the far side of the little swampy pond. Axel slowly turned his head, his eyes turning last 'cause he did not want to stop looking at the woman. Axel studied the far side for a short while but he did not see anything out of place, he looked back to the woman only to see her point at the far side once again.

"All right," he said softly. "I will go and look." Axel flew across the water and landed on the soft bank near the water's edge, as he dipped his hand into the water here he found it to be icy cold and fresh, an underground spring fed into this swamp. Axel fairly lapped up the water until he was satisfied and for a brief moment he had forgotten about the woman, until she once again rose up out of the water and stepped onto the soil near Axel, she moved past him and walked away without a backwards glance.

"Huldra!" Axel said under his breath as a terror deep in his chest grabbed him. He continued to watch her as she walked away, her pale naked body swaying with each step and her bare feet barely leaving any evidence of her passing through; the woman had a tail.

"Ello," the man called with a deep accent. "We don't see many people 'round here, you just passin' by?"

Axel had watched the tiny homestead for most of the morning before he had gone down to make himself known. There were two houses but only one had a family living in it, the man and his wife were old, their skin showing signs of aging, and they had four daughters, all of them grown women themselves.

"Just passing by," Axel confirmed.

"Told ya so, Papa," one of the women commented as she scraped at a squirrel hide that was stretched out before her, the man cleared his throat and smiled at Axel's raised eyebrow.

"We saw ya in yonder tree at first light and have been discussing what your plans would be all morning. We figured you were timid of strangers, and I do not blame ya on that, son, so we let ya come down in your own time."

"Oh," Axel said softly. "I thought I had a good hiding place."

"Ya did, son, but we are trackers, hunters, we have trained our eyes over many years to pick out certain things around us, we do not look for movements, but shapes and colors that do not blend just right."

"You are very handsome," the man's wife cut in as she reached out and fingered a lock of Axel's blond hair. Axel took a step back and the man took his wife's arm and brought it back down.

"Sorry, son," the older man said as he tucked his wife's arm into his own. "It has been a very long time since we have seen a young man come through. Please stay for a bite with us, and some drink. My daughters are all very good cooks and they would love for you to stay."

"I really should be going," Axel said slowly as he felt the presence of the four daughters surround him and a sinking feeling began to settle into his stomach.

"That's mole skin!" one of the daughters suddenly blurted out as she took hold of the cloak Axel wore. "Did you make it?"

"No," Axel said as he turned and pulled the cloak from her fingers, in doing so he backed into the old man and his wife, though they had also taken a step forward to make the encounter possible. The man's hands were suddenly clasped on Axel's shoulders and the daughters crowded in closer.

"Stay for a bite," the man said again. "You will not regret it. You and my daughters can share the other house tonight, it will make a beautiful home if only I had a son-in-law to live there. And blond babies would be such a blessing."

"No! Sorry!" Axel blurted as he suddenly ducked down out of the man's grasp and sprang forward knocking into the daughters' knees and bowling three of them over. The fourth daughter lunged at Axel, her hands reaching for his arm but she hit the ground and only found two wing feathers grasped in her hands, a sparrow flew straight up with a screech of anger and pain.

"I have something that belongs to you!" the woman called out as she waved the feathers around. "I will keep them forever and if you wish to come back for them...I will be right here!"

Axel flew awkwardly with the two missing primary feathers, he glanced back several times in case one of them could also fly but no one followed and after leaving that small homestead far behind he finally breathed easier and slowed his flight a little.

"Ouch," Axel commented to himself dryly when he landed later in the day and inspected his arm; the woman's fingernails had left four furrows across his forearm that leaked out little lines of blood. "Of course, I don't see a soul for days except for something that might eat me and the first normal-looking place I come across is filled with women who want to have babies."

Axel shook his head as he rummaged in his satchel and took out one of the small ointment jars, he dipped one finger into the brown paste and rubbed a little smear across each rip on his forearm.

"I suppose," Axel said and he continued to talk to himself. "I can walk for a while, maybe even run. That would please Landrew, to stay on top of my endurance."

And so for several days Axel ran, walked, took naps in sunny spots in the afternoons and talked to himself as he traveled on the ground giving his arm time to heal so he would have a full wing next time he needed to fly. He did not come across any other people, only the wildlife that merely glanced at him and sensing his calm un-harming attitude, they turned back to what they were doing and did not bother him. Several times Axel did steal an egg from a nest and ate them raw as he traveled. Late one evening he found a rabbit den and made off with a newborn rabbit, this he had to build a fire to cook and he ate nearly all of the sweet tender meat that very night. And so it was with a warm, cozy place to sleep, a quite night and a full belly that caused him to sleep past sunrise.

Axel was suddenly wakened by several sets of hands grabbing him and pinning him down, his first thought was the old man and his crazy daughters had found him, but soon as he opened his eyes he saw that it was actually four tall and manly figures with scarves pulled over their faces. Two of the men were pinning him down while the other two stood back and watched, they obviously thought their comrades could handle Axel alone.

With a cry Axel twisted his body around with a strength that caused surprised looks to cross the eyes of the two men. Axel hooked one leg around one of their ankles and rolled to the side, knocking the man's leg out from under him and nearly toppling him, the man fell to the side but he did not let go of Axel yet. Axel gripped his wrists in his hands and digging his fingertips into pressure points that caused the man's hands to spasm, he twisted them off and then, twisting his body around the other way he gave the other man a swift jab with his knee. For a moment that man continued to grasp Axel but then Axel gave him another jab and the man hit the ground and curled up like a child. The other two men were nearly upon him before he could get up, Axel swung one arm out and hit the man nearest in the stomach, this man faltered in his step but did not stop advancing. Axel had reached for his staff but found it was not where he had left it, they had flung it away from him as he slept, Axel also found his daggers to be gone from their sheaves.

"Damn me," Axel said as he considered for a moment if he had actually been sleeping so heavy that they could disarm him. Axel managed to get his feet under him just before they were upon him again, one of them was still on the ground, though he was attempting to get up now, the other three quickly made a triangle around Axel and fell into fighting stances; Axel did the same.

"Like to fight, huh," one of the men said from beneath the face scarf.

"You don't know who you are messing with," Axel said as his eyes quickly took in weak points of each man.

"Come on, pretty boy!" another man said as he took a step closer, Axel did not wait for him to make a move, instead he moved faster and swung his leg around to slam his foot against the man's jaw. The man's head snapped to the side and with a groan he hit the ground completely unmoving, his arms and legs laying in uncomfortable-looking positions.

"And then there were two," Axel said with a grin.

"Three," the man on the ground grunted as he finally managed to stand.

"Two and a half," Axel sneered as he shrugged his shoulders a little. Axel ducked as one man came forward swinging, then a second came right behind and landed a hard kick to Axel's thigh that made his leg go numb and nearly toppled him.

"We can go one on one if you really want to," one man seemed to chuckle.

"I got this," Axel said. "Just warming up...come at me!" The three men glanced at each other for a moment and then with a shrug they did, all at once. Axel leaned backwards as the closest man aimed his fist right for his face, the man's arm was now outstretched over Axel's body and he grabbed it in his hands. Gripping the man's arm, Axel turned on him and used his momentum to throw the man forward and away from the fight, from the corner of his eye Axel saw the next closest of the three and he kicked out and planted his foot firmly into this man's chest as he released the other's arm, both men went down hard and the third man paused for a moment. The two downed men looked at Axel with anger, and a hint of awe, then they shook off the hurt and was back on their feet going after Axel once again.

Axel took several well-placed blows and gritted hit teeth through the pain but he landed just as many blows against them, his limbs striking out faster and harder than they were and his moves better executed. After just a few seconds one of the men fell with blood gushing from his nose, he rose back up slightly and fell again, this time he stayed down.

"Two!" Axel shouted as he shoved another man back and immediately made an onslaught of fast, hard punches to the man still before him. The man went on the defensive and blocked almost everything Axel threw at him, his companion jumped back into the fray a moment later, making it two against one again. Axel narrowed his eyes and looked right into the eyes of one of the men, the man saw the power behind the glare and faltered for just a moment.

"One!" Axel shouted as he stepped into the man's body and gave him a powerful uppercut to the jaw, he then immediately stepped back as he barely avoided a well-aimed kick for his kidneys from the last man standing.

Axel and the remaining man stared at each other for a moment, then with a cry they each lunged at the same time, their fists swinging forward for each other's head. At the last moment Axel pulled his head down and was barely missed by the blow, the other threw up his arm and took the hit with his forearm but Axel could see in his eyes that it hurt him. Axel suddenly grinned, he had expected the man to block his blow, had hoped he would, and now that he was face to face with the man he grabbed the man by the shirt front with his free hand and slammed their foreheads together.

They both staggered a few steps back from each other and Axel blinked away the stars as he watched the last man crumple, he felt a tiny line of blood run down the bridge of his nose and he swiped his hand across his forehead.

"And then there were none," he said to himself since the four men before him were unable to hear at the moment. Axel looked toward his satchel that was several steps away and went to it, he sat down heavily and began to rummage through it looking for the jar of brown paste, he noticed a large shadow move across the ground near him and he looked up to the tree branches overhead.

"Well, damn," Axel said aloud as he suddenly noticed the others who had idly stood by and watched their fellow men be pummeled. Axel stood up and slowly turned in a circle as he silently counted the stationary men standing or sitting on the branches overhead, most of them had their faces covered like the first four, some of them had their scarves pulled down and some were even completely bare headed, their black and brown heads desperately needing a good haircut. Axel counted thirty-one of them by the time he made a full circle; he sighed as he dropped his satchel and picked up his staff instead.

"All right," he said. "Now there are thirty-one of you and only one of me, who wants to die with me?"

Without warning about half of the men converged upon him at once, leaping from where they were and falling straight down on top of Axel. Axel saw his dilemma and jumped up as if he wished to meet them in midair but instead he changed and tried to pass them. Axel beat his wings as hard as he could and almost made it past the group of falling men but one of them reached out and caught him by the foot, and in turn several of them grabbed that man and Axel found himself plummeting with the group. Axel immediately changed back, the staff still in hand, and began to beat the men around him. He managed to get several good hits in before they all hit the ground, Axel felt a pain in his hip and the air was knocked from his body with such a force that for a moment he feared he would pass out. Axel found himself immobile as he struggled to take in a breath, the staff was ripped from his grasp and as he looked up at the man now standing over him he saw a large bird just behind the man, flying toward them with large wings spread and bright red head blazing in the sun. Axel's own staff was swinging for his head when he suddenly realized who the bird was and a cry of Landrew's name escaped his lips just before the blow sent him plummeting once again, this time into darkness.

Chapter Thirty-five

Axel came to his feet ready to fight, he wasn't sure why, it just seemed like the right thing to do. He felt that he had missed something, he knew he had been fighting and then there seemed to be an empty space, where he just floated while everyone else around him was frozen. It was the last he remembered seeing and it stuck to his mind like a frozen land-scape and he was able to move around it and study the image before him.

Axel stood for a time, his feet planted and his fists raised, he shook his head and the frozen image dissipated to reveal a sunny spot in the forest with a handful of men milling around. A few of them looked at him but then continued with their tasks, most of them took no notice of him; Axel was confused. Axel saw his satchel and staff on the ground where he had been laying, his knives were back at his belt as though they had never been touched, Axel ran his hand through his unruly hair as he wandered if he had just dreamed the whole fight, but then where did these people come from? Axel tossed the satchel strap over his head and picked up his staff, he turned around in a circle looking for his hat and finally found it tucked away inside of the satchel, he pulled it out and fit it firmly onto his head. Axel began to walk amongst the men, his head swiveling back and forth as he studied what they were doing, he immediately noticed that there were no women, it was just like Hect's camp. One of the men passed by close enough for Axel to catch his sleeve.

"Where is Landrew?" Axel asked, but he didn't get much of a response, the man merely shook him off his arm and tilted his head in a direction. Axel looked toward the way the man had indicated and saw a circle of men sitting on the ground, pipe smoke curled up around them and each of them had some kind of container in their hand that they were drinking out of. A couple of millipedes were wrestling on the ground inside of the circle, each as thick and long as a man's leg. Axel immediately saw the red hair as Landrew sat facing away from him, he was sitting cross-legged and leaning over to watch the millipedes and poke at them with a stick.

"Landrew!" Axel called out. The man slowly turned toward Axel as Axel quickly walked toward him. That same large smile was on Landrew's face but Axel suddenly stopped when their eyes met, something was strangely different. They were the same eyes, same shape and color, but there was a wildness to them like Axel had never seen before.

"Come here, little brother!"

"You, are not...Landrew," Axel said as the man rose up and Axel took a step back. The man began to laugh and so did the others in the circle.

"No, I am not, but I am happy to see that my brother still does not tell people about us. I am Lando, Landrew's younger twin brother!"

Axel took another step back, still in shock that this man before him, who looked so much like Landrew, his mentor, his father figure, his best friend, and yet it was not Landrew. Lando grinned widely as he clasped his hands behind his back and rocked back and forth on his feet while he watched Axel, something Axel had never seen Landrew do before.

"Do you need to sit for a little while, little brother? Perhaps have a drink or two?"

Axel did sit down but he did not take any drink, he rubbed his hands over his face for a little while and kept looking at Lando with knitted brows.

"I am so glad you are not damaged," Lando said after several minutes of Axel scrutinizing him. "My big brother would never forgive me if something happened to you, he spoke so highly of you in his letter, he may just come and break my handsome nose if I had let anything bad happen."

"My head does hurt," Axel said from behind his hands.

"I just received Landrew's letter a few days ago and I have been out looking for you," Lando continued as though Axel had never spoken. "When I heard there was a stranger in the area I rushed right over, I knew it was you soon as I saw that unique blond hair."

"Unique, that's a big word for you, Lando," one of the nearby men laughed.

"Sorry I couldn't get to you sooner, lad, I would have saved you the headache and my fear of a broken nose."

"You didn't look so scared to me when I came around," Axel said as he glanced at the millipedes that were still entwined in mortal combat. "Looked like you were drinking, and gambling."

"Yes, well, I do have my vices," Lando chuckled as he rubbed his hands together.

"You are a lot wilder than Landrew, aren't you?"

"Yes, good observation, Landrew said you were smart. I do like to live on the wild side. My brother seems to have gotten all the virtues while I got all the vices. I am impatient and do not plan ahead very well, unless it comes to battle tactics, I like my drink and I love my women," Lando put an emphasis on the word "love" as he smiled devilishly. "But don't let some of the rumors fool you, they are spread by the ones who do not like me and wish to kill me, I am in truth a good man, just a wild one. But never fear, little brother, Landrew did right by sending you to me, I will look after you as well as he did and I feel we will be great friends."

331

"Great," Axel commented without enthusiasm.

Lando did live up to his word, he was wild, but he was a good man. Their little group traveled a little every day, hunting and enjoying a leisurely life. Each man had a pack of a few essentials, usually a bedroll or hammock, medicines, bandages, a few small tools and small weapons. Axel soon discovered why he had not seen any women, they were indeed there, but it was as though they were another little band of renegades all on their own. By the fourth day they appeared. Axel awoke to a big stir in the camp, when he asked Lando what was going on he answered with a giddy laugh.

"Women! The women are returning, with food and drink and they will be ready for lovemaking!"

"Oh," was Axel's only answer. The women did return that day, there was only fifteen of them and they were dressed like warrior princesses. Each had a few pieces of jewelry that they wore with a flourish, some had little sparkling tiaras woven into their dark wild hair, and each one had a long bow and some sort of short sword. They were dressed in well-fitting leather armor and walked with an air of authority. They seemed to appear from nowhere, one moment all the men seemed to stop what they were doing and turned as one and the women were stepping forth from the underbrush, as they did so Axel caught a whiff of perfume on the air. The women also carried a pack on their backs much like Lando's men, and they all had a wildness about them.

"They are not ordinary women, are they?" Axel asked softly.

"No, not exactly. This group of gorgeous ladies are actually all half-breeds, one parent was a Little Folk like us, the other was a fairy or forest spirit of some kind. You know the Bloody Bitch frowns upon that, many years ago she made a decree that all half-breeds would be put to death, these are some of the women she could not beat. A half-breed man can hide their looks much easier than a women, so these lovely ladies travel this area and find other half-breeds and help them hide from the queen's grasp…although there is an old rumor that the queen is a half-breed herself."

"Lando!" one of the women called out as she strode forward, Axel took an involuntary step back. This woman was a full head taller than Lando, with breasts that threatened to fall out of her straining shirt. Her arms were long and muscled and she carried a full barrel strapped to her back. Lando ran a few steps toward her and fairly jumped into her arms like a child would to his mother, except he immediately buried his face between the huge fleshy mounds on her chest.

"Costinier!" Lando cried out as she dropped him back to his feet. "My lovely queen of the woods! How are you and the ladies?"

"We are quite well, thank you for asking," Costinier spoke deeply, her voice resonate and strong. "We have not seen you all in such a long while, are you ready for some fun tonight?"

"Why wait till tonight?" Lando teased as he wrapped his arm around her thick waist and pulled her closer. It was strange to Axel to see Lando looking up to a woman, he was a tall and trim man just like Landrew. Axel shook his head, he still was not used to this not being Landrew.

"He is new," Costinier commented as she indicated Axel.

"That is my little brother, he has been staying with Landrew but got into a bad spot so he came to travel with me. He is a smart young man and Landrew would break my nose if anything were to happen to him."

"Do you wish for a woman tonight?" Costinier asked, Axel was slightly shocked at her bluntness and he felt his face grow hot.

"You are cute when you blush," Costinier smiled at him.

"No, thank you," Axel said. "I think I will take a turn as lookout now."

"Good, little brother!" Lando laughed. "But you know, it is okay if you have actually never been yet…just say the word if you want a young lady to warm you up, Costinier has a sweet young thing that will be gentle."

Axel merely walked away without answering.

"Something is hurting him inside," he heard Costinier say softly to Lando.

"I know," Lando said just as softly but with a gentle concerned tone in his voice that made him sound just like Landrew.

The merriment lasted all night and Axel was surprised that there were actually no naked bodies or couples sneaking off to have sex somewhere in the darkness. There was drinking and dancing and a lot of hugging and holding, kissing and caressing but everyone kept their clothes on, even Lando. Lando came looking for Axel late in the morning, his eyes were bloodshot from lack of sleep and too much drink but he was smiling, nonetheless.

"Not what you expected, huh, little brother," Lando said as he clapped Axel on the back.

"No, I thought it was going to be a big orgy or something."

"I am not that wild, we all have duties that we wish to fulfill and having children is not one of them right now. Costinier and her women are good people, but they would not be able to continue fighting against Queen Charlotte if they were pregnant or trying to raise a baby. But sometimes we all just need a really good cuddle, so that is what happens when our paths cross."

"Are you and Costinier actually sweethearts?"

"What do you mean, little brother?"

"Will you get married once all this is over?"

Lando regarded Axel for a moment. "You really did come from a noble family, and was very sheltered as a child," he laughed as he said the last part. "Little brother, you can lay with a woman that is not going to be your wife."

Axel's face changed a few shades and Lando laughed heartily.

"Is that why you ran away last night, little brother? You have a sweetheart somewhere back home?"

"Sort of," Axel sighed. "I pledged myself to someone, made a promise to her before I found out just how rotten she is. But she is so beautiful...," Axel sighed.

"There is something about promises that we lesser people believe, they are meant to be broken. Now you came from a good household and I understand if you wish to continue to hold to your promise, because I am sure you were taught that your word is your bond, but there is no need to be miserable for the rest of your life."

Axel nodded a little at this as Lando reached out to squeeze his shoulder.

"Now, you hungry? You have been out all night on guard duty, Costinier has informed me there is a grouse caught in a live trap not far from here, let us go get it and have a feast tonight!"

The bird was huge and they needed four men to finally subdue it, its leg was caught and it flapped wildly and fought every time one of the men got close to it. Costinier stood back and laughed at them every time one got knocked down by the bird, one of the men got a good peck to the back of the head and another was sent reeling cartwheels across the ground.

"Lando, some of your new men just might starve if they were ever on their own," Costinier commented as she watched, her large arms folded across her ample chest causing her breast to bulge even more. "Why don't you send in the cute one? I heard about his valiant fight against all of your men at once."

"Ah, that is just a rumor," Lando laughed as they watched yet another man get knocked down. "He beat four of them at once and then tried to flee once the whole lot of them descended upon him, he almost made it too."

"I hear his spirit is a cute little sparrow, I would like to see that some time."

"Hmmm, he has been having trouble with that though, being so far away from home, it tires him out immensely."

"Tssk," Costinier shook her head. "You know how these things fascinate me, I love seeing you Little Folk change because I, being a half-breed, cannot."

"Axel!" Lando suddenly cried out. "This has gone on long enough, show these idiots how to do it! Get above it, then dive down and break its neck!"

Axel nodded to Lando and a second later a brown sparrow flitted straight up over the grouse and, turning downward, pulled its wings in to speed up the dive. During the descent the sparrow changed back into Axel's human form and at the last moment he flung his arms out as his foot was aimed right for the bird's neck; he missed. Axel's foot parted the puffed-up feathers of the bird's neck and his body slide right past the bird's slender neck, but reaching out at the last moment he wrapped his arms around it and held on as tight as he could. The bird instantly began to flap and fling its body around as Axel tightened his grip, his feet finally touched the ground and he pushed backwards, forcing the bird to stumble forward and come off its feet. The bird could not breathe as Axel was choking it with his fierce grip and it only took mere moments for the bird to finally stop and lay still.

"Good save, little brother! Fast thinking to grab it around the neck when you missed like that, are you okay?"

"Yeah!" Axel said with a grin. "That was actually almost fun, I have never taken down a bird like this before."

"Well, I am sure it won't be the last time," Lando said as he grasped Axel by the shoulders and gave him a good hearted shake.

"Lando...."

"Hmmm?"

"Why do you and Landrew live so far apart from each other? Is there bad blood or something?" Axel had asked the question later on as everyone was feasting on the tender bird.

"Not exactly, not between him and I anyway. It's really because he has an obsession with Max, and the crimes he did a long time ago.... I do not blame him for still holding a grudge and it does not surprise me that Landrew never told you, he still grieves though you would never be able to tell," Lando became silent for a moment as he looked into the fire before them, then he tossed in the bone he had been gnawing on and leaned back against Costinier's ample chest, she put one arm around him in turn and splayed her hand across his chest, gently massaging it with her fingers.

"I have heard of that name on several occasions but once, when I asked who it was, Landrew just said it was no one for me to worry over," Axel commented.

"Max is actually our cousin," Lando said as his eyes seemed to turn hazy with remembrance. "We all grew up together like brothers, Max lost his parents in one of the wars. Because we came from slaves, my parents still worked in the courts of the Bloody Bitch, and so in turn we did as well soon as we were old enough. Landrew and I despised the fact that we were all slaves but Max looked upon it as a blessing and he loved the queen so much that I am sure he would have married her if he ever had the chance. Once our parents passed away from a sickness that went through the slave quarters, Landrew and I then made a plea for our freedom. We discovered that if we became good enough fighters we could become mercenaries, and the queen will actually pay mercenaries for every head they take on the battlefield. And so after several years of very hard training we were finally able to show our talent at the Pond Island meeting…hands down we won, beat every single one of the others, including the queen's favorites. So she actually granted us our freedom, this was during a time that she was actually a little bit generous, but she would not pay us since we came from a slave family. We traveled around and fought in a few wars and was able to make our way as assassins, but during all that time Landrew stayed in touch with a childhood sweetheart from the queen's court. Her name was Odessa Dale Hearting, a noble woman, and so beautiful. She actually worked within the queen's chambers, we all loved her, including Max, but over the years I did not stay in touch with her and Max only spoke to her because he wanted to be close to the queen, which eventually worked out for him because now he is one of her generals. Landrew though, he constantly wrote letters to her and eventually he left the battlefield, built a stunning little house with a few good neighbors in the area and she left the palace to be with him. They had three strong young sons and Landrew could not have been prouder. I came to visit quite often and was beginning to think of settling down myself. One thing never changed, though, Landrew and I hated the queen and what she was doing. Every chance we got, we would foil her attempts of using slaves on the battlefields, ambushing and releasing the poor souls she was using to fight her enemies. We stole from her as well, one time we made off with almost one hundred war horses, each one being ridden by a slave; that was a triumphant night. But eventually Max found us, he played it off as a social visit and though we were leery of him we never thought he would go as far as he did. He drugged the water and lit the house on fire. The drugs made us all dizzy, we could barely walk. I can remember seeing Landrew run through the flames, Odessa and the boys were still in the house, Odessa was screaming for Landrew. I ran in to help but the smoke was so thick I couldn't see anything. The roof collapsed on us, not quite burying us, but knocking us down. Landrew was knocked out and I was able to grab a hold of him and drag him back outside, I ran back inside though I could not hear Odessa screaming anymore, I did not know where she was; it was chaos. One of the neighbors had seen the flames and came to help, he actually saw me run back inside and went in after me, it's the only way I am still alive. We were burned, not too badly but enough to put us in bed for a while," Lando stopped for a moment and rolled up one sleeve to show a large red scar that covered his right shoulder. "Until that night Landrew and I were identical, he didn't get a scratch on him," Lando chuckled softly as he rolled his sleeve back down. "We would have only been in bed for a day or two but the drugs made us sick for weeks, and once Landrew realized what had happened he nearly gave up entirely. I convinced him that he had to stay alive to avenge Odessa and the boys, we had to continue to fight against the queen and now we had to find Max and kill him as well. He finally made up his mind that he would avenge Odessa but he decided he would not kill Max, at least he would not let the hatred consume him anyway. He is truly a better man than I am, I would have gone out of my mind trying to hunt Max down and kill him. But Landrew could always see into the far future and he is constantly thinking about how things are affected by people's actions and what the outcomes may be. Me, well, I just jump into anything with fists flying. Eventually we decided it was better if we continued to attack the queen from different areas, so we created different camps. At first it was just Landrew and I, but now there is Hector leading a camp, Costinier has her little group and we hear rumor there are two other camps that are masquerading as us, which is fantastic because it only confuses Max on where we actually are…so there is some history on the famous Land brothers, very sad but it is how we got to where we are now."

,

Chapter Thirty-six

Axel eventually did look upon Lando as a great friend, not quite a father figure like Landrew had been, more like the crazy uncle that everyone liked to spend time with. Lando's group was constantly moving, never staying in the same place for more than a day. They usually traveled in zigzags, sometimes they would circle around a large area and sometimes they would follow a stream or the edge of a pond for days. They would go for weeks of not seeing any other Little Folk, sometimes they came across forest people, fairy folk, Druids, the occasional Sprite, and once Lando had to save a couple of his men from a Huldra. The year went by quickly and Lando taught Axel everything he knew about reading the terrain, studying the weather and making maps, which was a pastime that Lando actually enjoyed. During this time Axel became much more in tune with the nature around him, he learned how to draw some power from the wood and in doing so was able to change to his sparrow form without much issue. Though Lando acted like an impatient child at times and was continually doing things without thinking, Axel was constantly amazed at his sheer knowledge of fighting and surviving without food or shelter on a daily basis. They saw Costinier and her women once more that year, this second time around Axel drank with Lando and woke up the next morning with his face against Costinier's chest, she was holding on to him as she slept reclining against a small tree. Axel decided he would not regret waking up like that.

Lando and his men stole from some of the people they came across, if they were loyal to the queen they usually took everything including their clothes and left them naked to the elements. If it was merely a stranger but had riches they usually took half of their wealth, and if it was a poor person, they would invite them for dinner and send them away with more than they had before.

It was a day in late spring when they got word of Max being in the area, one of the men had spotted the camp when they were out checking the traps they had set the day before.

"There is a clearing over yonder, to the east, I could smell smoke so I went to investigate and saw the camp. There are a lot of men there, four times as many as we have, and there are even more combing through the wood. They came across one of the traps and I suppose that is what set them off to search."

Lando rubbed his hands across his face and sighed, then he turned to the half-finished map he had been working on.

"The clearing is here," he pointed out as he leaned over the map.

"Yes, that's it," the guard answered. "And I saw signs of men through this area," the man ran his own finger across the other charted area of the map. "But no signs over here," then he ran his finger across an area that was barely mapped out.

"Well, we have been in worse scrapes. See if you can find the others who went to check the traps and we will leave this area as soon as they get back."

The guard nodded and as he turned on his heel he turned into a large hummingbird that made a loud buzzing sound as he flapped his wings mercilessly.

"Damn the luck," Lando said more to himself as he leaned over the map and studied all the delicate thin lines that he had spent hours working on, marking down the terrain around them as they traveled. Axel began to lean in and look as well, Lando leaned to the side to give him room and just at that second an arrow whizzed through the narrow space between their heads and thudded into the ground near Lando's knee. Lando and Axel didn't even take the time to see what had caused the air to stir and whistle, they knew it had to be an arrow and without hesitation they both rolled backwards and away from the map that was splayed out on the ground. Two more arrows hit the ground following Lando as he rolled away, each one just barely missing him.

"Follow and anticipate where I will be next!" Lando shouted as he jumped up and grasped a bow from the air that someone had tossed to him. Lando pulled one of the arrows from the ground and jumped straight into the air as yet another arrow barely missed him. It only took Lando a half-second to notch the arrow and pull it back in the bow, he pointed it in the general direction it had come from and released it. There was a shout as the hidden figure in the tree leapt out of the arrow's path.

"Got you!" Lando shouted with a laugh, then he gasped a little as an arrow from another assailant grazed his thigh and left a bloody line across the new rip in his pants.

"Damn my luck!" Lando shouted as they all looked up and saw men reigning down upon them, like locusts from the trees. Lando and Axel came together, each now grasping their own short sword, as they prepared to fend off the enemy that had somehow sneaked up on their little group.

"You ready for this, little brother?" Lando asked as he swung at the head of the nearest enemy.

"Of course, the great Land brothers are my teachers," Axel answered as he delivered a crippling kick to one man and swung a killing sword blow at another. Lando's men that were good with bows immediately took up places of defense, they were much quicker to take down the enemy bowmen than the enemy was at taking down them.

"Like a charm!" Lando cried out with laughter as his men took to their positions without hesitation or orders. They had all been trained well by Lando and being such a small band of men, they all knew each other and how to fight side by side.

"It is beautiful when my battle plan finally comes together and works so well," Lando called out to Axel as he dodged a spear.

"You really don't shut up, do you?" Axel called back as he grasped that same spear from the ground and sent it back into the body of another enemy.

"Of course not, there is so much I want to say," Lando then laughed as he charged into four men like a mad man and bawled them all over.

"Notice how they are pushing us toward the clearing, they probably have more friends out there," Lando called out. "Let's go meet them and give them a taste of our skill!"

Axel looked up as the men who could fly suddenly came together in a deadly flurry of wing, claw and beak, all of it led by a screaming redheaded woodpecker. Axel could not join for he was in hand-to-hand combat with two at the moment and one of them had his arm twisted and pinned behind his back.

"Aw, damn it," Axel said through gritted teeth as he felt the bigger man wrenching his arm at an angle it wasn't meant to go. The second man was attempting to pummel him but he had an arrow in his shoulder so his moves were weak, Axel leaned into the man holding him and kicked upwards, right into the other's injured shoulder. Axel cried out as he felt the pop in his own shoulder and then the pain and numbness go down his arm.

That's not good, Axel thought as he felt his arm suddenly give way to the terrible angle the man had it at. Axel bit back the pain and took the advantage of his injury as he spun upon the man holding him, the man tried to keep hold of Axel's arm as Axel tried to swing on him with his other but just before he managed to hit the guy an arrow beat him to it. Axel froze for a second as the arrow suddenly appeared in the man's chest, the man didn't even utter a word, he just loosed his grip on Axel's injured arm and slowly fell backwards. Axel took a step back, his left hand grabbing the shoulder of his right arm as he felt numbness and tingling continue to pulse through his shoulder and arm. Axel suddenly felt weak as intense pain hit him and his arm twitched from muscle spasms, he fell to his knees and let a cry of pain and rage escape his lips as he continued to hold his dislocated shoulder.

"Axel!" someone shouted right next to him. Axel looked up and saw Ben, one of the older men and the best bowman they had. "You all right, lad?"

Axel glanced around and noticed that there was no more fighting around him, all the others had gone to the clearing like Lando had suggested. He and Ben were actually the only ones left of their band at that spot, not even any of the dead were of their group of skilled freelance fighters.

"My arm," Axel said through gritted teeth. "Put it back in place."

"Well, sure, Axel, but you still won't be able to use it."

"I don't care," Axel growled.

"It's going to hurt a lot, and it doesn't always work the first time. Maybe you should wait for…." As Ben spoke he suddenly took hold of Axel's body, fairly bear hugging him with one hand firmly grasping his injured shoulder. The movement was fast and fiercely executed, Axel felt his shoulder roll back into position and then Ben slammed his palm into Axel's shoulder so hard and fast that it popped back into place. Axel sighed a little at some of the relief he felt, sweat beaded his brow as he looked at Ben and half smiled in thanks.

"Better? Good, but I suggest you don't use it," Ben said as he released the hold he had on Axel.

"Not a problem," Axel said as he picked up a sword in his left hand and got back to his feet.

Lando dived into a man on a horse and knocked down both horse and rider, he bounded across the ground in his woodpecker form like a giddy creature as he took bites at men's faces and knocked them over with his powerful wings. It seemed as though nobody could touch the madly dancing bird as it screamed out its enjoyment at each downed enemy. Finally he dived at a large man on the battlefield and as he did so he changed back and wrapped his hands around the man's neck.

"Surprise!" he shouted as he slammed his forehead into the other's face, breaking the man's nose and dropping him almost instantly.

"Ah! Little brother!" Lando cried out when he caught sight of Axel sword fighting with another not far away. "Putting your left arm to the test or is something wrong with your right?"

"I'll be fine," Axel shouted back as he downed his opponent and gave him a kick for good measure. The fighting raged on and slowly some of Lando's men fell to the enemy. Lando changed back and forth as he battled in the sky and on the ground, he was all over the place and his merriment sometimes worried Axel.

"You really are crazy, you know that?" Axel said once when they were fighting side by side.

"Makes it more fun, scares the hell out of the enemy and if I'm going to die I want to die laughing!" Lando shouted as he suddenly made a mad dash toward another man on horseback. Axel took a moment to watch Lando leap into the air, his arms outstretched and that mad smile on his face as both feet hit the unsuspecting rider in the side of the head. Lando turned toward Axel and shouted as he pointed upwards. "You should join me, little brother!"

"Maybe another time! My arm won't let me," Axel shouted back.

"Damn your luck," Lando laughed as he leapt upwards with a screech and looked for a new victim to dive into. Lando saw his next target but as he turned to dive he felt the cold rush of air under his wings and a huge raindrop landed on his back, then a second and a third right after. Instead of taking out another of the enemy Lando turned toward one of his wounded comrades and dived down to help get him off the field.

"Everyone, cover!" Lando shouted, and then the rains hit. Huge drops came down with deadly force on the Little Folk and their horses. Several of them instantly went down from the sheer pressure of the huge falling raindrops, one hit Axel on his right shoulder and he instantly hit the ground. Lando grasped his injured man and flew to the shelter of the forest, others followed close behind; some were his men and some were not. Lando looked back across the battlefield and could still see several of his men trying to get to safety, Axel was among them.

"Fly, Axel!" Lando shouted though he knew Axel could not hear him. Axel did try to fly, he leapt upwards, the form of a sparrow appeared but it faltered and fell.

"No!" Lando shouted as he saw Axel slowly rise up from the ground holding his right shoulder. "He's going to drown!"

"Don't go!" one of Lando's men cried out as he saw Lando preparing to leap. The man leapt onto him instead and though he nearly knocked them both from the shelter of the tree, he managed to keep Lando there.

"But it's Axel!" Lando shouted as he struggled against the man.

"He'll make it," the man said sternly.

"No!" Lando suddenly cried out, reaching toward Axel as a huge man suddenly rose up and towered over Axel in the rain. Axel stopped and stood stock still in surprise for a moment and it was all the man needed. Lando broke free of the man holding him as he saw the enemy soldier run a spear right through Axel's body. Axel stood for a moment, slightly bent at the waist, his left hand grasping the spear that was now squiring him, dumbly looking down at the spear as the heavy raindrops grew thicker and quickly knocked him and the enemy down. It all happened in mere seconds and Lando was nearly off the branch when several of his men pinned him down this time.

"Let go of me!" Lando shouted. A hand slapped him across the face.

"They're lost! It won't do them any good to go and drown yourself!"

Lando suddenly became limp as his men held him back and he sat there, becoming drenched and choking on the rain until his men pulled him back into the shelter closer to the tree trunk. The wind and rain raged on, lightning lit up the sky and clearing before him and Lando could feel the tree tremble and groan from the force of the storm.

"I have to get him back, I have to get him back. Oh, Landrew, Amy, I am so sorry, so, so sorry."

The rain had barely ended when Lando flew down to the battlefield and began to look over the dead, most of them had drowned in the rain. There were a handful of his own men but a majority were of the enemy, quite a good battle considering how many they were up against, but Lando had no time to rejoice. He had kept his eyes on the exact spot where he had seen Axel fall throughout the entire storm, the rest of the afternoon he refused to move as he stared into the heavy rain and saw the spear trust through Axel's body again and again. Lando found the body of the huge enemy, lying face first in the mud, the heavy raindrops having pelted him down as the rain continued. But he did not find Axel's body, only several discarded weapons, two swords and a spear.

"I don't understand," Lando said as he picked up the spear and examined it. "Where is he? Where is Axel's body?"

"Lando," a voice barely above a whisper came to his ears, Lando leapt up and looked toward the call. Axel was kneeling, not far away, and looking at Lando with a sad and pained expression. Axel had no shirt on and his skin glistened sickly pale, his wet hair was plastered to his face and his left arm was pressed across his body while his right arm hung loose, a large bruise blossoming across his shoulder. Blood was leaking from beneath his left arm, staining his abdomen and pants red, the rain had washed away all other dirt and blood. Lando rushed forward and fell on his knees before Axel as though to embrace him but stopped at the last moment and grasped his shoulders instead.

"How?" Lando asked hoarsely with a pained gasp.

"I don't know," Axel said mirroring that same gasp. "I have a hole right through my body but somehow I am still alive." Lando slowly looked down as Axel moved his left arm to reveal the gaping wound, an ugly thing in his belly that was still slowly leaking blood. Lando felt his stomach churn and he instantly pressed his own hands against the wound to help stop the bleeding. Axel groaned and coughed a little as he fell against Lando while they kneeled facing each other.

"I would have come to you sooner," Axel said softly. "But there is something wrong with my legs. I felt the spear grate against my spine and now my legs won't work right."

Lando held Axel close, one hand pressed against his stomach while he looked over Axel's shoulder at the gaping hole in his lower back; he circled his other arm around to press his hand against that wound as well.

"I'm sorry, Lando, I didn't mean to make you worry."

"Shhhhh," Lando hushed him as he tried to rise up still holding him. "Everything will be all right." Lando looked up to see several of his men running toward them, they stopped when they reached Lando and stared down at them, fearing their leader had found a corpse and was going to hang onto him even after death.

"Help me," Lando said. "He lives, now help me!"

For a moment they hesitated in disbelief, then Axel coughed softly and they leapt forward, hands gently grabbing him as they tried to help him lay back in the makeshift hammock they created with their arms. Axel gasped and stiffened, he reached out and grabbed Lando's arm with his left hand, his right attempted to move but fell back limp. Lando held his breath as he saw Axel's eyes slowly roll back in his head and he fell limp into the arms of the men. Everyone seemed to hold their breath with Lando as they all looked down at Axel's still body, then Axel took a breath.

Chapter Thirty-seven

"I can't work magic, I'm not a shaman," Cofter fumed as Lando hovered over him while he attempted to stitch Axel's wounds. "I don't even think a shaman can fix this! So don't be mad at me if he dies. Make yourself useful, you big lunk, wipe up the blood!" Lando had not said a word the entire time but his mere presence spoke volumes.

"He should be dead," Cofter continued. "First he got run through, then there was all that blood loss, I am thoroughly surprised he still has any left in him, then he was out on the field during that entire storm. I have never heard of someone surviving so much all at once like that."

Lando continued to remain silent as he watched Cofter clean Axel's wounds. They put a temporary bandage on his back while Cofter cleaned his abdomen and bandaged it properly, then they rolled him back over and did the same for his back, only this time Cofter thought it best to stitch the wound. Blood still slowly ran from the wound as Cofter worked on it and Lando silently wiped it up as Cofter had advised.

"I am not a doctor, I only know as much about wounds as the next man, I'm barely an herbalist, hell, I'm just good at stitches 'cause I fix everyone's clothes." Cofter continued to vent and fume as he finished up and Lando let him, knowing full well it was what the man did to ease his nervousness.

"You did a good job," Lando said softly as they washed the blood from their hands.

"I'm sorry, Lando, I wish I could do more. Have you sent a letter to your brother?"

"Ben wrote one for me and already sent it off, the wind will find him much faster than anybody else will."

Landrew looked up just as he saw Amy pluck the letter from the wind, she studied it for a moment and then her knees gave away and she sat down hard, one hand covering her mouth.

"Amy! What is it?" Landrew cried out as he ran toward his wife.

"We have to go, now!" Amy answered as she held up the letter.

Axel slept for four days and nights. Not moving or making a sound expect for his soft breathing. Lando hovered around him the entire time because no one else would. Whispers began to go through the band of men as they spoke of the young man who wouldn't die.

"Is it just dumb luck?"

"A curse, perhaps?"

"There must be more to it."

"Dark magic, he was always so strong."

Lando ignored the whispers and paid attention to the men who did not speak their concerns aloud for he knew they were the ones that posed the biggest threat to Axel. However, Lando began to fear a little himself when Axel sat up in bed on the fourth day and began to peel away the bandages.

"What are you doing?" Lando asked.

"My back feels weird, like there's something there that shouldn't be."

"You have stitches in your back," Lando said as he tried to stop Axel from unwrapping any more of the bandages, then he stared at Axel with wide eyes and took several steps back as he watched Axel run his hand across his abdomen, healed and with only a reddish raw place where the wound had been.

"Can you get the stitches out, they feel strange, and kind of hurt," Axel said as he also ran a hand across his back and picked at the stitches once he felt them.

"Yeah, just give me a moment," Lando said as he reached out and also touched the wound that had once blossomed over Axel's stomach.

"What's wrong?" Axel asked. Lando looked at Axel for a long moment and stared into his bright blue eyes, then he slowly shook his head and stood up straight. Lando turned and noticed many of the men crowding around and staring, some had fearful looks on their faces, Lando dismissed them with a wave of his hand and they slowly began to disperse. Lando went to the door and looked out to make sure the men were not milling around, he saw Ben slowly leaving as well.

"Ben, go and get Cofter, I need him to look at Axel's back," Lando said just before the older man walked away. Ben stopped for a moment and turned his head toward Lando.

"Perhaps not Cofter, sir, you know how he already wants nothing more to do with him."

"Are you saying I can't trust him?" Lando asked, dropping his voice so Axel would not hear.

Ben did not answer in words but let his eyes do all the talking.

"Very well," Lando sighed. "Do you fear him as well?"

"I do not, sir," Ben answered.

"I trust your judgment, old friend, bring me a sharp knife and inform me of anyone else who is frightened by all this so I can speak to them about it."

Lando carefully cut the stitches in Axel's back and pulled them free, the whole time marveling at how the wounds had healed and asking Axel over and over again if he felt all right.

"How long was I asleep?"

"I don't know," Lando answered as he next inspected Axel's shoulder. Ben had told him how Axel had dislocated his shoulder, he held Axel's arm out and slowly rotated it around several times.

"It doesn't hurt," Axel assured him.

"I just want to make sure," Lando said. Axel noticed how the men kept walking by and staring at him.

"What's wrong with them?" Axel asked as he nodded toward the men as they mingled not far away.

"They are scared of something," Lando said, he also looked toward the men and then sighed.

"Why don't you go for a walk, get some fresh air and sunlight."

"Yeah, I would like to, my muscles are stiff from laying here for so long."

"I will get you some clothes," Lando said as he started to walk away. Lando got some clothes for Axel and stopped to speak to Ben.

"Follow him, keep him safe. I am going to try and speak to everyone while he is away and address what they are so afraid of."

"Yes, sir," Ben said as he nodded and picked up his quiver of arrows.

Axel felt a little uneasy as he walked through the little camp, a few of the men nodded at him and said they were glad to see him up, some of them stepped aside and avoided his eyes while others just stood and stared at him. Axel went east and skirted around the edge of a stream, after a while he stopped and sat down, pulling his knees up and hugging them as he watched the water before him.

"I know you are following me," Axel called out after a short while.

"You are a smart lad," Ben said as he flitted down from a tree and sat down next to Axel. They both watched the water for a time and finally Axel spoke.

"What happened, Ben?"

"What do you mean, lad?"

"Why do they stare at me like that?" Axel spoke softly and without looking up from the water. Ben brought a hand up to his face and rested his chin on it, he looked up from the water for a moment to see a fox silently jogging through the underbrush on the other side; in a moment it was gone.

"I don't think that is something I can answer, lad."

"Something happened, Lando had a look on his face like I have never seen before, and some of the others looked scared."

"They fear what they do not understand. You should have died, and you didn't."

"But shouldn't they be thankful? I know I am."

Ben took in an audible breath and closed his eyes for a long moment. "Some of the men have seen strange things, things they did not understand, things that caused them great pain and sorrow. So when they come across another thing they do not understand they become fearful of it. Do not let it get to you, lad, Lando is going to speak to them. Do not be any different then what you always have been and everything will be all right in the end."

"Why are you not treating me like they are?"

"Because I believe differently than they do. I do not fear like they do. I have been around for a long time and have discovered that everything I feared only hurt me the more because I feared it."

Axel and Ben did not return until late in the evening, they had sat by the water for some time then they went hunting for eggs to eat. After stealing an egg and sharing the raw contents Axel fell asleep in the shade for a time while Ben sat watch just as Lando had asked him to, after some time, though, he woke Axel and told him it was time they returned before Lando started to worry.

"Axel!"

Axel and Ben both stopped walking and looked up to see Lando running hard toward them.

No, Axel thought. *Not Lando....* His heart suddenly leapt with the recognition.

"Landrew!" Axel called out. Landrew ran straight into Axel and hugged him, nearly knocking him down.

"Landrew! What are you doing here?"

"Oh, my boy!" Landrew cried out as he finally released him. "We were told you were dying so we came right away."

"We? Who else is here?"

"Amy, Allen, Kalim and Hect."

"You brought Hect? Why?"

"Well, I didn't exactly bring him, he heard about your injuries and came of his own accord. But look at you! Not even in bed!"

"Oh, I was. Must have been for weeks. Look at the scars," Axel said as he lifted his shirt to show the healed wounds. A look of concern flashed across Landrew's face when he saw where the spear had gone through his body.

"So it's true," Landrew said softly and glanced at Ben.

"What's true?" Axel asked, suddenly worried that Landrew would also begin to treat him differently.

"I wish I was still young and could heal like that," Landrew said with a laugh as he poked the healed flesh with his index finger. "Amy brought all kinds of herbs and healing salves but now she will be overjoyed not to use them."

"I don't know what Lando used but it has worked wonders, the wounds are not even sore," Axel commented as he dropped his shirt back down. "Come on, I want to see Amy, I'll race you back!"

"You have never beat me yet, little sparrow!" Landrew shouted as they both jumped into the air with wings spreading, Ben watched them go with a smile on his weathered face.

Amy met Axel with sobs and would not let go of him for a long time, Axel stood and held her as she pressed her face into his shoulder. Allen and Kalim both patted his back in greeting but Hect saw his chance to hug him from behind while Amy was in his arms, Axel kicked back at him and caught him in the kneecap. Hect quickly jumped back with a laugh and smirked as he studied Axel. Amy finally let go of Axel and took a step back to look at him as she wiped the tears off her face.

"Oh," she said softly. "You have grown a little beard, you look so grown up now with a beard." Amy reached up and placed her hands on either side of his face. Lando grasped Landrew by the arm and walked him to a less crowded area.

"Tell me now, what is going on with Axel? You have seen for your own eyes, he should be dead."

Landrew looked back at Axel as he was surrounded by his old friends.

"It is an amazing mishap," Landrew said softly as he cast his eyes down.

"How is this a mishap, big brother? What happened? My men are afraid it is dark magic or demons at work here, I almost had an uprising against Axel earlier today," Lando spoke with an edge of anger to his tone.

"The only thing I can think of, is when he had fought Martin, he was dying, and I sought out a Snow Fairy."

"Landrew! How could you!? You know how they play their tricks, only stupid people seek them out and ask for help. What if all this ends suddenly, what if everything that has been inflicted upon him suddenly comes back all at once and he dies a very painful death?" Lando fairly growled as he spoke and Landrew grimaced with each word.

"I was not thinking straight, brother, he was dying. He has been as a son to me, a very good friend and student. He is my prodigy, I have never met another like him before. Amy loves him as well and I just couldn't stand by and let him die because of something I encouraged him to do."

"You remember Leo? His wife asked a Snow Fairy to heal him that one time he almost died of frostbite?"

Landrew put a hand over his eyes and gritted his teeth.

"He survived, grew his fingers and toes back even, but for how long? Just a few years and his limbs slowly began to fall off until he had no arms and legs left, then he died from what appeared to be frostbite all over his body, he was in such agony. Why would you wish anything like that on Axel?"

"I don't know, I wasn't thinking," Landrew said with a grimace.

"You're the brother who always thinks things through, I'm the brother that jumps into shit without thinking, get it right!" Lando lightly smacked Landrew on the back of the head and then they both silently stood there looking at Axel as Hect tried to hug him again.

"I think Amy and I will stay for a while, I want to be here if anything happens."

"Are you sure about that, big brother? You may have brought doom upon Axel by asking that Snow Fairy for help; he could start spitting up blood and bleed to death."

"I know," Landrew said softly. "But whatever may come, I wish to be here."

Chapter Thirty-eight

Aandrew and Amy did stay, for several months in fact. Allen, Kalim and Hect returned after one week and Landrew asked Kalim to be leader in his absence. After much urging from Axel, Landrew and him began to train again just as they had before.

"I don't think you have forgotten anything I taught you, I'm proud of you, Axel," Landrew commented after several days of training.

"Well, Lando does keep me on my toes," Axel answered as he tossed a fighting staff toward Lando, he reached up and caught it from the air.

"Why did you stop fighting in the tournaments anyway? Landrew told me once that you are a better fighter than even him," Axel asked casually. Lando looked at the staff in his hand and rubbed his fingers across the smooth surface.

"For the love of a woman, why else," he said as he handed the staff off to another and turned to walk away.

"What?" Axel called as he jogged to catch him. "You never told me of this woman."

"It was a long time ago," Lando said as he continued to walk. "And besides, she is dead now."

Axel stopped and watched Lando's back for a moment. Lando continued to walk but then stopped several paces away and turned back to Axel.

"Let's get something to eat and I will tell you about her," Lando said with a wave of his hand.

"Her name was Ispsi, and though I know her death was not my fault I still feel responsible. When we first met her, her name was Tom, and though she did a good job to hide it, we knew she was not a man; I saw her bathing one day. For a woman to travel alone is dangerous, so it was common for the brave ones to cut their hair and pretend to be a man. Since we knew she was a woman we decided to offer her to travel with us, she took the offer and was with us from early fall until late spring, all the while thinking we still thought her to be a man. Her and I became very close and finally she told me her name was actually Ispsi, in which my reply was, 'That's good, because I don't really want a wife named Tom.' I will never forget that look on her face," Lando laughed at the memory then became silent. "We were going to get married but then a battle broke out near us, it lasted for a full week. During her time of traveling with us she had picked up the skills of a bowman and begged to go with us to the battle. At first I told her no but she went anyway, dressed once again as Tom. It was during this battle that she was killed by my own knife. I had done my best to protect her, though she didn't need much protecting, but one of the enemy had got to her, injured her leg badly and stood over her, ready to kill. I knew I would not be able to get to her in time so I threw my knife, and it would have struck true if the enemy had not seen it coming. He plucked my flying blade from the air as if it were not moving at all and stabbed Ispsi with it; she was dead before I could get to her. I lost my will to fight for a while and I suppose I never really got it back completely. In my prime I could take down eight men at once, now I am content with three or four at once."

Axel looked at his food, it was untouched. Amy and Landrew sat nearby, they had also picked at their food during the story.

"I'm sorry, Lando," Axel said softly. "I have never heard you speak of her before."

"It is in the past," Lando said. "Landrew always told me if he ever had a daughter he would like to name her Ispsi for she was strong and brave, but Amy cannot seem to have children. I am not upset over it, it is what it is."

Axel glanced toward Amy, he had heard how she was once married to another when she was very young, a man that beat her for several years and then abandoned her when she did not bare children.

"Ispsi is a nice name for a little girl," Axel said as he set his plate aside.

"Don't be so glum, it is in the past. I came to terms with what happened and I continue to live on," Lando picked up Axel's untouched plate and speared a piece of the meat out of the gravy-like substance it sat in, he looked at it for a moment and then stuffed the entire piece into his mouth.

The next morning seemed to dawn with an ill omen, it was cloudy and dim and had everyone feeling edgy.

"It feels like something is happening," Lando commented to his brother as they both searched for the sunrise in the clouds. "The air is alive with a storm, but the wind does not act like a storm is coming and it does not smell like a storm either."

"I don't like it," Landrew said as he turned away. Just then a breeze edged across the back of Landrew's neck and seemed to curl around his body and hold him in place. Landrew looked up and saw the thin piece of leather come streaking through the air straight toward him, the wind had an urgency to it that frightened him. Landrew's hands almost shook as he grasped the message the wind had brought him. It seemed to have been ripped from someone's shirt, bloodstains on one edge had turned it brown, letters in the same brown color had been hastily written out with someone's finger.

"Come quick, Max attacks."

Lando called out for his men's aid and within moments the little band had taken to the skies and were flying as fast as they could back toward Landrew's camp. A few of the men could not change and were riding on the backs of the larger birds, Amy hugged the back of one of the great redheaded woodpeckers as the two great birds flew side by side just ahead of the others.

In the last hours of the next day they finally reached their destination and for a long moment Landrew could only stand in place and stare at the bodies around them. The ground was burned and furrowed from the battle, men that they had known and been close to were sprawled across the ground. Now they were mangled figures of death. A few of the women were found struck down as well, one man was holding his wife in his arms trying to protect her when they both had been run through with a lance, another mother was found holding her child in her arms, the child had been struck by a sword and she had two arrows in her back. Some had limbs missing, some had no heads, some were disemboweled but they were all dead. Landrew knelt down next to one man that had been wearing a white tunic before the battle, now it was pock marked with droplets of blood and several arrows.

"Kalim," Landrew said softly as he reached down to touch him. Kalim was cold and unmoving. Amy and several others began to run from body to body as they checked for survivors, Landrew gently laid his cloak over Kalim and ran his hands through his flaming hair several times before he finally stood back up.

"Everyone is dead," Landrew said out loud to himself as he slowly turned in place and looked from one still form to another in disbelief and horror.

"I got someone!" came Axel's shout, everyone turned as one and converged upon Axel's position. Hect lay on the ground beneath a dead horse, his legs pinned. One of Hect's arms was clearly broken and blood was still slowly running from a deep cut across his throat, his breath faintly whistled through the wound.

"It's okay, we got you," Axel was saying in an attempt to calm him but Hect was beating at him with the fist of his good arm and trying to speak but he could only gurgle and cough, which caused more blood to run from his wound. Several men surrounded the dead horse and grasping legs and main they lifted it enough for Axel to pull Hect free, Hect continued to fight against Axel.

"Something is wrong," Landrew said when he reached them at that moment. Hect looked at his dear friend with a pleading sorry expression as he continued to struggle for breath. An arrow suddenly flew through the circle of men and embedded itself into Lando's chest. Lando barely flinched and looked down at the shaft that had struck him, his hands slowly raised as his knees began to buckle.

"Damn my luck," he said just as two of his men caught him.

"Down!" Landrew cried out as he turned in the direction of the attackers. The men rose up from the ground where they had lain amongst the dead. For a moment everyone regarded each other and Landrew's eyes narrowed as the enemy continued to rise until they easily outnumbered Lando's band of men. Amy was actually the one to make the first move, with a scream of rage she unsheathed her short sword and hurled it at the nearest man, the sword made three graceful turns through the air, the man began to duck down but it did not save him as the fast and powerful throw struck him in the forehead. Axel was still kneeling by Hect when he looked up just as the blow was dealt, two droplets of blood flew from the dying man's head and hit Axel on the cheek. Everything suddenly began to move very slowly and for a panicked moment Axel felt as if he were that younger version of himself, on a battlefield for the very first time, he looked toward Lando as his men dragged his bleeding body out of harm's way behind a stand of boulders, his breath caught in his throat and his palms suddenly went clammy, then Hect punched him in the face and he was able to move again. Axel half dragged, half carried

Hect to the sanctuary of the boulders as the small battle raged around him and his adrenaline began to flood his head and make his ears ring.

"Let me help!" Lando was struggling as Amy fairly sat on top of him to hold him still, her hands pressed against his wound in an attempt to stop the bleeding. Landrew found himself pitted against three swordsmen at once as arrows periodically continued to fly by them, some hitting their targets and some embedding into the ground or ricocheting off the rocks around them. Axel laid Hect down next to Lando and the exhausted man went limp as he continued to struggle with his breathing, he cradled his broken arm and as Axel glanced down his body he could also see one leg had been mortally cut but the weight of the dead horse must have stopped the bleeding and saved his life. Axel grasped his sword and leapt back over the boulder to find his own enemy to fight but his feet had barely hit the ground when an arrow struck him in the back and he fell prone. Landrew turned at the sound of Amy's scream and saw her leaning out of the cover of the boulders as she grasped Axel's arm and was trying to pull him to her, in that split second of glancing away from his enemy, one man ran the tip of his sword across Landrew's face and Landrew fell backwards, his face was suddenly on fire and he tasted blood in his mouth as his now sliced and broken nose began to fairly gush. The wound was just below his eyes, it went from cheekbone to cheekbone and had destroyed the bridge of his nose, Landrew fought the urge to put a hand over the pain as he gripped his sword and with a savage cry he leapt back at the three men. Landrew was already spurred on by his anger at the slaughter of his men, but now the pain amplified his speed and he fairly danced around the three men and took them down one by one. Block, thrust, slice, spin, kick, slice, and as soon as those three were dead he instantly leapt toward another group of three against one. Landrew's sword barely missed this man and it shot out several sparks as it struck a rock.

"You bastards," Landrew growled as he saw Lando's man fall prone to the ground, blood quickly staining the back of his shirt. The three men suddenly converged upon Landrew and as he blocked two of them he saw from the corner of his eye, the third man's sword coming for his head in a wide and powerful arc as the other two ducked down. Landrew began to duck as well but knew he would not be fast enough and yet he did not close his eyes as he watched the blade coming for his head. Suddenly a hand reached up and caught the swinging blade, blood almost instantly began to run down the man's wrist and forearm and Landrew gasped when he saw who had saved him. Axel stood between him and his killer, his right hand now bloody as his left hand was holding a knife hilt, the blade of the knife buried in the enemy's chest. Axel turned as he threw the other man to the ground and Landrew could see the feathered arrow shaft still embedded in Axel's back. Landrew swallowed hard and then quickly took the opportunity to turn and dispatch one of the two he was still fighting against.

"Axel," Landrew said between sword swings. "You are grievously wounded."

"I know," Axel said as he also swung a sword. "It hurts, could you pull the damn thing out when you get a second?"

Landrew turned toward him a moment later and grasped Axel's shoulder with one hand, he dropped his sword so he could grasp the shaft of the arrow with the other.

"Do it," Axel said between gritted teeth. With one firm and strong pull Landrew had the arrow free of Axel's flesh. Axel fell to one knee for a moment with a cry of pain but was back up almost instantly. Before Landrew could grab up his sword again a weaponless man kicked him in the back of the leg and Landrew fell forward, tingling pain running up and down his leg. He rolled over and barely had enough time to block another kick coming for his head. A second man appeared with a sword and Landrew rolled to his left to avoid the blow, he rolled into someone's feet and put an arm up for protection but saw it was Axel who stood over him. Axel's blue eyes were flashing as he leapt forward over Landrew and tackled the two men. His right hand went around the neck of the weaponless man and his left hand grasped the sword hand of the other man, effectively deflecting the sword away from his body so the tip of it barely broke the skin along his ribs. An arrow hit the ground right next to Landrew's face and he leapt up just as a second would have struck him where he lay. Landrew reached forward and grasped the enemy's sword right out of his hand as Axel continued to grapple with them both at once, he turned the sword and trust it into the man's side. Axel released the wounded man from his grasp and fell upon the other with both hands and broke his neck.

"Stay here," Axel told Landrew. "I am going to get rid of those archers."

"No, don't," Landrew pleaded but Axel took off toward the ridge from where the arrows were coming from.

"I got one!" came Lando's shout just as Landrew felt the presence of a person behind him only to have that enemy fall down dead at his feet. Landrew saw that though Lando's chest was still bleeding he had propped himself up and with Amy's help they were both now firing arrows from their sanctuary. Landrew fell to one knee as he took stock of his wounds, none were serious except for the cut across his face, he very tenderly touched it and found it to be deeper than he had originally thought and it slowly came to his realization just how close he had come to losing his eyes, for that was what the man had been aiming for. Blood was slowly clouding his vision and Landrew squinted through the redness as he saw who he thought to be Axel, still running like a madman, confronting anyone who stood against him and dispatching them quickly and effectively as he dodged arrows from the ridge. Axel topped the ridge and Landrew shielded his eyes as he looked into the glare of the sun now, but he continued to watch the dark figures on the ridge fight one another; however, after mere moments all fell except for one. Landrew slowly stood back up as the remaining men began to gather and move toward the boulder, some carrying the wounded between them and some limping on their own. Axel was slowly walking back toward them, his feet stumbling a little as he went, Landrew went toward him and was slightly shocked at the sight of the young man. Axel's blond hair was now stained with blood from him running his injured hand through it out of habit, he had a cut on his cheek that ran blood into his beard on one side of his face, he had two arrows in his chest and a knife in his back. Landrew watched as Axel pulled out the arrows and then bending to the side a little, he was able to grasp the knife hilt in his back, he pulled it out and after looking at it for a moment he threw it and buried the blade in the dirt.

"I let one go," Axel said tiredly as Landrew put an arm around him to support him.

"Why?" Landrew asked.

"I told him to warn his master, warn him I was coming. Do you know what he called me?" Axel paused for a moment to take a breath, Landrew waited for him to answer. "He called me the blond demon, said I was summoned from below to kill them all, isn't that funny?"

"Yeah," Landrew said softly as they slowly walked toward the others.

"Wow," Axel said softly as Landrew felt him leaning on him a little more. "Once the excitement is over I am actually very tired…and I hurt so much. I just need to sleep, just sleep for a little while and I will be fine, I'm sure I will be."

"I'm sure you will be too," Landrew said as another man came to the other side of Axel to help.

Amy and a few others looked over the wounded with grim determination. Hect's neck had been ever so carefully bandaged and he slept, still struggling to breathe a little but now the air did not whistle through the wound anymore.

"You still with me?" Landrew asked as he sat down next to Lando's still form, the younger brother slowly opened his eyes and wearily looked at the older brother.

"I think so. Damn, Landrew, what happened to your face?"

"Oh, you know, I got tired of looking in the water and seeing a reflection of you staring back at me, it's kind of creepy."

"Don't make me laugh, it hurts," Lando answered. "I have had arrow wounds over the years but this is the first one to strike me down so. I guess it is time to pay for all the terrible things I have done."

"You are not allowed to die, I am the older brother, I die first, remember."

"I guess I better not die," Lando said with a groan. "How is Axel, he looked pretty bad when you brought him over here."

Landrew did not answer right away and looked toward Axel's still form some paces away, Lando followed his gaze.

"The wounds he had should have killed him, and yet, he fought like someone possessed. He was angry out there and he went after those archers alone, all the way across the battlefield. Amy patched him up and he has a high fever now but even with such wounds he is still alive, just, sleeping."

"Do you think it is the Snow Fairy?"

"It must be, how else would he survive death so many times now? And that cut he had on his face, Amy washed the blood off and cannot find a wound, and yet I saw it with my own eyes." Landrew sighed audibly and though he did not show it so much on the outside, Lando could tell he was troubled.

"What are you thinking about, brother?" Lando asked after they were silent for some time.

"I was wondering how long it will last. How many times will he be injured to the point of death and not die? Is this just something that will wear out over time or have I truly cursed him? Will he eventually die of old age or have I stolen that from him as well? How will he live in such a condition? Foolish people search for a gift such as this, but what he has now, it comes with an even greater price. How many times have we ourselves watched friends die in battle, die in our arms, and yet we are still here and the pain and sorrow of their passing is all we have left? How can one live with an eternity of such pain?"

Chapter Thirty-nine

"Don't look at me like that, you old pervert," Axel said as he sat before Hect holding the bowl of broth and spices Amy had prepared for everyone. Hect half smiled and slowly reached his uninjured arm to Axel's face to poke him on one of his bare cheeks.

"My beard? I couldn't get all the blood washed out so I shaved it off."

"You know Hect likes guys with no beards best, that's why he keeps his own face shaved," Landrew commented from several paces away where he was aiding Lando with his own bowl of broth. Axel looked at him with narrowed eyes and Lando laughed a little, then he groaned as he put a hand to his chest.

"Just look at them," Lando commented once he caught his breath again. "As much as Axel dislikes Hect and yet he is playing nursemaid for him, it is Hect's dream come true."

Axel made a sound between a snort and a growl and looked back at Hect only to see him grinning pervishly again as his eyes wandered over his body.

"You are not that sick," Axel said as he put the bowl down and quickly walked away. Hect looked at Lando and clenched his fist threateningly.

"Sorry," Lando answered back.

"Here, you're not that sick either," Landrew said as he set down Lando's bowl and stood up to follow Axel, he stopped for a moment as his head became giddy from standing too quickly then he continued on his way.

"Well, damn our luck," Lando said to Hect as he carefully picked up his bowl and began to sip from it.

"Axel," Landrew called as he followed. Axel slowed for a moment but continued to walk with purposeful strides. Axel stopped at the edge of the grave, it still smoldered, thin curling lines of smoke going to the sky. Their small group did not have the time or strength to bury all the dead so they had carefully laid everyone in a low spot in the ground and piled dry leaves and branches on them. Landrew had wept when they had put flame to it the night before, but Axel had no tears to shed, instead the anger he felt inside steadily grew and it continued to smolder inside just as the pile of ash and bone before him.

"Some people wish to be burned so they can rise above everything here," Landrew spoke softly, reverently. "And some people wish to be buried so they can still hold on to this place. I think I would like to be burned, so I can go and find Odessa and the boys. Amy says she will be burned also, she wishes to join us, Odessa won't mind if Amy followed."

"It must be nice to believe all that rubbish," Axel said softly. Landrew sighed a little and raised his hand as if to rub his face but then put it down again.

"Two days ago you said you had let one go to deliver a message. I ask you not to follow through with that plan. Please, Axel, leave it be, let the dead rest. Allen and Kalim, they wouldn't want you to get killed trying to avenge them."

Axel's hand raised and he rubbed his palm across his chest, the wounds were still there but already they were healed enough that he was up and moving around with very little pain.

"I won't die," Axel said, his voice low, his tone harsh. Landrew was about to speak again but Axel turned to him with a look in his eyes that told him not to, so instead Landrew watched Axel walk away until he was out of sight. Axel did not return that evening.

"How can the day be so hot and the night so cold?" the man asked his companion.

"Shut up, I think there is something out there."

"You are like a rabbit, jump and run at any noise."

"I am serious, I saw something moving in the shadows," the younger man stepped in closer to the tiny fire at their feet and gripped his sword.

"Stupid, how did I get stuck with you tonight?"

"You should heed the fears of your companion." The voice leaked out of the darkness around them and both men suddenly came alert, the younger man squeaked in fear and the older man growled out a warning.

"Who are you? Show yourself!" The two guards turned in place as they searched the shadows around them, when the voice spoke again it was in the older guard's ear, hot breath rolled across his neck and he saw the younger guard fall, dead at his feet.

"I am your death."

Max let the woman's soft delicate hands untie the front of his shirt and run her fingertips down his chest. He reached up and clasped one hand in his and began to softly kiss the fingertips of that delicate hand. Axel stood just outside the large tent in the shadows and watched through the opening as the woman pushed Max into a chair and sat on his lap, her lips caressing his neck and her long black hair falling in thick waves to her waist. Axel's hands tightened and his jaw clenched until his teeth hurt, anger began to build in his chest, a different kind of anger that he had not felt in a long time. He watched as Florence placed both hands onto Max's face and began to kiss him passionately, Max's arms circling her body and his fingers entwining into her hair. Axel finally took a step forward and Florence saw the movement just outside the tent flap, she gasped and one of Max's hands instantly went for his sword hilt while the other brought her closer in a protective embrace.

"Who is it?" Max asked as he came to his feet. Florence had not recognized the figure lurking outside in the darkness, she buried her face in Max's chest as her hands grasped his tunic.

"You two suit each other quite well, both being murderers and all."

"Axel?" Florence breathed at the sound of his voice.

"You know him?" Max asked as Florence slowly lifted her head from his chest. Axel's hand came forward and drew the tent flap open, light from inside spilled across his body and Florence gasped again at the sight of him. Axel's face was set in grim anger, blood all down the right side of it from hairline to shoulder. His clothes were torn and bloody, the hand that held the tent flap left bloody fingerprints behind when Axel released the heavy fabric. Axel stood slightly stooped and he leaned on a sword he grasped in his other hand, he looked utterly exhausted but his eyes glinted with an angry energy and power from deep within; the stare shook Florence to her very soul.

"Guard!" Max cried out. For a moment Axel's lips twitched into a bloody grin and then went lax again.

"Guard!" Max cried out again as he raised his sword toward Axel.

"Max, Max, it's no use," Florence said as she placed an open palm against his chest. "He has killed them all."

"How!" Max suddenly fumed. "How could you, a single man, kill nearly two hundred men?"

"Have you not heard?" Axel said as he took another step closer. "I am a demon, an avenging demon called upon to kill you. But I suppose as luck would have it, I will also kill Florence."

Max held the sword up in a more menacing stance and he pushed Florence behind himself now.

"You will not touch her," Max said. Axel lifted his foot to take another step but faltered, he stopped in mid-stride and began to cough, he put his hand to his mouth and blood flowed out from between his fingers with each body-shuttering cough.

"You are dying," Max said as he reached out and pressed the point of his sword against Axel's shoulder, pushing him back toward the door of the tent.

"It may appear so," Axel said as he took control of his breathing again. "But you are wrong." Axel's free hand reached across his body and grasped the fabric at his opposite shoulder, his shirt had been torn and cut enough that it tore away when he pulled; as Axel's chest came bare Max gasped and Florence covered her face. His body was covered in grievous wounds, many of them appeared to be fatal and yet Axel still stood before them. The stump of a broken arrow shaft was sticking out of the right side of his chest, a strip of flesh hung loosely from his ribs below his left arm and numerous stab wounds were still bleeding and staining him in dark red blood.

"Florence," Axel said as he tapped his chest where the X scar had been. "It has disappeared over the years, and so has that promise I made, I am no longer in your service."

"Kill him, Max! Kill him!" Florence urged as she pushed Max forward from behind. Max suddenly struck out at Axel but Axel moved faster, he pulled up the sword he had been using as a cane and blocked Max's powerful blow. Max looked at the locked swords for a moment, his right eye twitching a little as he tried to understand what had happened. Axel raised his head to look at Max over the two swords and grinned, this time showing bloody teeth. Max pulled his sword back and struck again, cutting the tent fabric as Axel leapt backwards into the darkness outside.

"Coward!" Max called as he followed. As Max left the light in the tent he was momentarily blinded in the dark, Axel struck out, but he had his sword turned, the flat of it slapped across Max's thigh and left a burning line of pain across Max's leg.

"Does she toy with you?" Axel's voice creeped out of the darkness. "Does she promise to love you forever?"

"Shut up!" Max cried out as he leapt toward Axel, his sword cut through the figure but then the image of Axel disappeared like a shadow melting into the darkness.

"You poor man, you have not seen through her lies yet."

"Florence is pure like a child, how dare you smudge her name," Max blindly began to swing at the shadows before him. His sword struck something soft and yielding but before he could even smile at the blow he saw a boot appear swinging for his face. Axel caught Max's right cheek with the toe of his foot and Max's head snapped to the side as he fell, his sword was thrown from his hand and spun away into the darkness; they heard it thud to the ground a moment later. Max landed on his hands and knees and began to frantically reach across the ground in search of his weapon, Axel took a step closer and in the darkness Max's hand touched his ankle and he recoiled back with a snarl.

"You should hang on to your weapon better, but here, I am a good sport," Axel tossed his own sword aside and held his fists up as he slid his feet into a good fighting stance. Max got to his own feet and laughed softly.

"You fool," he said as he pulled out a formable dagger from behind him.

"Tssk, attacking an unarmed man, your poor bloodlines are showing," Axel said as he ducked several of Max's swings.

"You will see it someday," Axel continued to taunt Max. "You will be watching her and her beauty will melt away and you will see her for what she really is. Her soul is black as night and so ugly that you will weep when you see it."

"Florence is all things good in this world of pain and death, she is what I have searched for my entire life, you cannot mar the image I have of her," Max leapt forward and plunged the blade down into the top of Axel's shoulder at the base of his neck but before he could pull the blade free and jump backwards Axel's fist dealt him a powerful blow to the underside of his jaw. Max's head snapped back, his face now looking at the starry sky and for a moment he felt his feet leave the ground. Max stumbled backwards, his head spinning and his whole face in pain now, he looked at Axel just as Axel leapt toward him and he did the only thing he could think of, he flew. A great red cardinal streaked upwards and Axel's fist just barely missed him as it parted the feathers of a wing. Axel laughed and was instantly in flight as well, quickly closing the gap between them. The two birds circled several times and then charged each other in the air, they hit hard and dropped back to the ground like two stones, landing with bone-crushing force. For a moment they both changed and Axel punched Max in the jaw again while they were still prone on the ground. Max rolled away and his hand felt a sizable stone, he grasped it and rolled back toward Axel, slamming the stone into the stub of arrow that was protruding from his chest, Axel cried out in pain and rolled away. The cardinal flew again as soon as he got his feet under him but the sparrow hesitated for a moment before following, blood dripping from a wound in its side. With a scream the sparrow went straight for the cardinal's back and landed a painful blow. The cardinal turned, his wings enveloping the sparrow and the two changed into grappling men in midair. Max grasped the hilt of the dagger that was still embedded into the flesh of Axel's shoulder, one of Axel's hands closed over the dagger as well and held Max's hand there while the other went for Max's throat. They tumbled and spun through the air for several long moments and just before their bodies struck the ground Max saw Axel smile and heard him softly say, "I win."

They hit the ground harder than the last time and bounced away from each other. Florence had been at the opening of the tent the whole time and screamed when she saw Max lying dead, his face smashed and bleeding from striking the ground.

"You killed him!" she cried out as she rushed forward and began to strike her fists against Axel's body as he was trying to rise up. Axel staggered back several steps from her blows but still managed to stand, then he caught her wrists in his bloody hands and held fast, squeezing until she cringed and gasped in pain.

"Let go of me, you monster," she said.

"I told you," Axel said softly but with an angry tone that made Florence stop struggling. "I no longer serve you. I break the vow I made to you and now I am going to kill you."

"You are no gentleman, you do not deserve the three names of a noble family."

"And you are not as beautiful as the fresh spring morning anymore. Tell me, did you kill Harold, your very brother?" Axel asked through gritted teeth.

"Stepbrother," Florence spat. "And yes, I killed him, he was arrogant and I got tired of him ordering me around. He wished to kill you but I wanted to kill you as well, so I kept him from taking that away from me."

"How many? How many men have you snared with your beauty and sweet talk? Only to suck the life from their being and leave them to wander as empty husks, unable to love another because they still love you?"

Florence laughed then and her body went a little limp as Axel continued to hold her by the wrists.

"Oh, so, so many over the years. I couldn't even begin to count the numerous men I have played with. I started toying with them when I was still just a child, I had to help secure my father's position, and once I discovered the weak point of all you men, it was just too easy and I began to enjoy it."

"You little bitch," Axel breathed out as Florence began to laugh again, then she stopped and became silent. "But Max was different than all the others, we had an understanding that went deeper than anyone else I have ever met."

"An understanding that would only last until he did something against your wishes," Axel said. "Then you were going to kill him. Like you did to your first husband, and Harold and you were going to kill me and so many others...." Axel suddenly became silent as his eyes grew wide and he looked off to the right for a moment.

"And my father," he said slowly, his voice almost quivering. "You killed my father!" Axel suddenly shouted as his grip on her wrists tightened to the point of breaking her arms, Florence cried out in pain as her legs gave way beneath her and she was left with Axel holding her up.

"Yes!" she finally growled. "You are so very right, I am surprised it took you this long to realize it. Yes! I killed your father! And now I will kill you!"

Florence screamed and her arms suddenly disappeared in Axel's grasp, what was left in their place was the feel of cool smooth scales, and a muscled body as thick as Axel's own waist. Axel stumbled backwards as the snake rose up above him with a threatening hiss, it opened and shut its mouth several times as its tongue flicked in and out from between two glistening fangs. Axel kicked backwards and pushed himself away but she was too fast and struck out, grazing his leg. The poison warmed Axel's blood and he wanted to cry out in pain as he felt it spreading up his leg and down to his toes. He rolled to the right and fought off the urge to curl his leg up and hug it, from the corner of his eye he saw Florence pull her head back for another strike and he rolled again, feeling the side of Florence's reptilian head brush across his back. Axel rose up on his hands and knees but before he could get to his feet and stand up, the powerful snake body shot beneath him and curled up over him. Axel grabbed at a broken sapling that was still rooted to the ground but he was not strong enough and the anchor was ripped from his grasp as the snake pulled him into her coils. Axel gasped from the sheer strength of Florence as she coiled around him a second time and began to squeeze, he felt his ribs strain under the pressure and his vision began to fade in and out.

"Do it," Axel groaned between clenched teeth. "Kill me."

Florence hissed and brought her face closer, her yellow eyes with the black slit pupils seemed to glow in the darkness. Her head hovered over him as she held him immobile, they stared at each other for a time, then she brought her head right next to Axel's face and her long tongue slowly came out and curled around his ear and across his cheek. Axel turned his face away and this time she ever so gently pressed her face against his, then she pulled her head back and looked at him for a long moment again. Axel felt the upper coil around his body loosen, he wiggled his shoulders but could not free his arms, then she struck. Her fangs sank into his exposed shoulder and chest, Axel cried out when he felt the poisoned fangs cut through his flesh and disperse the burning liquid throughout his body. The coils fell away from him but she continued to hold him in her massive jaws, Axel's arms finally came loose and he pressed one hand against the side of her face as the other reached for his belt. The cool scales beneath his hand flexed as she tightened her jaws around his body, Axel felt his collarbone straining under the pressure and a new pain began to shoot through his already agonized shoulder. Axel cried out once more but this time in triumph as he raised his other arm and then slammed it into the side of Florence's head. The snake screamed out a hiss as she released Axel from her grip and she shied away from him as she curled around herself in strange positions in an attempt to rid herself of the pain. Axel fell to his knees and remained kneeling as he watched the giant snake move. After a short time its movements slowed and it shivered, then changed back to the form of a woman. Florence lay on the ground, one hand at her throat, a large broken snake tooth had been buried deep into the side of her neck.

Axel was still on his knees but he had slowly fallen forward and was cradling his head in his arms. He had passed out like this and was now slowly coming awake as the sun shone in his eyes, there was a noise, a loud high-pitched wailing assaulted his ears. Axel slowly pushed himself back up into a kneeling position and gritted his teeth as every wound in his body cried out. His eyes, still unfocused and feeling gritty, roamed over the area. To his right was Max's body with the broken head and bloody face, to his left was Florence's body, laying in a relaxed position as if she were merely sleeping with her hand resting at her throat. The wailing stopped for a moment and Axel felt his head falling forward again as his eyes involuntarily closed, then the noise came again with even more force than last time and he suddenly knew what it was.

Axel unsteadily got to his feet and managed to get to the tent he had found Max and Florence in the night before, he entered the spacious and well-furnished dwelling and found it to really be a tent with two rooms, toward the back was the second half that had been curtained off. Axel slowly walked to the second room and pulled back the curtain, and then he fell to his knees and let his head drop into his hands.

"Oh, Florence," Axel said through his hands. "If only I knew, I would not have killed you last night."

The baby stopped crying when the curtain was pulled aside and daylight filtered into her crib, she reached up for it and tried to grasp it, her young mind not yet knowing that one could not take hold of the sunlight. Axel got back to his feet and looked over the edge of the crib at the child and the child looked back at him with black hair that was already thick and dark eyes rimmed by long beautiful eyelashes. The baby suddenly smiled a toothless grin and reached for Axel's bloody fingers, Axel let her grasp them but when he saw the blood smudge her tiny white fingers, tears came to his eyes and he did not stop them.

Chapter Forty

Axel sat cradling the baby girl in his arms, he rocked gently back and forth as he hummed softly to her. He had traveled far already, stumbling over the ground but never falling as he held the moaning crying infant; she was hungry but he had nothing for her to suckle. He had sensed their presence some time ago, they were following him but had yet to show themselves, his best guess was that there was four of them. This was the second time he had stopped to rest and rock the baby, and it was the second time he felt they had stopped as well.

"I know you are out there," Axel called out, his voice sounding weak and cracked. "I have known for some time now, you carry an ominous presence. I know you have come for me but I ask that you allow me this one thing, please let me take this baby to safety. As soon as I hand her off, then you may take me and I will not fight you."

Axel looked around the area and after several long moments a figure seemed to melt out of the shadows beneath a heavy pine branch. The man was not tall, he actually looked to be just a little shorter than Axel, but he had broad well-muscled shoulders and a trim waist. He was dressed in midnight black, even his hands were gloved and a shroud covered his face with black mud smeared around his eyes, the only thing that was not black was the whites of the man's eyes. He had two short swords across his back, the handles of which were visible over each shoulder, and a dozen throwing knives across his chest; the weapons were also all black. Axel and this man in black regarded each other for a long time, but neither of them looked away, then the man finally gave one slight nod of his head and taking a step backwards, he disappeared back into the shadows.

Landrew stopped to lean on the staff he was using as a walking stick and watched the figure come nearer. His eyes were black and swollen from the wound he had across his face and everything was blurry, he could not tell if the figure was friend or foe.

"Who are you?" Landrew called. The figure did not answer but continued to slowly walk toward him.

"You look terrible," Axel said dryly just as he came close enough for Landrew to see who it was.

"Axel?" Landrew quickly stepped forward and placed a firm hand on Axel's shoulder to make sure he was real, Axel grimaced and his shoulder drooped beneath Landrew's grasp.

"You're hurt," Landrew said as he squinted at the blood, Axel's stance and how he was wearing different clothes than when he had left. He disregarded the wad of cloth that Axel carried in one arm until it moved of its own accord.

"I am fine," Axel said as he shifted the bundle. "Please, take this to Amy, I cannot care for her and she is very hungry."

Landrew let the fighting staff fall from his hand, it made a dull thump on the ground as he took the child in his arms.

"She is a strong baby and I hope Amy will accept her…."

"Of course she will," Landrew fairly gasped as he cut Axel off. "But where is her mother?"

"I killed her," Axel breathed out softly and with great remorse. "If I had known that Florence had a child, then this baby would still have her mother at least."

Landrew looked at Axel, his eyes searching the young man's exhausted features. "Florence?" he finally asked, Axel nodded ever so slightly. The baby made a squeak and then began to cry but it sounded weak.

"Come," Landrew said. "Let Amy look at you."

"No," Axel answered firmly. "Do not even tell her I am here right now, I cannot stay. I was followed here and I promised that once I got the baby to safety I would let them take me. Landrew, I am so exhausted, I killed so many, in the darkness. And I killed the only woman I have ever loved, and deprived this baby of her mother, my soul is dead, and I wish to follow it now."

Axel turned and started to walk away but then he stopped and looked over his shoulder back at Landrew.

"I have named her Ispsi, and I ask that you forget the anger you have carried for so long because Max is now dead."

Landrew felt his knees tremble and he could not find words to speak, he watched as Axel took several more steps away from him and suddenly several men converged upon him. Axel put his arms out before him and they knocked him to the ground as they quickly tied his hands and feet and slung him over the back of a large black steed, the horse snorted and stomped until Axel was secure then with one powerful lunge, his muscles bunching and stretching beneath his fine coat, the horse was gone. The four men all turned as one for a moment and looked toward Landrew, his blurred vision made it hard to distinguish anything about them, then as if they had never been there, they were gone.

Several days later a very dirty and half-dead Axel was dropped off the back of the snorting sweaty horse and dragged into a large hall, where he was dropped on the floor before a table that had four people seated at it. There was three men and one woman, all dressed in white, gold and light pink garments.

"Axel William Ramses," the woman was the first to speak. Axel stirred and managed to sit up, he looked at the four regal-looking people before him and then glanced around the great room they had brought him to.

"We are Thorndin," one of the men spoke.

"You have been brought to the Kingdom of the Rising Sun," another of the men spoke. "To answer for all the lives you took in the cover of darkness," the final man finished.

"I always thought this place was a myth," Axel said, his voice husky from lack of water during the grueling and torturous trip.

"Why did you kill so many, there was not even a battle going on," one of the men stood up and walked around the edge of the table toward Axel, his hands clasped behind his back.

"Do you know what kind of terrible things you have set in motion?" another man said as he too stood up but he remained behind the table.

"We have been trying to bring the people, all of the people, to some form of peace, and now there is going to be a whole new war because of the men you have slain in cold blood."

Axel snorted and the woman looked down at him with an air of disgust.

"I hate to be the messenger of bad news but it has been war out there nonstop for several generations now."

"Only is select areas," one of the men said.

"We have taken control of well over half of this land and have been snuffing out the need for such violence, and now you have given them another reason to fight."

"Where were you when my friends were all slaughtered?" Axel suddenly shouted. "Less than fifty men, some of them with wives, children, all living in that camp, against two hundred? Where were you then?"

The four suddenly converged upon Axel and surrounded him just outside of arm's reach.

"It was a necessary loss."

"A sacrifice for the greater good."

"They had sins of their own."

"And now the land has been cleansed of them."

"Cleansed?" Axel said as he forced himself to stand so they could not look down at him anymore. "If you want this land to be cleansed and to stop the wars, then the killing has to stop first. No more killing for the greater good, no more slaughter just because someone is stronger than the other. No more bribes! You are corrupt!"

All four lashed out at once, striking Axel from each side, he saw it coming, was trying to invoke them, and he did not try to block any of the blows. Axel hit the stone floor hard and instantly had a ringing in his head.

"We are finished here."

"You will die now."

"By hanging, I think."

"We will leave your body on the rope as a visual for others."

"So they will know what we will do to anyone who disrupts our plans."

"But do not worry, we will send your family your bones once you rot off the rope."

"Unless the scavengers eat you first."

Axel pulled his hands beneath himself and slowly rose back to his feet. "I will welcome death," he said as he ran his tongue over a now bloody lip.

Thorndin all stood in a row in the huge doorway of the great hall and watched as Axel was walked to the stone tower that was built just for hanging the ones they put to death. Axel's hands were bound behind him and a rope was secured around his neck, one of the guards took a step back and raised his foot to kick Axel off the ledge but Axel jumped before the guard was able to complete his task.

"He truly was ready for death."

"Did not even put up a fight."

"Too bad, it is sporting to watch them struggle."

The fourth remained silent and continued to watch as the other three turned away, a short while later they heard him shout.

"Something is wrong, I feel it, a great power...." The other three rushed forward and looked upon Axel as he hung from the end of the rope. The woman stepped into the edge of the doorway and jumped into the air, her flowing garments exchanged for feathers as she changed into a yellow and gray oriole. She streaked toward Axel and cut the rope just above his head, his body plunged toward the ground and everyone held their breaths but to their astonishment Axel landed on his feet and stood there looking up at the oriole as she circled overhead.

Landrew had traveled hard the last two days closely following the tracks the horse had left, he was not exactly sure why Axel had been taken, but he knew that they would kill him, and once they tried and discovered they could not.... Landrew did not want to think of what they may do to him then. Landrew had just come to the gates of the kingdom and asked of Axel when the guard there pointed to their right and Landrew could see a man hanging by his neck.

"An example of those who disrupt the order of things," the guard said as he turned away. Landrew caught his breath and his legs nearly gave way beneath him, he reached out and put a supporting hand against the wall but part of him was relieved as he thought of all his worries over Axel being cursed because of him. Just then an oriole flew directly over Axel and Axel's body fell, Landrew watched as Axel landed on his feet and his heart sank.

"They can't kill him," Landrew said in fear and wonderment.

Axel was standing before the four who called themselves Thorndin once again, his hands still tied behind his back and his head bowed, the rope still around his neck.

"What is this deviltry?" the woman was the first to speak again.

"You had been hanging for some time, how are you still alive?"

"There are other ways we can kill you."

"Tell us what kind of darkness you have called upon to make this happen!"

"I am sorry," Axel said with head still bowed. "I do not know why I am not dead. I did not ask to keep living."

"We shall call our Shaman."

"She will know what you have done."

"And she will remove what protects you."

"Wait!"

Though he barely moved, Axel's heart leapt at the sound of that voice, the four turned toward the shout and watched as a man with flaming hair and a wounded face struggle with the guards at the door. The guards had him pinned down before he could even cross the threshold but Landrew continued to shout.

"I know what has happened to him, I know why he won't die, please grant me council!"

"You know this young man?"

"Yes," Landrew said as the guards continued to hold him down. "He is like a son to me."

"Very well, we grant you council."

"Take Axel away."

"We will call upon him when this is done."

Axel walked between the guards down the dark hallways beneath the earth, the smell was overpowering and the noise almost deafening as prisoners all around shouted and banged against the stone and rattled chains. They reached for them but many were too far away and the others had their hands smacked by the guards. Axel felt a small hand brush his forearm, it was cold and he felt a shiver run across his skin as he had the image of a dead child's hand touching him. Axel glanced down and saw the small white hand but instead of a child, it belonged to a creature he had never seen before, one with white skin and a wide mouth full of small sharp teeth. Its eyes were huge, blue and they danced with an inner mischievousness as the creature looked at him.

"You are special," the creature sang softly. "Oh, so special!"

"Shut up!" one of the guards shouted as he hit the bars of the creature's cell.

"What is that?" Axel asked but the guards ignored him.

"What was that thing?" Axel asked again, he could still feel the coldness of the creature's touch. Still the guards did not answer him, Axel glanced back toward the place where the creature had been but it was gone, retreated back into the darkness.

"I am so sorry," Landrew said when Axel found himself before the four again the next day. Landrew had briefly and hurriedly told Axel what had happened when he had been laid low by Martin so long ago now. "I did not know it would turn out like this."

"Stop your crying." Thorndin suddenly spoke up.

"It appears there is no helping it."

"It is not known for how much longer you will live."

"Snow Fairies are the most powerful creatures known to man."

"Even if we bring forward the one we have imprisoned here, he will not be able to break the magic that binds you to life."

"So we have a proposition for you."

"Serve us, answer every call you can, until your sins have been cleansed."

"Or until you finally die, whichever comes first."

Axel stared at the floor for a long time, his jaw clenching and unclenching as he thought about their offer.

"What will you have me doing?" he finally asked.

"You will work with us and others bound to our bidding, to stop the wars."

Axel bit back what he wanted to say and looked toward Landrew but Landrew gave him no hints of what to do.

"Why don't you just imprison me?" Axel asked, his voice showing his unease.

"Because we can use more fighting men in our secret guard."

"And you, Axel of the Might, are a fighting man."

"However, you will not be called by that name anymore."

"You will be called Axel the Black."

"For your sins will show when you work for us."

"You will become what your soul looks like."

"And it is now black as a moonless night."

Axel looked back down and was silent for a long time but they did not pressure him to make a decision, finally he looked back up and nodded.

"Axel William Ramses," one of the men said as he moved forward.

"You have chosen right," another said as he followed.

"This is the only way you can be cleansed." They had all moved forward now and was coming behind Axel.

"We bind you to us."

"To our every call."

"You must answer."

"Or suffer great punishment until you do."

"This is your duty to us."

"You will hear the cries of the hopeless."

"And you will go to them and aid them."

"This is your punishment for those you killed." Axel felt the cool edge of a knife tuck itself into the back of his collar and then slide down as it cut open the back of his shirt, he tried to look over his shoulder but could only see them standing there, the woman was closest and the men stood behind her, each had placed a hand upon her back or shoulder.

"You are now ours," the woman said as she placed both her hands against the bare skin of Axel's back. Axel felt a burning jolt flash through him, it seemed to last for a lifetime as it flowed through every part of his body and back again. The deed only took a moment and Axel fell to his knees, eyes wide and gasping for breath, and then the next wave hit him. Axel cried out as he pressed hands to his head, the sound of endless voices filled him, crying, pleading, wailing. Tears instantly welled in his eyes and he thought his ears would start to bleed from the pressure he suddenly felt in his head.

"Make them stop," Axel cried. "The voices! Make them stop!" Axel's body began to shake and he fell forward, his hands still grasping his head, his forehead now pressed into the cold stone floor. He turned his head and could see Landrew fighting against several guards that were holding him back, Landrew was shouting but Axel could not hear him over his own screams and the voices in his head. It suddenly became too much and with a gasp Axel went limp as his senses left him.

The man leaned over Axel's inert form and grasped a handful of his golden hair, pulling on it until Axel was in a semi-upright position. The man pulled down the black cloth that covered most of his face and looked in Axel's dazed, half-open eyes. The man then leaned in close and whispered in Axel's ear, his breath hot against the side of Axel's face.

"Those voices, you will eventually get used to them. You will learn to tune most of them out, though it may take years, but I will train you. But not all of them will go away, for the loudest ones can never be silenced. You will want to help them all, you will want to fly to them and extinguish their pain and sorrow, but you can't get to them all. And you will know true anguish when you are on your way to help one but their life is snuffed out before you get there. You will feel all their fear and pain and the snap of death on their very soul, and you will weep."

The man leaned back for a moment and studied Axel's face, then he once again leaned forward and whispered.

"My name is Viseman, I am leader of the council's secret guard. I now own you."

Chapter Forty-one

The voice awoke Tulley like a thunderclap; he was up on his feet before he had his eyes fully open.

"Graven!" the voice screamed in his mind again. Danger! Tulley felt his skin tingle as the power of the Druid in the great tree pulled at his magic tethers and sent screaming words to his mind.

"What is it!?" Tulley cried out, not realizing he was not speaking back in the Druid tongue.

"Graven!" the spirit screamed again. Tulley looked toward Lance's bed, in the near darkness he could see Lance's form on the thin pallet, one arm hung over the side, his knuckles against the floor. Tulley rushed to Lance and shook him, his body was heavy and he did not wake to Tulley's pleas. Tulley leaned down and placed his ear near Lance's face, finally he felt the tiny warm breath escape Lance's mouth and he leaned back only slightly relieved. Tulley wiped a hand across his own face and realized he was sweating heavily, though it was not a warm night, he took a moment to take stock of himself and found his mouth to be dry and his stomach hurt.

"Poison?" he said aloud as he placed a hand on Lance's face and found it to be drenched in sweat as well. Tulley tried shaking Lance awake once more but when that still did not work he pulled Lance from his bed and half dragged, half carried him from their room. As Tulley pulled Lance down the hall and stairs he noticed how quiet the tree was and that many of the doors and curtains to the children's rooms were open. The rooms were dark and silent, Tulley looked inside as he passed them and saw that the small beds were all empty. Tulley laid Lance near the fireplace of the great room downstairs, he took a moment to stir the tiny glowing embers and coax the fire back to life before he rushed back up the stairs to find Jessica. She was in her own room, but she was sitting on the floor next to her bed, the covers pulled from the mattress as if she knew something was wrong and tried to get up but couldn't. Tulley did not stop to see if she was even breathing, he picked her up in his arms and cradled her as he rushed back down the stairs, her clammy face against his neck. Tulley laid Jessica down beside Lance and without a second glance he jumped up again and rushed outside into the darkness.

"Supea!" Tulley cried out into the night as he circled the great tree. Just a few days prior all the adult Druids had left for their annual hunting trip to gather food for the cold season, the women and children Tulley had saved from the slavers had gone with them. Their home region was in the same direction and they expressed great interest in going home, Jarsic had agreed to escort them so they would be safe. The only ones left at the tree now had been Jessica, Lance, Supea, all the children, himself, and Gensieco.

What a time to be raided, Tulley thought as he continued to circle the tree and call for help from above, for a brief moment he feared Supea and her children may have been poisoned as well, but then he received an answer back. Tulley had gone almost a full circle around the tree when Supea dropped out of the darkness and landed in front of him in a crouch, then she stood up, her long limbs and thin black body seemed to rise out of the very darkness.

"There is something wrong," Supea said before Tulley could speak. "My ancestor told me to hide with the children until he could awaken you, what has happened, Tulley?"

"I don't know exactly, all the children are gone and Lance and Jessica have been poisoned."

Supea suddenly pushed past Tulley and ducked into the open doorway of the tree, she moved fast and though Tulley was right behind her, by the time he also entered the tree Supea was kneeling with Jessica pulled onto her lap. Tulley watched as Supea twined her fingers through the air just above Jessica's heart, she rocked back and forth as she concentrated on Jessica's invisible life thread that she now held. After several minutes of this Supea then flipped Jessica over and pressed her hand into the middle of Jessica's back. Jessica coughed and gagged as a dark foul liquid splashed from her mouth and made a small puddle on the floor.

"It is poison," Supea said softly as she then pulled Jessica upright and continued to rock her back and forth as she softly called her name over and over again until Jessica slowly opened her eyes. Jessica stared ahead blankly and moaned, then she coughed again and a tiny trickle of the dark poison ran out of the corner of her mouth.

"Hold her, keep her awake," Supea said as she gently pushed Jessica toward Tulley. Tulley took Jessica into his arms and softly spoke to her, after a moment Jessica finally looked at him and seemed to recognize him. Supea went through the same motions with Lance but it took longer for him to open his eyes and once he did he closed them again.

"Wake up!" Supea suddenly shouted in his ear as she roughly shook him. Lance's body trembled as Supea held onto him and his eyes widely stared forward for a time.

"Tulley?" Lance finally managed to say. "What happened to Jessica?"

"You have been poisoned," Supea said softly. "Please stay awake, it is a sleeping poison, concentrate on staying awake or you may fall asleep again and never awaken."

"I am so thirsty," Jessica said softly, she was sitting up now but still leaned against Tulley for support.

"Stay here, I will get some water," Tulley said as he leaned Jessica against Supea's shoulder and slowly rose to his feet.

"I suggest you get fresh water," Supea said softly as she watched Tulley dip from the barrel that sat in the corner. Tulley glanced back at her and then took a small sip from the cup, he gagged a little and spit the water out. How could they not have tasted the grittiness before? He wondered as he wiped his hand across his mouth, he suddenly felt a little dizzy and had to put his hand against the wall to steady himself.

"I will send one of my older children for fresh water," Supea said as she motioned for Tulley to come back and sit down. "You need to be cleansed, Tulley, you are sick as well, you are very pale all of the sudden."

Tulley's skin crawled as he felt Supea's power flow through the magic tether she took hold of in his back, it did not hurt but it made him feel strange and he wished to shy away from her touch. Supea softly tugged at the tether and twined her fingers around as she sensed the poison in Tulley's body and gathered what she could into one place. Tulley's stomach began to churn and he groaned a little as he slumped forward and pressed his hand against his abdomen. Supea suddenly pressed her hand hard against his back and though Tulley did not want to, his stomach heaved and he threw up a foul dark.mouthful of the poison. Tulley spit several times as he tried to clear the taste from his mouth, his stomach still churned but did not feel like expelling its contents anymore.

"Thanks," Tulley said as he wiped his mouth on the back of his hand and accepted a cup of fresh water from one of Supea's children. One of the children whispered in his mother's ear and Supea nodded in thanks, then she looked at Tulley and softly spoke in Druid to him.

"I do not wish to alarm Jessica, so let us speak in my tongue."

Tulley looked at her for a moment and then nodded for Supea to continue. "My eldest son says he cannot find Gensieco, and the two horses are gone as well. The disappearance of the children, the poisoning, the direction they seemed to have gone; it appears that Gensieco cannot be trusted. What will you do, Tulley?"

Tulley set his cup down and slowly rose to his feet.

"I am going to eradicate that camp of slavers once and for all."

The leader of the slavers was a large man who called himself Durban. He was loud and vulgar and threw things at his men as he yelled about the death and disappearances of their hunting parties over the past three days.

"For some reason the lot of you filthy, no-good fucking bastards can't find any damn food without getting killed. And by what?! A single damn shadow, a man that appears out of no fucking where and can overpower five of you damn fools with just his bare fucking hands!"

"Seven," one man called out. Durban stopped in mid throw of a fist-sized rock and turned toward the man who had spoken up.

"Shit head!" he shouted as he hurled the rock at him instead. The rock barely missed the man's head as he ducked out of the projectile's path. Durban cursed at the man for ducking and hurled a second rock at him.

"Do I have to show all your fuck sticks just how to catch one bloody damn man?" Durban said as he turned around in the middle of the camp and addressed everyone.

"What a terrible noise," Tulley said to himself as he watched from above while the big man abused his men. Tulley sighed and looked toward the dead bodies he had stacked up on a large branch, in the gathering dusk they could be mistaken for a large knot on the tree.

"Well," Tulley said to the corpses as he stood over them. "I thank you all for your help thus far, the weapons you had carried will be quite useful tonight. Now just one last favor I must ask you," Tulley grinned as he put his foot on top of one of the dead men's head.

Body parts began to fall from above and thick, sticky blood dripped down like a light rain shower. At first Durban had continued to scream even after they had all heard the first heavy thump of a torso hitting the ground, then an arm landed right on top of Durban and knocked him down.

"The bastard's in the trees!" Durban yelled as he got back to his feet. A few of the men screamed when they realized what was happening, one young man saw a severed head bounce on the ground and roll toward him, his mouth was open in sheer terror as the head bumped against his ankle and he fell to the ground in a dead faint when he realized he recognized the face that now blankly stared up at him.

A few of the men heeded Durban's words and turned upwards to the tree that was suddenly raining down bits and pieces of their comrades but before they could reach him, Tulley was suddenly falling from the tree as well. He glanced at the handful of men that were climbing the trunk in an attempt to catch him and laughed. Tulley was dressed in black and in the gathering darkness he flitted from one man to another and dispatched them with such speed that a few men were left swinging their swords at shadows that they thought were him before they realized they had a grievous wound and fell to the ground. Six of them fell to Tulley's stolen blades before one was able to touch him with their sword, but even then it was a scratch across his shoulder that didn't even hurt and Tulley laughed in the man's face as he stabbed a small dagger right behind his ear.

"Hey, you bastard!" Durban suddenly screamed out and everyone seemed to freeze, including Tulley.

"I think I have something that you want. We found him wandering around the area and a little bitch told us you would protect him no matter what."

Tulley stood his ground but glanced toward Durban as he vaguely wandered if this villain was bluffing or not. Two men held up a body between them, a man with bowed head and hands tied tightly behind his back with a cord running to his neck, a man with thick scruffy black hair and beard, a man with one leg. Tulley did not make a move as he looked at Lance between the two men, they had already roughed him up, his wooden leg was gone and his face had bruises and a swollen eye.

"Just get out of here!" Lance shouted without looking up. Durban swung at Lance and buried his fist in Lance's stomach, Lance's body curled in on itself and the two men dropped him to the ground where he lay like a child and struggled to breathe.

"Do you know him?" Durban asked as he turned back toward Tulley, who was still standing between several men with weapons raised.

"I have never seen him before," Tulley said with a cold tone.

"Well, I suppose I can put the gimp out of his misery then. What bastard would want to live through life missing their damn leg anyway," Durban grabbed Lance by the hair and pulled him into a semi-sitting position, his hand flicked out and a small dagger appeared between his fingers, then the dagger was pressed against the soft flesh just under Lance's jaw. Lance gasped as the point broke skin but then the dagger fell from Durban's hand as another, smaller dagger, grazed his forearm and just barely missed cutting across Lance's face.

"Oh, you bastard, you are good," Durban said as he let go of Lance. "I do believe you lied to me. Now, if you want this whimpering pile of shit to live, then surrender to me."

Tulley held a second small dagger hidden in his hand as his eyes took one quick sweep across the area and he quickly counted the men in the image he now held in his mind. Twenty-two of them just there, at least a dozen more out of sight but ready at a moment's notice. Lance was too far away, he would not be able to get to him before someone killed him, even with four more of the small throwing daggers at his belt and all the other weapons still hidden on his body. Durban kicked Lance as he lay on the ground to speed up Tulley's decision making, Tulley fairly growled at the large man and then with a flick of his wrist the small dagger was buried up to its hilt in the ground just in front of Durban. Tulley unbuckled a belt that was laden with weapons and it dropped heavily to the ground, then he unclasped the short black cloak he had stolen from one of the men to reveal the three short swords he had strapped to his back.

"Don't do it," Lance managed to cough out from the ground, Durban kicked him again. As the weapons fell from Tulley's body he slowly walked forward, toward Durban and Lance, and now as the last one hit the ground Tulley suddenly leapt at Durban with his fist raised, Durban didn't have time to move and they both hit the ground hard, nearly on top of Lance. A second later the entire group of men converged upon them to take hold of Tulley, with fists flying and heavy stinking bodies they quickly piled up as they tried to overpower him. One man fell on top of Lance and with a squeak of pain, Lance passed out.

Lance awoke at daybreak, he was still laying where they had left him with his arms tied behind his back and that cord around his neck. His whole body hurt and he slowly began to wiggle himself around so he could see where everyone had gone, a great feeling of dread grabbed his chest when he saw Tulley. They had ripped his shirt off and Lance could clearly see the tattoos that decorated Tulley's torso, the hand-prints seemed to stand out more than ever. They had outstretched his arms and tied him up between a set of sapling trees, the thin cords were cutting into his wrists and leaving bruises on the already swollen skin as he was held just high enough off the ground that he could not kneel and it was difficult to stay on his feet when Durban was constantly knocking them out from under his body. Durban was standing before Tulley, slightly bent over with his head turned to the side so he could look Tulley in the eye, he held the end of a belt in his hand, the belt was wrapped around Tulley's neck and Durban tightened it and loosened it as he spoke to Tulley.

"I can do this all day, you little shit, so it is just a matter of time. Tell me, where is the man they call the Black Sparrow? You know the bastard, the one they made so many scary stories about...the Death Whisperer, the Cursed, the God of the Battle, the Dead Man Walking."

"The man you seek is dead," Tulley said, his voice straining from the belt that was choking him. Durban tightened the belt until Tulley's eyes rolled upwards and his straining body went lax, then

Durban released the belt and sneered as Tulley coughed and slowly came back to life.

"I don't like that answer, because you see, the bastard I am looking for is immortal, and it is rather hard to be dead when one is immortal," Durban waited for an answer but when Tulley remained silent he pulled the belt tight again.

"Stop it!" Lance managed to call out, his voice weak from lack of water. Durban looked toward Lance and smiled viciously.

"Aw, your little gimp is still alive," Durban said as he motioned for Lance to be brought closer. A man roughly grabbed the back of Lance's shirt and dragged him toward Durban, he was dropped on the ground several paces in front of Tulley. Lance looked at Tulley but was only met with his usual blank stare.

"I am sorry," Lance managed before Durban kicked him right between the shoulder blades, the toe of Durban's boot hit him in the spine and Lance felt lightning bolts of pain flash and spasm through his body.

"Don't touch him," Tulley wheezed but Durban only kicked Lance twice more before turning upon Tulley and kicking him in his exposed ribs. Tulley's body swung from the blow and he gasped but continued to hold his ground.

"Don't touch him again," Tulley said louder this time.

"Oh, like this?" Durban said he rounded on Lance once more.

"Durban!" Tulley shouted. Durban turned back to Tulley and grabbed the end of the belt in his meaty hand.

"Answer me, you stinking shit," Durban said as he tightened the belt. Tulley gasped and tried to speak but could not for Durban had pulled the belt to tightly, he released some of the pressure and sneered as Tulley coughed, Durban bent down slightly with his ear turned toward Tulley.

"You're gonna die," Tulley said hoarsely.

"That's not the answer I was looking for," Durban said as he tightened the belt yet again. Tulley's arms strained and he raised his body up slightly, this time Durban had completely cut off his air supply and was watching Tulley with a malicious grin as his face began to turn red and his body shook a little. One of Durban's men walked up to him then and Durban turned toward him, the belt still tight around Tulley's neck.

"Did you get that old bitch up?" Durban asked.

"No, sir, we can't seem to wake her, seems like she is in one of her trances."

"Dump some fucking water on her," Durban said in a sudden rage as he swung at the man. "For months now she has been dreaming of some bastard with handprints tattooed on his back and now that we finally find the shithead that old hag won't come to see him. Damn her! Toss her in the river if you have to!"

The messenger quickly left and Durban turned back to Tulley only to see he had choked him for too long, Tulley's body was hanging limp, blood ran down his forearms in tiny rivulets and his head hung down.

"Aw, damn it," Durban said as he loosened the belt and then gave Tulley several kicks and one good punch to his sides and chest. Tulley came back almost instantly, coughing and gasping, his arms once again straining against the cords that held them outstretched.

"You're gonna die," Tulley coughed out.

"Oh! Really!?" Durban said, still angry about the old woman who was not coming out of her tent, Durban grasped Tulley by the hair and forced his head back.

"You are not exactly in a good position to talk back, you bastard," Durban fumed. "I wanna see you talk back like this!"

Durban then pushed Tulley's head down into his crouch and began to thrust his hips back and forth as he held Tulley's hair.

"Stop!" Lance cried out as tears of pain and anger clouded his vision while he watched Durban humiliate his friend and he could not do anything to help him. The others in the camp began to laugh and cheer

Durban on as Durban continued to grasp Tulley's hair and press his face into his groin.

"Stop!" Lance cried out again as he tried to rise but with his hands still tied he only succeeded in wiggling around on the ground, his leg kicking toward Durban and his stump uselessly waving back and forth.

Durban suddenly cried out in pain and fell backwards, his hands going to a rapidly spreading bloodstain on the inside of his thigh. Lance looked at Tulley as Durban rolled across the ground still holding his inner thigh. Tulley's mouth was bloody and his eyes flashed with a murderous gleam as he spit out the mouthful of flesh he had just bitten off of Durban's leg. For a moment the men were in shocked silence as they looked at their leader curled up on the ground, his hands pressed to the tender inner flesh of his thigh, blood slowly but steadily staining the ground around him.

"Yes!" Lance suddenly cried out as he could not hold back the pride that suddenly swept over him as he looked at Tulley and how he had fought back just then. Durban was back on his feet in moments, his hands now slick with blood and his legs shaking, he yelled like an enraged animal and charged Tulley. Tulley could not block any of the blows, he could only continue to hang by his wrists as Durban rocked his body with each heavy punch and swift kick. Pained gasps and coughs escaped Tulley's mouth and his hands uselessly grasped at the air as he was pummeled. Durban managed to hit Tulley a half-dozen times before Tulley suddenly took in a deep breath and flexed his arms and shoulders so hard that Lance saw veins pop up all over his body. Then in a single quick, fluid motion, Tulley raised himself up and swung his legs forward to wrap around Durban's neck. The two saplings that Tulley was tied to began to bend under the weight of both the men, shouts of surprise erupted as three of the men quickly stepped in and tried to pry Tulley's legs off from around Durban's neck. Durban's mouth was wide open as his tongue lolled around in the dark opening, his eyes were huge and quickly becoming bloodshot. Tulley was choking him with the full intent of killing him and the panic registered on Durban's face as his legs flailed uselessly and his hands pried and beat against Tulley's powerful legs. A couple of the men fell upon Tulley as they tried to restrain him but with so many now holding onto Tulley, the saplings finally gave way, one bent at the roots and the other broke and toppled. All the men went down in a pile and Tulley sudden found his hands loosened, he immediately pulled the belt from around his neck with one hand while the other grasped a dagger that was at one man's hip. With the belt gone from around his neck Tulley suddenly seemed to double in strength as he took in one deep breath and roared at the men. He reached up and cut the cord that was around one wrist and then tossing the knife to the other hand he cut the opposite cord, one man was reaching for the knife while another held Tulley around the waist, the third was also trying to get Durban out of the death lock that Tulley still held him in. Tulley moved so fast that Lance had a hard time taking it all in. Tulley buried the knife into the back of the man who held him around the waist, the man cried out as the knife hilt made a hollowed thump against his back. Tulley then swung at the other two, one man felt the knife bite into his upper arm down to the bone, the other got his throat slashed and fell away with blood gushing down his chest, Durban was quickly losing consciousness and his legs were moving slower now as his face took on an ashen color. Tulley stabbed the man in the back again but the man still held him around the waist and kept him pinned down as the rest of the camp converged upon them. Tulley was just raising the knife for a third stab into the man's back when there was a sudden thunderclap amongst the men and a gust of air blew past them all.

Lance's whole body shivered and he felt goose flesh ripple across his skin as he saw the figure appear right next to Tulley. She was tall and very thin, with long thin limbs and long fingers as she was holding a hand out before her. She was as pale as fresh snow and her silver and white hair was long and hanging nearly to the ground with little trinkets woven into several thick braids. Her face showed many wrinkles and her body was bent with age and the weight of the heavy robes and more trinkets sewn onto them. In one ugly claw-like hand she grasped an animal's curved rib as a walking cane, the other hand was reaching out toward Tulley's left shoulder, but instead of grasping his shoulder, she grasped the air just above the shoulder and yanked her fist backwards.

Tulley suddenly went rigid and dropped the knife, his whole body began to tremble and he seemed to be having difficulty moving, his limbs had become stiff and only jerked in little spasms at his commands to move; the woman closed her eyes and sighed in exaltation.

"You have a strong magic tether," she said, her voice barely above a whisper. Tulley managed to turn his shaking head toward her and he looked at her with such a malicious glare that Lance was suddenly scared; the bent old woman laughed.

"Stand up," she said as she jerked on the invisible thread. Tulley was suddenly on his feet, his back was ramrod straight and his shaking limbs now hung uselessly. Tulley's feet left the ground and he hung in suspension for several long moments before the woman drove her fist toward the ground and Tulley's body followed. Tulley landed on his back and with such force that Lance heard the air rush from his body; he groaned as he took in a breath and the old woman leaned over him. Tulley looked up at her with his teeth bared and uttered one word as he reached a shaking hand across his body in an attempt to reach the magic tether at his shoulder. The woman then raised her cane and slammed it into the side of his head.

Chapter Forty-two

The old woman in white walked around Tulley as she gazed at his tattoos, sometimes reaching a withered hand out to run a finger down a line or pluck at something and laugh when Tulley flinched in pain. Tulley was kneeling, his head hung down and his arms were tied behind his back in such a fashion so that his forearms were on top of each other and the fingers of one hand was clasping the elbow of the other arm. A thin cord ran from around his neck to his ankles so when he was pulled to his feet he had to walk, shuffling his feet and slouched over lest he choke himself.

"How long have you had your magic tethers?" the woman asked, her raspy voice showing her age. Tulley did not answer and the woman smiled as she grasped a thread at his back and gave it a harsh jerk. Tulley grimaced as he felt her pulling at pieces of his very soul.

"Longer than you have lived, I'm sure," Tulley answered, his voice straining and sweat beading his forehead. The woman laughed as she walked around to stand in front of Tulley, she ran a hand down the side of his face and licked his sweat from her fingers.

"You think you know my age? Do you know who I am then?"

"I have a pretty good idea," Tulley said as he turned his eyes up toward her and stared harshly. The woman grasped the rib cane with both hands and bent down so she could look Tulley in the eye expectantly; though she was clearly old and carried the cane with her she walked without difficulty.

"Only a couple of races are said to be able to see someone's lifeline," Tulley continued. "That's why they are marked out in tattoos when one gets a tether inlaid."

"And I am very impressed with yours," the woman interrupted him and reached out with a knife to run the flat edge along one of the tattoos.

"You are not Huldra, for they have a tail and are mute unless they use some form of disfiguring magic. So you are a Druid, or were one."

A smile began to creep across her mouth as she gave the slightest of nods.

"But I am white, while Druids are black."

"I have heard of an albino Druid who became a magic eater. They call her White Willow."

"I am impressed," the old woman said as she once again circled around to Tulley's back to inspect the vivid black tattoos that were now shinning from Tulley's perspiration. She ever so gently ran her fingertips across Tulley's skin until she came to the handprints, she paused for a moment but then continued.

"Do you know how a shaman eats magic?" she asked as she leaned over Tulley. Tulley shied away as she breathed on his face, her breath was rancid and smelled like rotten meat.

"I do not know how," Tulley answered when she would not back away as she awaited an answer from him.

"Normally I can just grasp a tether and cut it free of the flesh, but yours…." She paused as she pulled at one of the threads. "Are woven in quite deep. It is a wonder the shaman who inlaid these did not kill you in the process."

"I am stubborn," Tulley said. Willow leaned in close to Tulley's ear and breathed on him again as she spoke.

"You have much power, it makes me giddy," she whispered. She raised the small knife she held in her other hand and made a shallow cut along one of Tulley's tattoos, just enough for the blood to color the edge of the blade. Tulley didn't even flinch but for a moment Lance saw his eyes narrow as he stared at the ground. Willow raised the knife to her face and sniffed the blood, she sighed audibly and then she licked the knife blade. A visible shiver ran through her body and she giggled like a demented child.

"Even your blood is ripe with power!" she said, hardly able to conceal her excitement. For a moment she did not seem like a bent old woman anymore, she stood up to her full and impressive height and stared at the knife blade as she held it over her head, her eyes dancing, she slowly licked off the last drops of blood, then she spun around and buried the knife blade into Tulley's shoulder.

Tulley was knocked over from the impact and Willow stood over him as she laughed again, her hand went to the fresh wound and she caught blood in it as she pulled the knife free, Tulley gasped and turned his face away from her as she licked the blood from her palm and fingertips.

"I will have your blood," she said between licks. "And I will have your magic tethers." Willow turned toward several of the men who had been standing guard and gave them a little nod, they stepped forward and grasping Tulley by the arms, they pulled him to his feet and began to shuffle him away.

"Where are you taking him?" Lance called after Willow as she turned to follow, she paused for a moment and looked back at him.

"We are just going to have a little talk. He knows where I can find someone, someone more powerful than he is. Don't worry, little man, I will bring your friend back to you."

Tulley was forced to kneel, they pushed him down and laughed when he nearly fell on his face.

"So," Willow said as she seemed to glide into the scene. "Where is the Black Sparrow?"

"You get right to it, don't you," Tulley said as he tried to adjust his knees, he was kneeling on a sharp stone, it felt like it had already cut his shin. "I don't know where he is exactly," Tulley answered as his eyes roamed to the guards around them.

"You will not escape me," Willow said snidely as she leaned closer and ran the tip of her small knife along another tattoo, blood instantly welled up and this time she pressed her mouth against Tulley's skin to lap up the liquid. Tulley pulled away from her with a hiss.

"Do I disgust you?"

"Yes, more than most I have met of late."

"That's lovely," she said as she ran her tongue over another small cut on the back of his shoulder.

"What is she to you?" Tulley asked. "Gensieco."

"I am the one asking questions," Willow hissed as she fairly draped herself over Tulley's shoulder and ran a claw-like hand across his bare chest, her long fingers leaving red marks where she dug in her nails.

"What is she to you?" Tulley asked again as he ignored her while she pressed her body against his. "Release her."

"Release her?" Willow laughed. "But I have no spell binding her." Willow hummed to herself as she tugged at a magic tether and Tulley's vision began to blur, Willow released the tether and his vision snapped back to normal; Tulley gasped. Willow laughed softly as she snaked her body around Tulley and was now sitting in front of him.

"Then why does she come back to…." Tulley suddenly became silent as a thought struck him, everything suddenly made sense. "Jarsic, why didn't you tell me?" Tulley said softly as he closed his eyes and shook his head.

"Jarsic, that is an old Druid name...come to a conclusion, did you?" Tulley opened his eyes and found the knifepoint right before his right pupil, his head snapped back but Willow's hand went behind his neck and held him still.

"Her father was a Druid. I had no daughters to pass on the knowledge of being a shaman so many years ago I sent several of my sons out to have children of their own. None of them returned, but sometime later I heard of a half-breed Sprite, she was shunned by her own people because her mother had been raped by a Druid. I bought her, and gave her love when she was small, treated her like she was my own, and she may even be my granddaughter. I taught her many things, and as she grew and began to come into her power I pushed her forward, trained her harder because, one day, she will rule all of this. Can you just imagine, the strength and magical ties of a Druid and the ability to make anyone bow to her whims like a Sprite. It is such a beautiful combination, and so very powerful. I will be by her side as she rules, advising what to do, we will bring these lands back together and all will love her whether they want to or not."

"You are sick," Tulley said as he struggled against her hand, the knife still so very close to his eye. "When I first found her she was being savaged by one of your men, you call that training?"

"Oh," Willow sighed as she drew the knife back but continued to hold the back of Tulley's neck. "I had hoped she had actually killed him on her own, the beatings helps to bring her powers out, helps her to practice. You know, it is actually very exhausting for a Sprite to take control of five or six men at once, but with her Druid half she can now pull on the magic of the woods around her and control so many more. Did it confuse you when she left with so many children?"

"No, I have experienced her power myself, I know she has more strength than a normal Sprite."

"And after I finally discover the Black Sparrow I will rid him of his magic tie and give it to her, she will be even more powerful. And I will suck out his immortality for myself. Oh, how it must taste sweet, so many generations of built-up power and the immortality granted him by one of the most powerful fairies of our history, the malicious Snow Fairy. If only they were not all killed off, I would just find those sinister little creatures and suck the life and power out of them, one, by, one," she spoke the last words slowly and tapped her finger against Tulley's nose with each word.

Tulley curled the side of his lip up and bared his teeth, Willow laughed as she brought her face closer to stare at his pale green eyes.

"You are hiding something, I suppose I was too busy to notice it before, but I see, in your eyes. What is it? A truth shroud? You must know where the Black Sparrow is then, but no matter. I will have the truth out of you before morning."

Tulley spit in Willow's eye then, a large glob of mucus he had been working up in his mouth all the while she was speaking. Willow fell back with a cry as she rubbed at her eye, the liquid ran down one cheek and glistened. Two men instantly pounced on Tulley and drove him to the ground as they beat him with heavy sticks, Willow sat down for a moment as she studied the spit on her hand, then she also lapped that up like an animal.

They brought Tulley back that evening and roughly deposited him on the ground several paces away from Lance. Tulley landed on his side, his back to Lance, slightly curled up from the way he was still tied, and remained thus. Lance could see fresh wounds on his body, all of them cuts and slices along his tattoos, his back was covered in them, blood still dripped out of some of them in small lines as gravity pulled them down.

"Tulley?" Lance said, his voice slightly cracked from fear. Tulley did not move and Lance called his name again, slightly louder but still fearful.

"I am here," Tulley answered. He tried to move himself around so he could face Lance but gave up after a few tries.

"Tulley, I am so sorry," Lance said, a sob entering his tone now.

"Sorry for what?"

"Everything," Lance said as he fought back the hot tears that burned his eyes. "You told me to stay, Supea told me to stay, even Jessica told me to stay. And I still sneaked out and followed you. I don't know what I thought I could do, I'm a terrible fighter and missing a leg...."

"You are a terrible fighter," Tulley cut him off and Lance choked back a sob. "But don't worry about all of this. We will be just fine."

"But she's going to kill you," Lance said between breaths.

"Nah, I have been in worse places. They are going to slip up, they always do. And when that happens I can kill them."

They were silent for a time and Tulley listened as Lance choked back the sobs that threatened to overtake him.

"Hey," Tulley called out to him. "It's all right for a man to cry."

Lance could not hold them back anymore, the tears ran down his dirty face and stung his cheeks, the sobs racked his aching body. The thin ropes around his wrists were leaving raw and bleeding cuts, he was angry at himself for their situation, he was hungry and he was ashamed that he had been caught, tied up and that he now stank like urine.

"Tulley," Lance gasped out finally. "I'm so scared, what are they going to do now?"

"Well, I hope they let you live," Tulley answered and Lance began to sob again. The sun had set completely now and left them in darkness, Tulley wiggled around on the ground again and finally managed to get into a sitting position and leaned himself against a sapling like Lance was doing. His body was turned so Lance could only see his left side in the darkness, but he could see the dark stain and glisten of blood that covered his right shoulder. Tulley closed his eyes and let Lance cry for a little longer before he spoke again.

"Willow can't pull my magic tethers out, so her last chance at claiming them as her own would be to take my blood, and tie it in with her own...."

"Please stop," Lance suddenly cried. "Why can't we just get out of here?"

"Just a little tied up at the moment," Tulley said dryly.

"You are terrible at humor," Lance said, but it calmed him and after a short while he was able to stop his sobbing.

"Why don't you just give her your magic tethers? You had told me once that you regret having them."

"It's not that easy," Tulley said as he turned his head upwards and looked at the newly risen moon shining through the branches. "My tethers are woven through my ribs and tied to my true magic tie near my heart, I can't just release them, they have to be ripped out."

"Will you die?" Lance asked, his voice on the verge of sobbing again. Tulley slowly looked down from the moon and stared at something just ahead of him.

"Some people have lived through it. But they were maimed, they lost their senses. They were blind, deaf, mute...some of them lost the ability to walk."

Lance closed his eyes and could feel the grittiness in them, he could not cry anymore, his tears had dried up and his face hurt from their bite on his raw cheeks.

"I suppose that is only if she rips out my true one as well," Tulley finished.

"But I don't want you to die," Lance said with such a sorrow in his voice that Tulley physically flinched.

"It will be okay, I have done everything else in this life, dying is the last thing I have left."

"Don't say that," Lance said. "Where is your old friend? Axel? Where is he? If we call to him won't he come? Isn't that what he is supposed to do? You have told me so much about him now, he is a good person, he will save us!"

"He, he does not wish to...." Tulley spoke slowly and then stopped as they heard footsteps coming closer and saw torches moving toward them.

"Are you boys having a good conversation?" Willow asked as she came into view. She reached out and caressed the left side of Tulley's face, he closed his eyes in a grimace but said nothing.

"I need your blood now," Willow said as she now ran her hand over Tulley's hair as if she were stroking a pet.

"Do whatever you want to me," Tulley said through clenched teeth. "But don't lay a hand on my friend."

"Oh, how noble," Willow said as she stepped back to allow her men to step closer. They grabbed Tulley by the arms and lifted him up, then they brought him forward and as they turned him Lance gasped and shouted in anger, the entire right side of Tulley's face was burned. The skin was red and blistered, his ear was gone and his eye socket was a dark shadow that still leaked blood down to his neck and shoulder.

"You monsters!" Lance cried out as he watched them drop Tulley to his knees before Willow. One man grasped Tulley by the hair and pulled his head back, Tulley looked at Lance with his one good eye and whispered, "Be strong." Then Willow slashed his throat with a knife.

Lance cried out as the men forced Tulley forward so his blood would fall into a bowl that Willow set on the ground.

"No! He was your friend!" Lance suddenly screamed out as he fell forward in some vain attempt to help. "Why didn't you come to save him? He defended your name! Are you really so selfish to hide and turn your back on the people?" Lance continued to cry and scream until someone hit him over the head and he fell flat on his face. Lance lay on the ground motionless as his head spun and he fought against unconsciousness. After a short while he heard the sound of something heavy falling to the ground, then the receding footsteps as the light of the torches also left. Lance pushed himself up enough to raise his head and look. Tulley lay on his face, his arms still awkwardly tied behind him, his back glistened in the feeble moonlight from the numerous cuts Willow had made along his tattoos; he was motionless. Lance let his head fall back to the ground and let his unbelieving mind go blank.

Sometime through the night a noise awoke Lance from semi-consciousness, someone nearby was sobbing. Lance lifted his head again and looked toward Tulley. Someone had cut his bonds and rolled him onto his back and now a small childlike figure was draped over his bare and bloody torso. Gensieco sobbed as she pressed her face against his chest and beat her tiny fist against the unyielding flesh.

"I'm so sorry, Tulley," she managed between sobs. "This wasn't supposed to happen, she promised not to kill you. I'm so sorry, I love you!"

Lance slowly let his head fall back to the ground and he closed his eyes again.

Lance was awoken again at daybreak, this time by angry shouts. Men were running back and forth and Willow was screaming at them all, Gensieco was gone. She had taken all of the children, most of the horses, and Tulley's body with her.

Chapter Forty-three

"Tell me more, about the man you call Axel," Willow said as she reclined on a pile of furs. Lance sat on the ground across from her, his hands were not tied anymore, they did not fear he would do anything now because they had broken his only good leg the day before.

"I have already told you everything I know," Lance said weakly. "And you have killed the only man left who personally knew Axel."

"Yes, I suppose that was a foolish thing to do," Willow said. She picked up some small cuts of meat from a plate next to her and dropped them into her mouth. The meat was raw and smelled like decay but Lance was so hungry that he watched her eat with longing for a bite of the fowl stuff. Next she picked up a cup and drank from it, there was a long thin knife resting in the cup and she slowly drew the knife out, Lance closed his eyes for he did not wish to see the thing on the knife blade again.

"Does this bother you that much?" Willow asked. "It is just an eye, one full of power. I plucked it from the head of its owner as punishment for disobeying."

"No, it is a lovely eye," Lance answered, it was what Willow had instructed him to say when he had first seen the blue eye skewered to the knife blade.

"It is lovely," she said as she placed it back in the cup and poured water over it again.

"I suppose I have no need of you any longer," Willow said as she took another drink from the cup. Lance's stomach churned as Willow waved her hand and someone roughly grabbed the back of Lance's shirt and began to drag him outside.

"No, wait!" Lance cried as he tried to pry the man's hand free. The man did not stop as he pulled Lance across the ground. Lance's leg shot pain through his hip and back, after several very short moments of fighting Lance became still as he tried to stay conscious and fight against the pain. Lance was released and left lying on his back, panting heavily and his vision fading in and out as he stared at the sky through the trees overhead. He didn't even look at the man who now towered over him with raised sword, instead he was squinting hard at the large shadow that was now clouding his vision. A black shadow, with wings spread as it dropped straight for him. Lance raised one hand slightly and the man's sword began to fall for him but before it reached Lance's neck the shadow was upon him. With a terrified cry the man was suddenly lifted into the air, the sword dropped from his grasp to land next to Lance's head and a wingtip, soft but powerful, brushed against Lance's face as the bird carried the man upwards with it. The man's head was clasped in the bird's clawed feet and the bird spun in circles as it rose higher and higher, the man's arms and legs flailing uselessly as he screamed. The shadow-like creature reached a suitable height and then released its hold on the man and watched as the man plummeted back to the ground, spinning and screaming, his arms and legs jerking back and forth.

The man landed near Lance with a sickening thud and Lance felt the wind of the impact and the man's hand brush his shoulder as it came to earth next to him, he dared a look at the man and instantly regretted it as the man's head was now at an odd angle from his body, blood leaking from his nose and mouth.

The area was suddenly alive with commotion as men ran forward, weapons in hand, all of them looking up at the bird overhead; one of them stepped on Lance and he curled up in pain as he attempted to make himself as small as he could. The bird suddenly dived and once again grabbed a man's head in his feet, only this time the bird plucked the man's eyes out with two quick movements of its black feathered head. The man screamed as his hands grasped the bird's feet, another man with a war hammer swung at the bird and struck it in the back, the bird screeched and spun away to land on the ground as a man dressed in black from his ankles to his wrists. The man in black leapt up as soon as he came to a stop and using just his hands he struck at two of the men and they immediately went down. Lance felt someone trip over him and he cried out in pain as his wounded leg was jostled, the man in black noticed and seemed to go into a rage as he bowled over three men, swung a wild arm at a fourth, ducked under two sword swings and broke the knees of two others on his mad dash toward Lance. The man came to a stop and stood before Lance, his bare feet planted and his fists at the ready. The black garb covered him neatly from head to foot, even covering his face so that only his eyes showed; they were bright blue and dancing with an inner power Lance had never seen in any man before.

There were fourteen men left, several of them took a step back as they looked at this stranger in black, two of them turned to run. With a thunderclap Willow suddenly appeared before the two fleeing and she reached a long fingered hand out. She caught one young man by the throat and held him, the other arm swung her walking cane around, the sharpened edge cut through the back of the other's neck and he fell in mid-stride, his body twitching. Willow looked at the man she still held in her grasp, she hissed at him and then with a flick of her wrist the man was thrown to the side. He landed hard and got back up holding his arm, he didn't even look back at the scene but ran as he cradled his injured arm to his chest.

"Who are you?" Willow called out, her very voice sent shivers across Lance's skin and he whimpered softly.

"The one you have been looking for," the man called back, his voice strong and unfaltering as he stood against the odds.

"I thought so!" Willow said as she clapped her hands, her voice suddenly bubbling over with excitement. "I have been searching for you. But why do you come to me now?"

"I did not come to you, he called me," the man indicated Lance. Lance slowly pulled his arms away from his face and looked upwards at the man in black, the man was looking back down at him, his eyes were the most vibrant blue Lance had ever seen.

"Oh! So I have been doing this all wrong, I should have just called your name. Axel, Axel, Axel…." Willow mocked as she seemed to dance closer. "I need your aid, Axel, give me your strength so I may become immortal."

Willow was standing face to face with Axel now and Axel slowly lowered his arms to a more relaxed stance.

"I give you my immortality, it is yours for the taking," Axel said softly as he raised his hands slightly at either side, palms upwards. Willow laughed and then with a speed and strength that denied her aged body she raised the rib bone walking cane and struck Axel in the chest. Lance cried out when he saw the end of the cane go clear through Axel and protrude out of his back, but not breaking through the black fabric so instead it made a tent-like shape. Axel grunted and hunched forward, his hands grasping the cane in front of him, Willow reached out and wrapped her hands over his, slowly she pulled his hands free and then continued to hold them as she leaned forward and pressed her lips against Axel's through the black shroud. Lance suddenly felt sick as he watched this unfold just above him. Axel's body went rigid and he was suddenly standing ramrod straight as a pulsing glow seemed to come from both of them. The remaining men began to step back as they watched Willow and Axel begin to rise into the air, their feet now off the ground and the pulsing growing brighter.

"No!" Lance moaned as he watched the two glowing figures rise up, Willow's hands now holding either side of Axel's face as she continued to kiss him. The pulsing glow quickly grew to a constant light that seemed to dim even the sun, then with an ear-deafening boom like the sound of a storm rolled together into a single second, the two broke apart and fell back to the ground. Axel managed to land on his feet but Willow lay sprawled across the ground, her arms and legs akimbo and her white garments flecked in blood. She screamed as she tried to get to her feet, blood streaming out of her nose, ears, eyes and mouth. Several of the men that were still standing looked at Willow and fled, the remaining men stood frozen until Willow's voice cried out over the clearing.

"Kill him! Kill him!"

Lance raised his head enough to see Axel kneeling several paces away from him, the rib cane still pierced through his body. Axel pushed himself up, his body slightly bent as he grasped the cane in both hands and grimacing, pulled it free from his flesh. Axel turned and faced the handful of remaining men, holding the cane before him like a sword, blood trickled from one eye and he wiped it away as if he were used to such things. From behind the black mask his eyes danced and Lance could tell he must have been smiling though the blood from his grievous wound was now dripping onto the ground at his feet.

"Kill him!" Willow screamed again as she continued to writhe on the ground. The men suddenly surged forward as one and would have started the fight nearly on top of Lance but Axel spun away and ran, causing the others to follow to a safer distance. Lance tried to turn himself so he could see but the movement caused his head to feel light and he was only able to catch snatches of the scene. Axel flipping through the air, a man's head flying without its body, another man held at bay by Axel using one hand to choke him while the other continued to swing the cane. Several men screamed as Axel kicked them in the chest and sent them flying backwards, a knife now stuck out of Axel's back, buried to the hilt. The men surged forward again, now a sword swung into Axel's thigh and cleaved a large piece of flesh loose just above his knee, but Axel continued without seeming to notice. Several more men fell and Axel rushed one man who had pulled an arrow from a quiver but the man was not able to notch it, instead he saw the black form rushing him and stabbed it into Axel's shoulder as Axel bowled him over and sliced his belly open with the cane, the man stumbled backwards, his ropey insides spilling out over his hands as he screamed and blood began to seep from his mouth; the man took several steps before his feet stumbled over his own guts and he finally fell prone. Lance's stomach heaved but he had no contents to throw up, instead he just curled up on himself again and heaved until he thought he would pass out.

Axel swung around and saw that only one man now remained, his whole body trembled at the excitement of the battle and it screamed at the same time as he began to feel the numerous wounds he had just received. The man and Axel regarded each other for a moment and then the fear appeared in the man's eyes just before he turned to flee, it was a look Axel had seen numerous times over the years, the realization that everyone around him was now dead and he was surely next. Axel sighed as the last man ran, he reached behind himself and pulled the knife free, it grated against his shoulder blade as he did so, and then with one sweeping arc of his arm the knife flew toward the man and buried itself into his flesh. The man screamed and fell, the knife now in his back; it was actually his own knife, Axel was merely returning it. The man squirmed on the ground for a long and agonizing moment before he finally became still and died.

Willow lay on the ground, staring up at the sky, her long lean frame shook as the blood continued to flow freely from her face and seemed to seep from her very pores as it was slowly staining her clothes from beneath. Axel limped toward her, using the rib cane to support himself, he jammed the cane into the ground near to her head and fell to his knees next to her.

"Can you smell it?" Axel asked. Her eyes, rimmed with blood as though they were tears, looked at him. "The blood, and the death," Axel continued. "It is what you live for, what you have always craved, isn't it? Does it make you feel powerful? Does it make you tremble with excitement?"

Willow tried to speak but blood only came from her mouth and ran down both checks as she gurgled, Axel shook his head.

"I tried to give it to you, I freely willed all my strength and power to you and yet you could not handle it. As powerful as you are and just a hint of my own power has boiled your insides."

Axel sighed a little as he used the cane to push himself back to his feet.

"You should have remembered the history better, others more powerful than you couldn't kill me, I can't even kill myself, so what made you think you would succeed?"

Axel did not wait for an answer, the rib cane rose above Willow's head and with a single swing the sharpened edge cut into her flesh and her head fell away from her shoulders. Axel continued to look down at the body as the shaking stopped and the eyes grew dim, then he turned and looked toward the curled-up figure of the Bard who lay on the ground some distance away.

"Here, drink."

Lance was not sure for how long he had had his eyes open, he was dazed and confused, his body hurt and his stomach was slowly turning itself in knots as it begged for food but also rebelled against the thought of it at the same time. Lance slowly turned his eyes toward the man that was sitting next to him and studied the black fabric that still covered his face.

"Axel?" Lance finally said softly. The man next to him blinked once and gave a small nod of his head. Lance realized the man was holding a vessel of wine up for him and he grasped it with both hands and began to drink without stopping to take a breath. The spiced juice burned as it went down his throat and memories suddenly hit him as the taste filled his mouth, memories of sitting with his father and listening to the stories of old, sharing a cup of wine between them as his father recited the stories from memory. The vessel was drained quickly and Lance let it fall from his grasp as he took a deep breath, his head suddenly became still but he knew it would start spinning again soon, but it would be a welcome feeling this time, a soft spinning that would make the pain go away. Lance looked back at Axel and squinted.

"I'm sorry," Axel said as he picked up the dropped cup. "I'm sorry it took so long for me to get here, I had to come from a...from a very long ways."

"But...you...." Lance slowly reached up and his fingertips touched the fabric that covered Axel's face. "....You...," he said again slowly, his voice sounding lost and confused. Axel sighed a little and reached up, his hands slowly unwrapped the shroud that covered his face. The skin was new and fresh looking, without a blemish on it, the face younger and clean, not dirty anymore, not bloody anymore, not who Lance had expected and yet, it was...tears suddenly clouded Lance's vision.

"Tulley!"

Chapter Forty-four

"It took several days for my body to heal enough for me to wake up again, by then Gensieco and the children had already traveled that far from the camp, and they had become lost, so I had to figure out where they were and turn them in the right direction first, then I had to find this camp back. I have not flown in such a long time, I had forgotten how exhilarating it can be."

"Gensieco must have been surprised when you woke up," Lance said, his voice slightly slurred, not from the wine but from the exhaustion.

"She stabbed me."

"Oh."

"She never thought that I could be the Black Sparrow."

Lance sat silently and studied the man before him, his face was healed though one could tell it had undergone an injury recently, the skin looked as if it had been scrubbed till it began to turn raw. His ear was whole again, as was his eye. His unruly hair had been trimmed, and instead of letting it fall across his eyes, it was now swept back; he ran a hand through it and Lance thought it already looked more golden then brown.

"Tulley," Lance stopped and shook his head a little. "I mean, Axel… ." The other flinched a little at the name.

"No one has called me that name in a very long time, I am unsure of that name now, please just call me Tulley."

"Tulley," Lance said, then he became silent and did not finish what he was going to say. Tulley glanced down at him as he paused in tightening the saddle on the horse, then he turned away and picked up the small satchel of items he had collected from Willow's tent. Blood dripped onto Tulley's hand and he wiped it away, he limped toward Lance and reached out for him.

"Come on," he said softly. "The sooner we get back, the better. I don't know how much longer I can keep going."

The horse was stumbling when they finally reached the tree, though they had stopped several times on their journey back Tulley kept urging the horse to continue every day until the animal was at its breaking point. Young Druids swung through the branches overhead, they had been sent out to watch for Lance and Tulley and now they went forward crying out their arrival.

"Gartanging!" they heralded as they continued ahead of them. Tulley was leaning forward, clinging to the horse's neck and Lance was clinging to him, Jarsic suddenly dropped from the branches overhead and grasped Tulley's shoulder, the horse was so exhausted it didn't even spook but merely stood with head bowed and feet widely planted.

"The children have been back for several days now, we were about to search for you, Gartanging."

Tulley barely nodded to Jarsic, then he turned slightly to speak over his shoulder.

"You still with me?"

"My body is," Lance softly groaned, Tulley could feel his hot forehead through the fabric against his back.

"Hang on, you will be in bed soon."

Supea then descended from the branches overhead and enveloped Lance into her long thin arms, she gently pulled him from the horse's back and carried him like a child, Lance did not object.

"So the veil has lifted and you truly are Gartanging," Supea said softly as she walked away.

"Never would have thought that is who you really were," Jarsic said as he held out a hand to help Tulley dismount. Tulley took the aid and stumbled when his feet touched the ground, he leaned onto the horse's shoulder as he covered his face with one hand. Two figures were suddenly on either side of him and took his arms over their shoulders, one was lean and famine and the other small and slight, Jessica's voice whispered in his ear.

"It's alrights nows."

"Will you disappear again, Gartanging?" Jarsic asked as he followed behind while Jessica and Gensieco walked Tulley forward, Tulley did not answer, he stared at his feet as he shuffled them forward and concentrated on not tripping.

"What does thats means? Gartanging?" Jessica asked. Tulley and Jarsic remained silent but Gensieco answered in an excited tone.

"It is what the Druids call Axel, the Black Sparrow."

Jessica suddenly stopped walking and the little trio halted, she let go of Tulley's arm and took a step away from him, letting his arm fall from her shoulders.

"What?"

Tulley looked up at her then and slowly nodded, she gasped for now instead of the darker green eyes he used to have, they shone back bright blue.

Jessica did not speak to Tulley for most of the afternoon. She stood on the far side of the room holding the bowl of sickly sweet-smelling water Supea had prepared and watched as Supea helped Tulley undress from the crusty blood-soaked clothes. Tulley sat on a chair before them, unashamed at his nakedness, as Supea scrubbed at the wounds with a wet cloth she had soaked in the medicine water. Many of the wounds had begun to bleed again once the black cloth was pulled away and drops of blood began to appear on the floor beneath Tulley's chair.

Someone knocked lightly on the door and asked to come in, Supea dropped a blanket onto Tulley's lap before she bid Gensieco to enter. The young Sprite looked at Tulley and a hand instantly went to her mouth as she gasped at the sight of so many wounds. Tulley had four stab wounds, one of them from Gensieco herself, two arrow wounds, a meaty piece of flesh barely clinging to his thigh, and a hole in his chest that seemed to match the one in his back. Tulley's face looked strange with the skin being reddish and raw on one side and firm and tanned on the other and his neck sported the red line that almost ran from ear to ear, inflicted on him from Willow's blade when she had cut his throat.

"I have something for you," Tulley said softly to Gensieco as he looked at the bandage that ran around her head and covered one eye.

"My eye?" Gensieco asked softly.

"It is in the saddlebag," Tulley answered. "She will never hurt you again." Gensieco looked down as a tear instantly rolled down her cheek.

"I will burn it tonight," she said softly. "Thank you." Gensieco's voice quivered as she spoke, then she turned and ran out of the room. Tulley sighed then grimaced as Supea tucked the tip of a knife and two slender fingers into one of his wounds, a moment later she extracted an arrowhead that had broken off below the skin.

Tulley glanced at Jessica several times as Supea cleaned and dressed his wounds but he was only met with a blank stare, after a while he kept his eyes downcast and looked at his battered knuckles instead. Finally, as Supea was wrapping up the last of Tulley's wounds, Jessica took a step forward and spoke.

"You had green eyes before," her voice was soft, shaky, and her accent was gone. Tulley glanced up at her and nodded slightly. "Why?" Jessica asked.

"I pulled magic from my tethers to shroud myself," Tulley's own voice trembled, giving away the true pain and exhaustion he felt. "What you see now is my true self. My face is young, my eyes are blue and my hair will grow out and become golden again instead of the brown I normally have. It was a constant mental drain and took years to master but, at least people stopped trying to kill me."

Jessica slowly came closer to look at Tulley, her brows knitted as she studied him, slowly she reached out a hand and touched his face.

"Are you still Tulley?" she finally asked. Tulley sighed slightly and like a child he leaned into her, she put her arms around him and felt just how exhausted he was.

"Yes, I am," he said softly as he pressed his face into her shoulder. Jessica sighed and hugged him closer as she brought her own head down to his shoulder.

"That's goods," she said softly. "I wouldn't wants yous to bes anyones elses."

"I thought you would be scared of me, like so many others. I thought you would…."

"Shhhhh," Jessica whispered. "You needs to rests nows. You looks terribles, Tulleys."

A small pained laugh came from Tulley's clenched teeth.

"I have not had such wounds in many years," he said, his face still against Jessica's shoulder. "I think I will sleep for a couple of days, but don't worry about me, I will be fine."

"I wills worrys," Jessica said, her motherly tone suddenly coming out. "You wills stays in beds tills I says you cans gets outs."

"Yes, maim," Tulley said, his voice suddenly slurred as his body leaned heavily against Jessica, Supea reached forward and grasped him before his unconscious weight knocked Jessica down.

Lance bowed deeply before the young king, the child had grown during his absence but the king was still merely a child, barely twelve years old now.

"You have been gone longer than expected," the young king called out, his voice still high but clear.

"I am sorry, your majesty," Lance said, his head still bowed. "I ran into some trouble during my travels and was laid up for some time." Lance had removed the new wooden leg Tulley had made for him and came before the king with a crutch to show he truly was missing a limb now.

"Very well, I can see that," the young king said as he sat down and pointed at a servant holding a platter with delicate breads and fresh fruits on it. The servant quickly came forward and kneeled at the king's side as he selected some of the food.

"But do you have a story for me? Something new and exciting?"

Lance finally looked up then but he looked past the king to one of the high openings that let in light to the large room. The sun was peeking through the window but Lance could still make out the figure of a man sitting there, his back leaned against the side of the window, one leg dangling down into the room; the man could have only gotten there if he could fly. Lance was reassured that Tulley had come to hear his story even though the guards had turned him away because he was a stranger, and the king had only requested Lance to come to him. Lance nodded slightly and then looking the young king in the eye he began to recite his tale in a loud clear voice, a voice that commanded attention, a voice that caused all others to hush, a voice his father would have been proud to hear.

Epilogue

Part One: For Want of a White Horse

This is a story of love and jealousy,
Some have said it is of the greatest bravery,
But many say and still believe,
It is of life, death, lust and treachery.

Axel was the son of a poor man,
He was a handsome and healthy youth,
Raised to someday be a true gentleman,
He was taught in the ways of truth.

His eyes were as light blue as the sky,
His hair as beautiful and golden as the sun,
Axel was borne of an old and dying race,
His blood made strong by what his ancestors had done.

Florence was a girl from far away,
With a father who was called a majesty,

With hair and eyes as dark as the night,
Axel fell in love with this foreign beauty.

But Florence was a girl of many whims,
Who was more devoted to costly things,
She was always wearing expensive dresses,
And owned many necklaces and rings.

Axel swore she was his only love,
He constantly told her she was the one,
He confessed his great love to her,
But her heart was not so easily won.

"You are no gentleman," she told him,
"My body is too frail for such a life,
Surely I would die bearing your children!
You live in such hardship, such strife!"

"What must I do?" Axel begged of her,
"I wish to be worthy of your love and beauty,
I could swear myself to your very will,
And follow your every order with great duty."

"Yes," Florence said, "Swear yourself to me,
And after some years of unfailing service,
Only then shall I give you my hand,
You cannot have me without sacrifice."

So Axel fell upon his knees before her,
And willingly swore his life away,
That he would do whatever she asked,
Until the time of their wedding day.

The poor boy, so young and tender of heart,
Could not see the trouble he had bound himself to,
The love he felt made him blind to all,
As he eagerly waited for something to do.

Florence smiled to herself wickedly,
Here was another lover, like some new toy,
She had had so many lovers in the past,
She thought, *He is stupid, but he is a handsome boy.*

"This is what I want you to do for me now, Axel,
There is a simple farming family by the calm sea,
They have a magnificent white horse,
They are mere peasants, steal the horse for me."

Axel caught his breath at her request.
"Axel," she said. "You must heed my word."
"Yes," Axel said as he turned away from her,
Then he jumped from her window and became a bird.

For a moment she feared he had killed himself,
But then she saw his wingtips caress the very sky,
As she watched the sparrow she felt jealousy growing,
For she herself could not jump to the air and fly.

Axel flew throughout the night,
And early the next day he came to the lake,
It was indeed vast like a calm sea,
Now he had to find the horse to take.

He soon found the white horse in a field,
It was huge, beautiful and wild,

But there was a small boy tending him,
A boy no more than a child.

Axel watched for the best time to take the horse,
Ignoring the terrible growing dread in his gut,
"It is not wrong for I do it for her," Axel repeated,
As he waited for them to fall asleep in their hut.

Finally, he thought, the time had come,
So he carefully sneaked down to the stables,
He gently pushed open the old heavy door,
But as he entered he tripped an alarm cable.

Without Axel knowing, bells rang in the hut,
Mother, father and son were soon on their feet,
The father grasped his bow and some arrows,
Planning to kill the thief he was going to meet.

Unaware of danger, Axel went to the horse,
The great white beast was in the farthest stall,
He was a huge and powerful-looking creature,
With rippling muscles, he was strong and tall.

For a moment Axel hesitated in his evil task,
But then slipped the bridle over the horse's head,
Axel had no warning or idea,
That in a short while he might be dead.

The stable door suddenly burst open,
The horse reared with hooves cutting the air,
An arrow was loosed from the bow,
But the aim was not taken with care.

The arrow grazed Axel's neck,
Axel cried out from the sudden pain,
The horse was frightened by things in the dark,
And bolted with Axel grasping his silvery main.

For a terrifying moment at the stable door,
Axel saw the boy, eyes wide with fear,
Then the great horse trampled the child,
And the screams was all Axel could hear.

It took some time to stop the horse,
And then Axel realized what he had done,
He tried to forget the mother's wails,
As she sobbed over her dead son.

Axel rode the horse back to Florence,
A great grief was sitting upon his chest,
Florence saw Axel and the horse coming,
So she went and dismissed her guests.

"You are back so soon, Axel," she cooed,
"Oh, he is the prettiest I have ever seen,
His eyes are bright, his body is strong,
And my stable man shall make his coat gleam."

"Your success was very good," Florence said,
"I shall tell my servants there is to be a thoroughfare,
It shall be a party in honor of my new white horse,
Oh, what a meal the servants shall prepare!"

"Florence," Axel said as he grasped her arm,
"You do not know what I did to bring you this beast,

I have killed a boy, no more than a mere child,
And you say, 'Come! Let us prepare a feast!'"

"Release my arm, you fiend!" Florence cried,
She hit Axel in the shoulder as hard as she could,
It was where he was wounded, and he fell to knees,
"Yes," Florence spat, "Kneel before me like you should."

Axel looked up into her beautiful face,
His eyes were very hurt and wandering,
Florence forced herself to kneel next to him,
An act she found almost humbling.

"Axel," Florence said, looking into his face,
"You have fulfilled the task I asked of you,
It is no concern to me if you have killed,
As long as you did whatever I asked you to do."

"I see that you love me very dearly," she said,
"I can see it in your eyes and the horse you brought,
Now come inside with me, my dear Axel,
You have been wounded and it must hurt a lot."

Florence took him to her own bed chamber,
And ordered him to remove his vest and shirt,
Axel spoke very softly, "As I look at your face,
I can feel no more sorrow, no more hurt."

Suddenly she was kissing him,
Hard and right on the lips,
She held tightly to his arms,
Digging her nails in with a fierce grip.

Axel groaned and pushed her away,
He saw that his wound was bleeding again,
He saw Florence look to her bed,
"No," he said, "It would be a sin."

Once again Florence was kissing him,
And she shoved him down onto her bed,
But just as Axel got his arm around her waist,
She grasped a vase and hit him on the head.

Florence let the broken vase fall from her hand,
And she screamed as she shoved Axel to the floor,
Then she ruffled the bedsheets and her black hair,
Just as there was a great hammering on her door.

Florence opened her bedroom door,
Her brother rushed in, eyes searching the room,
He saw the unconscious boy on the floor,
And his sister, full of some great gloom.

"Little sister, what just happened?
Who is this boy that lays on your floor?!"
"He is some murderer, I fear," Florence said,
"Lock him away so I see him no more."

And then with delicate acting,
Florence fell into her brother's arms,
"Florence! Oh, Florence!" he cried,
Thinking she had been greatly harmed.

"I shall be all right, Harold," she said softly,
With shaking hand she touched her head,

"It was only the shock of it all."
"Perhaps," he said as he laid her in her bed.

Guards were called into Florence's room,
They picked up Axel and carried him out the door,
The only things he left was his shirt and vest,
And two drops of blood on the polished floor.

Part Two: To Say Goodbye

Axel's fear was almost overpowering,
When he awoke in a cold and dark place,
His head was throbbing quite terribly,
And he felt a cut that ran across his face.

He slowly sat up and looked around himself,
With wide eyes searching the shadowy dark,
He tenderly touched the cut on his cheek,
He vaguely wandered if it would leave a mark.

Suddenly the dungeon door was opened,
For a moment the light made Axel blind,
As he tried to see who was coming to him,
He heard a voice that was soft and kind.

The door creaked closed,
Soon Axel could see again,
There was a woman with a lamp,
She also had food and clean linen.

"Well, young lad, what a mess you're in,
You had gotten quite a knock on the head,

The others could not wake you,
So they sent me down instead."

She set the glowing lamp on the floor,
And handed Axel some fruit and bread,
Axel ate the food without a word,
As she tended to his neck and head.

"So much a single girl can do," she sighed,
"I almost feel sorry for you, young lad,
But things will get better, I'm sure,
After a while it won't be so bad."

Axel did not look at the woman,
He could not look her in the eye,
Slowly tears began to run down his face,
She held him a minute and let him cry.

"It is good to cry," she told him,
"It can make a very strong man,
But in a short time you'll be in court,
So let's spiff you up if we can."

Axel spoke up then, "Why am I going to court?
I feel I should know, though I don't mean to be a bother."
"Oh, you do not know?" she said, sounding quite surprised,
"It is for the attempted murder of the majesty's daughter."

Axel suddenly felt sick and his mind began to whirl,
He slumped to the floor, filled with great shock,
He was so full of grief at this sudden news,
That he didn't hear the clicking of the door lock.

The guards came in to take him away,
Axel let them fairly drag him up the stairs,
He felt as though he had just been stabbed,
And what now may happen to him, he didn't care.

Axel walked between the guards,
With closed eyes and bowed head,
I am already condemned, he thought,
And tomorrow I will be dead.

A crowd of Little Folk was in the courtroom,
In an attempt to liven up their dull day,
They had come from near and far,
To see Axel and hear what he had to say.

Axel then saw one in the crowd and he felt a chill,
He had seen that face before, in a distant land,
It was the farmer that Axel had stolen from,
The man suddenly leapt at Axel with a knife in his hand.

Axel turned his bare chest to the man,
He was not saddened that this was his end,
But the knife did not strike home,
It was deflected by the guard's duty to defend.

The guards instantly came to Axel's defense,
They arrested the man and took his knife away,
But the man yelled and pleaded loudly,
Telling all of the evil deed done that dark day.

"He came and stole my white horse,
In the process he killed my only son,

My wife was so grieved that she has died,
And now I am alone for what he has done!"

"I can understand why you wish to kill him,"
The majesty said, "But not by your own hand,"
Then he turned to Axel and the guards,
"Bring him here," he said, "Make him stand."

The guards placed Axel in the middle of a large room,
A guard remained on either side of him,
But Axel stood with his head hanging low,
The people waited but Axel would not speak to them.

The majesty spoke, "Do you have anything to say?
Is it true that in your actions you have killed and stolen?"
Everyone was silent as they waited for Axel to speak,
But Axel's throat suddenly felt dry and swollen.

After a time one of the guards smacked Axel on the head,
It was then that Axel looked up and caught his father's gaze,
But his father looked away with shame covering his face,
Inside Axel a hatred toward Florence suddenly began to blaze.

Then Axel stood tall and began to speak,
"Yes, I stole a horse and I killed a boy,
But I was commanded to do such things,
And now your help I sincerely employ."

"I was forced to do those terrible wrongs,
I was taking orders from one I love dearly,"
But then Axel saw Florence watching him closely,
And the pleading look on her face he read clearly.

Florence spoke to him through her eyes,
How could you do such a thing to me?
Don't you know that I love you?
I feel like you are drowning me in the sea.

Axel looked away and he became quiet,
No matter what, he refused to say any more,
So the court was dismissed for a time,
And the guards led Axel away through the door.

Florence went right to her father then,
For her controlling ways were even upon him,
She looked at her father and smiled innocently,
She knew he would bend to her every whim.

"Father, dear," she said every so sweetly,
"I have looked long into this boy's eyes,
I have felt a tugging at my very heart,
For his penalty, can there be a compromise?"

The majesty looked at his beautiful daughter,
"Well then, what do you wish of me to do?"
"I don't want him to die," Florence said,
"You won't kill him, Father, will you?"

"He can live if you wish it, daughter dear,
But then what shall I do with this misguided lad?
There must be some form of punishment,
Or the people may think that I have gone bad."

An idea sudden came to Florence,
"Send him with the slaves, to the battlefield,

He is such a rugged young ruffian,
I'm sure he knows the use of a sword and shield."

"That is a good idea, my daughter,
That is a harsh punishment, all right,
I shall send for a blacksmith,
Have some armor made for him tonight."

"Oh, no," Florence said with a frown,
"The battles alone are not punishment enough,
Send him without armor or weapon,
We shall see if he is weak or if he is tough."

"But I thought you did not wish him to die?
A punishment like this is worse than the death sentence."
"Perhaps it is, Father, but he still has the chance to live,
And this will give him time for his repentance."

The majesty slowly nodded his head toward her,
"It is such a shock what he tried to do to you,
I would have gladly killed him with my own hands,
But I shall do with him what you are asking me to do."

Florence smiled inwardly to herself,
She watched as her father left the room,
Once again she had tricked a lovesick boy,
And now he would be sent to certain doom.

Axel was sitting in the darkness of his cell,
When he heard his father's soft voice at the door,
"Escape if you can and I will keep you safe."
And then his father left without saying any more.

As Axel's father quickly left the dungeons,
He ran into Florence as she was coming down,
"You are an evil little witch!" he spat,
Then he left Florence sitting on the ground.

A raging anger began to rise in Florence's heart,
And her dark eyes turned to a darker black,
She charged into Axel's dark cell,
And he felt her little hand give his face a smack.

"You terrible boy!" she fairly screamed,
"I have just saved you from a certain death,
And your ungrateful father calls me a witch,
Do you also have such hot breath?"

"No," Axel said, his face still hurting,
"I do not have such evil words on my tongue,
If I should ever say such mean things to you,
Then give me a rope so I might be hung."

"You still may suffer," she snarled,
"For your father's ill-said words,
But be thankful that I still love you,
I think I shall forget what I have heard."

Axel reached out and found her in the dark,
He drew her close and held her against his chest,
"Florence, I am sorry if I have ever hurt you,
I am just so confused, and don't know what is best."

"I am best for you," she whispered to him,
She kissed his neck then, "Don't forget me."

Then she turned away and quickly left,
But Axel found something in his pocket, a key.

Axel waited for the guard to bring his dinner,
Once the guard left he then quickly sneaked out,
I will be very far away, Axel thought to himself,
Before they can even send any tracking scouts.

He walked through many doors and empty hallways,
Like a shadow flitting though the dark,
Finally he came across two guards,
He did not kill them but he surely left his mark.

And then through the town Axel was running,
Going to the home that he knew so very well,
But as he came near he saw something was amiss,
He stopped in the doorway and onto his knees he fell.

The strong front door had been broken,
The table turned over and dishes smashed,
And there on the floor in the middle of it all,
Was his father, his face the color of ash.

Axel wept as he sat next to his father,
He touched his cheek as it was growing cold,
Then Axel saw something in his father's hand,
For even in death he grasped something in his hold.

Axel cried as he pried it from his father's fingers,
He didn't even notice the guards coming in,
Until one of them spoke to him roughly,
"We have you, now stand up, you vile vermin."

Axel never showed them what he held,
He kept it well hidden as he turned to stand,
It was a tooth from a poisonous snake,
That had been held in his dead father's hand.

At the doorway Axel stopped and looked back,
It broke his heart to see his father like that,
"Goodbye, Father," he whispered softly,
He paused a moment to pick up his father's hat.

Part Three: Landrew and the Unwanted Boy

Landrew was a man that many knew but not all liked,
Sometimes called a thief, or one lost in his ways,
He could change into a great redheaded woodpecker,
And is still known as one of the greatest fighters till this day.

The kind of work he did always kept Landrew on his toes,
He didn't like to stay for more than a year in the same place,
He was very good at hiding away and disguising himself,
So only his closest friends knew his true face.

It was a bleak day as Landrew traversed abroad,
It was this day he came across an old enemy,
They both gave startled and angry shouts,
But then suddenly Landrew turned to flee.

A redheaded woodpecker took to the air,
Flying quickly on widespread wing,
But following right on his tail,
Was a cardinal as regal as a king.

The two birds fought in the air,
Pulling out feathers and clawing with feet,
The woodpecker took a terrific blow,
And fled again lest he be beat.

He flew keeping just ahead of the cardinal,
He wished he had some sword and shield,
But he had no weapons of any kind with him,
But up ahead he spied a wide battlefield.

Like lightning from above,
The woodpecker dove straight down,
He made a bit of a rough landing,
And became a man running across the ground.

Landrew ran swiftly through the gloom,
He stopped for a moment to grasp a shield,
Then he ran on for his enemy was near,
And he still needed to find a sword to wield.

Landrew found a sword just as the other was upon him,
He spun quickly and blocked the savage blow aimed for his head,
"Ah, dear cousin Max, so we meet again," Landrew laughed,
But Max sneered at him, "So many times I have wished you were dead."

"Such words from the mouth of family,
What is this land coming to?" Landrew sighed,
"You are no family of mine," Max said fiercely,
"You are a cowardly villain that likes to hide."

They drew apart and faced each other,
Max was grasping a large battle axe,

Landrew shook his head slowly at his cousin,
"You were always such a disappointment, Max."

"Don't play any mind games with me,"
Max said as he slowly took a step back,
But Landrew just turned his sword to the flat edge,
And he gave Max a sharp stinging smack.

"All right, no more games then,"
Landrew smiled and swung again,
But Max leapt backwards and swung as well,
The axe barely caught Landrew on the chin.

Landrew touched his chin tenderly,
The cut wasn't deep enough to touch bone,
"I already shaved today," Landrew said,
Then he gave Max a hit that made him groan.

Max fell backwards and hit the ground quite hard,
The axe was thrown and lost from his hand,
But then Max drew forth a long thin dagger,
And threw it at Landrew as he began to stand.

The dagger caught Landrew in the hip,
He pulled it out and suddenly felt dizzy in his head,
He looked back at Max but the man was gone,
Landrew was suddenly attacked by an angry cardinal instead.

The bird beat at Landrew with his wings,
And stabbed at him with its beak and claws,
But the bird did not have a good shield,
And Landrew quickly preyed upon that flaw.

Using the dagger he had pulled from his hip,
Landrew hit the cardinal swift and clean,
For a moment the bird seemed puzzled,
He did not know what the pain could mean.

Then with a blur of scarlet feathers,
And a man-like scream,
The cardinal flew away from the danger,
Leaving Landrew's hands with a bloody gleam.

Landrew turned then and began to run,
He knew the camp must be somewhere ahead,
He wanted bandages for his bleeding hip,
Or some kind of healing salve instead.

Everything was quiet in the camp,
The fires were embers and the tents were dark,
Landrew stopped and felt his bleeding hip,
Though it hurt it didn't seem like much of a mark.

Landrew then sat in the shadows of a tent,
And it was a good thing he did,
For Max was inside speaking to someone,
"…Yes, Landrew! I believe he came here and hid."

Landrew froze at the sound of his name,
I guess I didn't hurt him much, Landrew thought,
Then he looked all around himself,
Oh, look at all the trouble I've bought.

Max and the other came out of the tent,
"Don't worry about him," the man said,

"Everyone will be alerted at once,
I will personally put a price on his head."

Max and the man walked right past Landrew,
There was no more words they spoke,
Oh, the great fools, Landrew thought,
I could have had them both by their cloaks.

Word spread quickly through the camp,
That the notorious rebel Landrew was near,
The news set most all the men on edge,
But the reward quickly overcame their fear.

Landrew quietly sneaked through the camp,
Then he slid into a deep ditch to hide,
But he was not alone in the mud,
For there was a boy with an arrow in his side.

The wounded boy awoke and began to sob,
"Shush!" Landrew whispered, "Or we'll both be dead!"
But the words only made the boy cry louder,
So regretfully Landrew struck him on the head.

Landrew lay silently in the cold mud,
All he could hear was the boy's labored breaths,
But once things quieted down Landrew rose up,
He briefly looked down then left the boy to his death.

But Landrew had barely climbed out of the ditch,
When his heart began to loudly cry out,
"You have left that boy in his grave!" it said,
And so after a pause Landrew turned himself about.

448

He slid back down into the muddy ditch,
And after a little struggle he managed to pick the boy up,
"What are you doing in a man's war?" Landrew said,
He looked the boy over, "You are still just a pup."

Landrew had trouble climbing out of the ditch,
The boy was a heavy burden in his arms,
But it was this muddy wounded boy,
That kept Landrew safe from harm.

Landrew was nearly out of the dark camp,
He could see the safety of the woods,
But then a voice called out to him,
So Landrew stopped just like he should.

"What's your business, be quick," the guard snapped,
Landrew told him, "My boy is in grave need of help."
The guard didn't even look at Landrew, only at the boy,
"Very well, but I don't think you can save the little whelp."

Landrew quickly ran into the safety of the forest,
He could hardly believe his sudden luck,
Now he did not mind carrying the wounded boy,
Or that they were both still covered in cold muck.

Landrew stopped and laid the boy down,
He carefully wrapped him in his cape,
And then carrying him in the makeshift hammock,
The woodpecker quickly made their escape.

Part Four: Among the Thieves

In a far, faraway part of the forest,
There is a well-hidden little glade,
In that place is Landrew's current home,
Truly, a better hiding place could not be made.

The great woodpecker screamed out his presence,
A handful of Landrew's men came to meet him,
Some of them rushed forward to take the boy,
As the woodpecker hovered amongst them.

"So happy to see you have returned," one man said,
Landrew smiled, "Good to see you too, Kalim,"
He looked to the boy as the men gathered around,
"Look after this boy, take good care of him."

"That I will do," Kalim said,
"But, should I call a doctor for you?"
"Oh, no," Landrew said as he limped away,
"There is nothing that my Amy cannot do."

"Amy," Landrew called out as he went to his home,
She embraced him, "Landrew, you were gone for so long."
"Do not worry, Amy, I am back for a while now,
I will stay right by your side where I belong."

Amy bandaged his hip with expert hands,
Then she bid him to stay in his bed,
"You will feel better after a good rest,"
She whispered as she kissed his forehead.

"Amy," Landrew said before she left,
"I brought someone back with me when I came,
I owe my life to him, but he may die,
And I don't even know the poor boy's name."

"Do not worry, my dear," Amy said,
"I shall look after him while you sleep,
And the men shall know that you are resting,
So the whole camp shall not make a peep."

Amy then left Landrew to his dreams,
And she went to aid the injured,
"There is nothing we can do," the doctor said,
But she would not be detoured.

"You barbaric men," Amy seethed,
"You pull out the arrow but don't clean him up much,
Landrew wishes for this boy to live, not die,
This poor boy needs a woman's healing touch."

"Everyone, out of here!" Amy said,
And she fairly chased them down the path,
"Only Allen and Kalim shall help me,
Now bring hot water so we can make up a bath."

All the men had a healthy respect for Amy,
Even on days that she was cranky and mean,
For like Landrew, she had a good heart inside,
So many gave her reverence like she were a queen.

Allen and Kalim did as they were told,
Bringing in water that was steaming hot,

Gathering together all kinds of healing herbs,
And cooking a nourishing broth in a pot.

"The bath is now ready, I think," Allen said,
"Good," Amy answered, "Now grind these and mix them in,
They are herbs to help clean and heal wounds,
Hurry or you will have to heat all the water again."

Allen and Kalim then slowly set the boy into the water,
Amy leaned down and gently began to wash his face,
The boy stirred and opened his tired eyes,
He slowly looked around the strange new place.

Then the boy looked up at Amy,
And, oh, what blue eyes he had,
Amy whispered, "You are with friends,
I am here to help for you are hurt bad."

The boy slowly closed his eyes,
And he weakly turned his head,
"Wait, what is your name?" Amy asked,
He took a labored breath, "Axel," he said.

He did not open his eyes again,
And he did not say anything more,
They finished his bath and put him to bed,
Then Amy greeted the man at the door.

"He is doing better," she said softly,
"But he needs his sleep and I am weary,
You should all be ashamed of yourselves,
Next time do not wait to come and get me."

452

Then Amy went to join Landrew in bed,
She awoke him as she laid her head on his chest,
"Go back to sleep," she whispered to him,
"I will be upset with you if you do not rest."

When Landrew awoke the next morning,
He saw that Amy was already out of bed,
He found her with the injured boy,
She was changing the bandages that had turned red.

"He is a handsome boy," Amy said,
"Now that he is all washed and clean,
His blond hair just shines like gold,
But he is terribly weak and lean."

"Has he woken yet?" Landrew asked,
"He did last night for a very short while,
He said his name is Axel but that was all,
And his eyes are so beautiful," Amy said with a smile.

"Already you are in love with this boy," Landrew grinned,
"Should I be afraid that he will someday take you away?"
But then Amy stood and she kissed Landrew on the lips,
"Do not worry so, with you I will always stay."

Landrew kissed Amy again and held her,
"I must write a letter," he said and Amy groaned,
"You always write to Max as though you were best friends,
Why don't you stop and just leave him alone?"

"Because I promised Max that every time I saw him,
I would remind him off all the evil he did."

Axel stirred in his bed and let out a deep groan,
"You do a good job here, Amy, and take care of the kid."

Amy walked with Landrew to the door,
Though he was a thief she still loved him,
For he was the one who saved her so long ago,
And now she could not deny that she was one of them.

When Axel fully awoke a few days later,
He felt as weak and limp as a rag doll,
His head was dizzy and throbbing hard,
Everything echoed like he was in a great hall.

Axel looked around the dim and spacious room,
He was beneath warm covers in a soft bed,
And to his right he could see a man in a chair,
The man was tall and had thick hair flaming red.

"It is good to see you finally awake," he said,
"You have been in a fever the past few days,
My wife is out gathering more healing herbs,
She has grown fond of you in some motherly way."

The man stood and came closer to Axel,
"I am Landrew," he said, "And my wife is Amy,
Are you hungry or thirsty right now?
Do you think you can eat some mushroom gravy?"

Axel very slowly nodded his head,
He was not sure if he could speak,
He coughed and Landrew gave him a drink,
"I have hardly eaten anything for weeks."

"Then you shall eat some, my boy,
But for now, just a little bit,
You shouldn't overeat while you are sick,
You are too weak to make much use of it."

Landrew called for Allan to bring food,
Then he called for another named Kalim,
"Go and tell Amy her patient is awake,
I am sure she would like to talk to him."

In a short while Amy came up in a hurry,
She had a basket tucked tightly under her arm,
"Oh, you look so much better," she smiled,
And her flushed face filled with charm.

"Thank you for taking care of me," Axel said.
"You are welcome, but you are not all well yet,
You still have some fever," Amy said softly,
"But I'll take care of you, so don't you fret."

Allan then came in carrying a bowl of warm soup,
"I can see why you call it gravy," Axel said.
Amy helped him eat until he had had enough,
"Now sleep," she said, placing her hand on his forehead.

"You fear for him," Landrew said as they left the tent.
"He still runs a fever but he is awake and that is good,"
Amy was frowning though, "Sleep heals the body,
He will get better just as a lad his age should."

But Amy had no reason to fear,
For Axel grew a little stronger every day,

And they all grew so fond of him,
That Landrew offered him a place to stay.

"My wife will be heartbroken if you leave," Landrew said.
"Well," Axel sighed, "I don't really have any place else to go,
I was so sure I would die as I laid in that muddy ditch,
Any days of my life worse than that, I will never know."

"There were times that men looked down at me,
 But they would just walk by me as I lay there,
They stole everything that was of value to me,
I wonder if they even remember how to care."

"No," Landrew said with a pained look,
"Perhaps don't tell Amy of this, she will have a fit,
She will singlehandedly try to kill that entire army,
That woman has such spunk and I love her for it."

Just then there was a shout from across the camp,
They both turned to see what it was all about,
They saw Amy chasing men from the cook tent,
And she was wielding a spoon as she ran out.

"Cracking heads again," Landrew laughed,
"Just watch her, oh! There she goes!
Don't touch her soup before it is done,
Axel, when you find the right girl you'll just know."

"I thought I had found the right girl," Axel said,
And with such a sadness that it squeezed Landrew's heart,
"What troubles have you faced, my boy?" Landrew asked.
"I will have to tell you," Axel sighed. "From the very start."

So Axel told Landrew of his life so far,
He told about Florence and the white horse,
Of killing the boy and his father's terrible death,
"For all my actions, I fell much remorse."

"I suppose love can sometimes make you blind,
Especially when one is young and stupid like me,
And yet I still feel such a great love for Florence,
You would think that I would have learned already."

"A very sad tale you can tell, my boy,
But I have something to take your mind off such things,
Come with me, I shall show you my second camp,
Do you think you are fit enough to use your wings?"

"I can try and see," Axel said,
He lifted his arms and changed into a sparrow,
Landrew watched him fly straight up,
Then he dived back down like an arrow.

Just before the sparrow hit the ground,
He pulled up and hovered in the air.
"A fine sparrow you make," Landrew said,
"Together we will make quite the pair."

So side by side the two birds flew,
Above and away over the trees,
It felt so good to be flying again,
Axel spread his wings and welcomed the breeze.

Then the woodpecker flew downwards,
And all too soon the flight was ended,

Axel landed unsteadily next to Landrew,
"I may not be completely mended."

"If you wish we will walk back," Landrew said,
"It is just a very short time to fly,
Of course it takes longer to walk,
We'll see how you feel as the day goes by."

So they walked through the camp together,
Landrew would stop often to greet someone,
They both had a right merry time with the others,
But then it was time to leave as the day was nearly done.

"Well, do you think you can fly?" Landrew asked.
"I believe I can make it back on my own."
"Good," Landrew said but then he became silent,
Axel was staring at someone, his face like stone.

"Who is that man?" Axel asked, "In the hat?"
Landrew looked over at the man as well,
"I don't rightfully know, he has his back turned,
And with the hat on I really cannot tell."

Suddenly Axel was walking toward the man,
Landrew had never seen the boy mad before,
A frightening sight Axel had quickly become,
His anger seemed to be coming right from his core.

"Where did you come by your hat?" Axel asked,
The man turned and for a moment his face went white,
It was then that Landrew recognized the man,
He bit his lip hoping that Axel would not start a fight.

"I took it from a worm in a ditch,"
The man said as he glared at Axel,
"He couldn't get up out of the mud,
Must've hurt himself when he fell."

"You said you would help me, you liar,
You pulled me up out of the mud,
Only to rob me blind," Axel spat.
"And why didn't you stay there, you grub?"

"I'm not a worm and I'm not a grub,
Now I demand that you give back what you stole!"
"I don't think I want to give anything back, grub,
You should go back to your ditch, you little dirt mole."

Axel suddenly leapt at the man,
His hands going for the throat,
But into the air flew a chickadee,
And Axel was left holding his coat.

Before Landrew could stop him,
Axel changed and quickly followed,
They collided in midair and hurtled back to the ground,
And when they hit the thud sounded painful and hollow.

Landrew suddenly leapt at the two birds,
He grabbed a hold of both of them,
But they flew again and left Landrew holding feathers,
And just before they did the chickadee bit him.

Landrew was suddenly outraged by these actions,
With an angry scream he jumped into the air,

The woodpecker grabbed both birds by their heads,
And he shook them until he felt feathers turn to hair.

Then he released the two stunned men,
And the woodpecker followed them straight down,
And when they all three landed in a heap,
Landrew had them both pinned to the ground.

Axel's face was white with pain,
He had blood coming from his nose,
The other already had a black eye,
And several large rips in his clothes.

"You are both in trouble!" Landrew seethed,
Then he grabbed the other man around the neck.
"How dare you bite me when I am not in the fight,
You know I am not afraid to kill you, Hect!"

Then Landrew made them get to their feet,
He angrily brushed the dirt from his coat,
Axel held an arm against his throbbing side,
 And Hect gingerly rubbed his now aching throat.

"Now you two shake hands," Landrew growled,
"Or I'll take off both your heads,
And then you two can finish your fight,
Among the graves of the dead."

They slowly held out their hands, "I'm Axel."
"Hector, but I prefer to be called Hect for short,
You're a pretty good fighter for a sparrow,
Have you ever thought of joining the sport?"

"Only if I can break your face," Axel said,
Hect laughed aloud, "You make a good jest,
But you should, you already have a great teacher,
Landrew here has always been known as the best."

"Only if I don't kill him before we get home," Landrew said,
"Now Hect, give back everything you have taken from this lad."
"Ah, Landrew, Axel, I am sorry for causing this trouble,
It's just that I was sure you would die, you were hurt so bad."

"I begged you to kill me back there," Axel said,
"But you only robbed me and left me to my pain."
"Perhaps I should have listened," Hect said,
"Then you would have never been able to rattle my brain."

"I would have done more than just that,
If you had continued to call me names," Axel said.
"I still have fire to spit," Hect growled.
Landrew cut in, "Stop it before I split your heads."

Hect placed all of Axel's belongings in the hat,
A strong belt, a thin necklace of gold,
Two pieces of silver and a small knife,
And finally, a ring that looked very old.

"Here are your things and more, little worm,
Don't lose them on your way back home."
"Get out of here," Landrew said,
Then he gave Hect a kick, "Leave him alone."

"Now I should make you walk home," Landrew growled,
"Let you feel the pain as you carry your pack,"

But then Landrew began to feel sorry for the boy,
"Amy will be worried so you better ride on my back."

Part Five: Lessons From Landrew

"Come on, boy, it is time to be awake."
"But Landrew, it is so early and still dark."
Landrew laughed, "You want to be a fighter,
Training starts now, and it ain't a walk in the park."

"But Landrew," Amy cooed softly,
"Hardly a day to rest, he's still sore,
You have all the time for this tomorrow,
Let him rest for just one day more."

"There you go again," Landrew said,
"You fuss over him more than me,
Ahhhh, he will only watch for today,
When he feels better, then we'll see."

And thus life went on for Axel,
Early asleep and early arise,
Was one of Landrew's sayings,
And *How can one know unless one tries?*

Landrew truly was a champion of fighters,
Tall and strong, he fit the job quite well,
He never seemed to give up a fight,
And if he was tired, Axel could not tell.

Axel was trained in the ways of the sword,
First he had many bruises from using sticks,

"I know you want a real sword," Landrew said,
"But you shall not touch one until you are quick!"

Then with busted knuckles and tender ribs,
Axel thought hand-to-hand fighting was the worst,
Until Landrew thought he would boost Axel's confidence,
So one fight he made sure Axel came out first.

Archery and javelin was also quite a test for the youth,
Axel crawled into his bed sore but satisfied every night,
Every morning Landrew would say, "Do you wish to quit?"
But Axel would get up and say, "No! I want to fight!"

And so fight he did,
For over three years he trained,
He became as tall and strong as Landrew,
And was proud of the knowledge he gained.

"And now, I have a final test," Landrew said,
And he showed Axel a paper with an announcement,
But Axel still was not so good with his letters,
So it took him a bit until he knew what it meant.

"The Pond Island Meeting?" Axel said,
"I don't think I have ever heard of the thing."
"It is like a great big gathering," Amy said,
"And it only comes every seven or eight springs."

"You may have lived too far away before,
It is said that all are required to go to it,
We have not gone for a while now,
But this year I shall go and look around a bit."

"I wish for you to go with me, Axel,
For there is always many sporting games,
And if you wish to participate,
You could gain so much fame."

"All right!" Axel said strongly,
"It sounds like it'll be fun."
So a few days later Landrew and Axel,
And some close friends, left with the sun.

The group of birds and a few butterflies,
Flew south for several tiring days,
But every night Axel continued his training,
Lest he should forget some on the way.

Finally they came to the pond with the island,
It was already crowded with Little Folk,
And Axel saw fairies for the very first time,
One bowed to him, "Blessings," he spoke.

Axel was stunned as the fairy walked away,
"My boy," Landrew said, "That is a great start,
Fairies tend to avoid us Little Folk,
He must have seen something good in your heart."

"He was so beautiful to look at," Axel breathed,
"Fair of skin and handsome as could be,
Do you really think he meant to say that?
"I mean, what's so special about me?"

"Much more than you know," Landrew said,
Then he pushed Axel toward a sighing table,

Landrew carefully read the names on each list,
"There!" he said, pointing, "Martin the Able!"

"Who is Martin the Able?" Axel asked.
"The only man to ever beat me," Landrew said,
"But your advantage is you fight from the heart,
While he just fights from his head."

"Come now, Axel,
We have much to do,
You shall see your opponents,
But they shall not see you."

So they all set out through the crowd,
With Landrew pointing out certain men,
Until late in the day Allen came running,
"I've found him!" he panted, "It's Martin."

They went to a very big arena,
Where a great fight was in tow,
"Martin the Able is tough," Landrew said,
"Learn his moves as we watch the show."

"Why do they call him 'The Able'?"
Axel's voice quivered a bit,
"Because no one has been able to beat him,
But you will so don't get into a fit."

"But just look at him," Axel said,
"He must be a full head taller than me,
His shoulders are just as wide,
And he's far in the lead, you see."

"Yes, I know," Landrew said,
"It is only the first day of the fights,
And already he is the favorite,
But they have not seen Axel of the Might."

"Of the Might?" Axel fairly squeaked,
"Yes," Landrew said, "That name suits you well."
"But that is only if I win the match,"
Axel shivered, "What happens if I fell?"

"I hope you are not scared now, boy,
I have trained you too hard to just walk away,
Here you shall fight Martin the Able,
And you shall beat him this day."

"But I don't want to fight him now," Axel said,
"Butterflies in my stomach have made me sick."
"Well, you may not fight him today," Landrew said,
"It all depends on who the judges will next pick."

Axel waited on the edge of his seat,
But the judges never did call his name,
At first Axel was relieved for that,
But then from his cowardice he felt shame.

The next morning Landrew awoke Axel quite early,
He was out of breath, "The judges all agree with me,
Come with me, my boy, your first fight has finally come,
Remember, fighting with your heart is the key."

"Landrew, wait!" Axel cried aloud,
"What is this that you are saying?

Am I to fight Martin this early?
Please tell me that you are playing."

"No, no, no, my boy," Landrew said,
"You are not to fight Martin this minute,
You will fight first-timers like yourself,
But you will get out of it what you put in it."

"Though your opponent may lack experience,
They may still be very smart,
So don't ever let your guard down,
And give it your all from the very start."

"I will do my best, Landrew," Axel said.
Landrew smiled, "That's good enough for me."
Then taking off his shirt Axel entered the arena,
And he displayed some skill for all to see.

Axel's first opponent looked to be a worthy match,
This man was taller and looked quite strong,
But Axel threw him from the arena,
Before the other knew what went wrong.

"A record time!" the judges yelled,
"Next opponent, Mason of Light!"
And though Mason put on a good show,
He really didn't know how to fight.

"You're doing great! Just great!"
Landrew said toward the evening hour.
"Yes," Axel said with a groan,
"But I feel like a crushed flower."

"Just a bloody lip and sore ribs,
Nothing that a good night's sleep can't help,
And then tomorrow you shall defeat Martin,
And show these people that you're no whelp."

"But Landrew, what if I don't defeat Martin?" Axel asked,
"When I hear his name, my stomach churns with fear,
I heard this morning that two men Martin fought are now dead."
"Shush!" Landrew said, "We shall not speak of that here."

"To get to the top, you must work hard,
Those achievements will last quite long,
But those who cheat to get to the top,
They will fall because they are not as strong."

"Wise words that are well spoken,"
Said a rough old voice from behind,
Landrew and Axel turned to see two fairies,
One was young and the old one was blind.

"My son has told me of your style of fighting,"
The old fairy smiled toward them,
"It is very noble to fight in the old ways,
But Martin is not noble, be wary of him."

Axel's fear only mounted with the fairy's words,
He gave Landrew a forlorn look as the two fairies left,
"Don't worry," Landrew tried to laugh it off,
"Just look Martin in the eye and give him a good right and left!"

But that night Axel had a troubling dream,
It left many uncertain thoughts running through his head,

He tossed and turned and hardly slept all night,
And the next morning Landrew had to fairly drag him from bed.

"Axel, what is wrong with you today?"
"It is Florence, she is haunting my very dreams,
I don't know what to think anymore,
There is nothing right or wrong, it seems."

"Don't let this ruin your chances," Landrew said,
"I have heard gossip that you are becoming the favorite,
So push Florence from your mind for today,
Now let us go and train, that should help a bit."

So Axel and Landrew trained,
With many spectators looking on,
They stretched, fought with swords and boxed,
Until all thoughts of Florence were gone.

"Now I know you can do this," Landrew said,
He wrapped Axel's fists and knuckles,
"You have come so far since we first started,
Now get in there and make Martin buckle."

"I can only do my best," Axel said coolly,
"Now that's the spirit, my boy," Landrew smiled,
On the inside Axel felt weak and shaky,
But outside he remained relaxed and mild.

The first round of the fight was grueling,
Many moves were made against each other,
But the worst was Martin's jeering and teasing,
"Ha!" he would say, "You fight like a grandmother."

Many hard punches were thrown,
And many crippling kicks were aimed,
But each assault was well blocked,
And neither of them were badly maimed.

"You are doing great," Landrew would coach,
"Just remember all that I have taught you,
And don't ever hold back, you hear,
Keep it coming hard, whatever you do!"

Axel did well in the second round,
He followed through with everything Landrew said,
But then in the third round something happened,
And it nearly cost Axel his head.

For only a second he had looked away from Martin,
And as his eyes glanced over the crowd,
There amongst the people stood Florence,
Her head was erect, haughty and proud.

For a moment Axel thought he had lost his mind,
For there she was, looking him right in the eye,
Her questioning stare caused a pain in his chest,
And he suddenly felt like he would sit down and cry.

Then Axel received heavy blows for his hesitation,
Martin hit him hard about his head and face,
But just as Axel started to fall he heard the bell chime,
So he forced his mind not to fall into unconscious space.

Axel slowly got back to his feet and looked around,
He limped and swayed to where Landrew stood,

"What happened?" Landrew asked as he helped Axel to sit,
"Everything seemed perfect, you were doing so very good."

"It was her," Axel panted, "Truly she is some demon,
I saw Florence in the crowd and she was looking right at me,
I don't know what happened because my mind went blank,
And though my eyes were open I just couldn't see."

"Allan! Kalim!" Landrew summoned his men,
"Search through the crowd right now,
Find the raven-haired foreign beauty,
And take her away from here, I don't care how."

All the men quickly jumped to Landrew's bidding,
They moved like shadows through the entire place,
"Now forget about her and think about beating Martin,"
Landrew said as he washed the blood from Axel's face.

Then Landrew suddenly became solemn,
"Axel, I feared the worst when you fell,
And if you would excuse the odd expression,
Truly, you were saved by the bell."

Axel smiled through the pain in his face,
"Landrew, were you scared for me?
Please don't think of fear as a weakness,
It's good to know I am in loving company."

The fourth round was the hardest yet for both fighters,
They were both getting tired and were rather sore,
Sometimes the punches weren't all blocked in time,
And Axel took a hit that shook him to his core.

Then after what seemed an eternity of fighting,
The fourth round finally came to an end,
Axel and Martin were both gasping for breath,
So the judges decided to give them a short time to mend.

"You have watched Martin fight," Landrew told Axel,
"And you know that no one has made it past the fifth round."
Landrew then became silent as he checked Axel's knuckles,
Making sure they were covered and securely bound.

"You truly have come far since we first met, Axel my boy,
This is not worth dying for, it is all right to have second place,
I know I have spoken highly of winning all these matches,
But Amy will grieve if she never again sees your living face."

"I'll heed your words of advice," Axel said as he stood,
"But I have been taught not to give up so easily,
Besides, Martin knows he can't win this now,
I see it in his eyes every time he looks at me."

Part Six: Landrew's Pleading

It was true that Martin did not think he could win,
Never before had he received such savage beatings,
But the blind fairy's words also rang with truth,
For Martin was suspected of some form of cheating.

And so as the fifth round began,
Axel saw a sudden change come over Martin,
He seemed greatly refreshed in some way,
And Axel did not like his knowing grin.

472

Martin suddenly came at Axel with a vicious left,
Completely throwing Axel off his feet,
But Axel was back up in a moment,
Swinging a heavy right for Martin to meet.

Martin reached out and grabbed Axel's swinging fist,
He grinned though the move hurt him quite a bit,
Then he punched Axel in the chest with his massive right hand,
Axel suddenly felt very strange and he did not know what caused it.

Axel staggered around a few steps with his head spinning,
He looked down and saw on his chest was four fresh scratches,
Martin was watching Axel with that grin on his face,
No, Axel thought, *I've come through too many matches.*

Martin seemed to think the fight was over,
The world around Axel began to tilt and spin,
It is now or never, Axel thought dizzily,
Just one more hit to try and win.

Axel forced his beaten body to move,
He turned and gave a strong, high kick,
Martin was not expecting this sort of thing,
He saw Axel's foot coming and suddenly felt sick.

Axel's foot couldn't have hit in a better spot,
There was a loud *Crack!* as it met Martin's head,
The kick was so powerful that Martin flipped head over heels,
And then he just laid there as if he were now dead.

Landrew jumped into the arena and rushed to Axel's side,
For in that last moment he had seen a strange look come into the boy's eyes,

Axel groaned as his knees slowly buckled beneath him,
His hands pressed to his chest and his white face turned toward the sky.

Landrew caught Axel just before he hit the ground,
They gazed at each other for a moment before Axel's eyes shut,
The crowd became deathly silent and hardly breathed,
Then Landrew saw on Axel's chest were the four oozing cuts.

Landrew looked to Martin's still form,
Then he closely inspected Martin's hands,
A cry of rage escaped Landrew's lips,
He picked Martin up and forced him to stand.

He fairly dragged the still senseless Martin to the judges' table,
Landrew conversed with them, then he angrily turned to shout,
"Beneath the wrappings of Martin's right hand," he told the crowd,
"Are four tiny spikes and they are dipped in poison, no doubt!"

Martin heard and understood what was said,
Fear hit him and his eyes opened wide,
He shoved Landrew away from him and tried to run,
But the angry crowd gave him no place to hide.

Martin was quickly caught by Landrew's men,
They pushed his face in the dirt as they held him down,
Landrew descended upon him from the judges' table,
He raised his arm to hit him but then lowered it back down.

The crowd parted and made a wide path for them,
They watched silently as Landrew and his men carried Axel away,
They took him to a good doctor and Landrew warned him,
"Take care of him, for if this boy dies so will you this very day."

Landrew looked at all his men gathered around the bed,
Then looking at Axel he said softly, "Look after him."
All the men bowed their heads in allegiance to Landrew,
Then Landrew turned and quickly left them.

Landrew had a plan of what to do,
He knew he had to save Axel's life,
Right now the boy was very near death,
His life was upon the sharp edge of a knife.

Landrew ran through the forest for quite some time,
Until he finally found a secluded little stream,
There was something strange about the water here,
Nothing was what it really seemed.

Landrew was stricken and weary from running,
He let himself sink down to his knees,
He kneeled there and just stared at the water,
When suddenly there was what he was hoping to see.

A small white face was in the water,
With tiny red lips and huge blue eyes,
The strange face appeared so very suddenly,
That Landrew jumped back in great surprise.

But then the face was gone,
And a great despair came upon Landrew,
"No! Wait!" Landrew cried out,
"Don't go, I truly need you!"

Landrew then stripped off his cape and shirt,
He looked at the water for a moment before he dived in,

475

Landrew was one of the many who could not swim,
But he had to find back that Snow Fairy again.

Landrew desperately fought the current of the water,
The whole time calling for the Snow Fairy to come back,
But then Landrew grew angry and hit the water with his hands,
The water splashed up around him and emitted a loud smack.

Landrew then struggled to get back to the shore,
But his attempts only drew him farther away from the bank,
His arms and legs were growing tired and he couldn't keep his head up,
How stupid I was, I am so sorry, Axel, he thought as he slowly sank.

Landrew felt like he was waking from a dream,
He could remember running through the woods but not the rest,
So he did not fully understand why he was all wet,
With some kind of weight sitting upon his chest.

That weight upon his chest was a small person,
It was strangely the size of a young child,
With skin as white as freshly fallen snow,
And blue eyes that showed it could be quite wild.

"You were looking for me, Landrew the woodpecker,"
The Snow Fairy's voice was gentle like a soft breeze,
The words swirled down to Landrew's ears,
And frolicked about in the leaves.

"How do you know me?" Landrew asked.
"We Snow Fairies are a very special race,
We know of everything there is to know,
All without needing to leave our sacred place."

"Then you know why I am looking for you," Landrew said,
"Yes," the fairy said, "But you must ask me of it anyway,
And then I will think upon granting your request,
But be careful, for you may come to regret this day."

"Please," Landrew said without a moment's hesitation,
"I have a good friend who has been poisoned and is dying,
His whole life has been difficult because of the sins of others,
He is not the one who deserves punishment for their lying."

"Well said, Landrew," the fairy said softly,
"But I do not think I shall help you,
There are so many others I could be helping,
There is so much more I could do."

The small creature then jumped off of Landrew's chest,
It seemed to glide across the muddy stream bank,
It began to descend back into the water,
But Landrew grabbed its arm before it completely sank.

"Wait, please!" Landrew nearly sobbed,
"This boy has been as close as a son to me,
I have watched him grow to nearly a man,
And I have hopes he will always be in my company."

The Snow Fairy rose out of the flowing waters then,
It turned and looked Landrew straight in the eye,
"You are a thief, Landrew the woodpecker," it stated,
"Your life is spun around revenge, treachery and lies."

"But tell me again, Landrew, what is it you want?
And I suggest you think hard on this matter first,

We Snow Fairies are known for our own trickery,
What you are requesting could turn for the worst."

"We shall face whatever hardships may come," Landrew said,
"I just cannot watch the boy die by the works of my own hands,
I will never be able to forgive myself if my friend dies,
Never again will I hold my head high when I stand."

"So you want him never to die?" the fairy asked,
"Yes!" Landrew said, "Just as long as he lives."
"Then go back to him," the fairy replied,
"For life to this boy I will give."

Landrew watched the Snow Fairy sink back into the water,
Then he turned and ran as if demons were on his heels,
Axel would live, but what events had he set into motion?
How had he now affected the future by turning that wheel?

Landrew came back to Axel in the middle of the night,
All of his men were still silent as they sat around the bed,
"The doctor feared that you would kill him," Kalim told Landrew,
"So he has run away for by morning Axel will be dead."

Landrew did not say a word at the news,
He held Axel's hand for there was nothing else to do,
Then Landrew felt Axel squeeze back just slightly,
Landrew smiled and whispered, "Thank you!"

Axel slept peacefully for several long days,
Landrew hardly left him for fear that Axel was not all right,
But as that morning dawned bright and fresh,
Axel got up out of bed as he always did at daylight.

Not a bruise or scratch was upon his body,
All soreness and sickness had gone away,
Axel looked to be healed and in good shape,
He was ready to face whatever came his way.

"So good to see you up," Landrew said truthfully,
"Now, to get your prize before all have gone home."
"You mean I did beat Martin?" Axel asked suddenly,
"Yes, Axel, you beat him, your name should be put in stone."

But suddenly Allan came to them all out of breath,
"You must fly, Axel, there is grave danger here,
For some reason men are searching for you,
And they may kill you upon sight, I fear."

"What is this!?" Landrew asked with gritted teeth,
"Why is he in such danger so very suddenly?"
"I can only tell you some of the story," Allan panted,
"For I heard a snatch of it as some guards passed me."

"I heard this just now," Allan said,
"These orders have come right from her father,
I do not know what she has against Axel of the Might,
But there is no other as spoiled as this man's daughter."

"I did not stay to hear anything more,
I came straight here to tell you,
For they were all fiercely armed,
There is no telling what they may do."

Landrew turned around and faced Axel,
"Florence," he stated, "Is that what this is all about?"

"I am now positive that it was her I had seen in the crowd,
Axel shook his head, "She is seeking revenge, no doubt."

Landrew placed his hand upon Axel's shoulder,
"You are wise and strong like any other man now, Axel,
Whether you stay to fight or you fly and hide,
The decision is yours, so please choose well."

Axel turned to Allan, "Thank you for the warning,
My problem seems great but I will not dwell upon it,
I think I shall go to see Florence right now,
I seem to owe her a long-overdue visit."

Part Seven: Traveling with Lando

Axel silently watched the guards walk past him,
They were swarming the area like fleas,
But Axel was well hidden as a blind beggar,
And no one had bothered to stop him and see.

Dodging the guards was easy enough,
He soon came to her tent and heard her voice,
She has cursed me somehow, Axel thought,
For she had said, "Axel, do you now feel remorse?"

"How did you know it was me?" Axel asked,
He slowly and cautiously entered the tent,
"I knew you would come to see me," she said,
"So when I saw your shadow I knew what it meant."

"Axel, you are so much more handsome than I recall,
Come and sit on the bed, right here next to me,

I believe we have an awful lot to talk about,
There has been nights that I have longed for your company."

"I have missed you as well, Florence, my sweet,
But I shall not sit next to you today,
I just wanted to see you once more,
Before I continued on my way."

Florence was beginning to grow angry inside,
Axel was not obeying what she had said,
"Well, now you have seen me," she scoffed,
"Now go away, if the guards catch you, you'll be dead."

"I just want to confirm our agreement," Axel said,
"How many more years of service until you are mine?
It has been nearly four years already, Florence."
"Many men want me, you'll have to wait in line."

"I shall have you as my own, Florence."
Florence stood up and looked Axel in the eye,
"But what if I don't want you anymore?"
"You still want me, Florence, you cannot lie."

Axel grabbed Florence and drew her close,
On her lips, face and neck he kissed her,
But suddenly someone else entered the tent,
Axel dropped Florence and spun around in a blur.

"You!" Harold growled like an animal,
"Have you come back to finish the job?
Leave my sister to what innocence she has left,
That is something I shall not let you rob."

Harold drew his sword then,
And Axel made a quick thrust,
"I don't wish to hurt you," Axel said,
"But it would seem that I must."

"I shall kill you where you stand," Harold spat,
Then he leapt forward to make his kill,
But Axel proved to be much faster,
He dodged and came back at Harold with a will.

Axel hit Harold squarely on the jaw,
Harold fell and did not move anymore,
"I will come back for you someday," Axel said,
Then he turned and raced away out the tent door.

Axel returned to where Landrew was waiting,
"Oh, Axel, what a grave thing you have done,
You are truly a dead man now,
I've just heard that you killed a majesty's son."

"He tried to kill me first, Landrew,
I had no other choice but to fight."
"And now we must run," Landrew said,
"They come now, haste, take to flight!"

Axel and Landrew flew away,
Just as the guards lunged at him,
They threw spears and shot arrows,
But luckily they all missed them.

"Landrew, why did you say that I killed him?"
Axel asked when they stopped that night,

482

"You have taught me so much about defense,
I did not hit to kill in that fight."

"Then it may not have been you," Landrew said,
"I never told you exactly how Harold was laid low,
He was stabbed through the back with a dagger,
He was not killed by a fisted blow."

"But this is still bad news, Axel,
For it seems that you are to take the blame,
You are now, without a doubt, a hunted man,
And your fighting career carries a blemished name."

"I ask of your advice now, Landrew,
What is it do you think I should do?"
"Go far from this place, so far in fact,
You must take dirt from your home with you."

"Yes," Axel whispered in deep thought,
"To keep the magic of the wood forever near,
I can carry the dirt in a pouch around my neck,
So that I can fly anywhere without fear."

"If you do not mind, Axel," Landrew said,
"I have a brother who would take you in,
Just give me some time to write a letter,
And once I get word back, your journey can begin."

So Axel waited for a while,
But he soon became impatient for the reply,
And so after memorizing directions from Landrew,
He thanked them all and kissed Amy goodbye.

Such sights Axel had never seen before,
As he spread his wings and floated on the breeze,
He watched the orange sunset every night,
As he would go to sleep on a bed of leaves.

But flying for several long days,
Got to be quite boring,
So Axel began to run instead,
Though it was much slower than soaring.

And so after many days of travel,
Axel stopped to rest upon the road,
It was a warm day and he fell asleep,
Listening to the nearby croaking of a toad.

Axel suddenly awoke when many hands grabbed him,
Instantly he began to violently fight back,
And though he successfully knocked down some,
He could not defeat the entire pack.

They rushed Axel and pinned him down,
"Let me up and I will beat you all!" Axel said,
But then Axel suddenly became very still,
For there stood a man with hair that was flaming red.

"Landrew!" Axel gasped in great wonder,
The man looked at Axel with raised eyebrow,
Then he suddenly began to laugh out loud,
"But Landrew," Axel said, "I don't understand…how?"

"You must be Axel then," the man said,
"If Landrew did not tell you then how could you know,

Landrew and I are identical twins,
 He is called Landrew, and I am Lando."

"I thought it was you for not many have that face of old,
That fair and noble race is nearly died out,
My brother only vaguely described what you looked like,
So when I first saw you I had my doubts."

Lando held out his hand to Axel,
"Sorry for the scare, Axel, we have reasons to hide."
Axel saw that Lando truly did look just like Landrew,
Except for his eyes, like his soul was wilder inside.

"You did not scare me at all," Axel said,
"At least, not that much," he added at the end,
Lando and his men laughed heartily,
"Come, little brother, I think we'll be great friends."

Lando placed his arm over Axel's shoulders,
Then surrounded by Lando's men,
Axel was lead deeper into the woods,
"Lando, why did you just call me kin?"

"As highly as my brother wrote to me of you,
I feel as if you are one of the family,
And if you are as good and courageous as I hear,
Then you shall be as a little brother to me."

"So why are you and Landrew so far apart?" Axel asked,
"Now that is a question I have asked myself many times,
But in the end I think the reason is our cousin Max,
Landrew is rather obsessed with Max's crimes."

"What does Max do?" Axel suddenly asked,
Lando laughed, "So many questions coming from your head,
It is a story best told over dinner and a campfire,
So who's hungry?" Lando looked up and said.

"So what about Max?" Axel asked later,
"Max is a man of the law," Lando stated,
He stopped for a minute to drink some wine,
Then he continued once his thirst was sedated.

"And as you may have already thought,
Law men and thieves don't see eye to eye,
But it wasn't until a cold winter's night,
That Landrew started to wish Max would die."

"When we were much younger,
Landrew was blessed with a wonderful wife,
We both had a love for her,
But it was to Landrew that she gave her life."

"Her name was Odessa Dale Hearting,
And she was calm but so very brave,
And they had three strong, young sons,
But in one night the four of them met their graves."

"Landrew had done something to make Max very mad,
And the night was cold when Max came,
Max said he wanted to heat up the night,
So he set Landrew's home to flames."

"Landrew and I could not stop him,
The house was engulfed within minutes,

486

And we could hear the screams,
Odessa and the boys were still in it."

"Landrew would have killed Max then,
But he had gone into the house to save his family,
I followed him into the burning flames,
The smoke was so thick we just couldn't see."

"And then the whole house caved in around us,
Landrew was lucky I was able to pull him out,
We both had injuries upon our bodies,
And may have died if the neighbor wasn't about."

"By the time we recovered,
Max was long gone,
Time has healed my pain,
But Landrew's pain still carries on."

They were all looking deep into the fire,
"Landrew never told me of this," Axel sighed,
"For Landrew to lose so much in one night,
How he must have hurt and cried."

"We still cry till this day," Lando said,
"But the crying is in our hearts,"
Then Lando stood up and yawned,
"Sleep now, we have an early start."

But Axel hardly slept that night,
His mind was filled with screams of the dead,
And the sound of Landrew's anguished cry,
Kept echoing in Axel's tired head.

"You don't look so good this morning, Axel,
Did the story give you bad dreams in the night?"
"No," Axel said, "I am not a child,
Stories like that cannot give me a fright."

"Then why do you look like you got no sleep?"
Lando asked as he gave Axel a plate of food,
But Axel did not answer the question,
And Lando sensed that Axel was in a bad mood.

Axel soon found that traveling with Lando,
Was much different than living with Landrew,
They did not have a central camp to live in,
They just lived off the land and what they knew.

They knew exactly when a storm was coming,
Most of the time a full day before it would hit,
They always knew where to find plenty of food,
And they knew all about herbs for their medicine kits.

They knew when someone was coming down a path,
And they knew if the person was rich or poor,
They were always kind when they did take from a person,
Not taking much unless they were rich, then they took more.

"Always be kind to the women," Lando said,
"Yes," Axel said, "Landrew would say the same thing,"
Some people thought it worthy to give to them,
For in the thieves world Lando was like a king.

"Kind kings, though, Axel," Lando said,
"For as long as you are kind and just,

488

Though we are called road robbers,
There are many that trust us."

Each man had his own little pack,
To hold food and medicines and other things in it,
And each man had his very own short sword,
And a warm and well-made blanket.

Axel soon found that he enjoyed traveling like this,
And very quickly nearly a year went past,
But then there came a dangerous day,
And Axel felt that such fun would never last.

It was nearing the early evening hour,
When a watcher whistled from a tree,
Lando turned into a woodpecker and flew to him,
But he was not at all happy with what he could see.

"There are men searching the entire wood,
And I saw Max riding a brown horse,
He has finally cornered me here,
He has come to kill us, of course."

"But we shall not go down without a fight,
Men, arm yourselves as best you can,
Fighting seems to be the only way out,
Unless any of you have a better plan."

So armed to the teeth,
Some men hid in the trees,
Others stayed on the ground,
And hid in the dead leaves.

Max and his men were just slightly surprised,
To see men rise up as if they came from the dead,
Lando leapt at a man and with one fatal strike,
Lando's short and powerful sword cut off the man's head.

The men in the trees then fell upon their enemies below,
Like hornets swarming from the skies,
They engaged in combat with their enemies,
With swords ready and fierce battle cries.

The battle then began to rage,
The warriors' cries were strong and loud,
And during all that fighting,
Not a single person saw the storm clouds.

Like waves upon the wind, the rain came hard,
Men dropped their weapons and ran from this death,
For Little Folk can easily drown in a rainstorm,
And truly that day many drew their last breath.

Axel saw the rain coming across the field,
He turned to flee from the deadly pelt,
But as he did he came face to face with an enemy,
And Axel gasped for a great pain he suddenly felt.

Lando looked across the field from the edge of the wood,
And there he saw a huge enemy warrior facing Axel,
The warrior had thrust a spear through Axel's body,
Axel stood for a moment in shock before he fell.

"No!" Lando cried out as he tried to go to Axel,
But his men grabbed him and held him back,

Lando yelled and fought against them all,
Until one of them gave him a hard smack.

"Look at me, Lando!" the man cried,
Lando forced himself to turn his head,
"We all loved Axel just as much as you did,
But now we must leave the dead to the dead."

The heavy rain killed many of the enemy,
And some of Lando's men who did not hide quick enough,
It made the remaining enemy flee far away,
And then the sun came out with clouds like puffs.

Lando ran to the place where he had seen Axel fall,
But on the ground he only found a broken enemy spear,
The rain had washed it clean of any blood,
Lando cried out, "Why is his body not here?"

"Lando," there was a faint voice not far away,
Lando looked up and his blood froze,
For Axel was standing in the middle of the field,
In wet and blood-soaked clothes.

Axel's face was deathly white,
But he was standing just there,
Lando got up and ran to him,
And hugged him gently with care.

"I saw you struck down by a spear,
It skewered you like a slab of meat,
And yet you are alive before me,
Standing on your own two feet."

"Just barely alive, I think," Axel said,
Then he moved his hand to reveal a gaping hole,
"I know such a wound should have killed me,
But somehow I still have a living soul."

Lando recoiled at the sight of the wound,
He could not understand why Axel was not dead,
But then Axel let out a gasping groan,
He fell forward as his eyes rolled back in his head.

Lando reached out and caught him in his arms,
"Just fainted," he said, "From loss of blood, no doubt."
"Lando, strange magic is at work here," one of his men said,
"We are frightened and want to know what this is all about."

Lando and his men looked at Axel's still form,
"I do not know the answer myself," Lando said,
"But I do know that I want him to live,
So we need a good doctor and a clean bed."

They really did not have any beds,
Since they always slept on the ground,
And though they had good medicines,
A good doctor could not be found.

But the men did the best they could for Axel,
Donating their blankets to make him a soft pad,
And Lando cleaned up his wounds some,
So it stopped bleeding and did not look so bad.

All the men thought Axel was cursed,
And on the fourth day they all knew magic was involved,

For that morning Axel rose from bed perfectly healed,
Lando wrote to Landrew hoping that this mystery could be solved.

Landrew was dismayed when he received the letter on the wind,
It spoke of Axel being hurt greatly during some fight,
"We must go to him, I must go to him!" Amy told Landrew,
"I shall not wait till morning, I wish to leave tonight."

So Landrew called for some good men to accompany them,
They hurriedly packed a few things they might need,
And in the light of a half-moon they flew toward Lando's region,
Asking the wind to go with them and give them more speed.

Sometime later Axel went out for a well-needed walk,
He was troubled by how the men looked at him in a strange way,
No one told him how he had healed as if magic was at work,
Axel just thought he had been very sick and had forgotten some days.

Axel turned when he heard his name called,
Lando was running down the path toward him,
But then Axel saw his eyes and knew it was not Lando,
For he could see the different soul shining from them.

"Landrew! Is it really you?" Axel asked,
They came into a back breaking embrace,
"Let me look at you, my boy," Landrew said,
"Amy will be so happy to see your smiling face."

"Amy is here with you?" Axel asked,
"Yes, so is Allan, Kalim, Hect, Zane and Leo,
You look well," Landrew avoided asking of the wound,
Lando had told him that it seemed Axel did not know.

"I feel well enough," Axel replied,
"I think I had been rather sick."
"Well," Landrew cut Axel off suddenly,
"Amy is waiting, let us get back quick."

Amy cried tears of joy when she saw Axel,
She hugged him close and didn't want to let go,
"You look so grown up and manly now," she said,
"But that mischievous youth in your eyes still shows."

Lando then pulled Landrew aside from the reunion,
"Brother, what of these happenings can you tell?"
"The only thing I can think of," Landrew replied,
"Is that once I asked a Snow Fairy to make Axel well."

"Landrew! You know that Snow Fairies enjoy their tricks!"
"Yes, I know. But it was when he had fought Martin,
Martin had poisoned him and he was dying,
So I found a Snow Fairy and wished him well again."

"I wonder what evil you have started, brother,"
Landrew and Lando both turned to look at Axel,
"I think Amy and I will stay," Landrew said,
"Amy will wish to look after Axel and be sure he is well."

So for many weeks, Amy and Landrew stayed,
Landrew sent the rest of his men back,
"Hect," Landrew said, "You can be in charge,
I think you are worthy enough to lead both packs."

Then at Axel's urging and with Lando's help,
Landrew and Axel began training hard again,

Axel grew so strong with knowledge from the two brothers,
That even against a dozen men he would win.

"Lando," Axel asked one night,
"Why did you stop your career in fighting?
I have heard Landrew say you are better than him,
Your punches are true and your kick like lightning."

Lando turned his eyes up to his brother,
Landrew looked down upon the ground,
"I'm sorry," Axel said, suddenly feeling awkward,
Perhaps this was a story not meant to be passed around.

"I will tell you why I stopped, Axel,
But this story still sometimes grieves my heart,
I know Ispsi's death was not entirely my fault,
A few others played a hand in that part."

"Ispsi was to be my own dear wife,
She was tall and strong as any man,
She had grown up in hardships,
And was wise by the work of her two hands."

"We met her while Landrew and I were traveling,
Back then we were known as the Land Brothers Fight Team,
She had disguised herself as a man and called herself Tom,
She then asked us to train her, said that fighting was her dream."

"We had our suspicions that she was a woman,
But we had decided not to say anything,
She traveled with us and we trained her,
She was Tom from late fall to early spring."

"It was then that she confronted me,
She told me that she could not hide anymore,
She said that she loved me so dearly,
More than any man before."

"We were going to be married that summer,
A better bride I would never find,
But then we were caught up in a small war,
And I bid Ispsi to stay behind."

"She argued with me for a time,
Saying she was as good a fighter as any other,
So against my infallible better judgment,
She dressed as a man and called herself our brother."

"She fought so well beside us in the battle,
For her, fighting came so easy,
As easy as the hiss is for a snake,
Or the buzz for a bumblebee."

"But tragic things will happen to us all,
I turned to see that an enemy had her down,
She was bleeding from a bad leg wound,
And all she could do was fight from the ground."

"I yelled at the man and took out my knife,
I threw it so it would lop off his head,
But without even looking he grabbed it from the air,
And I watched as my knife killed Ispsi instead."

"I killed the man who had killed Ispsi,
Then I held her close to my side,

Her face was so beautiful and calm,
I kissed her though she had already died."

"Landrew once told me, if he ever had a daughter,
He thought Ispsi would be a good name,
But I am afraid that will never happen,
Don't worry, Amy, you are not to blame."

Axel looked up at Landrew and Amy,
They were tightly grasping each other's hands,
"Axel, Amy suffered a terrible fate many years ago,
Her last husband used to beat her till she could not stand."

"She had finally ran away from her cowardly husband,
And she came to the war areas looking for her brothers,
The scar she carries on her lovely face is from that man,
And though you cannot see the injuries, there are others."

"At one point after we married she became very ill,
I looked after her as best I could but she just became sicker,
The illness robbed much from her, I am afraid to say,
Even though we have never had any children I still love her."

Everyone was silent for a time and stared at the fire,
Once again Axel had stories running through his head,
He would have sat there all night thinking,
If Lando had not announced, "Everyone to bed."

The next day seemed to dawn rather dreary,
Hardly anyone said "Good morning" when they awoke,
Everyone still seemed to be thinking of Lando's story,
Breakfast was rather quiet and nobody spoke.

Then suddenly they all looked up at once,
Landrew reached up and snatched a letter from the breeze,
It seemed that drops of blood was on the soiled page,
And everyone crowded close so they could see.

It read, "The encampment is under attack,
Many of us are dying or very sick,
Max has found where we are,
Bring reinforcements quick!"

Part Eight: Axel Avenged

Within the hour Lando gathered all his men,
They left to lend their aid to their fallen brothers,
But by the time they got there, it was too late,
The destruction was horrible and like no other.

Everything was broken and burnt to the ground,
They searched for survivors but had found none,
Landrew kneeled on the ground next to Kalim,
"Oh, Max," she said, "Look at the evil you have done."

Landrew gently laid his cape over Kalim's still form,
"This fight was not theirs, why did he have to kill all of them?"
"Remember, brother," Lando said, "He killed Odessa and your boys,
Max seems to have no human sympathy left in him."

"Landrew! I have found one still alive!" Axel cried out,
Axel was walking toward them and in his arms was Hect,
Hect had several deep wounds upon his beaten body,
And he could not speak because of a gash across his neck.

"Let him rest here, near this boulder," Amy said,
Axel very gently lowered Hect to the ground,
It seemed that Hect was trying to speak to them,
But all he could manage was a deep gurgling sound.

Suddenly Axel let out a cry of pain,
His body fell forward and was laid across the boulder,
Amy let out a terrified scream for there was now an arrow,
It was stuck deep in the back of Axel's left shoulder.

Amy grabbed Axel's arm and pulled him to the ground,
Lando snatched up a bow and arrows that were close by,
They could now see figures standing on the ridge,
Lando released a shot and a moment later they heard the cry.

Another arrow came quite close to Amy's ear,
She gasped and drew closer to Landrew,
"It is an ambush and Hect was trying to warn us."
Lando shot again, "If only we knew!"

Lando stood up again to shoot,
But before he could duck down again,
An arrow took him and he fell,
"Ah," he sighed, "This is for all my sins."

"No," Landrew said sternly,
"You will not die while I am here."
Amy pulled the arrow from Lando's chest,
"Amy, I must go fight, but have no fear."

But before Landrew could go, Axel grabbed his arm,
"Pull this arrow out of me," he said through gritted teeth,

"You stay here with Amy," Axel ordered, "I have nothing to lose,"
So Landrew pulled the arrow out and Axel got to his feet.

They all watched with abated breath,
Axel grabbed a sword as he ran from them,
Some of the enemy were quite a ways off,
But Axel dodged arrows and quickly dispatched them.

Then suddenly four more men appeared,
"I have to help him," Landrew said,
He jumped up from the shelter of the boulder,
Only to meet a sword swinging for his head.

Landrew ducked the sword just in time,
He found he was facing several armed enemies,
Landrew dived for a sword to defend himself,
Then he taunted, "Come on, your dirty little fleas!"

The men swung at Landrew from all different sides,
Landrew managed to barely hold his own,
He lunged toward one but the enemy ducked,
And Landrew's sword emitted sparks as it struck stone.

Amy managed to fit an arrow to the bow,
She was not the best shot though,
So she helped Landrew to sit up,
And he fired the arrow from the bow.

One enemy fell to the ground dead,
But suddenly two more sprang up in his place,
Landrew managed to kill one more on his own,
But another left a terribly deep gash across Landrew's face.

Landrew fell back when he felt the pain in his face,
The men were suddenly upon him like some savage beasts,
Hitting and kicking while Landrew could hardly defend himself,
In their eyes, Landrew saw they were like animals ravaging a feast.

Landrew's sword was lost from his grasp.
One of the enemy raised his sword to make the kill,
But there was a sword swipe from behind,
And the man fell, his blood did spill.

Suddenly Axel was fighting amongst them,
His sword cutting the air and taking men down,
He fought like an enraged animal,
Protecting Landrew, who was still on the ground.

Only once before had Landrew seen Axel truly mad,
But the anger he saw now couldn't even compare,
Never before had Landrew seen such a savage fight,
The enemies were clearly frightened by this demon with blond hair.

And then suddenly it was all over,
Axel stood in the middle of the fallen enemies,
He turned and looked at Landrew,
And slowly he fell to his hands and knees.

Axel had a knife thrust deep in the middle of his back,
And there were two arrows buried in his heaving chest,
Axel gritted his teeth as he pulled them all out,
"I let one go," he said slowly, "To tell the rest."

"To tell them what?" Landrew asked with concern.
"That I would be coming for them," Axel said,

"These were all my friends but they are gone now,
And I shall be the one to avenge the dead."

"You won't be going anywhere," Landrew said sternly,
Axel coughed quite hard and then looked at Landrew,
Bright red blood dripped from his lower lip,
"Just rest some or these wounds will kill you."

So they found some shelter from a half-burned tent,
Amy tended to the men while Landrew buried some of the dead,
"How are they faring?" Landrew asked her late that night.
"Hect and Lando will live but Axel has such a fever," Amy said.

Landrew sat down next to Axel,
He replaced the cooling cloth on his forehead,
That Snow Fairy must have cursed you, Axel,
Landrew thought, *That's twice now you should be dead.*

The next morning Axel was up with the sun,
He bandaged his wounds and put a black shirt on,
Landrew was waiting for him outside the tent,
"I wanted to talk to you before you were gone."

"What is it?" Axel asked.
"All this killing," Landrew said,
"I say to just let it be,
You do not need to avenge the dead."

"So you say I should let Max live?"
"Yes, just forgive and forget."
"What about the death of Odessa?
Or have you forgotten about it?"

Landrew did not say anything to this,
He just watched as Axel gathered some weapons,
But Landrew began to feel an ache in his heart,
As he watched Axel disappear into the sun.

"Where is Axel?" Amy asked a little while later,
"He has gone to fulfill an avenging duty," Landrew replied,
"But he will be killed, Landrew, you must stop him!" Amy said,
"No, I shall not," Landrew said and Amy sat down and cried.

Axel traveled throughout the entire day,
He did not stop though his wounds bled,
He ignored the sometimes intense pain,
And through his anger his energy was fed.

"It is so cold out here," a border guard said that night,
"The moon is in shadow and I can see my breath."
"Shush!" the other guard said, "Who comes upon us?!"
Axel came into the firelight. "I am your death."

Not a sound was heard in the camp,
Axel went from tent to tent like a demon,
He left behind him darkness and hate,
And a camp of some two hundred slaughtered men.

Finally there was just one tent remaining,
Axel came upon it silently,
There were two people inside
And Axel recognized one of them immediately.

Florence kissed Max with a passion,
They were both sitting on the same chair,

Max held one hand on the small of her back,
And the other he brushed through her raven hair.

Neither of them at first knew Axel was there,
Axel saw the wedding bands upon their fingers,
Then Florence suddenly looked up and gasped,
For standing in the tent door was a dark figure.

Max grabbed up his sword and turned,
But Axel knocked it out of his hand,
"Florence, I am no longer in your service."
Max watched Axel closely as he started to stand.

"What are you going to do?" Florence asked,
Axel heard genuine fear in her quivering voice,
Axel felt no shame as he smiled at himself,
"I have come to kill you, I see no other choice."

"How did you get past all my men?" Max asked,
"What men?" Axel asked mockingly,
He looked around himself for a moment,
"A camp full of corpses is all I see."

"You killed them all?" Max said,
"But, how…?" Then Max looked down,
Max smiled for at Axel's feet,
Was a puddle of blood on the ground.

"Ha, you are wounded quite badly, I see,
How will you kill me if you are not at your best?
Tell me, Axel, if it is true,
My men said you were shot twice in the chest."

504

"It is true," Axel said with narrowed eyes,
"But don't let that stop you from killing me,
I just killed off your entire encampment,
So I suppose that makes me your worst enemy."

Axel placed his toe beneath Max's fallen sword,
"Defend yourself," he said as he kicked it into the air,
Max caught the sword and then suddenly pounced,
"Attacking an unarmed man," Axel said, "That's not fair."

But Axel ducked blow after blow that Max dealt,
Slowly Max had backed Axel out of the tent,
"So tell me," Axel hissed, "does she toy with you?
Does she swallow up your life until it is spent?"

"How dare you say such things of Florence!"
And Max struck out with more savage blows,
"She is the one I have searched for all my life,
Her love for me is strong and truly shows."

"I grow tired of this ducking," Axel suddenly said,
He grabbed up a sword from beneath a dead man,
Max made a killing strike but Axel flipped over the blade,
Then Axel came upon Max with a sword in his hand.

The fight would have been great entertainment,
If only each man did not have the intent to kill,
Max was a worthy opponent with a sword,
But Axel was better because of his duty to fulfill.

Then there was a moment when they came close together,
Max reached out and delivered a hard blow to Axel's chest,

Axel fell back coughing with blood upon his lips again,
Then he attacked more fiercely, for he wouldn't let Max be best.

But Max knew Axel truly had a weak spot then,
For he had seen the pain come to Axel's eyes,
Max laughed horribly as he leapt into the air,
And his laughter turned to a cardinal's cries.

Axel dropped his sword and quickly followed,
Both birds climbed high into the chilly night air,
They collided with each other and then changed to men,
Fighting, kicking, punching and grasping handfuls of hair.

They fought savagely as they fell from the sky,
But just before they hit the ground they flew again,
Only this time it was to stand away from each other,
And each watched the other in the form of men.

Then suddenly they ran at each other,
And they both leapt into the sky,
They collided again and fell to the ground,
And Florence released an anguished cry.

Max was dead when he hit the ground,
Axel heard the satisfying snap of his neck,
Axel rose from the ground and turned upon Florence,
He was ready to kill but held his anger in check.

"You killed him!" Florence screamed into the night,
"How could you have done such a wrong?"
Axel was suddenly disgusted by her beauty,
"Was Max the evil one? Or were you working through him all along?"

"I am an evil being!" Florence cried,
She looked at Axel, "To that I'll admit,
I began hunting you to kill you,
I met Max and he just fell into it."

"You suited each other well since you murder people,
How long have you been married to him?
Were there others like me that you toyed with?
And what of Harold? Did you dispatch him?"

"Yes, I killed Harold and many others," she sobbed,
"I just let them think they had fallen into a wonderful dream,
But they all discovered the truth at their moment of death,
I am a killer!" then Florence let out a hideous scream.

Her scream changed to a threatening hiss,
And her body took the form of a poisonous snake,
Suddenly Axel knew who had killed his father,
And his anger toward Florence turned to a raging hate.

The large snake turned upon Axel,
He knew the snake planned a fatal strike,
But he let the snake coil around his body,
And he allowed the snake to give a deadly bite.

But suddenly in Axel's hand was the snake tooth,
He had carried it with him for so long,
And now after so many years of waiting,
He gave the tooth back to whom it belonged.

He made one sure strike at the snake's head,
The snake seemed to scream and Axel came unbound,

The snake twisted around and shivered and then changed,
And with the tooth in her neck, Florence lay dead upon the ground.

Axel sat down for a long time as he looked at her,
Slowly the sunrise cast light on all the dead enemies,
Axel slowly stood up to leave but he stopped and turned his head,
For coming from Florence's tent was the frantic wails of a baby.

"No...," Axel sighed deeply to himself,
 "Florence, I am sorry, if only I had known,
But from all this wrong I shall do a right,
This baby shall not be neglected and alone."

So Axel once again entered the tent,
He followed the sounds of the baby's cries,
When he looked upon it the baby became silent,
And looked back at Axel with Florence's huge black eyes.

It was late in the afternoon of the next day,
When Landrew looked up and saw Axel arrive,
He dropped his tools and ran to meet him,
"So good to see that you are still alive!"

"Is Amy in the tent?" Axel asked.
"Yes, she is looking after Hect and Lando,
But I shall tell her that you are here...."
"No," Axel said, "Don't let her know."

"I'm afraid I was followed here,
The Rising Sun Guards are right behind me,
I would have let them take me already,
But I had to bring you little baby Ispsi."

Axel then carefully unwrapped the small bundle,
"If I had known then Florence wouldn't now be dead,
Take Ispsi to Amy and take good care of her for me,
She needs some fresh milk and some kind of bed."

Landrew took the sleeping child from Axel,
Then he looked long into Axel's eyes,
"She's a strong baby," Axel said softly,
"She lifts her head up, or at least she tries."

Axel then got up to leave but stopped,
"Don't try to stop them when the guards come for me,
My soul is dying from all those I killed in that camp,
I will face what is coming now, I do not wish to flee."

Axel took a step forward but then stopped again,
"And one more thing," he added as he turned his head,
"Do not let the sun set upon your sorrows or anger again,
Release your pain, Landrew, for Max is now dead."

Axel then left Landrew and the child behind,
And Landrew watched helplessly as the guards took him,
Axel held out his arms and allowed them to drag him down,
He did nothing at all to stop them.

Part Nine: The Death of Axel of the Might

The Sunrise Guard are only the best warriors,
They protect the legendary Kingdom of the Sunrise,
And they do whatever the council may bid them to do,
They hunt down and kill evildoers and spies.

Axel was taken to this land of far away,
He was imprisoned where he could not see the sun,
While there he had to face the four on the council,
He tried to stay strong as they discussed what he had done.

Axel did not deny what the council accused him of,
He stood and waited before the men and woman,
They did not see him as one who could surpass their own guard,
To them he was just a murderer in torn and dirty linen.

"Axel," one of them said, "We know of your crimes,
Though the evil deeds were done in the dark of night,
Everything has been made known to us,
Your whole life has been brought to light."

"You have not asked for forgiveness," another said,
"Even if you did, your crimes are too much to forgive,
It is not your place to take such matters into your own hands,
For so many unnecessary deaths, we cannot let you live."

Axel solemnly looked down at his feet,
So much pain he had suffered in his young years,
He hoped his death would be clean and swift,
He closed his eyes so the council could not see his fear.

"You shall be hung by the neck until dead,"
The council woman then looked at the guard,
And as the guard led Axel away his heart felt lighter,
He thought, *A hanging shouldn't be very hard.*

Axel was led outside to the hanging platform,
He was to be killed for what he had done that very minute,

He stood for a moment and looked at the heavy noose,
Then bowed his head as they put him in it.

Landrew had traveled without rest for several days,
He thought to help Axel by standing at his side,
And telling of how the whole story unfolded,
For the council may want to know it from another's eyes.

But when Landrew finally came to the great kingdom,
He found that the front gates were closed that day,
"Please, you have to let me in," he told the guard,
"I'm here to see Axel and I have come a long way."

The guard pointed for Landrew to look through the gates,
Landrew saw a man hanging there and knew Axel was now dead,
But then he saw someone cut Axel's body down,
Axel landed on his feet, "They can't kill him!" Landrew said.

Everyone was surprised to see this happen,
"What is going on here?" a guard said,
Axel looked oddly at him and coughed a bit,
Someone ran to the council shouting, "He's not dead!"

Axel was taken before the council again,
He was forced to kneel before them all,
The noose was still around his neck,
The council was conversing at a far wall.

"What magic is this?" the council woman asked,
"Why does this brute stand before us again?"
"Something is not right," a man said,
"He must be a demon trapped among men."

"If he is a demon,
Then his life we must take,
Beat him to death,
Then burn him at a stake!"

"Wait!" someone shouted above them all,
Everyone except Axel looked toward the door,
A man with flaming hair was fighting past the guards,
But he was quickly taken down and held to the floor.

"Do you know something of this demon?" a man asked,
He pointed to Axel as he kneeled before them.
"Yes," Landrew said, out of breath from the struggle,
"I can tell you exactly why death does not take him."

"Take this prisoner, Axel, away," the woman said,
"We shall talk to this newcomer alone."
So Axel was taken away to his cell,
And Landrew came forward and made it all known.

Landrew then went to Axel with a heavy heart,
"I'm sorry, but when you were dying after fighting Martin,
I made a wish to a Snow Fairy that you would not die,
But now I see that my wish became a terrible sin."

"I am the cause of all your suffering, Axel,
I wish I could bear all the pain you feel,
I wish I had let you die that day,
I wish all this now wasn't real."

Axel grabbed Landrew's shoulder,
"Don't wish such things," he said,

"I am happy that you took care of me,
I am happy that I am not dead."

"But there is sorrow in your voice," Landrew said,
"Yes," Axel replied, "I have a heaviness on my heart,
I have sat here and thought for a long time, why am I alive?
Landrew, I just wish you had told me all of this at the start."

"I just hope the council won't decide to imprison me forever,"
Axel slowly lowered his chin until it rested upon his chest.
"When I told the council of your plight they seemed understanding,
Now all we can do is wait for their decision and hope for the best."

They did not have to wait for very long,
Landrew and Axel were summoned that same day,
Axel's punishment was suddenly changed,
But Axel was unsure if it was in a better way.

"Axel of the Might," one man said,
"We have a sort of proposition for you,
Landrew has told us of your good fighting spirit,
So we would like to see what it can do."

"The land is terribly troubled now,
And we cannot help all of the suffering,
We want you to work for us, fight for us,
It is very hard and can also be humbling."

"Do as we say and help the ones in need,
We see a great asset in a man that cannot die,
We want you to become one of our special guards,
And you would be a fool to pass this offer by."

"What of my punishment?" Axel asked.
"It is true that you have killed many men,
And we have not forgotten about that,
But we cannot kill you to atone for your sins."

"So we shall change your name,
Now you will be known as Axel the Black,
You shall forever hear the cries of the hopeless,
And wear your sins like a cloak upon your back."

"You shall no longer be a brown sparrow,
But one born from evil and night,
A black sparrow is what you shall become,
Your feathers dim and no longer bright."

"So this will be my punishment,
I think I shall accept it," Axel said.
"Then we bestow a new curse upon you,"
The woman said as she shook her head.

Thousands of sorrowful, pleading voices filled Axel's mind,
Axel cried aloud and grasped his head as he fell upon his knees,
"There are so many of them asking for help," Axel cried out,
"It hurts my head to hear them, make it stop, please!"

"No, Axel, for this is your punishment,
From now on your time you must give,
Listen to the voices that cry out to you,
And help them for as long as you live."

So thus was the death of Axel of the Might,
And he is now forever known as Axel the Black,

His punishment is to lend help to any in need,
And black feathers now cover his sparrow's back.

And so as Axel helped people in their strife,
Their voices reminded him every day of his sins,
He would proclaim a message to many he met,
"Forget your anger, for nothing good comes from revenge."

CPSIA information can be obtained
at www.ICGtesting.com
Printed in the USA
LVHW081351050321
680689LV00032B/458